PRAISE FOR
Michael Sinclair and the 1920s Mystery Series

"Michael Sinclair displays a mastery of pace and mystery in this suspenseful and satisfying historical thriller."

—Amazon.com

"*An Unfortunate Coincidence* is a delight to read, filled with complicated and duplicitous characters all of whom look guilty until the final surprising end of this mystery. The plot is perfect for the 1920s and the characters have so many secrets it takes till the end to figure out the truth. Well-written and worth the read. Enjoy!"

—Marcia Rosen, author of *Murder at the Zoo*,
The Senior Sleuths and *Dying to Be Beautiful* mysteries

"It's been a long time since I've enjoyed a mystery as much as this one. The historical background in 1927 was fascinating. The suspense was so effective that I wanted to keep reading and not put it down. The characters were cleverly drawn and believable. Highly recommended."

—Goodreads.com review of *Murder in Cucumber Alley*

DARKER THAN THE NIGHT

A 1920s Mystery

MICHAEL SINCLAIR

By Michael Sinclair in the 1920s historical mystery series:

An Unfortunate Coincidence
The Consequences of Murder
Murder In Cucumber Alley
Darker than the Night

DARKER THAN THE NIGHT

© 2023 by Michael Sinclair
All Rights Reserved

ISBN: 978-1-78324-290-0 (paperback)
ISBN: 978-1-78324-291-7 (ebook)

First Edition
Published by Wordzworth Publishing

The right of Michael Sinclair to be identified as the author of this work has been asserted by him in accordance with the Copyrights, Designs and Patents Act, 1988.

Darker than the Night is a work of fiction. Names, characters, places and incidents are the products of the author's imagination or are used fictitiously. Any resemblance to actual events or persons, living or dead, is entirely coincidental.

Author's Note

Harmanus Bleecker, a prominent lawyer and businessman, was born in Albany, New York in 1779 and died there in 1849. In 1889, a public hall bearing his name was erected to serve as a community center and city library. It highlighted performers of stage and screen. The new city library, also bearing his name opened in 1924. Harmanus Bleecker Hall caught fire in 1940 and was later demolished. The current Albany Public Library, which opened in 1973, is located on its former site. The Ivory Theater was fictional although The Strand was a real theater on North Pearl Street before becoming a victim of the wrecking ball.

Barbara La Mar was a popular actress of the silent era. She died on January 30, 1926, of tuberculosis at age twenty-nine. The League of Women Voters began in 1920 by Carrie Chapman Catt. The speech she delivered in front of the New York State Capitol in 1926 as described in this story is fictitious. The characters and incidents in this novel are also fictitious. Any similarity to anyone living or dead is entirely coincidental.

Michael Sinclair

Dedicated to my parents, my first readers,
and to the memory of Elizabeth Ferrars,
who encouraged me to keep writing.

CHAPTER ONE

December 1925

Albany, New York

Illuminated by glittering floodlights, proudly emblazoned on its marquee the latest hit rendition of the popular musical *A Lucky Break*, the Ivory Theater stood majestically off North Pearl Street, tucked away on a side street, rather forlorn and apart from other playhouses, nonetheless welcoming theater goers to enter its opulent and grandiose atrium. The elegance of its patrons matched the theater's illustrious presence. The evening's performance brought chauffeur driven cars to pull in front of the theater. Men dressed stylishly in three-piece suits and scarves. Women wore evening dresses, adored with furs, wraps and elegant cloche hats.

Considered a mecca of world-renowned entertainment, many popular performers graced its stage. Versatile in its divertissements, The

Ivory highlighted plays, concerts, magic acts and current films. Fanny Brice, Ethel Barrymore and Marie Dressler performed to outstanding reviews. Ruth Etting sang to standing ovations. Harry Houdini enthralled audiences with his mystifying illusions. Norma Shearer gave an outstanding performance in the hit movie *Lady of Burlesque.*

Tonight's performance of *A Lucky Break* and the featured performer, Miss Penelope Barker, certainly the most celebrated of the cast, drew crowds for another sold-out performance. Thunderous applause greeted her as she stepped onstage from the wings. It was obvious to those watching that Penelope Barker had an enduring appeal. All eyes focused on her magnificent delivery, her poise, her sultry voice and the dexterity in which she played her part.

Upon its conclusion, a standing ovation and more deafening applause beckoned her for a second and even a third bow. Her fellow actors reveled in her superb performance, appreciated and envied her in equal proportions. After the last curtain call and finally subdued in her dressing room, she exhaled a sigh of relief, sat at her vanity table before a large mirror, and lit a cigarette.

While she charmed her audience and the press, Penelope Barker offstage was a different person, given to bouts of anger and erratic behavior. She threw fits if something did not go her way and while delighted by her stage persona, many in the theater avoided her at all costs, especially after the performance. She took a drag on her cigarette, looked at herself in the mirror. She pushed back some hair from her forehead and began to remove make-up with a tissue.

She was thirty-four, healthy, clever and had been described more than once as handsome, with a fine figure, radiant facial features and an alluring, albeit deceptive smile. Her brown hair, worn in the bob style, accentuated her flapper appeal. The *Brooklyn Daily Times* had snapped pictures of her as a vivacious stage star, with a wide popular appeal.

Throughout her stellar career, she found many of her peers envious of her success in the theater. But Penelope paid them little attention. She knew how to manipulate the system to get what she wanted.

A knock came on her dressing room door. A costume fitter, Cora, a gentle woman in her seventies with a solemn expression, entered. "Good show tonight, Miss Barker. Everyone's talking about it. I just made a fresh pot of coffee. I'll bring you a cup."

Penelope looked at her through the mirror. "No thanks, Cora."

"I heard there's an after-hours party at that speakeasy on Sheridan Avenue," Cora told her. "Why don't you go? Do you good to get out of this stuffy theater."

"Not for me," Penelope said. "I'll be on my way soon, thanks just the same."

Cora shrugged, wished her a good night and left the dressing room. Penelope extinguished her cigarette in a nearby ashtray, changed into a dress of navy blue, along with a string of pearls, adjusted her lace-trimmed cloche hat and applied lipstick. Studying herself in the mirror, her mind drifted to her acting career, although sometimes she wondered why she had ever decided to become an actor in the first place. She had tired of the endless rehearsals, catering to the whims of producers and the insecurities of the other actors. The highlight of her career came at the Cohoes Music Hall in neighboring Cohoes, where she starred with such renowned players as Sarah Bernhardt, John Philip Sousa, Lillian Russell and Eva Tanguay. Her talents eventually took her to New York City, where she earned the reputation as one of the most popular stage stars of 1925.

She put on her fur coat and collected her purse, taking a last look at herself in the mirror. Smiling in satisfaction, she opened the dressing room door, looking up and down the hallway to be sure no one was about. Furtively making her way to the backstage door, and pleased the guard was not there, she found freedom in the chilly night air. She breathed in the refreshing cold and relished in it, feeling rejuvenated from the rather claustrophobic feel of the theater.

She walked to North Pearl Street and jumped on a trolley, headed for State and Broadway. It was crowded, being a Saturday evening, and she had to stand for a while before a seat became vacant. She got off at North Pearl and State Streets with a sizeable crowd. She walked down State, took a left on Broadway until she came to Union Station. She made her way to the information booth and inquired about trains to New York City. The young man behind the counter handed her a timetable of trains headed to Grand Central Station.

She left Union Station and stood hesitantly on Broadway. If the weather was pleasant she walked to her apartment on Lancaster Street, but it was too cold, and not wanting to sit on a crowded trolley again, she decided to hail a taxi. While in the cab, she noted the heavy traffic and the crowds, enjoying the plentiful restaurants, shops and theaters. North Pearl and State Streets were a sea of bright neon lights, pedestrians, trollies and traffic. The cab passed several department stores, all adorned with Christmas decorations. How pretty they looked, Penelope admired from the cab. Glancing at her watch, she saw it was ten minutes to eleven. She would pack her suitcase and get the first train to New York City tomorrow. Her life had been threatened, and she was afraid. She thought of informing the police, but that would mean negative publicity for her. She would be safer in New York City. She felt satisfied with her plans.

The taxi pulled up in front of her building. Snow showers and a gusty wind greeted her as she stepped out of the cab. She paid the driver and watched as it sped off. It was quiet on Lancaster Street and Penelope felt uneasy. Then she shrugged it off. Nothing would happen here, she was at her apartment building and home was just a step away.

She was about to take the key out of her purse and climb the steps of the opulent brownstone when she realized someone, or something was behind her. She was unaware of danger, but it came silently and quickly. She was too late to fight off her attacker, too late to ward off the piercing knife, until the final agonizing end came, and she sank onto the steps into a dark and permanent oblivion.

Excerpt from the *Knickerbocker Press,* Albany, New York, Monday, December 7, 1925.

LOCAL ACTRESS MURDERED

Miss Penelope Barker, glamorous stage star and Albany native, met a tragic end over the weekend. Miss Barker was found lying on the steps in front of her apartment building on Lancaster Street in the city, the victim of an apparent homicide. Robbery did not appear a motive in this grievous deadly attack. A Mr. and Mrs. Fleming, who live at the apartments, discovered her body at two a.m. Saturday. Miss Barker is well known for her stellar performances at the Strand, the Ivory and the Cohoes Music Hall as well as numerous theaters in New York City. Police are asking anyone with information to contact them as they continue their investigation.

CHAPTER TWO

January 1926

Albany, New York

It was almost one o'clock on a snowy Monday afternoon when Alan Cartwright's secretary, Mrs. Russell, entered his office on the second floor of Harmanus Bleecker Hall and handed him a memo from the executive director. It detailed the proposal Alan had been exhausting his resources to either postpone or nullify. After reading it several times, he tossed it aside, sat back in his desk chair and signed in trepidation.

Over the last several weeks, he had worked tirelessly to prevent a dance marathon from taking place at Harmanus Bleecker Hall, a major entertainment venue. Mr. Ferguson, the executive director, was adamant, noting that the publicity meant more financial benefits.

As the assistant manager, Alan had diligently brought increased business to the Hall. Audiences marveled at the Marx Brothers and W.C. Fields, the most popular acts he arranged. Over the years, dances took place in the Hall's fabulous ballroom, usually to coincide with a special event. But a dance marathon? That would be a first. Of course, dance marathons were all the rage and growing in popularity.

His mind flew to Penelope Barker, an Albany celebrity. On numerous occasions, he tried to schedule Miss Barker for a singing performance. He remembered her rave reviews at local theaters and was shocked upon reading about her death in the newspaper. His conservative mother contributed it to the decline in morals in today's youth. She spoke quite negatively of Miss Barker. She grumbled that the most despicable thing known today, what Miss Barker epitomized, were the flappers. The newspapers and magazines glamorized such a lifestyle, as though they bowed to its popularity and encouraged it, according to his mother. Alan did not quite agree with her but kept his opinion to himself.

At twenty-nine, Alan Cartwright was in his sixth year as the assistant manager at Harmanus Bleecker Hall. Upon graduating from Hamilton College in 1918, where he studied business and finance, he worked various managerial jobs in Albany before landing his current role.

On his desk the January issues of *Photoplay, Screenland, Vanity Fair* and *Motion Picture* magazines beckoned him to read about the celebrated lives of film and radio stars, which he frequently consulted to acquire talent for future bookings. Like many readers, Colleen Moore, Charlie Chaplin, Clara Bow, Mary Pickford and Lillian Gish fascinated him. And while the eccentric lives of actors portrayed in print intrigued him, the behavior exhibited by his generation alienated him to some degree, although he did find the flappers rather appealing. Certainly, many girls admired the tall, handsome, intelligent Alan, but he was neither married nor engaged and showed no inclination to change that status. Always dashing in his pristine vest, formal dress slacks, shirt and tie, his brown hair, worn slicked back from a prominent forehead and his expressive green eyes highlighted a gentle face. He lived with his widowed mother in the house he grew up in, a wonderful old brownstone on fashionable Elk Street, one of the most prestigious neighborhoods in Albany. It also was not far from Harmanus Bleecker Hall. He contemplated renting an apartment, but Elk Street was equidistant to work, so he decided to stay put.

Glancing out the windows, overlooking Washington Avenue, he noticed snow showers were numerous, and it remained cold. He turned his attention again to the memo from Mr. Ferguson. He realized he had called a meeting in the second-floor conference room, to discuss the dance marathon proposal. He had summoned numerous staff and his presence was expected. The meeting was to start at one thirty and it was already one ten. So much for advanced notice, he thought. He straightened his tie, vest, and left the office. He mentioned to Mrs. Russell in the outer office that he would attend Mr. Ferguson's meeting in the second-floor conference room. She smiled wryly, knowing from long experience what board meetings were like, having been employed at the Hall for over thirty years.

He left the office, making his way rather cautiously along the hallway to the conference room, not sure what to expect. Upon entering, he heard voices and to his chagrin, most of the staff, including Mr. Ferguson, was already there.

Upon entering, he noticed that those already present were consuming cigarettes and coffee in equal proportions, most likely in an attempt to remain alert during what was destined to be a long and tedious narration on the benefits of sponsoring a dance marathon.

Alan knew from experience that once Mr. Ferguson started to speak, he would never finish until his objectives were met. He lit a cigarette and settled back in the hard chair, uncomfortably. A quick glance made Alan realize the board of directors were present. He acknowledged everyone and then turned his attention to the elderly gentleman at the head of the table.

Mr. Gerald Ferguson, the executive director, a robust man of seventy-five, with a thick head of white hair, sprinkled with gray and rather dark, commanding eyes, considered Harmanus Bleecker Hall the epitome of entertainment in Albany. Many people found Mr. Ferguson sincere and unpretentious in his endeavors, while others thought him extreme and thickheaded. He approved of Alan's efforts to bring top performers and first-run movies to the Hall but, Mr. Ferguson, a staunch Democrat, was more politically minded. In 1922 and 1925, he promoted functions for the mayoral campaign of William Stormont Hackett, which ensured victory for the Democratic candidate.

He greeted his audience pleasantly, shuffled a few papers and began speaking. Twenty minutes later, a quick glance around the table made Alan realize Mr. Ferguson had already lost his listeners and he seemed blissfully unaware of it. He knocked ash from his cigarette and glanced out the tall windows onto Washington Avenue, as snow pelted the windowpanes and pedestrians scurried to catch the trolley. He returned his attention to Mr. Ferguson, who continued driving home his points as he had done since the meeting began.

"I am proposing a dance marathon here at the Hall, for later this month. January is the ideal time for hosting it. Many people find themselves at home, settling by their radios, reluctant to get out due to the cold temperatures. I believe a dance marathon will bring increased publicity. Dancers will pay a fee of fifty cents per couple to participate. The admission fee of twenty-five cents will entitle the audience to watch as long as they please. The prize money will be five hundred dollars for the couple that remain dancing the longest. We will launch a campaign of unprecedented exposure, advertising in newspapers not only locally but in different areas of the state." He paused in his exuberance. "I see a dance marathon as worthwhile and expedient. It will provide an excellent source of revenue."

A low murmur of assent was audible but Mr. Ferguson, undaunted, cleared his throat and lingered on the advantages of such an event. Alan did not think he would ever stop; reaching the point of a monotonous and redundant babble, as though by repeating his objectives he would ensure his decision was made. The various people seated around the long table listened attentively albeit disproportionally as the agenda was proposed. Opinions divided amongst the board members as to the feasibility and the rationale of sponsoring a dance marathon.

To Alan's right was Mrs. Jeanne Churchill, a formidable presence and a retired manager of Harmanus Bleecker Hall. Certainly, of considerable age, Alan wondered if she were eighty or close to it. She was well dressed and well kept, in a black dress, a string of pearls, little make-up and a doleful expression as though she couldn't bear to listen to Mr. Ferguson and wished he'd end it. Next to her was young Miss Norma Smith, a Hall employee, quite the modern woman, with her exaggerated bob-style hair, excessive make-up, bright lipstick and rather provocative dress of bright blue. She smiled, smoked and listened attentively to Mr. Ferguson, although Alan could not determine if she comprehended what was being said.

Across from him sat the other board members. Edward Flynn, Ed to his associates, was rather a strange sort, Alan thought, observing his dark brows, his sullen manner, rather aloof and distant. He smiled occasionally and chain-smoked nervously. Alan knew Ed was about his own age, that he worked at city hall but what his job there was he did not know. Next to Ed Flynn was John Whitmore. Alan did not know much about John, except that he worked at the Strand Theater on North Pearl Street as an assistant manager. He had had numerous occasions to speak with him by telephone, regarding talent for future shows. He was severely dressed in a dark suit and looked around thirty-eight or so, although Alan noticed lines around his eyes and gray patches in his hair that made him look older.

Alan's eyes then moved to the last attendee and board member, Lester Cavanaugh. From previous experiences at meetings, he considered Lester even stranger than Ed and John put together. He could not determine if Lester was snobby, naturally quiet or just shy. Lester Cavanaugh was about thirty-five at a guess and an employee of Harmanus Bleecker Library, Albany's brand-new public library. He also wore a dark suit, held a cigarette and blew smoke upwards as though in an attempt to stay alert. Alan remembered how he had been involved with Penelope Barker. They were quite an item once. He never knew what happened to them, although he figured Lester must have moved on, tiring of Penelope and finding someone new. But then he remembered that John Whitmore and Ed Flynn had also been involved with Penelope Barker.

Alan wondered how Ed Flynn, John Whitmore, Lester Cavanaugh and even Norma Smith, ever got on the board of directors. Mrs. Churchill had been with the Hall forever it seemed, so her stature was assured if rather exacting. He felt somewhat irresolute as though the attendees would not reach an agreement and that this meeting would end up a complete waste of time, despite Mr. Ferguson's demands. An awkward silence ensued until Mrs. Churchill, realizing no one else dared speak, cleared her throat and rose to the occasion.

"Frankly, Mr. Ferguson, I do not see the advantages of a dance marathon. I know you've sent memos on this before the holidays, but

I cannot lend my support to this ludicrous idea." Her tone was brusque and to the point but did not faze Mr. Ferguson in the least.

"What is your opinion, Alan?" he asked him.

All eyes turned to Alan, who crushed his cigarette and feeling rather ill at ease, looked first at Mr. Ferguson then at the board members. "It'd bring publicity for the Hall, but the expense wouldn't compensate." He paused, as Mrs. Churchill and a few others nodded in agreement. "Are you willing to keep the Hall open all night and into the next day or even longer? Where will you get the music? Who would monitor the dancers?"

Mr. Ferguson cast a rather shadowy look at young Alan, more affected by his comments than those of staid Mrs. Churchill. The older man cleared his throat, looking at his papers.

"In this proposal, I have already secured music provided by several area dance bands. Their rates are reasonable."

Norma Smith nodded. "Sounds good to me, Mr. Ferguson."

She lit another cigarette, casually depositing the match into an ashtray and seemed nonchalant about the whole thing. Ed Flynn and John Whitmore agreed about the difficulties of keeping the Hall open for extended periods, especially during the winter, with heating an issue, but again Mr. Ferguson had his bases covered. He explained he proposed keeping his maintenance team abreast of heating issues and providing plenty of food, water and cots during breaks for the participants. He contacted area caterers who were willing to provide these provisions at nominal costs. He included his active participation at the event as an emcee, while other Hall employees (he cast a quick glance at Alan) would also serve in that capacity, ensuring round the clock supervision of the dancers.

Lester Cavanaugh blew a cloud of smoke and asked what the total cost of this event would cost the Hall. Mr. Ferguson mentioned he did not have the final tabulations but did not see expense as an issue.

Changing course, with a more somber tone, he paused and then took a deep breath. "I had hoped to bring Miss Penelope Barker here. Her singing and presence would've enticed the public to attend." He paused again, morosely. "Sadly, Miss Barker met an unfortunate end last month…" His voice trailed off. "I had known Miss Barker for several years. She was a distinguished actress and singer, highly respected in the Albany theatrical community."

John Whitmore agreed. "Her performances at the Strand always sold out. Her loss is still felt by the actors circle here in Albany."

"She was popular with the mayor, too," Ed Flynn commented. "She'd visit him in city hall every so often. The police didn't think it was a random act. Who'd want to kill her?"

The question remained suspended in mid-air, as though no one wanted to ruminate on such a horrendous event. Lester Cavanaugh cleared his throat and broke the uncomfortable silence.

"She was always cheerful when she came into the library," he said.

Norma Smith cleared her throat. "I found her loud and boisterous, rather stuck-up, if you ask me. She came to the Hall a few times, putting on airs. Personally, I couldn't stand her."

Mr. Ferguson cast a disdainful glance at Norma. Ignoring her unmannerly comments, he looked at a calendar that was underneath his papers. "I propose Friday, the 29th. Today is Monday, the 11th, so that gives us over two weeks. Registration for the dancers will take place either in person here at the Hall or by mail. I recommend a cut-off date of the twenty-seventh. As I mentioned, I made preliminary contacts with caterers and a few bands, which I will finalize this week. I've sent a memo to several employees, including the cleaning staff and the legal department. Now, we need to advertise." He paused. "Alan, you will handle advertising. You'll need to mention the date and the cut-off of the twenty-seventh, the cost for participants, the cost to attend and the prize money."

That's all he thinks about, making money, Alan thought. He sat up and blinked a few times. "Of course, Mr. Ferguson. I know editors in newspapers locally."

Mr. Ferguson nodded, smiled and thanked the board members for attending. The meeting adjourned. A murmur of unintelligible words was heard before chairs were scraped back and everyone stood, the men shaking hands with Mr. Ferguson as they filed out of the room.

Officially, the dance marathon had been scheduled for Friday, January 29th.

Mrs. Jeanne Churchill descended the stairs, to avoid the rickety old elevator that she considered slower than molasses. She glanced as the other members scattered in different directions, seeking their own sense of privacy. She made her way to a small office on the first floor, opened the door and found contentment in solitude. She smoothed down her iron-gray hair in a wall mirror and sighed in consternation.

Mrs. Churchill had a reputation as a cantankerous old matron, outspoken and forthright, who ruled with an iron fist and had little patience with those who did not share her perspectives. A widow with no children, she was inclined to firm control over others, and most people were terrified of her. Even her deceased husband exercised caution with her. Her sharp sense of humor and quick tongue reduced most people to a stunned silence. On the other hand, board meetings usually flustered her.

And how could they not? Mr. Ferguson's preposterous ideas. She was intolerant of the current staff, board members and even Mr. Ferguson, who she found incompetent and lacking in ethics. A dance marathon? Such foolishness, she thought irritably, fingering her string of pearls absently. The young people of today were hideous, with their drinking, smoking, dancing and other unscrupulous activities she dared not linger on. She was perturbed that the members did not share her opinion, although Mr. Cartwright reiterated her concern. She had been employed at Harmanus Bleecker Hall for over thirty years and even in retirement; she maintained an office and worked part-time. God only knew they needed extra help, she thought contemptuously.

She gathered her coat and purse from the cabinet where she left them and was about to leave but decided to sit at the only desk in the room and catch her breath. Something nagged in her mind, but she couldn't quite place it. Something Mr. Ferguson said. Oh, of course, Penelope Barker. Now why did he mention her? No need to bring her into the conversation, foolish young woman. Perhaps if she hadn't gallivanted all over town, she'd be alive today. She remembered the problems she had with Miss Penelope Barker and Miss Betsy Donovan several years ago, causing great turmoil in her life. Realizing it was getting late, she put on her coat and cloche hat. Once outside she breathed in the refreshing air. Neither Miss Penelope Barker nor Miss Betsy Donovan need distress her any longer

It was nearly four fifteen and dusk settled over Albany. Though the holidays were over, city residents knew winter was just beginning.

Wind increased, scattering snow flurries and hastening the steps of pedestrians. Traffic and trollies clogged Washington Avenue. It was a busy evening as the Albany Institute of History and Art hosted a painting exhibit and Harmanus Bleecker Library hosted an author event. Quite a hectic but exciting rush hour in Albany.

John Whitmore and Edward Flynn stood on the corner of Washington Avenue and Dove Street, debating whether to hop on a trolley or just walk. They left Harmanus Bleecker Hall and exchanged comments on the dance marathon proposal, although after walking down Washington Avenue and braving the bitter cold, they were more intent on seeking shelter.

"My apartment's on State," John exclaimed, burying his chin in his scarf, lowering his cap on his head and bundling his coat tighter. "Where do you live, Ed?"

Ed Flynn lit a cigarette as though to keep warm. "On Elk Street, an apartment convenient to city hall, where I work," he said, his teeth chattering. "Not far from Alan's house."

John rolled his eyes. "Sounded like he wasn't too keen on the dance marathon."

"I know Alan pretty well," Ed said, exhaling a large puff of smoke. "He'll go along with whatever old Ferguson wants. After all, he works there, he really has no choice."

They exchanged a few trivial words, while pedestrians brushed by, and the snow continued to fall. Several trollies passed but they were crowded, so they decided to walk.

"Strange Mr. Ferguson mentioning Miss Barker, isn't it?" John said, unexpectedly.

Ed shrugged, avoiding his gaze. "Maybe. She was a flirt and liked to carouse around city hall, trying to impress the mayor."

John agreed. "When she'd perform at the Strand, she was great for business. The public loved her, but she was a tyrant afterwards. Nobody could stand her backstage."

Ed nodded, smoking incessantly. "John, we'll talk again later. Great seeing you again."

John shook his hand. "Same here, Ed. I'm sure we'll be an integral part of this dance marathon Mr. Ferguson's proposing."

Ed winced, as though the idea of the dance marathon repulsed him. He headed south on Washington Avenue toward the State Education Building and Elk Street. John watched as he walked off. He then crossed Washington Avenue with a heavy crowd, and headed south on Dove, turning right onto State Street. He arrived at his apartment, but within an hour was out again, as he planned to get drunk at a local speakeasy, where he was a regular.

Ed Flynn, arriving at his apartment on Elk Street, headed straight for the kitchen, where an unopened bottle of whiskey awaited him. He bought it last night in the black market near the Hudson River downtown, where bootleggers proliferated. Opening it quickly and filling a glass, he relished the taste of the bourbon, settling his nerves, pouring more and lighting another cigarette.

As they had done many times before, John Whitmore and Edward Flynn drowned their contemptuous thoughts of Penelope Barker and Betsy Donovan with liquor that night.

Norma Smith returned to her office on the second floor, not far from Alan's office. She gathered a few papers that needed attention and attempted to return to work, then realized it was almost time to leave for the day. She wondered if Lester would want to see her tonight. He was so busy at the library, although she never pictured him the bookish type.

Norma Smith was twenty-five and had a voluptuous figure, fine brown hair in the bob-style and an outgoing personality that most men were drawn to, and most women envied. She was fascinated with current fads and trends; dieting, make-up, certainly lipstick and cigarettes, jazz music, liquor, dance halls and speakeasies, petting parties and mixing with the right people, especially eligible males. An Albany native, her parents divorced years ago, her father remarrying and settling in Rochester, her mother living in Schenectady with her elderly mother. Norma lived in a furnished room in a boarding house on State Street not far from Harmanus Bleecker Hall and the Harmanus Bleecker Library, where Lester worked. She would often stop by to see him and on summer days, they would have lunch in the park behind the capitol.

Well, why not, she thought, after all, she was young, assertive, attractive and demanding and Lester was personable enough to live up to her expectations. Although, she admitted, he did have a darker side, moody, incommunicative and withdrawn. Part of his appeal, she smiled, lighting a cigarette. Her mind turned to Alan Cartwright, just down the hall. Certainly, a looker, handsome, better than Lester, but nothing daredevil about him, too refined and sedate. She preferred a challenge and Alan Cartwright did not seem to fit that bill.

She was a secretary at Harmanus Bleecker Hall and soon applied for the board position. Mr. Ferguson heartily welcomed her, citing her youth and exuberance, her positive attitude, and she charmed him every step of the way.

She straightened the candlestick phone on her desk. Odd that Mr. Ferguson mentioned Miss Penelope Barker, someone she had had run-ins with in the past. She was glad she never got to perform at the Hall.

Bad enough she had visited more than once. Her presence at a dance marathon would have ensured disaster for sure.

Just then, someone knocked on her office door. Without looking up, she assumed it was Alan asking for certain documents, although he had his own secretary, elderly Mrs. Russell, who had worked there forever and looked a hundred. Instead, she saw Lester Cavanaugh in the doorway, smiling mischievously, smoking and apparently reeking of alcohol. Didn't take him long to hit the bottle, Norma thought wryly.

"Where did you get the booze?" she asked him. "Smashed already?"

Lester puffed on his cigarette and entered the small office, sitting at a chair in front of her desk. "I'm not drunk, Norma. But a flask serves it purpose, especially after listening to old man Ferguson and his ideas about a dance marathon."

"I wouldn't say that too loudly," she warned him. "People eavesdrop and gossip around here." She paused. "I think the dance marathon will work," she said, puffing at her own cigarette. "If that's what he wants, then I'll help put it together."

"Always the pleaser, aren't you, Norma," Lester said sarcastically.

She smiled uncertainly. She had seen Lester inebriated in speakeasies around the city. She knew he could be capricious and difficult when intoxicated.

"Why don't you stop by my place later," he suggested. "You know where I live. The door's always open." She watched as he swayed slightly walking out of the office, heading for the stairs.

Norma looked after him, finishing her cigarette. She wished she had brought her own flask, because she could use a drink to steady her nerves right now. Was it Lester Cavanaugh that was bothering her? No, she knew Lester and his moody ways, certainly nothing new, they quarreled every so often. He was rather odd at times. She wondered if he had secrets he kept from her. She then realized what was at the forefront of her mind.

It was Mr. Ferguson's abrupt mention of Penelope Barker. Her thoughts turned to that hideous woman, her many visits at the Hall; miss la-de-da, her air of superiority, showing off with her diamonds, her lovely pearl necklace and fur coat, the most stylish and expensive cloche hat, acting like the queen of the cinema.

Norma put the thought of Miss Barker out of her mind. In a few moments, she put on her coat, her cloche hat firmly on her head and left for the day.

It was a little after five o'clock when Alan decided to leave Harmanus Bleecker Hall. He had finished reviewing an expense report and other important papers. Putting them aside, he rubbed his tired eyes and stretched. Looking out his office window, he saw the snow continuing to fall and the wind howling. Fortunately, Elk Street was an easy walk, although he knew he would freeze on the way home.

Gathering his coat and cap from the rack in the corner, he entered the outer office and noticed Mrs. Russell had already left. Hastily descending the stairs, and upon exiting he said good night to a few employees. As he expected a gust of wind and snow showers stung his face and shoulders. Turning left on Washington Avenue and heading south, he brushed past the after-work crowd, as he steadily made his way toward Elk Street.

Passing the Albany Institute of History and Art and the monumental State Education Building, he cut across Academy Park, arriving at his mother's grandiose brownstone in a few short steps. Fumbling for his keys in his pocket, his fingers practically numb from the cold, nevertheless he managed to open the front door and was greeted with warmth and the smell of something delightful from the kitchen. He took off his jacket and cap and leaving them on a chair, he removed his shoes, stomping them on the hallway mat, as he knew his mother hated his tracking slush in the house. He had no sooner done this than his mother appeared from the kitchen.

"Hello, dear," she called pleasantly, wiping her hands on her apron. "I've made beef stew, your favorite. Warm us up on a night like this, too. Dinner will be ready soon."

Mrs. Bernice Cartwright was in her mid-fifties, charismatic and outgoing, a widow who lost her husband during the flu pandemic in 1918. Her brown hair was tastefully arranged and the dress she wore was simple, yet appropriate for her trim figure. She wore little make-up as her natural radiant features invoked simplicity rather than excess. Her personality was kind and caring if rather protective at times.

With almost thirty years as a librarian at the New York State Legislative Library, Bernice enjoyed her work at the capitol and it was convenient too, located on Washington Avenue, across from Academy Park, within walking distance. She had never owned a car and frowned upon its popularity. She took great pride in her house, one of many old brownstones in a row on fashionable Elk Street. It was Victorian in style, with three levels, a large staircase against the right wall and three rooms on each floor. The Cartwrights lived in their magnificent brownstone since they were first married, and Bernice intended to stay. She smiled at her son and asked him about his day.

Alan forced a tired smile. "Mr. Ferguson wants to schedule a dance marathon at the Hall."

He had followed her down the hallway to the kitchen, where the table was set for two. Bernice went to the stove, retrieved the pot containing the beef stew, and served up the delicious meal in bowls. She placed one in front of her son and then one for herself and sat at the head of the table. Alan looked at his mother, surprised she did not comment. Perhaps she did not really understand it. On the other hand, perhaps she had not heard. He repeated what he had said and this time Bernice, looking up from her food, addressed her son.

"I already know about it, dear."

Alan was taken by surprise, putting down his fork. From where had his mother heard about the dance marathon? He did not think it was common knowledge, as it had not been promoted yet. "I spoke to my brother. He mentioned Betsy heard about it from someone at the bank where she works. Someone from the Hall had gone there and mentioned it to her in passing." She paused, swallowing some of the delicious stew. "News travels fast in this city. You know your cousin, Betsy." Her tone implied disapproval.

Alan nodded. Indeed he did know his cousin Betsy Donovan and his Uncle Carl, who lived just three doors down on Elk Street. He was never fond of Betsy. She was too impetuous and outspoken, and Uncle Carl could not handle her. He was surprised she could even hold a job, especially at a bank.

They continued eating in relative silence. Bernice mentioned a few friends would be stopping over for their bridge game and Alan was welcomed to join but he declined. As much as he liked card games, he was not in the mood this evening for bridge. He helped his mother clear the table and wash and dry the dishes, then went to the living room to listen to the radio. He turned the knob to his favorite station, WGY, to hear the latest headlines, sports and weather. He sat in an easy chair comfortably and was about to light a cigarette when his attention was focused on the radio. He listened as the announcer spoke about the murder of Miss Penelope Barker. No new leads had been uncovered and the police urged anyone with information to contact them as they continue their investigation. Bernice entered at that moment, looking at her son curiously.

"Is there something wrong, dear? Is it about the dance marathon? Sorry if I upset you."

Alan shook his head. "No, Mother, I just heard a report about Penelope Barker."

"It's best not to think about Miss Barker," Bernice said, sitting opposite him on the sofa. "I'd prefer not to discuss her or for her name to be mentioned in this house. I talked to her a few times when she had the occasion to visit the capitol. She was extremely crass and uncouth, not to my liking. Obviously, she got herself into trouble of some sort. Perhaps if she had been more careful, it would not have happened. The police will discover what happened sooner or later."

Her tone implied it was nothing of any great importance. Alan puffed at his cigarette and although he knew his mother's dislike of Miss Barker, her reaction still surprised him. Of course, he knew flappers and actors were not to everyone's liking. Stage stars tended to be flamboyant, as he knew from actors he booked for performances. He was never successful in booking Miss Barker for one reason or another. He shrugged it off, crushed his cigarette in an ashtray on the coffee table and realized she was still speaking to him. She suggested he call John Whitmore, to see if he could stop over but Alan shook his head.

"Not tonight, Mother. I'll listen to the radio upstairs in my bedroom."

Bernice smiled. "Sometimes I forget about your own radio. We're fortunate to have two radios in the house! Is there anything I can get you before the ladies arrive for our bridge game?"

Again, Alan shook his head. He extinguished his cigarette, and then made his way to the hallway and the staircase, to the second floor and his bedroom. Changing into more casual clothing, he then turned the radio to WGY. Stretching his long legs on his bed and lighting another cigarette, he listened to the news, the political commentaries and reviews of current films. Certainly, President Coolidge was the popular man of the day. Silent Cal they called him. Rudolph Valentino, Mary Pickford, Charlie Chaplin and Clara Bow dominated entertainment news. Announcements promoting *Listerine, Dentyne Chewing Gum* and *Lipton Tea* were broadcast before the weather report. The announcer continued animatedly but Alan's mind was cluttered, only half-listening.

He wondered as he had many times before why mentioning Penelope Barker caused his mother such extreme loathing and disapproval. He also wondered if there was something about Miss Barker he was unaware of.

CHAPTER THREE

I n a comfortable brownstone house on Columbia Street, just around the corner from Elk Street, Mrs. Eleanor Whitney sipped her morning coffee and looked across the kitchen table at her daughter, Evangeline, who was engrossed in the current issue of *True Story* magazine while crunching a piece of toast and also sipping coffee.

Eleanor sighed, folded back the front page of the Tuesday morning edition of the *Times Union* and scanned the headlines. Eleanor Whitney was in her mid-fifties, of medium stature, highly intelligent and articulate, with fine auburn hair, and deep green eyes. She dressed fashionably and, thanks to Evangeline, she was introduced to modern styles, extolling the right look, cosmetics and perfume. She did not consider herself a true flapper, but she marveled at the looser morals and values, especially for women. Eleanor admitted she enjoyed reading *True Story* as much as her daughter. Once she read an article about an introverted middle-aged divorcee who got involved with gangsters! Such is life, she thought wryly.

She often played bridge at Mrs. Cartwright's house with other women, as she did last evening. She stayed clear of their gossip. She steadfastly affirmed her personal life her own business. However, she kept her eyes fixed on a certain man, and she made her interests known. She admitted she enjoyed the attention. If a man found her appealing, how could she help it? The truth was that many men found her appealing. Divorced for over ten years, her husband having left her for a much younger woman, she kept her eyes open for another suitor. Her former husband remarried and lived in Dunkirk, on the western side of the state. He had little contact with Evangeline, so it was just mother and daughter in the big old brownstone house on Columbia Street. Her job at city hall, a five-minute walk away, meant the most to her. She looked at her daughter with a worried expression.

She was proud of the young woman across from her. Evangeline Whitney, at twenty-five, was, in her own words, a flapper in the sense of fashion and cosmetics, but not one for late nights, drinking or smoking. Her black hair, tastefully arranged in the bob-style, a clear white skin and an easy, overall serene expression highlighted her pleasing appearance. Like many young people, she loved dance halls and parties. She had dated Ed Flynn and John Whitmore but found them reserved and distant. She had enjoyed the company of Alan Cartwright, but he was so devoted to his mother. She knew Norma Smith had her eye on him as well as Lester, although what those men saw in Miss Smith she could not imagine. She kept her distance from Norma Smith as well as Betsy Blake, both of whom she considered unscrupulous and desperate for male companionship.

On the other hand, she did keep her eyes open for an eligible bachelor; one she hoped played the stock market wisely, ensuring a life of complacency as a housewife and mother. She was employed as a bookkeeper at Whitney's, one of Albany's fabulous shopping meccas on North Pearl Street. After graduating college, she started at Whitney's in billing and was promoted to head bookkeeper. She enjoyed her position and the busy downtown Albany scene. She walked to work and took pride that her father was the great-grandson of the founder. She didn't expect any preferential treatment, but the Whitney name carried certain prestige.

She took her eyes away from *True Story*, put down her coffee cup and looked at her mother carefully, and asked if something was wrong.

"I don't think it's wise for you to stay out late," Mrs. Whitney said.

"Mother, I can take care of myself," her daughter pacified her, returning to *True Story*.

"Are you seeing Mr. Flynn or Mr. Whitmore again?"

Evangeline shrugged. "I gave them my phone number."

Mrs. Whitney nodded in agreement. "Of course, dear. It's only appropriate for a man to call a woman, not the other way around."

"I've called them in the past and asked them out," Evangeline told her. She paused, seeing her mother's startled expression. "Well, why not? This is 1926, you know. I'm not waiting around for them to ask me. Or anyone else for that matter."

"You aren't associating with Betsy Donovan, are you?" Eleanor asked cautiously.

Evangeline put down her coffee cup. "I rarely see her and when I do, I don't talk with her. She tried to interfere with my relationship with Alan, you know."

"Her behavior is atrocious," Mrs. Whitney said with tight lips.

Evangeline agreed, and then changed the subject. "Aren't you interested in her father?"

Mrs. Whitney was appalled. "Evangeline, how can you suggest such a thing? I am *not* interested in Mr. Carl Donovan. Besides, I prefer…"

At that moment, the candlestick phone from in the hallway rang shrilly surprising them, as it was still quite early. Evangeline got up to answer it, leaving Eleanor alone at the kitchen table. It seemed like mother and daughter touched on a forbidden subject, the Donovans.

Too bad they lived so close by, Eleanor thought contemptuously. She could hear her daughter talking in the hallway. Within a few moments, she returned, telling her mother it was her supervisor at Whitney's Department Store.

"I have to report earlier today," she explained, finishing her coffee. "They want me on the sales floor. One of the salesgirls is out sick, so they asked me to help out."

"The sales floor?" Eleanor was surprised. "You're the bookkeeper, not a salesgirl!"

"Mr. Whitney wouldn't ask me if he didn't think I couldn't handle both jobs!"

She then ran upstairs to dress, leaving her mother alone again. Eleanor folded the paper, turning to the cinema section. She returned to the front page and an article on Miss Barker. She remembered her performance at the Cohoes Music Hall. She admired her beauty, her poise, her delivery. Miss Barker was the epitome of success in the capital city.

Eleanor sat brooding; moodily sipping her coffee, realizing it was cold and scowling in distaste. With gangsters, bootleggers and criminal activity flourishing in Albany, she worried about Evangeline. Young people were so carefree these days. Eleanor enjoyed her evening and early morning strolls, but with the recent crime, she wasn't so sure it was wise to walk alone.

She turned the page and started to read the local headlines, blocking the hideous thoughts of Penelope Barker and Betsy Donovan from her already troubled mind.

Carl Donovan rose early and slowly descended the stairs on his way to the kitchen. It was only seven o'clock, but he could not sleep much longer, preoccupied with his workday, new clients to attend and a meeting in the afternoon. Glancing out the kitchen windows, he saw it was still dark and cold, but the snow had finally stopped. Maybe the sun would come out. He would listen to the radio for a little while. He approached the stove and began to prepare breakfast.

Carl Donovan was divorced and at the point in his life where money meant a great deal to him. Of course, caring for his rambunctious daughter, Betsy, was a priority, too. His ex-wife remarried and settled in Ithaca, so he thankfully never saw her. She had little contact with her daughter, as she relinquished authority to her husband in the divorce proceedings. That was ten years ago, just as Betsy graduated high school. Carl bitterly thought his ex-wife made such a decision to avoid future responsibilities of her troublesome daughter, casting that burden on Carl.

Of medium height, with crisp brown hair and dark eyes, he wore a solemn face, rather hardened by the unfairness of his life, but optimistic about his future. His accounting firm downtown had prospered since opening just three years ago and Carl, at only fifty, reaped the benefits of not only his prosperous business but also his expedient stock market investments. Certainly, the dividends enabled him to maintain the old brownstone house he still lived in on Elk Street. He kept in touch with his sister, Bernice and his nephew, Alan, just three doors away and with their help; he tolerated his daughter's lively shenanigans.

Turning from the counter with a pot of coffee and a bowl of oatmeal, he placed both on the table and then entering the hall, he approached the front door. Opening it, he grabbed the paper on the step, allowing a swish of chilly air to enter the hallway before quickly closing it. At the same time, Betsy appeared at the bottom of the steps. She exclaimed her dismay to her father.

"Another cold morning, Dad. I can feel it already. You should be more careful, you know. I can't afford to get sick!"

Carl glared at his shallow daughter, ignoring her superfluous remarks, finding it too early to address them. She entered the kitchen, helped herself to coffee and sat opposite Carl at the table. Usually mornings were not the best for Betsy and Carl knew to proceed with caution when it came to his daughter's flippant remarks and her moodiness. Underneath he thought she was just shy and scared and put on a front as though to hide her true self. He sipped his coffee, ate some of the oatmeal and opened the paper, ignoring Betsy until she finally spoke.

"I see there's more about Penelope Barker." She leaned over the table to read the article on the front page that her father had not seen. Carl folded the paper back.

"Well, it says the police are investigating," he commented, adding nothing more. It did not affect him, so he was not even following it. He had heard about her murder on the radio but paid little attention. Betsy, on the other hand, seemed fascinated by it.

"A local actress murdered," she commented breathlessly. "I wonder what Alan thinks about it. Didn't he try to book her at the Hall a few times?"

Carl murmured that he did not know if Miss Barker performed at Harmanus Bleecker Hall and his tone implied he could have cared less. He kept reading the paper all the while drinking his coffee and eating the oatmeal. Betsy helped herself to more coffee and a bowl of oatmeal.

Betsy Blake was a feisty and energetic twenty-eight-year-old, petit, blonde, usually full of make-up, and naturally inquisitive. She had a rather foolish nature and lived up to the flapper standards she read about in True Confessions, Love Stories, Cosmopolitan, and True

Story. Many people found Betsy's outlandish personality alluring. Others, like her father and Aunt Bernice, found it revolting. Her cousin Alan kept neutral and like her father, ignored her behavior.

She easily interfered in friendships and romances and freely spread malicious gossip to suit her purpose. She had an outrageous egotism and a voice that could be as sweet one moment and then mean and vindictive the next. She exuded a certain captivating ambience of wealth and high class, thanks to her ambitious and money-hungry father.

While she enjoyed the company of several young men, she was not interested in the marriage state, at least not any time soon. She spent time with eligible locals such as Edward Flynn, John Whitmore and Lester Cavanaugh, finding their company a diversion. She did find Lester rather intriguing. She liked to pick on her cousin, Alan, telling him to 'loosen up.' Her position at the Albany Savings Bank was beneficial and many welcomed her lively and vivacious personality in an otherwise humdrum environment. Personally, her father wondered how she could handle money, accounts, stocks and figures but she had been employed there for over five years, so he decided not to say anything.

As usual, father and daughter exchanged morning small talk before retreating upstairs to prepare for the day. Carl handed her the sections of the paper he finished. Betsy again mentioned Penelope Barker, rereading the article on the front page.

"Too bad they haven't caught the killer," she lamented. "Although I have my suspicions."

This time Carl did look up at his daughter. Not believing half of the things she would say, he felt a strange premonition. He addressed her in a serious tone.

"If you have information to help the police, you should go to them. After all, a killer is loose here in the city. He could strike again."

Betsy laughed. "Oh, Dad, do you really think they would listen to me? Besides, I'd rather tease Alan about it. Rather fun, you know."

Carl put his head back down on the newspaper, ignoring her comments. Betsy mentioned the dance marathon that Mr. Ferguson was preparing for later in the month at the Hall. Carl mentioned rather irritably that she told him about it already last night when she arrived home.

"A teller at the bank told me she heard about it from someone at the Hall. Now that would be the bees' knees for sure! I would love to take part in it. I've read about them in Boston, Baltimore and in New York City. Now we'll have it in Albany! I wonder what Alan thinks. He must be involved with it somehow."

"Why don't you ask your cousin when you see him?" her father asked her.

Betsy murmured that she planned to do just that and then continued sipping her coffee. Carl continued reading the paper. The usual morning silence between father and daughter ensued before they trekked upstairs to prepare for the day.

In a short time, Carl came downstairs, dressed in his best three-piece suit. He stood at the hallway mirror, combing his hair and arranging papers in his briefcase. He would wait to see if Betsy would want to walk with him to catch the trolley on Washington Avenue. Certainly too cold to walk in this weather.

Betsy looked pretty in a dark green dress, a string of pearls, with just enough make-up to highlight her small face. She stood at the top of the stairs and as usual, slid backwards down the banister, triumphantly, giggling, obviously enjoying herself. Carl, annoyed beyond words, found his voice, and scolded his daughter as though speaking to a child. He had a long day ahead and did not want to get upset by her foolish behavior.

"Betsy, must you slide down the banister! I find that extremely juvenile!"

Betsy laughed. "Oh, Dad, I've done it before! Let's go or we'll be late for work." She grabbed her fur coat from the hall closet and opened the front door, not waiting for her father.

Carl had put on his coat and fedora hat. He glanced back at the staircase, thinking her foolishness of sliding down the banister must stop. He shook his head, then closed and locked the door. He hurried to keep up with his energetic and vivacious daughter, crossing Academy Park on the way to Washington Avenue to catch the trolley.

CHAPTER FOUR

Alan arrived at Harmanus Bleecker Hall just before nine o'clock. Bundled up in his winter jacket, his cap firmly on his head, he traversed the slushy sidewalk, braved the chilly air, brushing past the morning crowds on Washington Avenue. It remained cloudy, with more snow to follow.

The gloomy weather did not dampen his spirits. Albany in winter was for Alan the best of seasons. The fireplace in the living room flaming brilliantly, trollies at a snail's pace, packed with pedestrians. He even enjoyed walking through the snow on his way to work.

Approaching Harmanus Bleecker Hall, he spotted Mrs. Russell alighting from a trolley. Faithful Mrs. Russell, over thirty years at the Hall and the best secretary ever. She saw him near the entrance and steadily approached him.

"Good morning, Mr. Cartwright," she exclaimed, her face blotched from the cold.

Alan smiled. "Good morning, Mrs. Russell."

His breath froze in the air, and his legs felt like blocks of ice. Realizing they were practically blocking the main entrance, they hurried inside with a group of employees and then made their way to the staircase. Mrs. Russell did not believe in elevators.

"Never been on one and never will," she told Alan. "Don't trust the things. It's so slow, although Henry knows what he's doing."

Alan looked in the direction of the elevator and spotted Henry, an amicable middle-aged man, securing the occupants, closing the gate, before it began its slow ascent to the upper floors.

Mrs. Russell gave a snort as she mounted the stairs. "People should use the stairs. Healthier, wouldn't you say, Mr. Cartwright?"

"Indeed, Mrs. Russell," Alan remarked, walking beside her.

"Quite a steep ledge, those upper floors," Mrs. Russell said, arriving at her desk in Alan's outer office. "Maybe that's why some people prefer the elevator. I'm afraid of heights."

The staircase, wound on both sides, with the one elevator in the middle, brought people to the upper floors on a steep grade. Although only five floors, the building rose dexterously, and the upper levels were quite steep. Alan did not suffer from vertigo, but he knew his mother was not fond of heights. Apparently, Mrs. Russell was not either.

He settled at his desk, turned on the banker's lamp, lit a cigarette and looked at the stack of papers awaiting his attention. He remembered several he already addressed so those he put aside. One came from the agent of Fanny Brice, who requested her booking for a future performance. Another from Groucho Marx, praising the Hall's fine auditorium and acoustics. He planned to contact the Marx Brother's agent again soon. He noticed another memo from Mr. Ferguson on the dance marathon. It was official; the date was the twenty-ninth. Of course, Alan knew that from the board meeting, but he hoped Mr. Ferguson might have changed his mind, given the reluctance of the board members to concur with his suggestion. Certainly, Mrs. Churchill did not share his enthusiasm. His lifted his head as he heard voices in the outer office. Mrs. Russell was speaking to Norma Smith.

Soon enough Norma stood in the doorway of his office.

"Good morning, Alan," she said, entering and sitting at the chair before him. She thought nothing of calling him by his first name, while most associates referred to him by the more professional Mr. Cartwright. "I think we need to discuss the dance marathon. We only have two weeks to prepare."

Alan set aside a report, his attention diverted from his work. He did not invite Norma to his office much less to sit down. He eyed her carefully. She certainly played the part of the modern girl, appealing to men, although her flamboyance and excessive make-up were a little much for him. The black dress she wore along with the string of pearls accentuated her slim figure. She repeated her concerns about the dance marathon. He wondered if she wanted to ask him to lunch. They had dated off and on and he was never sure of her feelings for him. Admittedly, he was unsure of his feelings for her.

"I'll contact the caterers Mr. Ferguson spoke with to secure their participation, along with the dance bands. He's already circulated a memo to different departments here. I'm sure everyone knows about it already." She paused. "We can play phonograph records, too. That'll save money. You'll handle the advertising part, won't you?"

She made it sound like an ultimatum as though she made the final decisions. Alan reiterated that he planned to contact newspapers but added nothing more.

"It'd be appropriate to honor Miss Barker," Norma suggested, fingering her pearls. "She never played here, but she was an Albany native. What do you think?"

"I'm sure we can mention Miss Barker as Mr. Ferguson suggested," he managed to say, although not seeing the relevance. "She was from Albany, as you mentioned."

He knew there was bad blood between her and Penelope Barker, so he was surprised she would even mention her name. An awkward silence followed. She mentioned she would contact WGY and other radio stations, as well as the Harmanus Bleecker Library.

"Lester works there, so he'll be my contact," she said.

Alan was sure Lester Cavanaugh was her contact in many ways. He had seen them together downtown evenings and weekends. Of course, Alan did not really care what Norma did during her free time. It was none of his business. He turned his attention back to her.

"It'll be great publicity for the Hall," she said brightly. "And a real money-maker, too."

He did not realize she was so concerned about the Hall's financial status. Her role as a secretary did not involve high-level decisions, but her position on the board was another matter. He felt she used it to her advantage, siding with Mr. Ferguson, even if she disagreed.

"Evangeline may want to attend," Alan put in, watching her reaction.

"Didn't you go out with her before, Alan?"

Alan fought the urge to tell her to mind her own business. He noticed some envy in her tone, as though she resented his previous relationship with Evangeline Whitney. Irritably he puffed at his cigarette, trying to find a way to have her leave his office.

"I'm sure Betsy will want to attend, too," Norma added, getting up from the chair. "She never wants to miss anything." She expected Alan to comment on his headstrong cousin, but he remained silent, his cigarette between his lips.

"I'll take care of things on my end," she mentioned, turning back to look at him. "I'll type a report of what I accomplished and give it to you and Mr. Ferguson."

She stood framed in the doorway, awaiting a response. Alan realized that maybe she really did like him and perhaps hoped he would reciprocate those feelings. Maybe she was lonely, after all, and knew she could trust him.

"Thanks, Norma," he said and offered her a reassuring smile.

Opened in 1924, and in less than two years, the Harmanus Bleecker Library saw tremendous growth in patronage. Conveniently located on the corner of Washington Avenue and Dove Street, it was a stone's throw from Harmanus Bleecker Hall and within walking distance of many Albany landmarks, including the State Education Building and the capitol.

This morning it was business as usual at the busy library. Politicians and state employees utilized resources and staff scurried to find the information they needed. A librarian, highlighting the marvels of the children's room, entertained a school group.

Lester Cavanaugh was sorting reference books. He soon received requests for numerous volumes in the basement, where older books were stored. It was Lester's duty to retrieve them, as the library did not allow patrons on the lower floor.

He had no sooner returned to the main floor, his arms loaded with three volumes on Albany history as requested by an elderly man, when he spotted Mrs. Churchill at the circulation desk. She nodded at him and was about to turn to leave when she suddenly addressed him.

"Hello, Mr. Cavanaugh, good morning. Looks like you're weighted down with books."

She sized him up quickly. Certainly, a strong and capable young man, broad shouldered, with a fine head of blond hair, his brown eyes intent and alluring. Dressed in a clean, white shirt, tie and vest, well-mended dress slacks, he was handsome in a traditional style. She knew little about him, but she imagined his appearance and demeanor would be attractive to young women, even one a bit older. She assumed he was somewhere in his mid-thirties, certainly a desirable age for any female. She remembered seeing him out with Penelope Barker, several years ago. He must have tired of her, which Mrs. Churchill understood. She wiped the unpleasant memory of Miss Barker from her mind and looked carefully at Lester Cavanaugh.

He placed the heavy volumes on a nearby table, where the elderly man was waiting. He then reluctantly turned his attention to Mrs. Churchill. Her tone was pleasant and polite, but Lester was not one to be caught off guard. While he admired her perspicuity and fortitude in her work at the Hall and as a board member, he never felt comfortable in her presence, perhaps because he knew of her reputation, that she was demanding and painstakingly meticulous.

"Good morning, Mrs. Churchill. I see you have a book to read."

"Grace Livingston Hill's new novel," she explained, looking at the book in her hand. "A favorite author of mine." She hesitated, letting a few people pass, and then lowered her voice, almost to a whisper. "Mr. Cavanaugh, what do you think of this dance marathon idea? You are a board member, after all. I made my opinions clear at the meeting."

Lester sighed inwardly, not wishing to discuss anything with this bossy, meddlesome woman, whom he personally found untrustworthy. He cleared his throat and mentioned tactfully that he would agree to it if Mr. Ferguson wanted it, after all, he was the Hall's executive director.

He regretted even saying that to her. Upon seeing her expression, he added that he had his reservations, but with enough planning, he thought it could be pulled off without a hitch. Mrs. Churchill clicked her tongue disapprovingly.

"Well, Mr. Cavanaugh, you certainly are entitled to your opinion. I assume that the impetuous Miss Donovan will attend once it's made public. I do not understand why her father does not control her. She is a menace to the community."

She made it seem as though Betsy Donovan was a plague that was contagious and would wreak havoc anywhere she went. On that, Lester silently agreed with her, having had more than his fair share of bad experiences with Miss Donovan. On the other hand, he knew Mrs. Churchill was old-fashioned and her perceptions of young people, especially young women, was extremely archaic, to say the least.

"We've had enough negative publicity here in the city with the recent murder of Miss Barker," she said with tight lips. "I do not feel we need any more negativity."

Lester was surprised she would mention Penelope Barker. It seemed so long ago, over a month now, and her murder was still a topic of discussion. He stepped aside as more patrons milled about the library. He glanced over to the circulation desk, realizing his services were needed, which was a perfect excuse to get away from this overbearing matron. He scurried over to the main desk, leaving Mrs. Churchill rather rebuffed, before she took a last look around and left.

Lester began assisting patrons, locating materials and answering questions. Although his attention was drawn to his work, his thoughts returned to Miss Betsy Donovan and Miss Penelope Barker. Strange Mrs. Churchill mentioning them, as though she had a personal vendetta with them.

Like we all have, he thought grudgingly. He knew Ed Flynn, John Whitmore, Norma Smith, even Mrs. Churchill, Evangeline Whitney and her mother and Alan Cartwright and his mother had gripes with both Betsy Donovan and Penelope Barker.

Betsy was Alan's cousin and his mother's niece. How could they stand having her in the family? Although Betsy's father, Mr. Carl Donovan, seemed decent enough, but too good to have such a high-strung daughter. On the other hand, perhaps he had issues with her no one knew about.

He remembered how Norma threatened Penelope Barker in a heat of anger about something. Lester was not fond of her, either. And he remembered when Penelope and Betsy argued at a local speakeasy, both drunk out of their minds. Like most people who knew her devious ways, Miss Barker's demise was not a total surprise, as though she had it coming to her.

A woman requesting his assistance occupied his thoughts. He looked forward to the end of the day, when he could forget his troubles at a local speakeasy, where plenty of liquor and female attention awaited him.

As the noon hour approached, Alan decided to call John Whitmore at the Strand Theater, to see if he was available for lunch. Glancing toward the windows in his office overlooking Washington Avenue, he noticed the sun made a brief appearance, although he doubted the temperature had changed significantly from when he first arrived at the Hall this morning.

He picked up the handset of the candlestick phone on his desk and asked the operator to dial the Strand Theater. After a few connections with the switchboard there, he was connected to John Whitmore. He asked him if were available to meet for lunch.

"Hey Alan," he exclaimed. "Lunch? Sure, do you want to come here to North Pearl Street? There's the diner across the street."

Alan told him he would meet him in front of the Strand Theater in about fifteen minutes. Finishing with a few papers on his desk, he grabbed his jacket and cap from the rack behind the door, told Mrs. Russell where he was going and headed for the main exit and the blustery cold outside. Crossing Washington Avenue, he hopped on a trolley, which took him to the corner of State Street and South Pearl Street. Crossing at the light with a sizeable lunchtime crowd, he walked briskly up North Pearl Street until he came to the Strand Theater. He saw John at the entrance waiting for him. They greeted each other amicably and then John told him he needed to go to the bank, as he was low on money.

Before Alan could ask which bank, he followed him down North Pearl Street, crossing the busy intersection, arriving in front of the Ten Eyck Hotel and then the imposing Albany Savings Bank. Alan marveled at the beauty of the building, a white marble masterpiece, with ornate columns and a dome ceiling. It was busy with lunchtime workers, seeking to withdraw funds and conduct other business. John soon approached a teller and in no time was stuffing cash in his wallet. They were about to leave when they were suddenly hailed.

"Well, hello you guys. Must be my lucky day!"

It was Alan's cousin, Betsy Donovan, who stood in their path. She looked extremely well-dressed as always, with a provocative green dress highlighting her excellent figure, a great many shiny teeth, round blue eyes, enough rouge and lipstick, certainly coquettish around men.

"What brings you two here today?" she inquired sweetly.

Now why would we come to a bank, Alan thought irritably. Sometimes he thought his cousin extremely stupid. John broke the silence, keeping his temper at bay.

"For some cash, Betsy, what else," he said as though reading Alan's mind.

He knew his cousin worked at the Albany Savings Bank but hoped they would not see her, as from long experience he knew encounters with her were usually unpleasant. The times he spent with her were best forgotten, even while growing up, so the less he saw of her the better. He wondered if John felt the same. He remembered they had dated a few times, but John had broken off with her, so there could not have been any love lost between them.

"Of course, John, silly of me to ask," she smiled again and batted her eyelashes. The bank was getting crowded and Betsy, in her conniving way, led them over to her desk and invited them to sit. The murmur of voices was a steady hum. More customers entered and it was quite busy. John and Alan told her they did not have time but thanked her and started to head for the exit when Betsy said something, stopping them in their tracks.

"I hear there's a dance marathon at the Hall in a few weeks."

Alan decided to press her for more information.

"Oh, I think someone from the Hall mentioned it to a teller," she said. "I hear everyone at the Hall's talking about it, too. A dance marathon here in Albany! I can't wait to attend!"

"We haven't finished the arrangements yet," Alan said, trying to keep the irritation out of his voice. His glance went to John, who appeared equally annoyed.

Betsy went on babbling sweetly with words that were seldom more than a cover up for most likely inappropriate thoughts. Suddenly she mentioned the murder of Miss Barker and how people were discussing it here at the bank. Such a shame wasn't it, a popular actress, too.

Now why would she mention Penelope Barker, Alan thought. He remembered hearing how they had quarreled bitterly at a speakeasy, and it almost turned into a catfight. He noticed John was becoming increasingly impatient, anxious to leave.

"Dad and I will stop over to see you and Aunt Bernice real soon, Alan," she said and smiled. "We hardly ever see you even though we live so close by!"

"We really need to get going, Betsy," John finally said, cutting her off.

"Oh, well, it's nice seeing you both again," she remarked.

Alan thought his cousin looked so relaxed and composed, as though nothing could disturb her serenity, that she would look calm in the middle of a cyclone or a rescue at sea, if it suited her purpose. While he and Betsy were related and only lived a few doors away, they had little in common. Although he enjoyed the company of his Uncle Carl, his daughter Betsy was someone he preferred keeping a safe distance from and his mother agreed. He admitted to himself that he was rather embarrassed to let anyone know he was related to her.

Wind seized them the minute they stepped out onto North Pearl Street. Snow showers increased and the few glimpses of the sun Alan saw earlier faded behind thickening clouds. They walked up North Pearl until they found the diner. They sat at a booth a family had just vacated. Taking off their jackets and caps, the waiter soon appeared with menus.

Sandwiches, French fries, ice cream, coffee and cigarettes, a satisfying lunch enabled them to forget their encounter with Betsy and enjoy their meal. They discussed Babe Ruth, the favorite of the upcoming baseball season, the current movies with Valentino and Colleen Moore and the latest hit songs by Ruth Etting and Bessie Smith. It was close to one o'clock and John mentioned he needed to return to the theater. They paid the check and upon exiting, he said goodbye to Alan and that they would talk again soon. He crossed North Pearl

Street while Alan waited to catch the trolley uptown. It was only a few minutes before one pulled up and he quickly boarded. Seated between an elderly woman loaded down with packages and an executive reading the *Wall Street Journal*, he wondered about his infuriating cousin, Betsy. She had interfered with so many people's lives. He was certain she affected Evangeline Whitney, Mrs. Whitney, Ed Flynn, Norma Smith and Lester Cavanaugh. She made an enemy of them as well as Miss Barker. A sudden horrid thought crossed his mind. Was it possible that Betsy was involved somehow with Miss Barker's murder? No way, his cousin could not possibly be a murderer!

The trolley, snaking its way up Washington Avenue, soon arrived at the intersection with Lark Street. Alan jumped off, briskly heading back to Harmanus Bleecker Hall, reminding himself that his cousin Betsy usually meant trouble. And that perhaps there was more trouble to come.

Downtown Albany during the lunch hour was a busy place. Dodging pedestrians and snow showers as he walked steadily up State Street, Carl Donovan kept his head down, fighting the gusty wind on his way to city hall. The trench coat and fedora hat he wore kept him warm, but the cold seemed to go right through him. Finally arriving at his destination, he let several people pass before entering. He was greeted by warmth and a busy atrium, with several disoriented individuals, unclear where to turn for assistance. Fortunately, Carl knew right where to go. He headed for the taxation office on the first floor, as he needed to secure documents for a client. After filling out the required papers to obtain the records, he waited for no more than fifteen minutes before his request was ready.

Satisfied his trip to city hall was a success, and not too time-consuming, he was about to head for the exit when he noticed Mr. Flynn and Mrs. Whitney. He had seen them on previous visits to city hall, as he knew they worked in the building, but what their jobs entailed, he had no idea. It seemed to him they were engaged in a rather intimate conversation. He knew Mr. Flynn lived on Elk Street, not far from his house and Mrs. Whitney lived on Columbia Street, just around the corner. He preferred not to greet them as he was in no mood for small talk but as usually happens in such cases, they turned and saw him just as he reached the exit and greeted him politely.

"Well, Mr. Donovan," Ed said, shaking hands with him. "What brings you to city hall?"

Carl thought some people asked the most foolish questions. Hadn't Mr. Flynn seen him in here before? Mr. Flynn and Mrs. Whitney knew of his accounting practice, so why the surprise of seeing him? Unless he was just being polite, which Carl thought was most likely the case.

"My accounting position often requires retrieving financial documents," Carl said rather uncomfortably, as though he needed to explain his presence. "City hall is the place to find them." He smiled and was about to take leave of them when Mrs. Whitney spoke, taking him off guard.

"How is Betsy, Mr. Donovan?" she asked, sounding genuinely concerned about his daughter's well-being. "Is she still working at the Albany Savings Bank?"

Carl looked at Mrs. Eleanor Whitney carefully. A handsome woman, tall and slender, quite stylish in a floral dress, rather becoming, her hair tastefully arranged. He had thought more than once of asking her out, but hesitated, knowing she and her daughter Evangeline did not like his daughter Betsy. Therefore, he was taken aback by her question, as though she had a sudden change of heart about his daughter. On the other hand, was she just being polite too or perhaps nosy?

"She's fine, thank you," Carl said, somewhat uneasily.

"Mr. Flynn mentioned there's a dance marathon at the Hall soon," Eleanor commented as though Carl was involved with it.

Ed smiled. "Well, we haven't gotten everything squared away yet," he told them.

Carl thought Ed Flynn seemed like a well-mannered young man. He was handsome enough, his vest and dress shirt fit well around his broad shoulders, his brown hair and green eyes were impressive. Hadn't he and Betsy gone out a few times? Like she had with several other local men. But it seemed Betsy had a way of destroying relationships, so even if Ed Flynn were interested in his daughter, he did not think he stood a chance. Which he considered for Ed's sake was probably for the best.

"It'll cost the Hall a lot of money," Eleanor said, as though thinking to herself.

"We haven't worked out all of the financial arrangement," Ed mentioned. "It'll be our first marathon, so we'll see how it goes. People are talking about it already, so the word is spreading."

"What is your position here, Mrs. Whitney?" Carl asked her, surprising himself.

"I'm a secretary in the Department of Public Works," she answered him politely.

"I work in Licensing and Permits," Ed volunteered.

Good positions with the city, Carl thought, a little enviously. A strange silence ensued. More people brushed pass them, heading for different departments. Carl mentioned he needed to see a few clients this afternoon. He wished them well and turned rather eagerly toward the exit. He hurried down the steps, and instead of going down State Street, he turned right, walking past the Court of Appeals and the County Court House, walking south on Columbia Street for the short distance to his office on Broadway.

He saw Union Station ahead of him. A jewel of a building; it was across from the Peter Schuyler Building, where his accounting practice prospered. This strategic location enabled him to serve a vast array of clients from all over the state. Carl smiled to himself, knowing he was quite an affluent man. His stock market investments accentuated his wealth, too. Thinking of his financial stability helped to deflect the rumination pressing to the forefront of his mind.

Mrs. Whitney mentioned Betsy, he thought irritably, avoiding more pedestrians. Why would she ask about her? Perhaps there was something he did not know, but what? Young people today were so brazen, outlandish, and ostentatious. And deceptive, he thought grimly.

He put it out of his mind as he arrived back at his office, the work-day still ahead of him.

It was after five o'clock when Alan walked through Academy Park, evening settling over downtown Albany. Washington Avenue was a sea of radiance; the capitol lit brilliantly, city hall gleamed with light, the State Education Building was on full display, showing its grandeur with unequaled splendor. Traffic and trollies jammed the roadway, the sidewalks were full. There was a sting in the frosty air with intermittent snow showers.

Alan glanced to his right, observing the new Philip Schuyler statue in front of city hall, a spotlight highlighting it vividly, certainly a proud display of the city's heritage. Even the Court of Appeals was decked out in lights. Approaching the house, he noticed there were no lights on, and as he unlocked the front door, he saw it was completely dark. His mother had yet to arrive. He reached for a hallway lamp at the same time the telephone rang, startling him in the silence of the big house. Upon answering, he heard the comforting voice of his mother. She explained she had to work late but would be home soon, as the Assembly was still in session and the library remained open. She mentioned there was food in the icebox for him to start dinner. Alan assured her he would have it ready when she got home.

Removing his jacket, cap and shoes, he rushed upstairs to change into clothing that was more comfortable before descending to prepare the evening meal. He made coffee, as he knew his mother always enjoyed her evening coffee. Soon enough, chicken and rice were ready, although Alan admitted he was not much of a chef. He had no sooner lowered the burner on the gas stove, than the doorbell rang. Finding it strange his mother would use the doorbell, unless she forgot her key, he hurried to the front door. Upon opening it, he saw Mrs. Churchill, holding a basket and shaking from the cold.

"Hello, Rodney," she said pleasantly. "I made sweet potato pie today and wanted to bring it to your mother. I know how much she likes it."

Alan stepped aside allowing Mrs. Churchill to enter. He explained his mother had yet to arrive from the library. He took her coat and welcomed her to the kitchen, where he poured two cups of coffee, one for her and the other for himself. Sitting opposite her at the kitchen table, he wondered what Mrs. Churchill had in mind, knowing she was never at a loss for words.

"Alan, I must reiterate my disapproval of this dance marathon. I do not like it at all. I think it will draw unsavory characters to the Hall and end up a disgrace. You must do something to stop Mr. Ferguson for going ahead with it."

Alan sipped his coffee and lit a cigarette, stalling. Certainly, Mrs. Churchill meant well, but her ideas were so old-fashioned. Although he was not keen on the dance marathon initially, he gravitated more toward it as an expenditure of great value for the Hall. Of course, he did not say that to Mrs. Churchill. His response was delayed as the front door opened, letting in a whisk of cold air. Soon, Bernice appeared at the kitchen doorway.

"Hello, Alan dear. Mrs. Churchill, what a pleasant surprise! How nice to see you."

Mrs. Churchill eyed her carefully and smiled. Always charming and pleasant, Mrs. Cartwright, and certainly handsome in her dark blue dress with a lovely string of pearls.

"I made my sweet potato pie for you, Bernice," she said warmly. She was on a first names basis with both Bernice and Alan, considering them not only neighbors but friends. Usually stringent in her relations with outsiders, Mrs. Churchill was never so informal with most people, and certainly not with people at the Hall.

"Please stay for dinner," Bernice told her, sitting next to her son at the table.

Mrs. Churchill finished her coffee. "No, I've already eaten, thanks just the same. I stopped over to give you the pie." She hesitated. "Bernice, what are your thoughts of this dance marathon?"

Bernice glanced at her son. Having just arrived home, she was not quite in the mood for a discussion of something that was really of little importance to her. Sensing the urgency in the older woman's tone, she cleared her throat and commented that it was certainly hard to phantom, such an event occurring at a renowned place like the Hall.

"It's a disgrace," Mrs. Churchill said disapprovingly. "It'll bring out the worst people in the city. Mr. Ferguson wants to advertise in newspapers, doesn't he, Alan?"

Alan nodded. "I've already placed ads in papers in Albany and Schenectady."

"Ridiculous," Mrs. Churchill added with tight lips.

Bernice smiled. "I'm sure it's nothing to worry about, Jeanne. After all, dance marathons are quite popular. It could be a great draw for the Hall and make a lot of money, too."

"Do you see your niece often, Bernice?" she asked her, changing the subject.

Bernice was rather taken aback. "No, I do speak with my brother, but Betsy I hardly see."

She did not understand why Mrs. Churchill would mention Betsy, as she knew she was not fond of her. Given the proximity of where they lived, it was inevitable Mrs. Churchill would see the Donovans, too. There must be a reason why she would mention Betsy, of course. She waited for her to elaborate, but she remained oddly quiet, sipping the coffee.

Alan mentioned he would serve the chicken and rice, but Mrs. Churchill was adamant she needed to leave. She planned to shop this evening at Whitney's. Bernice and Alan followed her to the front door, Bernice thanking her again for the wonderful pie.

After dinner and washing up, Bernice retreated to the living room, where she settled with a slice of Mrs. Churchill's pie and coffee. She put on the radio to hear the news, weather report and a documentary on the current economy. Alan joined her, with a slice of the rich pie and then lighting another cigarette, reading the evening newspaper and the January issues of *Popular Science*, *Vanity Fair* and *Reader's Digest*. Bernice sensed her son was restless. She asked him what was troubling him.

"I wasn't thrilled about the dance marathon," he explained, stubbing the cigarette in an ashtray on the coffee table. "It's in the planning stages now, so I'm sure it'll be worthwhile."

Bernice took out some knitting she kept near her favorite armchair. "Well, I wish you'd be more careful, Alan. Like Mrs. Churchill says, a dance marathon could bring out the worst people."

"Mr. Ferguson wants us all to attend. He hasn't divided up the roles yet."

"I may attend, too," Bernice said, smiling, looking up from her knitting. "I've never attended a dance marathon. Should be exciting to watch."

They continued listening to the news and the political commentary on the Democratic Party and the presidency of Calvin Coolidge. *The Atwater Kent Hour* came on next and relaxing symphonic music filled the living room, creating a wonderful calming atmosphere. It was almost ten-thirty when Alan mentioned he planned to turn in for the night; he wished his mother good night and climbed the stairs to his bedroom. Within an hour, his mother went to bed, with the lights off downstairs.

Soon houses took on their usual nighttime silence; lights off, windows shuttered, and people gone to bed. Darkness had settled over the brownstones on Elk Street.

It was about one o'clock in the morning when Alan was awakened. Glancing at the alarm clock on his nightstand, he rolled over on his right side and tried falling back to sleep. But however hard he tried, sleep would not return. He lay still, listening to the wind push against the windows overlooking Academy Park and another sound he could not quite determine. He tried to concentrate on sleep, but he heard it again. A high-pitched wail from somewhere outside.

He pushed back the blankets and got up, rather irritably, thinking perhaps it was a stray dog. He crept to the right window, his bare feet freezing from the drafty cold. He lifted one of the slats of the blind just enough to see.

In Academy Park, in the distance near Washington Avenue, he saw a man and woman. They looked like they were arguing. Maybe they had come from a speakeasy and were drunk? He looked carefully, shivering slightly and wishing he had put on his socks. He then realized it was Betsy he saw in the distance. She was conversing, quite animatedly, by waving her arms and appearing upset. But whom was she speaking to? And what was she doing out at one in the morning in this frigid weather? Perhaps a clandestine meeting? A sudden horrid thought came to Alan. Was his cousin involved with illegal drugs or bootlegging?

At that point, they parted and wandered off in the direction of State Street. Alan last saw them as they rounded city hall. He lowered the slat as the snow continued to fall, returning to bed, shivering, his feet practically frozen.

From a distance and in the steady snowfall, he recognized his cousin. What was Betsy doing in Academy Park at one in the morning? Did Uncle Carl know she was out at this hour? His mind was churning over innumerable thoughts. It was after two o'clock when he finally dozed off. Less than five hours later, his alarm rang, waking him from a restless sleep.

CHAPTER FIVE

I t was still dark when Alan awoke, the alarm interrupting his early morning slumber. He brushed a hand over his face, and then swung his long legs over the side of the bed. He reached for his robe and slippers and then opened the door. He was glad his mother had turned the heat up. Even in the hallway, he could feel the drafty cold. Downstairs he heard her in the kitchen and the smell of coffee was a pleasing aroma. Descending the stairs, pulling his robe tighter around his waist, he entered to see her busy at the stove. She smiled upon seeing her son.

"Good morning, dear. I'm fixing a nice breakfast this morning. I invited Uncle Carl, Mrs. Churchill and Mr. Flynn to stop over on their way to work. Betsy may drop over, too."

Not fully awake, Alan yawned, greeted his mother, poured coffee from the pot on the stove, sat at the kitchen table and reached for his cigarettes in his robe pocket. He needed his first morning cigarette and coffee to wake up.

Bernice joined him at the table, with her coffee. "I don't have to go to work until noon today, so I invited them for breakfast. We are neighbors, after all."

Still not quite awake and given his tumultuous sleep last night, Alan yawned again, sipped his coffee and lit a much-needed cigarette, depositing the match in a nearby ashtray. Bernice looked at him with concern, noticing his tousled hair, drawn eyes and tired expression. She asked him what was wrong.

Alan hesitated, exhaling a great puff of smoke. He then took a large sip of his coffee. He decided to tell her about seeing Betsy earlier that morning in Academy Park. "Around one o'clock, I heard something outside. I went to the window and thought I saw Betsy talking with someone. I couldn't see who it was. Could've been a man or a woman."

Bernice put down her cup. "Why would she be in Academy Park at one in the morning?"

"If Uncle Carl comes here, why don't I ask him?"

Bernice disagreed. "It may not be the right time, dear. My brother tends to get upset over his daughter's behavior. That girl is so wild and uncompromising. She does whatever she wants."

She got up and put two pancakes and sausages on a plate for her son. At the same time, the doorbell rang. Wiping her hands on her apron, Bernice went to answer it. Alan could hear several voices, and soon enough his mother returned with Mrs. Churchill, Ed Flynn and his Uncle Carl. They greeted Alan pleasantly and then Bernice invited them to sit at the table while she prepared more pancakes and sausages.

"I brought the maple syrup," Mrs. Churchill said, extracting a rather tall bottle from her pocketbook. "Straight from Vermont, too." She looked pleasant and fresh in a black dress, pearls and her white hair fixed tastefully.

"The pancakes smell delicious, Bernice," her brother exclaimed, helping himself to coffee. "I can't stay too long as I have a client coming at nine."

"Same for me," Ed Flynn said, accepting a cup from Carl. "It was really nice of you to invite me here this morning, Mrs. Cartwright. I hardly ever see you or Alan."

He sat at the table, opposite Alan, and they began to converse about work, sports, Babe Ruth, the weather and the inevitable, the upcoming dance marathon. Alan sipped more coffee and tried to steer the conversation away from the marathon, but Ed seemed intent on discussing it, with Mrs. Churchill adding her two cents, or Alan thought more like fifty cents, to the discussion.

"A waste of time and money," she said, again voicing her opposition. She sipped coffee, speared a sausage and cut into the pancakes. "It'll end up costing more than Mr. Ferguson realizes. I do not like the idea of the Hall being open twenty-four hours a day or longer, either."

Carl swallowed some pancakes. "I agree, Mrs. Churchill. I can see Mr. Ferguson wanting to promote the Hall, but a dance marathon is ludicrous."

"Alan and I are on the board, along with Mrs. Churchill," Ed said. "We listened to his rationale. Personally, I think it's worth the risk. Could be the start of something great for the Hall and for Albany."

Alan glanced at Ed Flynn. Although he found him strange at times, there was something about his personality he liked. He was about his age, tall, well dressed, and certainly professional. He knew he spent much time at speakeasies and drank quite heavily, from his own admission, but Alan did not let those habits affect his attitude toward him.

Ed's exuberance was met with a silence so thick you could cut it with a knife. Only Alan concurred and voiced the same optimism.

"What could possibly go wrong at the dance marathon," he asked, as though anyone at the table had an answer. "At first, I didn't think it was a good idea but like Ed said it'll be great publicity for the Hall."

"Where's Betsy, Carl?" Bernice asked her brother, hoping to change the subject. She looked at him in his three-piece suit, looking appropriate but rather drawn, as though work pressures and the ruthless schemes of his high-strung, flapper daughter were too much for him. Her temper grew just thinking of her wild niece and the effect on her brother.

"Still sleeping," Carl explained, as though relieved. "I don't think she wanted to come here this morning. She doesn't usually eat breakfast, anyway." He paused. "I went to bed early last night, so I don't know if she was out. She's always doing something evenings."

Alan thought it sounded as though he were making excuses for her. The fact he went to bed early showed he did not know what his daughter was up to. He wanted to ask him about her nocturnal visit to Academy Park, but a quick glance at his mother silently conveyed to him that the present was not the right time.

"Do you plan to attend the dance marathon, Mrs. Churchill?" Carl asked her.

"Well, Mr. Ferguson may want my help," she said reluctantly. "Although it'll be a waste of my time. Friday nights I attend a Bible study at my church." She clicked her tongue, showing her extreme disapproval. "The young people today are too carefree, concerned with parties, dancing, smoking. In my day, a young woman knew her place, isn't that so, Bernice?"

Bernice put down her coffee cup. Although she was not Mrs. Churchill's age, with a twenty-year age difference, she did agree with her.

Mrs. Churchill shook her head. "I don't understand the younger generation."

Ed grinned. "Please, Mrs. Churchill, we're not all that bad! Alan and I have our feet firmly on the ground! We have good careers and act reasonably."

Mrs. Churchill smiled wanly at Ed Flynn. "It's a pleasure to associate with you and Alan."

Carl looked at his watch and finished his pancakes. "I really need to go, Bernice. Thanks for this delicious breakfast! You're the best sister ever." He got up and hugged her, excused himself and made his way to the hallway and the front door.

Ed Flynn also mentioned he needed to leave, telling Alan he would be in touch soon. Mrs. Churchill finished her coffee and thanked Bernice for the wonderful breakfast. She mentioned she planned to work at the hall for half the day and then visit relatives in Schenectady. Bernice joined her to the front door, and then returned to the kitchen, where she began to clean up.

"Lovely having company isn't it, dear?" she asked her son, beginning to wash the dishes. "I so enjoy entertaining our neighbors. I think I'll do it again sometime."

"I didn't mention seeing Betsy in Academy Park this morning," Alan said, still at the kitchen table, finishing his coffee. "I got the cue from you not to mention it."

Bernice nodded, washing the skillet. "My brother looks ragged. He works awfully hard, and his hideous daughter is too much." She spoke vehemently. "I cannot tolerate her at all."

Realizing he needed to leave soon himself, Alan left the kitchen and bounded up the stairs to the second floor to his bedroom. He arranged his clothes neatly on his bed and then removed his robe, pajamas and underclothes. He entered the bathroom, where he showered and shaved. His black dress slacks, vest and clean white shirt with a navy tie were immaculate. His hair, center parted, and enough after-shave helped to buoy his appearance and confidence.

Buttoning his shirt cuffs on descending the stairs, he noticed his mother had entered the living room. She was reading the morning newspaper, with the radio on, soft music a pleasant background.

"I'll be home the usual time, Mother," he said, putting on his jacket and cap. He stood in the entranceway to the living room, looking at her, although he could sense something was wrong.

"Short day for me today," Bernice told him, looking over the top of the newspaper. "The Assembly isn't in chambers today."

He said goodbye to her, closing the front door behind him. Cutting through Academy Park, he thought of his mother's negative attitude toward Betsy, and of seeing his cousin here in the park at one in the morning. His mind then drifted to the dance marathon. It was a harmless event, he told himself positively, walking briskly toward Harmanus Bleecker Hall. He even looked forward to it! With all the preparations, it would go off without a hitch, he was sure of it.

Amidst lingering snow showers and a sidewalk full of pedestrians, he continued up Washington Avenue, unaware of the impending calamity that lay ahead.

W.M. Whitney & Company, commonly known as Whitney's, was one of the most popular department stores on North Pearl Street. It catered to everyone, and it was not uncommon to see it busy during the lunch hour, when employees of nearby office buildings went there to eat in the cafeteria, to shop or simply to browse.

Evangeline Whitney's office, on the lower floor, did not see much of the customer traffic. In her role as principal bookkeeper, she was responsible for the daily cash flow as well as ensuring money was distributed for expenses, store layouts, designs, and other expenditures.

While on her lunch hour, she could not help but go to the ladies hat department on the first floor and browse the latest designer hats.

Evangeline considered a cloche hat an integral part of her apparel.

While looking at the pretty hats on display, Evangeline thought of her longing to meet the right man. She had dated Ed Flynn, John Whitmore and Lester Cavanaugh but she fixed her eyes on Alan Cartwright. She knew that was a difficult one, as Alan was so glued to his mother. On the other hand, that showed his devotion and if she only could steer that toward herself, she might have a chance. Evangeline considered herself a modern woman, but not to the extent of other flappers she knew. She smoked and drank on occasions but not excessively and was more intent on finding the right man than attending the next party. That her mother and Alan's mother were good friends helped. Her mother played bridge at the Cartwright's house with that old matron Mrs. Churchill. Maybe one of these days she will take an interest in bridge. She picked up a hat and looked at herself in a counter mirror next to the display.

She studied herself in the mirror and was pleased with her reflection; that of a bright, exuberant, fresh-faced young woman with a fine head of black hair with brown eyes, a soft complexion and just enough make-up not to overwhelm anyone. Her navy dress hung loosely in the current style and the string of pearls accentuated her thin neckline.

She found another cloche hat, this one from France and endorsed by Coco Chanel. Eagerly she placed it delicately on her pretty head, turning different angles and liking it immensely. She was about to catch the eye of the salesgirl when an unwelcomed female voice spoke to her.

"Why, Evangeline, the perfect hat. Now if only you had occasion to wear it."

Evangeline turned and saw Betsy Donovan standing behind her. As usual, Betsy wore her make-up excessively and her black and white dress was provocative and alluring, highlighting her svelte figure. Evangeline admitted her looks were appealing but her demeanor was not to her liking. She wondered what she was doing at Whitney's. She figured she would be off with some man during her lunch hour. God only knew she had had plenty of them in her life.

Betsy looked around casually, as though she could choose whatever she wanted at the drop of a hat, literally. "That is a very pretty, Evangeline. Perfect with your blue dress, too."

"Well, thanks, Betsy," Evangeline said gratefully, ignoring her previous snide remark. "I just love hats, especially the ones Coco Chanel designed!"

Betsy agreed, and then tried on a few hats, too. While taking one off and putting on another, she asked Evangeline about the dance marathon and if she planned to attend. Evangeline looked sideways at Betsy, rather taken aback, not sure how to respond.

"Mother mentioned it. I really don't know if I'll attend. I'm not one for a lot of dancing."

Betsy tried on yet another hat and looked at herself in a counter mirror. "I do say this is the most beautiful new hat for me. Another Coco Chanel creation! My, that woman over there in France knows how to design hats, wouldn't you say, Evangeline?"

Evangeline nodded, rather embarrassed by her flamboyance and loud voice. She choose a cloche hat and was about to ask the salesgirl to put it in a box when Betsy surprised her by asking her if she was going out with Alan.

Evangeline turned to look at her. It was none of her business whom she socialized with. She could easily ask her the same question. She did not think she had a steady beau, as she knew Betsy was a party-girl, who lived the flapper lifestyle much more than she did.

"No, Betsy, I'm not going out with Alan," she answered briefly, her tone implying it was none of her business who she went out with.

Catching her even further off guard, Betsy asked her what she thought about the murder of Miss Penelope Barker last month, before Christmas. Did she read about it in the papers? It was just so terrible, wasn't it? Poor Miss Barker, how could anyone do something so cruel to a brilliant stage star! And the police haven't caught the person responsible either, how dreadful. Betsy lamented the murder of Miss Barker as if she were a close friend or relative, as though it was foremost on her mind.

Evangeline caught a tone of mockery in her voice, as though Betsy knew things she did not know, or anyone else for that matter. She found her phony sincerity and flashy attitude unbecoming. Why would she mention the murder of Miss Barker? Why would she even care? She did not think Betsy could think of anyone other than herself.

"I've been seeing Lester," Betsy added. "He's quite a man, you know."

Evangeline really did not care if Betsy went out with Lester Cavanaugh. Betsy knew she had once dated Lester too, so she must have found great pleasure in bringing that up. Finding the perfect excuse, Evangeline glanced at her watch and exclaimed she had to return to work. She knew she had plenty of time, but she used it as a way to get away from the wrath of this infuriating female fox before she devoured her.

The salesgirl took the hat and gently placed it in a box, ringing the sale at the register. Glancing over her shoulder, she noticed Betsy trying on hats again, making a scene of doing so, apparently annoying a salesgirl, obviously showing off.

Thanking the salesgirl, Evangeline collected her hatbox and eagerly made her way to her office on the lower floor. Returning to her desk, her thoughts turned to Betsy. She was curious why she mentioned the murder of Miss Barker, so unexpectedly. She wondered too if she knew more about it than she let on.

After lunch, Alan decided to go to the Harmanus Bleecker Library, as he wanted to research theaters and promoters in Yonkers and Brooklyn. He told Mrs. Russell he would return shortly, and then proceeded down the stairs. He crossed at the light and although only a short distance, he hopped on a trolley, bringing him to the corner of Dove Street and Washington Avenue in no time.

It was still blustery, and the fierce arctic wind, blowing off the Hudson River, was laden with icy moisture, the frigid cold heavy in the air. He felt as though it were seeping into his bones. Descending the trolley, he huddled further into his coat, turned the collar up and his cap lower, in a futile attempt to ward off the biting wind and the persistent snow showers.

He arrived at the Harmanus Bleecker Library and had no sooner entered when he almost collided with Lester Cavanaugh in the lobby. His arms were full of books and magazines, which he barely held onto. They exclaimed surprise at seeing each other and then Alan cleared his throat, not wishing to waste time.

"Good to see you again, Lester. I need to find information on a few theaters and promoters in Yonkers and Brooklyn. Are the city directories in the same spot as the local city directories?"

Lester nodded and showed him where the directories for Yonkers and Brooklyn were located as well as the Albany and Schenectady directories. He also pointed him to the *Reader's Guide to Periodical Literature* to search for information on theaters. Alan thanked him and began to look at the directory for Yonkers when he noticed Lester hovering nearby. He turned and looked at him inquiringly.

"Something wrong, Lester?" he asked.

"Just wondering about the dance marathon." He hesitated,

fingering his tie nervously, pulling the vest lower on his waist. "I don't know if it's a good idea, although I don't think Mr. Ferguson will think differently."

Alan replaced the Yonkers directory and picked up the Brooklyn directory. He could not help noticing that Lester seemed nervous, perspiration on his forehead. "We hope to secure Eddie Cantor, Helen Hayes and Janet Gaynor at the Hall," he said, trying to change the subject. "Miss Hayes was terrific in *The Last of Mrs. Cheyney* on Broadway and Mr. Cantor had excellent reviews in *Make It Snappy*. His song *Yes! We Have no Bananas* is still played on the radio! And Miss Gaynor is one of Hollywood's leading ladies."

Lester waited for him to finish then brought the conversation back to the dance marathon. He expressed his concerns. Alan mentioned if it was Mr. Ferguson's intention to host a dance marathon that he would help wherever possible. He hoped the conversation would end there.

"Are you going out with Evangeline or Norma anytime soon?" he asked Alan.

"No, not in the foreseeable future," Alan said, keeping his patience, while thumbing through the Brooklyn directory. He did not think Lester was the inquisitive type. His contacts with him at board meetings and out on the town usually revealed him as laconic, a man of few words. He wondered if he harbored another side, jealousy a part of it. "What about you, Lester?" he asked, rather boldly. "Aren't you and Betsy an item? Haven't you and Norma been out recently? Or are you dating Betsy, Evangeline and Norma at the same time?"

"Not quite," Lester said, his voice lacking enthusiasm. "I think John's going out with Betsy or Evangeline, maybe both." He hesitated. "But then he's a womanizer, anyway."

Alan was surprised he would refer to John Whitmore in such a derogatory way. He did not perceive John as a womanizer, although he knew he enjoyed nights on the town, which for John usually meant getting drunk at a local speakeasy. But that was his business. Alan considered Lester more of a womanizer, given his shady background. He thought he and Betsy were an item. They certainly seemed to share the same loose morals. Wasn't he arrested once for disorderly conduct? As though reading his mind, Lester remarked on his previous arrest.

"My probation officer came by to see me the other day," he said, as though confiding in Alan. "He's pleased with my work. Guess I need to control my drinking and behavior in public."

He paused. "I heard someone earlier mention Miss Barker and her murder. Must still bother some people. Seems so long ago."

Alan did not know what to say, so he decided not to say anything. He wondered if Lester was trying to feel him out, to see his reactions about the dance marathon and the murder of Miss Barker. Such a strange person and unscrupulous, too.

Just then, a supervisor called Lester to the front, where his assistance was needed. Alan continued looking at the Brooklyn directory, making a few notes of theaters and phone numbers on a pad he brought with him. Satisfied with his research, he replaced the directories on the shelf and took a quick look around the library.

His attention was drawn to several patrons near the circulation desk. He recognized Ed Flynn and Mrs. Eleanor Whitney. They seemed busy, checking out a few books, most likely researching topics for their work at city hall.

Alan avoided contact with them. He milled about; looking at a few magazines and noticed Ed Flynn had left. He saw him on the sidewalk through the large windows overlooking Dove Street. He noticed Mrs. Whitney, speaking to Lester, a rather private conversation from all intents and purposes. He then saw her leave, although he could not read the look on her face.

Alan knew Lester had been involved with the underworld of this city, the nefarious gangsters that were prevalent in Albany. Neither he nor his cousin had notable reputations. He wished his uncle would discourage Betsy from associating with Lester. As kind as his uncle appeared, he would consider it meddling and would even tell his nephew to mind his own business.

On the other hand, Penelope Barker did not have a good reputation, either. He did not know her personally but despite her popularity, her standing in the theater community was abominable. She made enemies easily and her stage persona did not mirror her identity. Certainly, her behavior when visiting the Hall reflected her deviousness. He knew stage stars could be rather tempestuous, but Miss Barker was altogether too unpredictable.

Upon leaving the library, with snow and ice pellets stinging his face, Alan trudged along the busy sidewalk. Something was brewing, but he could not quite pinpoint it. He had only to wait and see what would happen.

CHAPTER SIX

I t was a week later when Alan was summoned to Mr. Ferguson's office.

The preparations for the dance marathon were slowly and steadily coming to fruition. The dance bands were booked, the caterers secured, phonograph records were collected to replace the bands as needed, medical supplies were on hand in case of injuries, and cots were rented for rest periods for the dancers. Radio stations in Albany and Schenectady heavily promoted it as well as local newspapers. Mr. Ferguson was interviewed in the *Times Union, Albany Evening Press, Knickerbocker News* and *Schenectady Gazette*. The Harmanus Bleecker Library and Albany City Hall displayed a poster, extolling the latest thrilling event at Harmanus Bleecker Hall. Even Mayor Hackett expressed interest, encouraging citizens to attend and participate.

On a cloudy and cold Wednesday afternoon, Mrs. Russell entered Alan's office and told him Mr. Ferguson wished to see him at once, although from her tone, he could tell it did not sound too promising. Certainly, the preparations for the dance marathon were progressing smoothly. He straightened his tie and vest, smoothed down his hair and left his office, heading for the stairs.

He wanted to call Evangeline, to see if she was available this weekend. He would prefer calling her at Whitney's rather than at home. He found her mother rather strange, almost reclusive and protective of her daughter.

Arriving at the fifth floor, just outside Mr. Ferguson's office, he noticed Norma in the hallway, pacing back and forth, a cigarette between her fingers. She smiled briefly when she saw Alan and asked him if he was there for the same reason.

"About the dance marathon?" she offered before he had a chance to speak. "Can't be too bad. He should be pleased with the work we've done."

Alan thought Norma covered all of her bases as though she feared any retribution. He opened Mr. Ferguson's office door for her. They saw their boss seated behind his large desk, littered with papers, a candlestick phone on one end. It was a small office, not large enough for such a big desk, Alan thought sensibly; a filing cabinet was located in a corner. Two chairs were in front, and Mr. Ferguson motioned them to sit. He took his time before speaking, shuffling papers, clearing his blotter and then he looked up at the young people before him.

"Alan and Norma, I have been impressed with the work you have done to bring together the dance marathon," he said, rather jovially.

Alan felt a weight lifted off him and by a quick glance at Norma, could tell she felt the same. While he respected Mr. Ferguson, he knew from experience his demands exceeded normal rationale at times. He waited to hear if there was anything more. He certainly did not call them to merely congratulate them.

"However, I've been aware of negative publicity," he said gravely. "While I understand people will talk and voice their opinions, any negativity could hurt attendance." He paused, lighting a cigarette. "The purpose of the dance marathon is to increase the profits of Harmanus

Bleecker Hall. I want more than just to break even with the investments we are making."

"What do you want us to do, Mr. Ferguson?" Alan dared to speak.

"Radio station WGY in Schenectady will be here tomorrow to interview us. I've already spoken with them by telephone. I decided to have the reporter speak first with you, Alan and then to you, Norma. I want you to debrief them on all the particulars in a positive light..."

"What negative publicity have you heard?" Alan asked, rather meekly.

"Many of the older residents of this community are not in favor of it. Several prominent families been quite vocal in their disapproval. While I understand this is a first for the Hall and for Albany, I do not like negative publicity, which may impact sales."

"Mayor Hackett is supporting us," Alan reminded him.

"Even the library and city hall," Norma added. "I think we'll have a good turnout, Mr. Ferguson. People will talk, but they can't stop it from taking place."

"If they have enough support, the police could shut it down," Mr. Ferguson pointed out. "Especially if anything illegal goes on, like alcohol." He paused. "Alan, will you give me an update, please?"

Alan proceeded to review the details so far. They planned on a starting time of seven p.m., that Friday, with the couples arriving at six. Each couple will have a number, worn as a bib, around their necks to identify themselves. Music will begin with the first band, scheduled to perform for three hours. There will be phonograph records after the first band finishes. The next band begins at one a.m. and will end at four a.m. There will be breaks of up to fifteen minutes for participants, including the band, giving the dancers time to rest, use the facilities, eat food the caterers provide and change clothes, shoes and socks. Alan mentioned he contacted Albany City Hospital to have a nurse available. He arranged through a furniture store to rent cots for those wishing to rest.

Mr. Ferguson nodded. "Excellent work. I do not anticipate any problems; however, I am concerned about drinking."

"We won't have alcohol at the marathon, Mr. Ferguson," Norma assured him.

"People bring in their own alcohol, Norma," he said dryly. "A dance marathon may draw such unscrupulous behavior, from participants and attendees."

"Wouldn't the participants want to stay awake?" Norma said. "I can't imagine them drinking during the event. It'd be counterproductive!"

"You would think so," Mr. Ferguson remarked. He sighed in trepidation. "We will reiterate to WGY that the dance marathon is a family event. There will be no alcohol permitted."

"We have twenty-two couples so far registered," Alan said, as he was in charge of registration and procuring payments. "But we have another week, so we may get more."

"Excellent," Mr. Ferguson said again. "The ballroom will serve as the ideal space for the marathon. Alan, you will work Friday evening as an emcee. I will be there as the master of ceremonies. Norma, you will be on hand, to assist as needed. I have designated other Hall employees to work the midnight hours. Both of you can leave after the eleven o'clock hour, as there will be replacements." He mentioned other Hall employees, from secretaries, cafeteria cooks and custodians. "Mrs. Churchill will also serve as an emcee, but she told me she just wants to watch on Friday evening. I have already contacted Mr. Whitmore, Mr. Flynn and Mr. Cavanaugh. They will serve as emcees on Saturday and Sunday."

"How long do you anticipate the marathon lasting, Mr. Ferguson?" Alan asked him.

The older man wrinkled his face in a sardonic grin, butting his cigarette in the ashtray. "With a dance marathon, Alan, it can last for several days, maybe even a week. If we have a good crowd, it could go on for a while, which is excellent publicity for the Hall."

Alan cringed inwardly as he spoke about publicity. Is that all this man thought about, the publicity and the financial benefits? Of course, he was an executive, so he would see it through the commercial aspect. Initially, Alan wanted to stop or postpone it, then changed course and accepted it. He only hoped it would go off without any problems.

Mr. Ferguson cleared his throat, signaling an end to the meeting. "Remember, tomorrow a reporter from WGY will be here to speak to you."

Alan and Norma left the office. Norma headed for the elevator but changed her mind and joined Alan down the long, wide stairs. He realized she was speaking to him.

"…will work out fine, Alan. It'll be the talk of Albany. I may even dance a bit, too!"

Coming out of his reverie, Alan nodded, only half listening. He could not focus on what she was saying. He hung onto the banister on descending the steep, curvy staircase. Upon reaching the second floor, Norma walked off to her office, while Alan headed for his own sanctuary.

Greeting Mrs. Russell, he found refuge behind his desk. A growing sense of unease overwhelmed him as he attempted to concentrate on his work.

On Friday evening, Bernice invited Mrs. Whitney and Mrs. Churchill for a game of bridge and coffee. An avid bridge player, Bernice knew she needed a fourth but unable to secure anyone, she settled on just three. They would improvise and she would take two hands, not to worry, she told Eleanor on the telephone the evening before. She called her brother to see if he was available, but Carl told her, rather vehemently, he was not interested in bridge but thanked her just the same.

After finishing dinner, she washed the dishes, and then set the table for the women who would soon drop by. She fussed about, cleaning here and there, preparing the coffee and icing a chocolate cake she had baked last night. She set the deck of cards on the table, along with coffee cups, a jug of cream, plates, forks and spoons. Satisfied with her plans, she went into the living room to turn on the radio. She twisted the dial until she found *The Atwater Kent Hour*, the soothing symphonic music soon filled the room. She turned the volume up so it could be heard in the kitchen, where she returned to check on the coffee.

Alan descended the stairs and looked into the kitchen, to see his mother busy at the sink. It was close to seven o'clock, dark and bitterly cold. He was about to tell his mother of his evening plans when the doorbell rang. Going to the hallway, he opened the front door, to see Mrs. Whitney and Mrs. Churchill, bundled in their coats like Eskimos. He stepped aside, taking their coats and hats, quickly closing the door. Bernice entered to greet her visitors.

She led them to the kitchen, where they sat at the table and were soon discussing this and that, the winter weather, the snow, the slushy pavements, the church rummage sale, sales at Whitney's and of course the upcoming dance marathon, just a week away.

Alan joined them in the kitchen and heard their comments on the dance marathon. He expected Mrs. Churchill to chastise him for agreeing to it. Instead, she offered him a rare smile and invited him to join them, as his mother dealt the cards and the game got underway.

"Looking forward to the dance marathon, Alan?" Mrs. Whitney asked him pleasantly.

Feeling somewhat uncomfortable, he helped himself to coffee from the pot on the stove, to avoid the women at the table. He put sugar and cream in his cup and stood by the sink, too deep in thought to actually hear what they were saying.

"Alan, Mrs. Whitney is speaking to you," his mother said, looking at her son.

"Oh, I'm sorry, Mrs. Whitney. I'm meeting Ed, John, Norma and Evangeline in a little while. I've got a lot on my mind."

Mrs. Whitney smiled. "Evangeline mentioned you are going to a speakeasy tonight?"

"There's a coffee house on Broadway," he lied, as he knew his mother did not approve of speakeasies. "Probably we'll go there."

"Betsy, too, dear?" his mother inquired innocently.

Alan looked at his mother, knowing full well the casual comment was a cover for a more decisive tone. She would prefer her son not to associate with his cousin, under any circumstances.

"I really don't know, Mother. She may have a date tonight."

"Miss Donovan is nothing but trouble," Mrs. Churchill said. "I know she's your niece, Bernice, but I am not in the least comfortable around her."

"The dance marathon is just a week away," Mrs. Whitney commented, stirring her coffee.

Bernice smiled. "It's just a harmless dance marathon. Rather exciting, really."

Mrs. Churchill looked at her with raised eyebrows. "Do you plan to attend, Bernice?"

She shrugged. "Perhaps. I've never been to a dance marathon. I've read they are quite the entertainment. Or as the younger people say the bees' knees."

"What is your role going to be, Alan?" Mrs. Whitney asked him.

Alan stood at the counter, sipping his coffee, wondering why Mrs. Whitney was showing such an interest. Maybe for Evangeline. He did not think she was interested in it herself.

"I'll be there as an emcee," he told her. "Mr. Ferguson is paying us overtime for working at the dance marathon. Everyone will be working the marathon in some capacity."

"Does that include you, too, Jeanne?" Bernice asked her.

Mrs. Churchill grimaced, and then reluctantly answered. "Yes, I told Mr. Ferguson I'd be there over the weekend. It's an abomination and a waste of the Hall's resources."

"I may drop by, too," Bernice said, with a mischievous smile. "We can go together, Eleanor. Maybe kick up our heels! I haven't danced in years."

Bernice and Eleanor laughed but Mrs. Churchill was silent, sipping her coffee.

"Well, to each his own," she said dryly, as she played her cards. She sipped more of her coffee. "Mark my word, Bernice and Eleanor, nothing good will come from this ridiculous dance marathon. Trust me when I say that. I mean *nothing*!"

Her words were like a judge's gavel, pounding the word *nothing* explicitly, as though pronouncing judgement. They continued playing bridge, with little conversation, as though Mrs. Churchill's words had a distinct impact.

Alan retreated to the living room, with a strong desire for solitude. Sitting on the sofa, loosening his tie, he sipped his coffee, lit a cigarette and listened to *The Atwater Kent Hour*. He picked up from the coffee table the current issues of his mother's favorite magazines; *Vanity Fair,* *Photoplay* and *The Saturday Evening Post,* and glanced through them.

Why did Mrs. Churchill make such a negative pronouncement? He assumed in her rather old-fashioned way of thinking, she saw modern ideals as festoons of discomposure, perhaps an injustice, certainly a disservice. He blew smoke, hearing the howling wind against the windows. It's just a dance marathon; he told himself repeatedly, a harmless dance marathon.

The side streets off South Pearl Street harbored many small shops, cafes and businesses. In a nondescript old building on Howard Street, a tailoring and dry cleaner, well established in the community and catering to local residents, did exceptional business by day. Evenings, a speakeasy with quite a notorious reputation was in its basement, to which the owners turned a blind eye, as they were not the proprietors. As usual, customers needed a password, a door attendant quite vigilant and disconcerting as to whom he allowed inside.

It was to this place of inebriation that Alan, along with Ed, John, Norma and Evangeline ventured that Friday evening. After leaving his mother, Mrs. Whitney and Mrs. Churchill at their bridge game, Alan walked to Washington Avenue, where he hopped on a trolley to take him to the corner of State and South Pearl Streets. Once there, he made his way to Howard Street, where he met Ed and John outside. He smiled upon seeing them.

"We're waiting for the girls," Ed said, puffing away at a cigarette. "Norma called me earlier and said she'll meet us here."

"I spoke to Evangeline, too," Alan told them, his face red from the cold. "Let's go inside before we freeze to death."

"Should be a good crowd tonight," John said eagerly, already slurring his words.

The young men approached the door and Ed knocked, waiting for the door attendant. Upon the small window opening, he spoke a code that Alan did not hear and then the door opened, allowing them to enter.

To their surprise, they saw Norma and Evangeline there already, waiting for them, near the entrance. Norma had a drink in one hand, a cigarette in the other. She smiled upon seeing the young men, her black dress rather provocative, clinging to her shapely figure, her bobbed hair fixed tastefully. Evangeline held a cigarette and a glass of ginger ale, looking pretty in a chiffon dress and high heels.

"Sorry, guys, but we weren't going to wait outside in the cold," Norma chided them.

They took off their coats and caps, leaving them with the cloakroom attendant. Alan glanced around, taking in the scene before him. It was small, noisy, and smoky, but much more crowded than the last time he was there, which was several weeks ago. Perhaps the cold weather was making people desire to drink, he thought. There was a band playing popular tunes and the dance floor was full. John went to the bar and ordered drinks and with Ed's help, they carried them to the table where Alan, Norma and Evangeline were sitting.

Ed asked Norma to dance, and before long Alan and Evangeline were on the dance floor, enjoying the music. John was chatting up a blonde-haired woman, who he was quite smitten with and, to Alan, was making rather a fool of himself. Obviously, he already had a little too much to drink, but the blonde-haired girl held his attention, and they continued chatting quite amicably.

The evening wore on with more dancing and drinking, with

revelers packing the already crowded club. Ed and Norma were still on the dance floor, enjoying a lively Charleston. Alan and Evangeline returned to the table, squeezing their way between tables and couples. They had just sat down when Alan and Evangeline looked up and saw Betsy with Lester beside her.

"What's she doing here?" Evangeline said, finishing her cigarette, clearly annoyed at seeing Betsy. "Of all nights for her to come here. Why couldn't she find another place?"

Alan watched as his cousin sauntered across the floor, clearly enjoying the glances men gave her as she headed toward the bar, looking chic in a low-cut beige dress, with sparkling earrings, diamonds on her fingers and a lovely string of pearls, and stylish high heels. Lester followed, looking ever the professional in a dark suit and tie, handsome, debonair, charming and rather reckless. He noticed several women eyeing him carefully, smiling and hoping he would ditch the girl he was with and approach them.

Alan finished a cigarette and lit another, emptying his glass of beer. It would be a long night with them here and he wondered if they should leave, knowing Betsy once inebriated, usually meant trouble. He glanced at Evangeline whose thoughts mirrored his own. He then looked at the dance floor to see if he could find Ed and Norma. They were lost in a sea of dancers. He looked to his right and noticed John still talking to the blonde-haired girl. They were laughing, talking and smoking, obviously enjoying each other's company.

Alan spotted Betsy and Lester talking and laughing with a few people they seemed to know near the bar. Lester ordered drinks and before long, he and Betsy had glasses and cigarettes in hand. Alan was glad they stayed near the bar and did not venture to a table. He looked up to see Norma and Ed approaching, smiling and rather flustered from dancing.

"Hey everyone," Norma said breathlessly, Ed trailing behind her. "That was quite a dance!"

"It'll prepare you for the marathon," Ed laughed.

"Please, no mention of that tonight," Norma said jokingly.

Ed lit a cigarette and one for Norma. "You dance a mean Charleston, Norma."

"I have Arthur Murray's dance school to thank," she joked. "Those lessons were worth it! And Vernon and Irene Castle, too. They're the bees' knees in dancing!"

They laughed and the atmosphere was light and amiable. Evangeline noticed a few girls she worked with at Whitney's. She motioned them over and the party continued its lively discourse, laughing, drinking, smoking and enjoying the ambience. Ed volunteered to order more drinks and he soon returned with beer, gin for Norma and another ginger ale for Evangeline.

Through a cloud of smoke, Alan noticed Betsy and Lester. They approached the dance floor, watching the dancers before turning to find an empty table. As there were none available, he saw they were about to head back toward the bar, when Lester spotted Alan. He motioned to Betsy to follow him.

"Hey Alan, great seeing you here," he said jovially, acknowledging the rest. "Great night, isn't it? I've never seen it so crowded. Must be the cold bringing everyone out tonight."

Lester began conversing with Alan and Ed. John soon returned and was talking with Lester, the blonde-haired girl at his heels. Norma and Evangeline were laughing, chatting, and smoking and it seemed to Alan as though they were talking mostly in an attempt to ignore Betsy, who remained standing, clearly perturbed at having been left out. She sipped her gin cocktail in great gulps and puffed furiously at her cigarette, her temper rising.

While Alan listened to his friends, his glance returned to his cousin, who he knew was far from content, standing near their table, brooding. He motioned her to find an empty chair and to join them, but Betsy was clearly not having it. Evangeline and Norma were not paying her any attention; Ed and John were both entranced by the blonde-haired girl and by now were too intoxicated to even know Betsy was near them. He looked around to see if he could find an empty chair, but he did not see one anywhere. His glance returned to Betsy, knowing something would soon happen, something ugly.

The music continued loud and inviting, the dance floor full, amidst more drinking, smoking and tantalizing conversations. Ed was on the other side of the club, talking with a few girls he recognized. John and the blonde-haired girl retreated to the dance floor, while Alan asked Evangeline to dance. She graciously accepted, both eager to escape Betsy's anticipated wrath. Lester left Betsy's side and sat in the chair Evangeline vacated, striking up a conversation with Norma, lighting her cigarette and seemingly enthralled by her seductive prowess. Despite the loud music and raucous behavior of the crowd, Betsy's volatile aggression could not be mistaken or overlooked. Several heads turned her way as she lashed out at her targets.

"What the hell is going on?" she flared, aiming her fury at Lester and Norma. "You came here with me, remember, Lester? You're nothing but a lounge lizard! And you, Norma dear, are nothing but a gangster's moll."

Lester and Norma looked up at her, fury and contempt in her eyes. Norma, drawing on her cigarette, spoke mockingly, edging her on.

"Well, Betsy darling, I wouldn't talk about molls. Haven't you been involved with gangsters long enough? That bathtub gin you sell on the side, without your father knowing."

"Join us, Betsy," Lester implored, trying to maintain a semblance of peace and finding humor in the situation. "Let's have a good time tonight, after all, that's why we came here."

Norma laughed, exhaling a large cloud of cigarette smoke. Alan, Evangeline and Ed returned to the table at that moment, followed by John and the blonde-haired girl. Betsy remained standing, obviously livid.

"Watch out, everyone," Norma berated. "Betsy's peeved off, so take cover!"

"Oh, you are acting so hotsy totsy, like the whole world owes you everything!" Betsy retaliated, quite loudly. "You think you're so swank and ritzy, you man stealing hussy! Try this on for size, Norma dear!"

Before Norma could shield herself, Betsy hurled the remainder of her gin, which was not much, at Norma's face. The liquid splashed over her dress, causing quite a mess. Lester tried to calm Norma, but it was to no avail. Enraged, she got up and was at Betsy in two steps. She grabbed her by the hair and spun her around, causing her to fall, Norma delivering punch after punch. Betsy flung her arms wildly, screaming invectives at Norma, kicking her, causing her to be thrown off balance. They struggled furiously, where Norma practically had Betsy by the throat.

The crowd had either cheered them on or gasped in horrified silence. Lester, Ed and John broke them apart, before Norma was able to strike her again. Alan and Evangeline got up and attempted to calm Norma while Lester took Betsy by the hand and guided her to the front entrance. By now a bouncer, a large heavyset middle-aged man, approached them and quickly dispelled anything further from happening, telling them to leave.

As they made their way among the people in the club, Alan noticed it did not appear to faze anyone at all, as though a catfight was not something out of the ordinary. The rowdy crowd continued dancing, drinking, laughing, talking and smoking just as though out of the ordinary had happened. Gratefully taking his coat and cap from the attendant, he helped Evangeline on with hers and then he, Evangeline, Norma, Ed and John walked out of the club onto Howard Street. The chilly night air seemed to restore their vitality. He noticed Norma was still in a vile temper, but John and Ed attempted to pacify her.

"It's too cold to walk home, so let's get the trolley and call it a night," Ed suggested. "Don't worry, Norma. Nobody likes Betsy; you're not the only one."

"I could kill her," Norma breathed, grinding her teeth. "Give me a cigarette, with you, Ed?"

They walked south on Howard, turning left on South Pearl Street, heading for State Street. Alan thought Norma seemed to relax some and gain her composure. Evangeline helped to calm her down. John told her not to worry about tonight, Alan and Ed saying the same. Norma apologized profusely for her behavior, but Alan reiterated not to worry, that they understood perfectly. He apologized for his cousin's outlandishness.

It would have worked too, Alan thought, if they had not spotted Lester and Betsy on the corner of South Pearl and State Streets. Lester was in the process of flagging down a taxi when Betsy turned and made eye contact with Norma. As they were less than one hundred yards apart, Norma had the last gushing blow. Between puffs of her cigarette, she lashed out verbally, regardless of who heard her.

"You haven't seen the last of me, Betsy dear. You made a fool of me. I'll get even with you if it's the last think I do, and believe me, I will."

A cab had pulled up. Lester opened the door for Betsy, who merely laughed, albeit nervously, at Norma as she entered. Lester followed and closed the door as the taxi sped off.

They crossed State Street in silence and in no time, a trolley arrived.

Alan settled next to Evangeline, with Ed, John and Norma in the back. He could hear them talking, but his mind was elsewhere. He glanced at Evangeline, who was quiet and appeared morose over the ordeal. The trolley rounded the curve in front of city hall.

Alan realized he was soon home and wanted nothing more than to crawl into bed, hoping by morning the whole episode would have been just a bad dream, easily forgotten.

At around the same time Alan left to meet Ed, John, Norma and Evangeline, Carl Donovan was ensconced in his favorite armchair in the living room of his well-furnished brownstone on Elk Street, a fire warming the room comfortably. The radio played symphonic music, as Carl enjoyed *The Atwater Kent Hour*, one of his favorite programs.

The current issues of *The Saturday Evening Post*, *Popular Science* and *Readers Digest* were on the end table, along with a cup of tea and a pack of cigarettes. On the coffee table in front of him were Betsy's magazines, but Carl was not interested in *True Confessions*, *True Story* and *Harper's Bazaar*. He attempted to steer his daughter's reading interests in more scholarly and meaningful directions, but he had not been successful.

At the moment, he was reading the *Albany Evening Journal*. He noticed an ad proclaiming the dance marathon at Harmanus Bleecker Hall all the rage for Albany, set for next Friday, the twenty-ninth. He turned the page rather quickly, his eyes drawn to an article about the murder of Miss Penelope Barker. He read it several times, frowning. He ruffled the pages and put the newspaper aside, reaching for his cigarettes.

He heard the grandfathers' clock in the hallway chime eight o'clock. It was so damn early, he thought irritably. He was alone, not the preferred evening of choice for a middle-aged divorcee, but he learned to live with it. Betsy was already gone for the night, so he did not know when or if she would return. He lit a cigarette and blew smoke impatiently.

His mind drifted to Mrs. Eleanor Whitney, a divorcee, living just around the corner on Columbia Street. He thought more than once of asking her to dinner or the theater but decided against it. He knew Betsy and Evangeline did not get along. Admittedly, he found Mrs. Whitney rather odd. Didn't he see her carousing over Ed Flynn, especially since they worked in city hall? On the other hand, was it John Whitmore or Lester Cavanaugh?

Carl continued smoking, his mind turning once again to Penelope Barker. He found his temper mounting. Few knew of the time she entered his office, vehemently demanding he give her a tax break. She was delinquent on her taxes for 1923 and she wanted a break for 1924. He told her that was impossible. She then set out to damage his business reputation, spreading malicious gossip, which made its way back to him. He had enough contacts in Albany to see her finished off, ruining her theater career in the city.

Finishing his cigarette and the tea, he picked up the issues of *The Saturday Evening Post*, *Popular Science* and *Readers Digest*. Flipping the pages of *Popular Science*, he contemplated the sudden death of Miss Barker. He was not in the least concerned that she came to a bad end.

CHAPTER SEVEN

On Saturday morning, the sun made a weak appearance, and it remained cold, although the wind had subsided. Alan savored the warmth from his blankets, stretching luxuriously in bed, knowing he did not need to prepare for work. A quick glance at his alarm clock told him it was almost eight thirty, quite a late time for Alan to sleep in. He felt comfortable in his warm blankets, and was prepared to fall back to sleep, when the memories of last night's ordeal at the speakeasy came flooding back, like a giant tidal wave sweeping him off his feet. The memories were so strong he sat up and brushed a hand over his startled face. He looked around as though he did not know where he was, then immediately thought of his cousin and uncle, only a few doors down. And if Betsy told her father about last night, if she went home at all.

He threw back the blankets and reached for his robe and slippers. Upon opening the door, the usual aroma of coffee was a wonderful reminder of the serenity of this big old house. He could hear his mother busy in the kitchen, the smell of oatmeal wafting through the hallway. Upon reaching the kitchen, he saw her at the table, sipping coffee. She looked up upon seeing her son, commenting on the late hour. From her demeanor, he could tell she was not pleased about something; he could make a good guess what irritated her. But how did she find out so fast? Not wasting time, Bernice cleared her throat and spoke firmly.

"Your uncle called me about an hour ago while you were still sleeping. He told me all about last night's episode at the speakeasy." She paused, putting down her coffee cup. "You told me you were going to a coffee house last night."

Alan poured a cup of coffee from the pot on the stove, sleep still in his eyes. He then joined his mother at the kitchen table, fumbled for his pack of cigarettes in his robe packet and was about to put one to his lips, when Bernice spoke again, this time more firmly.

"Alan, you are not a child, so I do not feel I need to reprimand you. But I do not like you to go to speakeasies. I believe I have made that clear. As long as you are living here, then you must respect my wishes. What you do when you are not living here, is your business."

Alan sipped the coffee and sighed inwardly. Sometimes he wished he lived on his own. Certainly, Ed and John seemed content living alone. Even Norma in her rooming house seemed satisfied. And Lester had a nice place near the river. Perhaps it was time for him to move out. He could afford to live on his own. He did not say that to his mother, of course.

Bernice pushed back some gray hair from her obstinate forehead. It was obvious she was angry with her son. She told Alan her brother mentioned that upon arriving home last night, Betsy was extremely upset, crying heavily, almost delirious, and Carl had all he could do to calm her down. She mentioned how Norma Smith had threatened her in a heat of anger and was physically abusive. Lester Cavanaugh accompanied her and spent time with them in the early morning, finally leaving about one o'clock, helping Carl to settle Betsy, assuring them he'd stop by in the morning.

90

Alan waited for his mother to finish, and then put down his coffee cup. He lit his cigarette, bringing smoke into his lungs and then exhaling in great satisfaction. In listening to what was obviously Betsy's side of the story, he wondered if she told her father that she instigated the whole ordeal, by throwing her cocktail in Norma's face. He puffed at his cigarette and asked his mother just that, to which Bernice nodded.

"But Miss Smith attacked her first. Did you see it, Alan?"

Alan felt his stomach in knots. Since when did his mother defend Betsy? He thought she was supporting her brother more than she was supporting her deplorable niece. He looked at his mother through a cloud of smoke.

"Yes, Mother, I saw the whole thing as did Evangeline, Ed, John and Lester. Betsy was angry that Lester was talking to Norma."

Bernice nodded. "My niece is a hot-headed young woman. I'm not defending her. She may press charges against Miss Smith for assault. I am thinking of the shame and humiliation my brother will experience, especially if people talk."

"Do you think Betsy will report this to the police?" Alan asked his mother.

Bernice shook her head. "Your uncle didn't say much, he was rather upset by his daughter's behavior. He'd like to speak to Miss Smith, although I advised him not to."

Alan sipped his coffee, deep in thought. It didn't occur to him that his cousin could press charges over Norma's display of aggression, even if Betsy provoked it.

"This is embarrassing for me, too, dear," Bernice said, rising to fill her cup and then returning to the table. "Betsy has brought shame and disgrace to this family. I have an important job at the capitol, and nothing can jeopardize it."

Alan looked at her incredulously. "Mother, I hardly think what happened between Betsy and Norma would ruin your position at the library. How would people there even know?"

Bernice set her mouth firmly, still rather angry. "Alan, are you forgetting that people will talk? Albany is not so big that people know everything that happens. Your uncle is well known in his accounting firm and people know he is my brother." She paused, seething in apparent disgust. "Anyone could figure his daughter is my niece."

Alan thought she was so humiliated by the relation that she would prefer to go into hiding than admit she was the aunt to Betsy Donovan. Personally, he did not see the big deal, but given the older generation, they would make it seem so scandalous. Betsy came out of it relatively unscathed. His reverie was interrupted by his mother, placing a bowl of steaming oatmeal in front of him, gently sprinkled with nutmeg.

"And have you forgotten, dear, that Mr. Ferguson will learn about it? I hardly think it would look good for Harmanus Bleecker Hall, since Miss Smith is employed there. Exactly the sort of conduct he and Mrs. Churchill detest; wild, aggressive, drunken behavior. Certainly, a bad image for the dance marathon, too."

She mentioned the milkman was delivering this morning and that she planned to go grocery shopping on Lark Street. She disappeared upstairs, leaving Alan alone at the kitchen table.

Between a spoonful of oatmeal and sips of coffee, his mind turned to the dance marathon. His mother was right; Albany was small enough that people would know what happened. Certainly, Mr. Ferguson would have found out soon if he had not already. If Betsy were foolish enough to bring charges, it could cause negative publicity for the Hall, certainly for Norma and even Uncle Carl's accounting practice.

Smoking one cigarette after another, his coffee cold, Alan felt an overwhelming sense of impending doom, rather strongly as before, as though a foreshadow of misfortune was brewing.

The Cathedral of All Saints, on the corner of South Swan and Elk Streets, was one of Albany's distinguished places of worship. Completed in 1888, it maintained a steady group of parishioners and hosted multiple events.

It was later in the morning when Mrs. Jeanne Churchill, a communicant of the cathedral, left her brownstone on Elk Street. Braving the chilly air and the slushy pavement, she walked the short distance. As a member of the women's group, she was involved in several functions, one of which was the planning of the annual rummage sale. She made her way to the rectory and upon entering, was greeted pleasantly by several friends and associates.

"Well, good morning, Mrs. Churchill," Mrs. Norton smiled, a fellow volunteer. She was quite friendly, with an outgoing personality. "The members are here, so you can get started with the sorting, if you'd like."

Mrs. Churchill took off her winter coat, leaving it on a chair, and immediately began to help. It was rather a chaotic scene, with women rushing about, depositing items in boxes, pricing this and that and deciding what to eliminate and what to include. The afternoon wore on, with most items sorted into boxes, ready for the upcoming sale.

Afterwards, the volunteers settled in the kitchen for coffee and Mrs. Churchill gladly joined them, rather tired from the arranging of the various items. She enjoyed chatting with the members, most of whom she had known for years and were friends. She was eager to hear any news in the neighborhood. In this case, she was not disappointed.

"My granddaughter went to that speakeasy on Howard Street last night," Mrs. Glasgow, a chief volunteer said, sipping coffee. "There was quite a row there, I understand."

"What happened?" another woman asked.

"Well, my granddaughter told me there was a fight between two girls, can you imagine? It was that Miss Betsy Donovan and Miss Norma Smith. They must've been drunk to act in such a repulsive manner."

A low murmur of assent was heard. Another volunteer, Mrs. Clark, commented on the corrupt youth and such a shame to the community, too.

"Miss Donovan and Miss Smith?" Mrs. Churchill said, feeling a lump in her throat. She put down her coffee and looked at Mrs. Glasgow across the table and at the other women.

Mrs. Glasgow nodded. "I guess there was a catfight. Miss Smith really slugged Miss Donovan. Must've been quite a show!"

A few laughs went around the table, while another volunteer brought over a coffee cake. Several members helped themselves to the delicious confection, but Mrs. Churchill remained numb, rather in a state of paralysis. A member asked if she was feeling all right.

Mrs. Churchill blinked. "Oh, I'm fine, dear, just rather tired. The cold gets to these old bones, you know."

That the majority of the volunteers were roughly the same age or older than Mrs. Churchill, they concurred with her, smiling and laughing, chiding that she was young and full of energy. Mrs. Churchill was undaunted by what Mrs. Glasgow told them. She pressed her for more information.

"I'm afraid that's all I know," she told the group. "Isn't that the same Miss Smith who works at the Hall, Mrs. Churchill?"

Mrs. Churchill set her lips firmly. "Yes, her name is Miss Norma Smith. She is quite a character. I don't know her too well, but she is one of those modern young women, you know."

"You mean the flappers," someone added.

"Disgraceful," another woman said, to which they all agreed.

"Who is this Miss Donovan your granddaughter mentioned?" Mrs. Norton asked.

"Mr. Donovan's daughter," Mrs. Glasgow said, finishing a piece of the coffee cake. "He's an accountant on Broadway. He prepares our taxes every year. Does a good job, too. His daughter is quite the flapper, drinking, smoking and keeping late hours."

A brief discussion of the lack of morals and values in young people began in earnest. A volunteer mentioned she had seen Miss Donovan frolicking on Lark Street, acting untoward with a young man in her company. A click of tongues and murmurs of dismay. Just what was the youth coming to, they pondered, such appalling behavior.

"Exactly what we don't want at the dance marathon," Mrs. Churchill said. "Miss Smith works at the Hall. Her behavior is totally out of line."

"Another terrible ordeal in our city," Mrs. Glasgow lamented. "Last month it was the murder of Miss Barker, on Lancaster Street, not far from here."

"Albany used to be such a refined city," another member added nostalgically. "Now it's overrun with wild young people, gangsters, and bootleggers."

Mrs. Glasgow commented that they had accomplished what they set out to do and that she needed to leave, as her daughter and son-in-law were visiting later in the day. Several of the women rose to leave, but Mrs. Churchill remained seated. Mrs. Norton asked her if something was wrong.

Mrs. Churchill, always in control, smiled. "No, I'm fine, dear. I must leave, too."

The ladies wished each other well, and then exited the rectory. Mrs. Churchill walked south on Elk Street, just as light snow started to fall, deep in disturbed thoughts.

So, Miss Donovan and Miss Smith had a row last night. Well, she would not think about Miss Smith. But that repugnant Miss Donovan was another story. Mrs. Churchill had had her fair share of problems from both Miss Barker and Miss Donovan. At least Miss Barker was out of the way. Now if only the same could be said for Miss Donovan, too.

At the Donovan's house on Elk Street, Carl was in the living room, reading the morning paper, trying to forget the deplorable incident between his daughter and Miss Smith. Betsy slept until almost nine o'clock, having settled down after arriving home late last night with Lester.

It was almost nine-thirty and Lester had arrived fifteen minutes earlier. Upon entering the living room, he again apologized to Carl for what occurred at the speakeasy last night.

Carl returned to his armchair and looked at Lester Cavanaugh. He invited him to sit on the sofa, across from him. Certainly, a hand-some young man, he could understand Betsy's draw to him. He knew of his reputation with numerous women in Albany, one of whom was Miss Penelope Barker. Now he had seduced his daughter or had his daughter seduced him? He came out of his reverie to see Lester lighting a cigarette and casually depositing the match in the ashtray on the coffee table.

"Perhaps if you hadn't spoken to Miss Smith none of this would've happened," Carl said abruptly. He had mentioned that last night and reiterated it again. "You can see how my daughter would become jealous over *your* behavior."

Lester avoided his eyes. "I meant nothing by it," he lied. Ever the playboy, Lester always played the field. He would not mention that to Mr. Donovan, of course. Betsy referred to him as a lounge lizard, which to him was simply fine.

"How is Betsy this morning?" he asked, hoping to change the subject.

"Why don't you ask her yourself," Carl said dryly, lighting a cigarette.

At that moment, Betsy slid down the banister as usual, and entered the living room, looking more serene and composed. That she slid down the railing told her father she was feeling much better. Her floral dress and string of pearls were quite pretty. She smiled upon seeing Lester and sat next to him on the sofa, mentioning she was feeling better. Carl decided to speak to them again, direct and to the point.

"Betsy, your behavior last night was appalling," her father told her. "I am a successful businessman here in Albany. I will not have any disgrace brought to me, my company or to the Donovan name. Do you understand?"

Betsy nodded, rather meekly. "I'm sorry, Dad, but Norma got the best of me."

Lester crushed his cigarette in the ashtray and suggested they go out for breakfast, but Carl was not in the mood for eating out. He was still irritated over the incident but found the complacent behavior of the young people in front of him more aggravating. Did they not realize the seriousness of the situation?

"Will you press charges, Betsy?" Lester asked her.

Betsy smiled, rather coyly. "Well, I'm not sure, Lester dear." She squeezed his hand. "That certainly would shake Miss Smith up, wouldn't it?"

Again, the unruffled attitude they exhibited disturbed Carl. He knew his daughter had enraged so many people in the community over the years by spreading malicious gossip, in one form or another, tarnishing reputations. Even Lester had not escaped her wrath. Carl was surprised Lester would even bother with her, but he had a feeling he knew the reason. Her behavior reminded him of Miss Barker, manipulative, vindictive, and cunning. He did not raise his daughter to be vengeful but blamed his bitter divorce and his inconsiderate ex-wife for ruining Betsy. He realized his daughter and Lester were in the hallway. He joined them, asking where they were going on such a cold morning.

"Downtown," Betsy said, bundling her fur coat, her cloche hat firmly on her head. "It'll do me good to spend money and enjoy a good meal!"

She was out the door and almost across Academy Park. Carl looked at his high-strung daughter in the distance, and then turned to Lester, who seemed confused by the ordeal, which surprised Carl. He always believed Lester was level-headed but by his facial expression, it was obvious he was preoccupied, whether for Betsy, Miss Smith or himself. He asked him what he thought of his daughter's predicament.

Lester looked drained of energy as though the situation was out of his realm and he could do nothing to rectify it. "Darker than the night," he mumbled, resorting to a euphemism. He caught up with Betsy, leaving Carl staring after him.

CHAPTER EIGHT

Friday, the twenty-ninth was another cold, blustery January day, with more snow predicted for later in the afternoon. The day looked ominous, with dark storm clouds rolling in by late morning. The snow meant little to Alan except in a busy city like Albany, the nuisance of slushy sidewalks and riding on crowded trollies.

Upon waking that morning, he had no foreboding of disaster. He felt confident with the preparations in place, everything would go as planned. He wondered if the forecast would stop people from attending the dance marathon. Certainly, a heavy snowfall could curtail attendance.

Alan was glad he would have the afternoon free. Mr. Ferguson told his staff to work a half the day in the morning and then return before six, when the participants would arrive. He added that overtime pay would accrue, so participation would be rewarded monetarily, to everyone's satisfaction.

Lazily getting out of bed, he tied his robe around his waist, slipped his feet into slippers, and then put the radio on. After listening to advertisements for Rudolph Valentino's new film, Lillian Gish appearing at the Strand Theater and commercials for *Listerine, Wonder Bread,* and *Borden Milk*, he heard the weather report. Snow, heavy at times, starting late this afternoon and continuing into the evening and overnight. He padded to the right window, lifting the blind, to look out onto a frozen world of whiteness, glimmering in the weak sun in Academy Park. He yawned, still not quite awake, and scratched the stubble on his face.

After showering and shaving, dressing in his customary shirt, tie and vest, he descended the stairs, to see his mother at the kitchen table, reading the morning paper. It was the usual routine, but there was tension evident. Would she still harbor anger over his going to the speakeasy?

He poured coffee from the pot on the stove. Bernice looked up from the paper and asked her son if he planned to attend the dance marathon this evening. Alan found her question rather superfluous; she knew he would be attending and participating.

"I work half a day today," he reminded her, realizing the tension was the dance marathon. "I'll be home after one, and then I go back for six when the dancers start to arrive."

"Humph," was all Bernice said, her curt answer enough for Alan to realize her displeasure. She hesitated, as though she wanted to add more, and then returned to reading the paper.

Changing the subject, he mentioned he would shovel the steps and the sidewalk in front of the house when he returned this afternoon, as well as put the garbage out and do the laundry.

"I may attend this evening, too," Bernice said, surprising him, reconsidering her opinion. Alan swallowed coffee, almost gagging upon hearing her affirmation. "Are you serious, Mother? I didn't think you would go."

"Uncle Carl told me the other day he plans to attend, so I may as well. I'm sure there is no harm in it. Your cousin will be there, too."

"You may enjoy it, Mother," he said encouragingly.

Bernice nodded. "Carl didn't mention if Betsy plans to participate, but you know Betsy. She never wants to miss anything." She paused. "I hope there will not be friction between Betsy and Miss Smith. I assume she will be present, too."

Alan explained that Norma would work at the marathon, but he doubted if anything would pass between her and Betsy. Mr. Ferguson would not allow it. He had already spoken to Norma about the speak-easy incident and expected the utmost professional behavior on her part. He thought there was something more to what his mother was alluding to about Betsy. He agreed that his cousin was not one to miss anything, especially an attention-grabbing event like a dance marathon.

"I'm sure she'll be the center of attention," Bernice continued, with tight lips. She added nothing more, looking again at the newspaper.

Alan sipped coffee, puffed on his cigarette and later that evening would remember his mother's exact words. Betsy would certainly be the center of attention, indubitably.

As predicted, the snow started to fall steadily just as the afternoon progressed. Upon returning from the Hall, Alan shoveled the steps and sidewalk in front of the house, but after completing his task, he realized his efforts were in vain. The snow left a fresh blanket of white where he had already shoveled. Rather than fight a losing battle, he shook snow off his boots and found relief in the shelter of the warm house. He removed his boots, socks, jacket and cap, his cheeks flushed from the cold. He had no sooner hung up his jacket than the telephone rang. Thinking it was his mother, John or Ed, he was surprised to hear the excitable voice of his cousin. She spoke so quickly he could not get a word in.

"Alan? This is Betsy. What time does the dance marathon begin tonight? I can't wait to start dancing! I'll dance the night away! It'll be the best time ever!"

Alan grimaced, hoping she forgot or had other plans. Of course, with the publicity on the radio and in the newspapers, he knew that was impossible. And with her father attending, how could she not go? He kept his voice level when addressing his overzealous cousin.

"At seven, Betsy, but I don't remember receiving your registration for the marathon."

"Oh, I may decide to dance a little," Betsy said, laughing and sounding extremely childish. "I'm sure there'll be lots of people there. I can't wait for the fun to start!"

Alan was surprised when Betsy asked him to take her to the marathon. Lester or even John or Ed, would surely accompany her? He hesitated, not knowing what she had in mind. Ed's apartment on Elk Street was at the end of the street; certainly, she would rather go with him. He mentioned this but she simply brushed his comments off. He relented and suggested they meet in front of the Boys Academy at five-thirty. He hung up before Betsy could add anything further.

Entering the living room, he turned on the radio and heard another advertisement for the dance marathon, an enthusiastic announcer inviting everyone to attend.

A worthwhile and timely event for this new year of 1926, ladies and gentlemen, the first in Albany! The dance marathon, at Harmanus Bleecker Hall, begins this evening at seven o'clock. You don't want to miss it!

The latest hit song by Ethel Waters, followed by commercials for *Dentyne Gum* and *Carnation Evaporated Milk*, diverted his attention.

Alan knew Norma, Ed, John, Evangeline and Uncle Carl would attend. His mother and Mrs. Churchill would make an appearance. He wondered if Mrs. Whitney would attend.

He put his feet up on the coffee table and chain-smoked, flipping through the pages of the latest issues of *Popular Science*, *Ladies Home Journal* and *Readers Digest*, until it was almost time to leave. He realized he had a long evening ahead of him. Mr. Ferguson should have his head examined for this harebrained idea, he thought irritably. Initially he was against it, and then he changed his mind. Now that it was upon him, he was having second thoughts.

Finishing a last cigarette, he flew upstairs and dressed in his best shirt, tie and vest, his dress slacks recently pressed at the dry cleaners, along with his two-toned shoes, the perfect ensemble. He slicked back his hair and applied aftershave, looking quite debonair. Glancing at his watch, he saw it was already five thirty-five. Rushing downstairs, he put on his coat and cap and flew out the front door, almost forgetting to lock it. He crossed Elk Street and saw Betsy waiting in front of the Boys Academy, a hard look on her face.

"You said five-thirty, Alan," she said impatiently, looking chic in her fur coat, her cloche hat resting daintily on her head. "I don't like waiting outside in this frigid weather! You could've gotten here earlier, you know."

Was five minutes so important, Alan sighed inwardly. He suggested they hop on the trolley to escape the cold. They crossed Academy Park, waiting on Washington Avenue and soon enough a northbound trolley appeared, crowded with many attendees and participants, headed for Harmanus Bleecker Hall. The trolley soon arrived at the corner of

Washington Avenue and Lark Street. Alan and Betsy disembarked, in a heavy snow shower.

A large banner above the front entrance proudly proclaimed *ALBANY'S FIRST EVER DANCE MARATHON FOR 1926*. A momentous and certainly highly anticipated event, with people milled about the entrance, as though debating whether to go in.

Brushing past the assembled crowd, Alan and Betsy entered and saw quite a busy scene. The doors to the ballroom were wide open, and the dance band was already on stage, practicing their set. Alan spotted Mr. Ferguson, looking rather debonair in a tuxedo, acting quite the master of ceremonies, standing at the ballroom entrance, beckoning participants and attendees to enjoy the evening at the dance marathon. It was an important occasion; radio station WGY was there, reporters from the *Albany Evening Journal* and the *Times Union* were on hand as well as an official from the mayor's office. Newspaper reporters from Utica and Ithaca were also there.

Alan and Betsy greeted Mr. Ferguson pleasantly. After a few minutes of idle chatter, Betsy appeared restless. At first glance, she took in the scene then wandered off, as though she planned to enjoy herself and did not need the company of her cousin Alan. Looking at her as she strode around the large atrium, Alan wondered what she was up to. He followed Mr. Ferguson's eyes. They saw Betsy, chatting with a group of people, laughing and talking quite loudly.

"You brought your cousin with you, Alan?" Mr. Ferguson asked. His tone held disapproval.

"No, my cousin asked me to take her," Alan explained rather defensively. He did not know what else to add, so he thought it best to remain quiet. Sensing the growing anticipation as more dancers and attendees filled the atrium, headed for the ballroom, he felt a strange premonition as though something unplanned would occur. He saw

Betsy talking and laughing with another group of young men, flirting girlishly. He wondered if she had already had something to drink, as he knew she kept a flask tucked away in her stocking.

He told Mr. Ferguson he would return shortly; he wanted to leave his jacket and cap in his office and proceeded to the second floor. He needed a few moments of respite, because he knew deep in his heart it would be a long and unsettling evening.

It was an energetic group at the start of the dance marathon. Twenty-two couples kept time with the lively music, which included jazz, blues, swing, polkas, waltzes, fox trots, and the Charleston. To the right was the rest station for male competitors and to the left was the rest station for females. A nurse was available, and cots were ready in each area.

Alan stood next to Mr. Ferguson on the stage, observing the scene. He noticed the food booth, between the rest areas. Mrs. Churchill and Norma helped the caterers with the concessions, including sandwiches, cookies, coffee, tea and lemonade. During the fifteen-minute break times, dancers could eat, use the bathroom, sleep or change shoes and clothes or ask the nurse for assistance. As it was just starting, Alan did not think the nurse would be needed yet.

On the stage, Mr. Ferguson spoke into a microphone, graciously welcoming attendees, who eagerly filled chairs around the dance floor. It was arranged similar to a boxing ring; as guard ropes protected the dancers, with chairs around the perimeter. Much excitement was evident as Alan heard squeals of delight, amazement and surprise from the audience, watching in fasciation as the dancers twirled around the floor. Friends and family cheered some couples on. Others exhibited rather flamboyant dips, to the astonishment and approval of the crowd.

On the wall across from the stage was a banner than read ONE DROP AND OUT. Alan found that rather amusing, but he knew the rules of a dance marathon; participants must remain upright while on the floor and if they dropped just the once, they would be eliminated.

He continued watching the dancers, admiring their graceful and sometimes comedic moves and certainly enjoying the lively music of the band, tapping his foot in rhythm. He spotted Betsy in a corner among the attendees, having what appeared a lively discussion with several young men, appearing to edge them in obvious flirtatiousness. He hoped she would not walk over to the concession area and spot Norma. Of course, that area was strictly for the dancers but knowing Betsy, she would go wherever she wanted.

He glanced at the ballroom entrance and saw Ed and John. They looked around, taking it all in, as though they had other plans but wanted to see what was happening first. Alan hoped they were not intoxicated, as he knew they were inclined to drink excessively. He was not sure they would attend opening night but as they were board members, Mr. Ferguson must have insisted. Within a few minutes, he spotted his mother, Uncle Carl and Mrs. Whitney walking in practically together, followed by Evangeline. His mother looked pretty in a floral dress, pearls and high heels, his uncle in a business suit. Mrs. Whitney and Evangeline appeared smart in dresses and pearls, Alan thought Evangeline looked forlorn, even lonesome. While observing the dancers, her mother was talking almost nonstop with his mother and Uncle Carl. He then saw Evangeline start to talk with his mother and Uncle Carl began chatting with Mrs. Whitney, quite animatedly. He wondered if Uncle Carl and Mrs. Whitney would become an item.

In less than ten minutes, Alan noticed Lester casually stroll into the ballroom, like he was a movie star or someone of great importance, as though everyone would stop and take notice of him. His cap was lowered cunningly below his right eye, giving a rather seductive aura about him. He walked with an arrogant self-confidence, looking quite dashing in a suit and bow tie. His handsome appearance would certainly draw females to swoon over him, which Alan knew he relished. Sure enough, Alan saw several females turned in his direction. Like John and Ed, he appeared to take everything in at once, as though sizing up the situation and trying to determine if it was worth his time. But like with John and Ed, Mr. Ferguson most likely required his attendance, as he was a board member. Alan wondered if he too was intoxicated, as he knew Lester had a notorious reputation to drink.

The dance marathon continued, with more people arriving to watch, exclaiming gleefully at the participants and the thrilling sounds of the dance band. It was a festive event, with much merriment and scintillating conversations. As Alan stood on the small stage alongside Mr. Ferguson, observing the dancers and the attendees, he was glad it had gone off without a hitch.

"Excuse me, Alan," Mr. Ferguson said, turning to him. "I'd like to introduce you to Senator Walter Miles and his charming wife, Louise. They are here as our guests. Would you show them around the Hall? Mrs. Miles has never been here before."

Alan smiled and shook hands with the elderly couple, certainly a distinguished pair. He led them to the ballroom entrance, past many attendees, to the large atrium, where several people congregated, enjoying the festive music. Several people were even dancing.

"Quite a lively evening here," Senator Miles observed, smiling at the crowd.

"The music's so great that people are dancing here, too," Mrs. Miles said, as they entered the atrium. "Makes me what to kick up my heels and join them!"

"Not at this time, dear," the Senator said, putting his wife in her place.

Alan looked at people dancing in the atrium, which he found rather bizarre. He did not know if he should break it up or let the attendees enjoy themselves. Mr. Ferguson did not mention anything about dancing among the attendees. Of course, the music was so enticing; he felt he would have wanted to dance himself. He did a double take when he saw his mother dancing with Ed Flynn and Mrs. Whitney dancing with John Whitmore. He then noticed Evangeline dancing with his Uncle Carl. Why not, he thought, they seemed to be enjoying themselves. Isn't that what the dance marathon was for? He spotted Betsy dancing quite ostentatiously with Lester, laughing and acting boisterously, causing several heads to turn in her direction.

Alan led the Miles up the left staircase, to the second, third, fourth and fifth floors, climbing the steep marble stairs carefully, noting the reception rooms, planning areas and Mr. Ferguson's executive office on the fifth floor.

"Quite a place," Mrs. Miles observed, obviously impressed, looking down at the atrium from the fifth floor. "The marble staircases on both sides are just beautiful and so ornate. Although that is quite a drop to the bottom. I've always been afraid of heights."

From the fifth-floor passageway, they could hear the band playing great music in the ballroom. Below in the atrium, attendees were still dancing, rather playfully, enjoying the rhythms and the buoyant atmosphere, without the stress of competition.

"I agree with you, dear," Senator Miles said, looking away from the ledge where they stood. "Rather makes me dizzy. Why don't we return to the ballroom?"

Alan was about to lead them down the left staircase, the way they came up, when he felt a draft of cold air around his legs. He turned and noticed a fire door, slightly ajar. He told the Miles to wait at the top of the staircase, and then walked over to the door. Upon inspecting it, he noticed snowy footprints leading to the right staircase. He knew the fire escape went down to the parking lot in the back. His first thought was that someone got in this way without paying. Opening it further, he did not see footprints on the snow-covered steps, although it appeared there were footprints on the landing just outside the door. The maintenance crew, he realized, shoveling snow.

Alan secured the fire door and then walked along the passageway, joining the Miles. Descending the marble staircase and skirting around the dancers in the atrium, they entered the ballroom and met up with Mr. Ferguson. He was soon enraptured by the excitement of the dance marathon, the open fire door and the snowy footprints forgotten.

It was close to eleven o'clock and so far, none of the participants had been eliminated. With plenty of break times, they managed to stay upright, although slouching was evident. Alan helped Norma and Mrs. Churchill with the concessions, while Ed and John mingled with the other attendees, asking girls to dance in the atrium and apparently enjoying the music.

"Quite a spectacular, isn't it?" Norma said to Alan, handing a cup of lemonade to a dancer.

"It's the bees' knees," Alan said enthusiastically. "Mr. Ferguson seems pleased, too."

"Alan, I'm sure you know Miss Sarah Evans," Mrs. Churchill introduced a young woman to him. "She works in the kitchen and is helping with the concessions."

Sarah Evans mentioned to Alan that she had seen him during the day at the Hall but had never had the chance to converse with him. She was about twenty, medium height and slender, with large brown eyes and a perpetual excitable personality. It seemed Norma was already acquainted with her. Watching her rush back and forth to assist the dancers during breaks, Alan smiled in spite of himself, thinking Miss Evans was exactly who Mr. Ferguson would want to assist with the festivities. Her enthusiasm was evident and very pleasing, he noted.

Mrs. Churchill had just handed a sandwich to a young dancer when Ed Flynn came up to them. Alan could tell he had been drinking and wondered why tonight of all nights, he had to drink.

"Hey, Alan, Norma and Mrs. Churchill," he slurred. "Hey, Miss Evans, how's it going? Great party, isn't it? Norma, do you want to dance? What about you, Mrs. Churchill? How about shaking a leg with me?"

"Mr. Flynn, I hope you haven't been drinking," Mrs. Churchill said, with much disfavor.

Ed laughed, loosening his tie. "I'm in control, Mrs. Churchill, but I'm here to have fun, too." He laughed, obviously tipsy, and Alan could see the anger flushed in Mrs. Churchill.

Norma told Ed she would dance with him in the atrium, excusing herself from Alan and Mrs. Churchill. Alan thought she wanted to get him away from Mrs. Churchill as she could also tell he was drunk. He hoped she would not encounter Betsy, who he knew was still in the atrium. They walked out of the ballroom, leaving him alone with Mrs. Churchill and Sarah Evans.

"Just what we didn't want, Alan," Mrs. Churchill commented. "His behavior is deplorable. Although, I am sure he is not the only one."

Alan looked toward the stage and observed John conversing amicably with Mr. Ferguson. He then approached the concessions booth.

"Hello Alan, Mrs. Churchill," he said pleasantly, looking dapper in his suit, vest and tie. "There's another party of sorts in the atrium. Lots of dancing and Betsy acting her old silly self!"

Alan and Mrs. Churchill looked at each other curiously. They knew there was informal dancing going on, but with Betsy, just about anything could happen. As though by silent agreement, they followed John out of the ballroom, leaving another kitchen helper in charge of concessions. Sarah Evans and another kitchen worker joined them, standing at the bottom of the right staircase, admiring the merriment in the atrium. Alan noticed it had gotten more crowded, some people dancing, obviously enjoying the great music from in the ballroom, others watching and milling around, pleased to attend an actual dance marathon.

"I'm surprised Mr. Ferguson is allowing this," Mrs. Churchill remarked to Alan.

Alan chose his words carefully, knowing Mrs. Churchill did not approve of loud, aggressive behavior. "Well, I'm sure it's just harmless fun, Mrs. Churchill. If I wasn't working here tonight, I'd be dancing, too!"

"That hasn't stopped Miss Smith," Mrs. Churchill remarked dryly.

They watched as Ed and Norma were dancing a fox trot, along with Lester and Mrs. Whitney, Carl and Evangeline, and Bernice and John. Alan was surprised he did not see Betsy until he heard her laughing loudly with a young man, who was twirling her around the dance floor, obviously enjoying being the center of attention as usual. The fox trot soon ended and then a polka began, with more twirling and circular movements. Alan marveled there were two dance marathons:

one in the ballroom for competition, the other in the atrium, purely for amusement. Bernice saw her son and went over to him.

"Hello, dear," she exclaimed, catching her breath. "I can't remember when I've enjoyed myself so much. The music is just wonderful! I haven't danced like this in years."

Mrs. Churchill set her mouth firmly. "I'm glad you're enjoying yourself," she said dryly.

"We'll dance again later, Mrs. Cartwright," John told her and smiled.

Norma and Ed approached them. "You're the best dancer, Norma," Ed told her.

"You dance very well, Miss Smith," Mrs. Churchill complimented her.

"You shake a mean leg, too, Ed darling," Norma said, smiling.

"You're quite the dancer, Miss Whitney," Carl remarked to Evangeline.

"Who is Betsy talking to near the staircase?" Evangeline asked, looking in that direction.

"Oh, that rude niece of mine," Bernice said, looking after Betsy.

Betsy had made her way to the top of the marble staircase. Despite the music and dancing, she managed to grab nearly everyone's attention below in the atrium.

"My goodness, what is she doing now?" Bernice exclaimed, horrified.

"Betsy, come down here!" Carl ordered his daughter as though speaking to a child.

Alan thought his uncle often spoke to his daughter as though speaking to a child. Certainly, her outlandish behavior justified it. Betsy had rapidly climbed the right staircase, reaching the fifth floor. She looked down at the atrium, laughing girlishly, pleased to have an audience.

It was a few moments later when Mr. Ferguson entered the atrium. "What's going on here?" he demanded, obviously perturbed, coming up to Alan and Mrs. Churchill. He joined the others in looking upward at Betsy, who was enjoying make a spectacle of herself. "Miss Donovan, come down here at once!"

"A show-off," Norma said, looking up at Betsy. "She loves the center of attention."

"Stupid girl," Mrs. Churchill remarked. "Just what does she think she is doing?"

"She's making a fool of herself," Ed commented wryly.

"I do hope she's careful," Mrs. Whitney worried.

"Why must she act like that tonight," John said irritably.

"Betsy, come down here right now!" Lester demanded, having come from the ballroom.

"Oh, Lester, you're all mine, baby!" Betsy giggled, knowing she had an audience. "This is how you slide down a banister. I'm a pro and it's so much fun! The bees' knees, for sure! Watch me show you all how to do it!"

Out of long habit, and laughing quite loudly, she perched herself on the marble banister at the top of the staircase and began to demonstrate how to slide down, much to the astonishment and horror of everyone below. But it did not go as planned. While beginning to glide along the railing, very carefree, she lost her grip, slipped and screaming horrifically, fell five flights below, crashing down horribly onto the marble floor of the atrium.

For a stunned moment, nobody moved. Betsy lay sprawled, spread-eagled on the hard floor, hideously twisted and broken. Collecting himself, Alan moved quickly with Mr. Ferguson and Carl behind him. With Carl's assistance, Alan tried to find a pulse, feeling her wrists and then shaking her face lightly. Carl and Mr. Ferguson

113

shook her wrists and legs, hoping to bring blood back into circulation. Carl was beside himself, trying in vain to resuscitate his daughter.

By now, the others had gathered, forming a small circle. Someone asked for Lester, but nobody could find him. Ed told them he would get a bag of ice. Evangeline and Mrs. Whitney mentioned they would go for the nurse. Bernice went to call an ambulance, while Norma and Mrs. Churchill attempted to control the attendees. They pressed forward, wondering what happened. Alan looked up into the startled eyes of Mr. Ferguson and his uncle. He swallowed hard and his face turned a pale white.

"She's dead," he gasped, registering shock and horror. "Betsy is dead!"

CHAPTER NINE

E xcerpt from the *Albany Evening Journal*, Saturday, January 30, 1926.

ENTERTAINMENT NEWS

A horrific scene last night at the dance marathon at Harmanus Bleecker Hall. Miss Betsy Donovan of Elk Street, Albany, was killed in a tragic accident. According to witnesses, while on the top floor, Miss Donovan lost her footing and slipped on the stair railing, falling to her death. Because of this unforeseen calamity and the effect it had on participants and attendees, the executive director of Harmanus Bleecker Hall canceled the remaining event. Her father, Mr. Carl Donovan, also of Albany, survives Miss Donovan. An official police investigation is underway. Anyone with information is asked to contact Harmanus Bleecker Hall or the Albany City Police. In other entertainment news, actress Barbara La Mar has died of complications associated with tuberculosis in California at the age of 29...

By late Saturday afternoon, Alan and his mother had helped Carl as much as possible. He had spent Friday evening with them, and was not up to returning home, at least not yet. Bernice prepared breakfast, lunch, and was in the process of making dinner. She found the more she kept busy, the less she thought about what occurred at the dance marathon.

Alan joined Carl in the living room, bringing him a fresh cup of coffee and a corn muffin, but Carl had little appetite. He had eaten nothing at breakfast and only picked at the chicken Bernice prepared for lunch. He sat in one of the armchairs near the fireplace, deep in thought, staring straight ahead, a blank, exhausted expression on his face. He looked up at his nephew as though just realizing he was there. He tried to formulate words but found speaking an effort.

"Betsy was a good girl, basically," he mumbled, dazed and rather incoherently. "She had her faults, but she had a good heart. She didn't deserve this, Alan."

Alan sat across from his uncle on the sofa, feeling helpless. It had been a long evening and a longer day today, with acquaintances stopping by to pay respects to Carl. Mrs. Whitney and Evangeline visited in the morning, while several neighbors came by to offer condolences, some bringing bread and baked goods. But Carl was too anxious to even acknowledge their presence.

Alan had just lit a cigarette, depositing the match in an ashtray, when the doorbell rang yet again. He wondered who it could be now. Upon opening the front door, he saw Ed Flynn and Mrs. Churchill on the doorstep, looking anxious and rather perplexed. He stepped aside allowing them to enter. Taking their coats, he mentioned Carl was in the living room.

"Mr. Donovan, I am so sorry," Mrs. Churchill said sympathetically, upon entering and seeing Carl in the armchair. "I am profoundly sorry for your loss. Please accept my condolences."

Joining them in the living room, Alan looked at his uncle pitifully. He did not get up to greet Mrs. Churchill or Ed Flynn, almost as though he wished they were not there. As remorseful as he felt, he could tell his uncle had heard enough condolences, especially from this infuriating old woman, who he knew his uncle personally could not stand. Alan had heard Mrs. Churchill apologize repeatedly to him last evening, so why keep saying it? He knew Mrs. Churchill did not like Betsy, so he found her sentimentality rather difficult to take. And Ed Flynn, too. Why in the world would Ed care about Betsy? He knew Betsy had gone out on several occasions with him, but she had dropped him like a hot potato, for reasons he never knew. He regretted not having a closer relationship with his cousin, but given her disposition, how could he? He blinked as he realized Mrs. Churchill and Ed were talking to Carl.

"If there is anything I can do to help, Mr. Donovan," Ed said, "please let me know."

Carl forced a tired smile. "Thank you, but there is nothing anyone can do. I will plan for the wake and funeral, of course, at St. Mary's Church."

Mrs. Churchill nodded. "I still do not understand how it could have happened. Betsy was in control. You've said she always slid down the banister!"

The image of Betsy sliding down the banister brought back memories for Carl and Ed, even Alan mentioned he had seen her doing just that several times. As much as he disapproved of his daughter behaving in such juvenile ways, Carl admitted it was part of her persona. Only Mrs. Churchill remained tip lipped, disapproval distorting her wrinkled face.

"I told Mr. Ferguson nothing good would come out of this dance marathon," she said, irritably. "The Hall will end up losing money." She cast a quick glance at Carl, who was still sullen and quiet. "I am so sorry, Mr. Donovan. It was most inconsiderate."

A strange silence followed. Alan looked first at his uncle, who understandably remained withdrawn. Mrs. Churchill was obviously perturbed, although Alan could not tell if she was perturbed over Betsy's death or the negative publicity for the Hall. Alan noticed Ed's face was blank, either too shocked to reveal his true feelings or harboring guilt about something.

The silence was broken by the arrival of Bernice, who stood in the doorway, announcing dinner was served. She greeted Mrs. Churchill and Ed and invited them to stay, but they declined.

Seeing Mrs. Churchill and Ed at the door, Alan then joined his mother and uncle in the kitchen, where a sumptuous meal of ham and hot biscuits awaited him.

After dinner, Lester called Alan and invited him to his apartment. He wanted to offer his condolences to Carl, but Carl refused to speak to him. Bernice told her son not to bother with Mr. Cavanaugh, but Alan held his ground.

"I'll be back later, Mother," he said, putting on his jacket and cap. He stood in the doorway to the living room, looking at the rather pathetic figures of his mother and uncle, sitting in the armchairs near the fireplace, listening to the radio and reading the evening paper. He felt deep remorse for his uncle but did not know what more he could do for him. Suddenly, he felt stifled, with an uncontrolled urge for fresh air. He was out the front door in three quick steps and once outside, breathed in the invigorating cold air. He walked through Academy Park, over to Washington Avenue, crossing at the light and stood in front of the capitol, awaiting the next southbound trolley.

For a Saturday evening, it was busy and when a trolley finally arrived, it was crowded. He sat between a middle-aged man, on his way to Union Station to catch a train to Utica and a young woman, who was engrossed in *Gentlemen Prefer Blondes* by Anita Loos, all the rage when published last year. Alan decided he would eventually get around to reading it.

The trolley turned left onto State Street and at the corner of State and Broadway, he disembarked. Lester's apartment overlooked the Hudson River, not far from the imposing Delaware and Hudson Railroad Building. Walking the short distance, he climbed the snowy steps of the building and pressed the buzzer. The door clicked open and once inside, he mounted the stairs to Lester's apartment.

After knocking and waiting, he could hear voices and to his surprise, Norma answered the door. She moved aside, allowing him to enter. Taking off his jacket and cap, he was greeted by Lester, who shook hands with him, and then welcomed him into the living room. To Alan's even further surprise, he saw Ed, John and Evangeline sitting around the spacious living room, drinking, smoking and talking. With everyone assembled, Lester gulped a large swallow of Scotch and spoke abruptly, getting straight to the point.

"I want to talk about what happened to Betsy. That's why I asked everyone here tonight."

Alan was rather taken aback by Lester's bluntness and concern for Betsy. He did not think him capable of such profound emotion or that he even cared for Betsy so much that he would ruminate over her untimely demise in such a grievous manner.

"You said you think it wasn't an accident?" John asked him, sipping his Scotch and puffing away on a cigarette.

"Better watch what you say, Lester," Ed warned him. He too was drinking quite heavily and smoking one cigarette after another.

"Honestly, I don't know what to think," Lester admitted irritably, refilling his glass and offering more Scotch to whoever wanted it.

Alan accepted a glass from Norma, sipping the hard liquor, lighting a cigarette and sitting on the sofa, next to Evangeline. He noticed she was stoic, almost immobile, too shocked to speak. Ed and John were sitting in armchairs near the windows, close to drunkenness, which he supposed was their way of coping. Norma sat on the floor, smoking and sipping the liquor. She seemed the only one composed, almost relieved. Lester was indignant, although Alan could not tell if his wrath was toward Betsy or something else. He listened as he continued talking.

"How could she have slipped off the railing?"

"It happened so fast," Evangeline spoke up, catching them by surprise. "She was acting her normal self and then she fell so hard on the ground. I couldn't bear it."

"Evangeline, we all saw it," Norma spoke assuredly. "Betsy met with a terrible accident."

"The ambulance crew pronounced her dead," John commented. "They told us there was nothing more that could be done. Death was instantaneous."

Evangeline shuddered and even Alan felt a degree of anxiety. He listened while John and Ed discussed what happened to Betsy, like playing a phonograph record repeatedly. Norma poured more Scotch and retrieved another pack of cigarettes from her pocketbook. Lester sat brooding, listening to John and Ed and finally having enough, telling them to stop talking. He had everyone's attention again as he spoke.

"Listen, we all had bad experiences with Betsy. If the police investigate this, as it says in the paper, we may be questioned about our relationship with her." He paused. "That could open a new can of worms, you know."

"We have nothing to hide," Ed said sensibly, finishing his Scotch.

Lester smirked. "Are you serious, Ed? Norma and Betsy had a fight at the speakeasy, are you forgetting? Betsy knew of my involvement with the local bootleggers and criminals. She broke up with you and John, threatening to expose secrets."

John cleared his throat. "I'd rather not discuss that, Lester."

"Yes, I agree," Ed said. "Betsy spread unfounded rumors about all of us. She had a reputation for destroying lives."

"She wasn't the type to confide it," John said, sounding regretful at his previous involvement with Betsy. "She was a two-faced person. I never trusted her one bit."

"Like Penelope Barker," Ed mumbled.

Lester nodded. "Penelope and Betsy had practically the same temperament."

Even Evangeline agreed. "She resented my dating you, Ed. When she found out I was seeing Lester and John, she was enraged."

"Didn't she resent your dating Penelope, too, Lester?" Norma asked him.

Lester cast a glance at her. "Yes, she certainly did resent it. I tried to keep it a secret from her, but she found out. She confronted Penelope about it, too."

"There's no reason to mention Miss Barker," John said firmly. "I prefer not to discuss her. She has nothing to do with this unfortunate occurrence with Betsy."

Norma agreed. "Betsy did make trouble for me, too. She was jealous of my relationship with Lester and tried to break us up."

By looking at their faces, Alan could tell they had been hurt and angered by his cousin, who maliciously spread gossip in downtown Albany, a tight-knit community where nearly everyone knew everyone else. He listened as Lester continued talking.

"Something must've happened to Betsy while on that banister," he exclaimed.

John shrugged. "Like what, Lester? She just lost her grip and fell. Simple as that."

"Is it really?" Ed said, lighting another cigarette.

"What are you implying, Ed?" Evangeline asked him, a frightened tone in her voice.

"Well, I don't know," he answered. "I really don't know."

"We all saw it," John insisted. "It was simply an accident, that's all."

"Enough for now," Norma said, hotly, almost slamming her glass on the coffee table. She got up in a huff, going to the windows overlooking the Hudson River. She turned and addressed them, a slight tremble in her voice. "Lester's right. If the police investigate Betsy's death, we may be under suspicion of murder."

"Murder?" Evangeline said, clearly in shock. "But she just lost her balance and fell! As John said, we all saw it. There was nobody with her on the stairs."

They continued discussing what happened to Betsy, offering suggestions and finally ending it when Lester put his foot down, suggesting they break open another bottle of Scotch and discuss other matters of interest. Alan wondered where he got the liquor from, and then remembered Lester knew bootleggers in the city. Norma poured more of the liquor for everyone, and Lester turned on the radio. Ed and Norma danced to the latest tunes by Duke Ellington and Ruth Etting, while John and Lester chatted about the upcoming basketball game at the YMCA and the new Mary Pickford film. Evangeline and Alan spoke about their work, the Marx Brothers and Buster Keaton movies.

As Evangeline was speaking, Alan's mind returned to his cousin Betsy on the railing and the faces of those around him; startled, horrified, aghast. Persistent memories kept pulling at him. The snowy footprints near the top of the stairs, leading from the fire escape. The maintenance crew, of course, he reminded himself stubbornly. He listened and smiled as Evangeline continued talking, rather nervously, but he could not concentrate on what she said.

There was something wrong with this whole situation he thought uneasily, something horribly, terribly wrong.

CHAPTER TEN

It was a somber atmosphere at Harmanus Bleecker Hall on Monday. After spending the weekend assisting his mother and uncle, trying to bring some semblance of normalcy to their lives, Alan returned to work, albeit preoccupied about Mr. Ferguson. He had not spoken to him since the incident Friday evening, and he was anxious to find out what his boss would tell them. He assumed he would call a meeting on Monday. He had no sooner arrived at his office, when Mrs. Russell entered, telling him he was requested by Mr. Ferguson in the meeting room.

As he expected, Norma was there as well as Mrs. Churchill but Ed, John and Lester were not. Of course, Mr. Ferguson could not expect them to leave their jobs at the drop of a hat for a meeting at the Hall. Alan noticed other employees, including maintenance workers and secretaries from the first-floor offices. His tone was solemn yet controlled, although it was obvious, he was deeply affected by Betsy's death. He cleared his throat before speaking.

"I called this meeting to discuss Friday night's unfortunate accident as well as the impact it will have on the Hall. It was indeed an accident, but I saw no other recourse than to cancel the dance marathon. We are in the process of sending refunds to the participants." He paused. "I would like a return to normalcy, as President Harding used to say."

"Exactly what we want, too, Mr. Ferguson," Norma acknowledged.

"I am concerned about the negative publicity this will have on future bookings," Mr. Ferguson continued. "We cannot afford to lose entertainers otherwise we may be forced to close."

While he understood his concern about the Hall's reputation, Alan thought he was carrying it too far. He listened as Mrs. Churchill spoke, quite firmly, as though her point of view was the only one that mattered.

"Mr. Ferguson, I do not see how Miss Donovan's accident will have a negative impact. We have always had a solid reputation, so I do not foresee any future problems."

Norma puffed at her cigarette. "You did the right thing in canceling the rest of the marathon, Mr. Ferguson."

Alan suddenly spoke, even catching himself by surprise. "Why don't you ask the local papers and WGY to interview you again?" All eyes turned to him. "That way, you can clarify why you canceled the marathon and your regret over what happened."

Mr. Ferguson nodded. "That is a particularly good idea, Alan. I may just contact the papers. WGY expressed interest in speaking to me again at the conclusion of the marathon, but since the accident has appeared in the papers, it'd be better if they hear about it directly from me."

A murmur of assent was evident in the conference room. Mr. Ferguson then cleared his throat again and spoke even more forcefully.

"The police will be here later today to speak to us. I spoke with them earlier and assured them it was only an accident. They want to look at the banister where Betsy fell and speak to those who were here Friday night. In cases of sudden death, even an accident, they get involved."

"I do not see the need for that, Mr. Ferguson," Mrs. Churchill commented. "If the police make a report, the newspapers may find out and cause even more negative publicity."

"I am afraid that is out of my hands, Mrs. Churchill," Mr. Ferguson said regretfully.

The head maintenance man, by the name of Harvey, reiterated Mrs. Churchill. He was a tall, heavyset middle-aged man, who had worked at Harmanus Bleecker Hall for many years. He was jovial and trustworthy, and well liked among employees. "If Miss Donovan slipped, it had nothing to do with us. We didn't wax the banister, so we can't take any blame."

Mr. Ferguson agreed. "I know that Harvey, but they will be here to speak to us, regardless. Certainly, we do not want people coming here to gawk at the top right-hand banister to see where Miss Donovan slipped. People are curious over things like that."

"If the police determine it was not an accident, they'll investigate even further," Norma said. "We'll be looking at a murder charge. We'll all be under suspicion."

Mrs. Churchill coughed. "Miss Donovan simply fell, an unfortunate accident. Have we considered that Miss Donovan was intoxicated at the time of her fall? Regarding the police, they have better ways to use their labor. They have not discovered who murdered Miss Barker and that was well over a month ago."

"I remember Miss Barker was involved with Mr. Cavanaugh," Harvey, the maintenance man added thoughtfully. "I think Miss Donovan was seeing him, too. My wife and I saw them on Lark Street when we were out for dinner once."

"That isn't relevant," Norma said firmly, butting her cigarette in an ashtray. "There's no reason to discuss Miss Barker. As Mr. Ferguson mentioned, we have to be concerned with the Hall's future. We can't allow negative publicity of any kind."

Alan was impressed that Norma would take such a stand. Obviously, she was trying to impress Mr. Ferguson and, he thought, she was doing a good job of it. He also thought she wanted to avoid any mention of Lester.

Mr. Ferguson than adjourned the meeting, thanking everyone for their time and effort for the dance marathon. People filed out of the room, Alan, Norma and Mrs. Churchill walking out together. Mrs. Churchill mentioned she needed to leave and headed down the stairs for the main entrance as though she could not get out fast enough, leaving Alan and Norma to return to their offices. Norma made a few casual comments about Betsy, as though nonchalantly casting aside her death as trivial, inconsequential. Alan had the disturbing feeling he was seeing a side of her that he did not fully understand.

Standing in the doorway to Mrs. Russell's office, he watched as Norma walked down the hallway, mumbling to herself. He wondered what was passing in her mind.

Mrs. Eleanor Whitney folded back the *Albany Evening Journal* and handed it to Evangeline. They were in the living room of their spacious brownstone on Columbia Street, having recently finished dinner. Eleanor was about to continue with the sweater she was knitting for Evangeline, when she decided to let her see the article on the death of Betsy Donovan for herself.

It was close to seven o'clock, dark and bitterly cold. Eleanor finished her shift at city hall and upon returning home, prepared dinner. Within the half hour, Evangeline entered, stomping her boots on the mat in the hallway, and eagerly taking off her fur coat and cloche hat, joined her mother in the kitchen for a hearty dinner consisting of roast beef, vegetables and rice. Afterwards they relaxed in the living room with coffee. Evangeline turned on the radio to *The Atwater Kent Hour*, her mother's favorite program and the wonderful soft music filled the room. Settling in an armchair with the latest issue of *True Story*, her favorite magazine, Evangeline looked up to see her mother holding the *Albany Evening Journal* out to her, beckoning her to read the article she pointed to. Evangeline did not need to ask what the article was about. She glanced at it and then cast it aside casually on the coffee table, returning to *True Story*, of more importance to her. Her mother looked at her, rather curiously.

"The article was about Betsy, dear. Did you read it?"

Evangeline looked up from her magazine. "Yes, Mother, I looked at it. I don't feel I need to read any more about Betsy falling from a banister. It's been in all the papers, people at work have talked about it and the radio stations keep mentioning it. Will it ever die down?"

Eleanor continued knitting. "Well, dear, it is newsworthy. Certainly looks bad for the Hall. Poor Mr. Ferguson must be beside himself. After tall, the Hall is his lifeblood."

Evangeline continued reading, not taking her eyes from the magazine. "Betsy was foolish to put on a show like she did. Who cared if she slid down the railing? She was always such a showoff. The banisters are marble, so I imagine they'd be slippery."

Eleanor made no comment. She continued knitting while listening to the symphonic music on the radio. Mother and daughter sat silently for quite a while, tumultuous thoughts running through their heads. Finally, Evangeline put *True Story* on the coffee table.

"Do you think there is more to what happened to Betsy, Mother? I heard on the radio earlier at work that the police plan to investigate.

What is there to investigate? It's not anyone's fault, except her own. She was showing off and lost her grip."

Eleanor agreed and paused in her knitting. "Someone at city hall told me she heard it on the radio today, too. I don't understand why the police of this city need to waste their time looking into a simple accident." She paused. "Have you spoken to Alan lately?"

Evangeline sighed. "Just at Lester's on Saturday."

Eleanor continued knitting. "He is such a fine young man, dear. You should try to spend more time with him."

"What do you think happened to Betsy, Mother?" Evangeline asked.

Eleanor looked up from her knitting. "What do you mean, dear?"

Evangeline was obstinate. "Do you think it was just an accident?"

"I believe it was just that, dear, an accident." Eleanor's voice was rather firm. "I don't know what they'll find, of course."

"If they determine it was not an accident, it'll be a murder charge," Evangeline continued. "Norma mentioned that at Lester's on Saturday."

This time Eleanor put down her knitting. "Did she say that now? Miss Smith has a rather active imagination. Didn't she and Betsy have that terrible catfight at the speakeasy recently? If it is determined to be murder, I imagine Miss Smith would be a prime suspect. She had problems with Betsy previously, too."

The Atwater Kent Hour was interrupted briefly for the evening news. The radio announcer commented on the growing stock market, President Coolidge's recent visit to his home state of Vermont and the rising popularity of automobiles, with Henry Ford's *Model T* at the forefront. The announcer broadcast the weather prognosis of snow this evening and continuing during the overnight hours. Commecials for *Jell-O*, *Camel Cigarettes* and *Borden Ice Cream* finished, as the announcer continued:

...A strange death occurred over the weekend during the dance marathon at Harmanus Bleecker Hall. Miss Betsy Donovan of Albany apparently lost her grip on a railing and plunged to her death. Police will investigate this mishap. You will remember another young woman in our city, Miss Penelope Barker, a local actress, met an unfortunate end outside her apartment in December. Police are not alluding to any connection between these two deaths...

Eleanor and Evangeline looked at each other in shock. Evangeline had gone chalk white while Eleanor was clearly alarmed. The same thoughts permeated their minds, like a roller coaster out of control. Was there a connection between Betsy's death and the murder of Miss Barker? Eleanor wondered if others involved, including Mr. Ferguson and Alan and his mother, heard this unsettling and rather preposterous proclamation. But then radio announcers usually exaggerated stories, she thought sensibly. Certainly, Mrs. Churchill would have heard this same announcement, as she knew she always listened to *The Atwater Kent Hour* in the evenings.

Neither mother nor daughter spoke, too stunned to annunciate words. Refusing to discuss either Betsy or Miss Barker, Evangeline picked up *True Story* and immersed herself in an article while Eleanor bent her head down to her knitting.

Outside the wind had increased but it had not yet begun to snow.

Later that evening, Lester stood on the balcony of his apartment on Broadway in downtown Albany, with a hard-set look to his face.

It was one of several well-kept brownstones. His apartment was on the top floor, offering majestic views of the Hudson River and beyond. He looked across the dark night to the frozen waters of the river. Heedless of the cold, and deep in troublesome thoughts, he continued puffing at his cigarette, intermittent snow showers brushing his face and shoulders. It was quite late, and he had had a long day at the library, but with plenty of liquor and cigarettes, he managed to keep his sanity. He considered dropping by his usual speakeasy, but Betsy's death curtailed his plans. He could easily find a female companion but not tonight. The parties and the women had to be put on the shelf, at least temporarily.

His bootlegging contacts kept him well plied with liquor. He smiled to himself, as he made money with that endeavor, too, so he had no complaints. His kingpin, an Albany gangster and his associates, considered Lester one of their elite circle and he knew better than to turn his back on them. If he ever did, he knew he would end up with his face in a ditch and a knife in his back.

He finished the cigarette and flicked it over the edge of the terrace before turning to go back inside. Closing the sliding door, he walked over to the kitchen table, where a half-empty bottle of Scotch stood. He poured a glass and swallowed with great satisfaction. He had no sooner taken another cigarette from the pack in his pocket and lit it when the telephone in the hallway rang. He wondered if it was Alan, John or Ed, asking to get together tonight. Upon hearing the voice on the other end, he was annoyed, speaking belligerently and to the point.

"You've got to stop calling me here. Get yourself together. Goodnight."

Puffing at his cigarette, he replaced the handset and returned to the living room. He swallowed more of the liquor and sat on the sofa, rather irritably. He exhaled a large cloud of smoke and knocked ash into an ashtray on an end table. Taking off his shoes and socks, he tried to relax, stretching his long legs, although he was finding that extremely difficult.

His mind returned to the phone call. Poor dumb fool, he thought, hanging around him when she could have any man. She knew he had a criminal record, that he was on probation and involved with bootleggers. So what was the appeal? His good looks, rugged face, broad shoulders, muscular physique and daredevil grace. Part of his charm, he laughed crudely, swallowing more of the liquor. He continued smoking, his mind now turning over the events from Friday evening.

At least Betsy was out of the picture, he thought grimly, like Penelope Barker. He need not worry about their interference. Betsy believed he belonged to her, as though he would be stuck with her the rest of his life. He used her whenever he wanted, and it was a convenient arrangement. The similarities between Betsy and Penelope were amazing, he joked. Like Penelope, Betsy came from money and with her father's lucrative accounting practice; she would be well off financially. Their brownstone on Elk Street certainly reeked of money. Some men would have hung onto either one, but Lester, ever the lounge lizard, played the field. After all, he had no plans to settle down with just one woman when there were so many interested in him.

He marveled at his own vanity, his alluring warmth and manipulations to get his way. He had seduced countless women, Betsy and Penelope Barker included, and he enjoyed his conquests, finding pleasure at his notorious reputation as a ladies man. His job at the library paid the bills but his bootlegging activities enabled him to afford expensive clothes and keep his physique in top shape through a YMCA membership. Of course, he was still on probation, so he had to play his cards right and exercise caution. His mind returned to the telephone call he just received. Glancing toward the terrace, he saw snow showers increasing prodigiously. He drew smoke into his lungs and exhaled almost angrily.

As long as you keep your mouth shut, he thought spitefully, as though talking to himself. I don't need you at all, but you'll never know it.

CHAPTER ELEVEN

Late on Tuesday morning, Alan asked Mrs. Russell to hold phone calls and with too much on his mind, he sat for a long time at his desk, turning over the recent events. He had already spoken to the police yesterday afternoon regarding Betsy's death and again this morning. By all accounts, it was now a formal investigation; the police officers mentioning detectives would be assigned to the case. Which Alan knew meant more interrogations, probing and questioning. He mentioned the snowy footprints near the fire escape, which the police jotted in their notebook as a possible lead in the investigation, although Alan did not see the relevance.

The police officers who spoke to him also met with other Hall employees, including Mr. Ferguson, Norma and Harvey, the head of maintenance. They spoke with many Hall employees who were present at the time of the accident. Most answers, including those of Mr. Ferguson, Norma and Harvey, were perfunctory, except for Alan, who unwillingly added more complicity to a growing situation. After obtaining the names of Hall associates who were present during the accident from Mr. Ferguson, they also planned to speak to Mrs. Churchill, Mr. Flynn, Mr. Whitmore and Mr. Cavanaugh. Having spent the majority of the morning at Harmanus Bleecker Hall, the police officers finally left much to Alan's relief.

It was almost noontime and he had accomplished nothing. He needed to draft reports, contact agents and plan future bookings, but his mind was elsewhere. He lit a cigarette, loosened his tie, unbuttoned the top of his vest, put his feet up on the desk and sat back on his swivel chair, regardless if Mr. Ferguson walked in. He knew his boss did not approve of lounging, but at the moment, he needed what he considered a breathing spell and a cigarette and stretching his legs helped. He looked up to see Mrs. Russell in the doorway.

"Mr. Cartwright, I don't mean to intrude," she said, looking worriedly at the young man at the desk before her, "but Mr. Ferguson spoke to me late yesterday afternoon about what you told the police. Did you mention it to them again this morning?"

Alan puffed on his cigarette and took time in replying. "Yes, I did mention it to the policemen yesterday and this morning." He could tell Mrs. Russell wished he would elaborate. "I told them I saw the fire escape on the fifth floor ajar and footprints leading to the right staircase."

Mrs. Russell asked him what significance that may have on Miss Donovan's accident. Alan leaned back on his swivel chair and exhaled a great puff of smoke before speaking.

"I don't know what it means, Mrs. Russell."

"When did you notice the footprints?"

"When Mr. Ferguson asked me to show Senator Miles and his wife around the building. Mrs. Miles had never been here before. I brought them to the fifth floor, where we looked down to the atrium. There were people dancing there and it was really a festive occasion."

"I still don't see the significance," Mrs. Russell said, rather confusedly.

"Neither did I, at first," a strong female voice spoke from behind Mrs. Russell.

It was Norma standing behind her, looking severe and irritable. From her tone and superfluous remark, Alan assumed her displeasure centered on him. Mrs. Russell turned and seeing Norma, excused herself, feeling rather uncomfortable. Norma entered Alan's office furtively, noting his relaxed posture, commenting that Mr. Ferguson would not approve of his feet on top of the desk and his rather disheveled appearance.

"Is that why you're here, to comment on my feet on the desk?" Alan asked her, his voice tinged with sarcasm.

Norma sat in the chair in front of his desk, a firm look on her face. "Why didn't you tell us about the footprints on the fifth floor over the weekend?" she asked, getting straight to the point. "You told the police yesterday and they discussed it with Mr. Ferguson. He mentioned he spoke to you about it yesterday, too. The police brought it up again today."

"I didn't think anything of it," Alan explained, then extinguished his cigarette. He removed his feet from the desk and sat upright in the swivel chair. "I'm not convinced it means anything at all." He did not think he owed Norma an explanation, even though she was an employee. She used her weight as a board member, which he personally found irritating.

"According to Mr. Ferguson, the police seem to believe it does," Norma said. Before Alan could speak, she continued. "They seem to think it may tie in with Betsy's accident."

"In what way?" Alan asked.

"From the first report of the police who were here over the weekend, they told Mr. Ferguson the banister was slippery."

Alan looked incredulous. "The banisters are always slippery. How could they determine that in the first place? They are made of marble, after all."

"Because Mr. Ferguson told me the police are investigating if something may have been applied to the banister to make it slippery."

"It doesn't make sense," Alan argued. "We didn't know Betsy would slide down the banister when she did!"

Norma agreed. "Since she had an audience watching in the atrium, she enjoyed every minute of it. And we all knew she liked sliding down banisters."

Alan was silent, thoughtful. It did not occur to him that the footprints that led from the fire escape to the top of the staircase had anything to do with Betsy's accident. Although now, it may not have been an accident at all. As though reading his mind, Norma reiterated what she mentioned at Lester's apartment on Saturday night.

"If the police really believe something was done to the banister, then Betsy's fall was not an accident."

Alan was so stunned he did not notice Mr. Ferguson walk in. He blinked several times as though to orient himself, before realizing Mr. Ferguson was speaking to him.

"I overheard what Norma just told you, Alan," he said, looking disgruntled, wearing a three-piece suit, much older than his years as though Betsy's mishap aged him terribly. His voice held strict disapproval. "I do not understand why you did not mention to me that you noticed the fire escape open on Friday night."

"I apologize, Mr. Ferguson. First I thought someone got in without paying, but when I opened it further, there were no footprints on the steps, just on the landing outside the door. I noticed the footprints leading from the door to the top of the staircase."

"Which means someone could have rubbed snow on the banister, making it extremely slippery," Mr. Ferguson said thoughtfully.

"Although it would have melted, of course."

"It would still be slippery," Norma observed. "Betsy would not have noticed it."

"If she did notice it, it was too late," Mr. Ferguson added. He paused, meditatively. "This looks extremely bad for the Hall. If it gets out to the press, they will have a field day with it. The headlines would read Murder at the Dance Marathon or some such nonsense. In addition, our business would dwindle. Who would want to come here if there was a murder under our roof?"

Alan had seen Mr. Ferguson annoyed and upset on various occasions in the past, but this was the worst. He knew he directed part of his wrath at him.

"I would have preferred that you told me this at once, Alan, when you first noticed it."

"What good would that have done, Mr. Ferguson?" Norma asked.

Alan was glad she asked that question instead of him. What good would it have been to tell him, anyway? It did not occur to him to check the banister, as the last thing he would have thought of was someone applying snow to make it slippery. Perhaps Mr. Ferguson was looking to cast the blame on someone, so Alan knew he was the scapegoat.

"The police asked me if Miss Donovan had enemies," Mr. Ferguson said, his face rather twisted, obviously disturbed. "I told them Miss Donovan was not popular with many in the community." He paused. "Surprisingly, they also mentioned Miss Barker. I didn't see the relevance with Miss Donovan's accident. I said she had never played here at the Hall and as far as I knew, she had no contact with Miss Donovan."

"The police haven't found who killed her yet," Norma murmured.

The uncomfortable conversation ended by Mr. Ferguson mentioning again the possibility of something slippery on the banister, shaking his head in disbelief. Norma got up to leave when he spoke again, addressing both Alan and Norma.

"If it's determined it wasn't an accident, I'd hate to think of what it would be."

"What is that, Mr. Ferguson?" Alan could not quite grasp all that was happening.

"Murder," Mr. Ferguson said grimly.

"Miss Donovan —your daughter—may not have been the victim of an accident."

It was a difficult and somber atmosphere that evening in the living room of Carl Donovan's brownstone on Elk Street. Carl sat in his armchair near the fireplace, with a cup of tea and cigarettes. He had yet to return to work, entrusting his associates to carry on the business efficiently. He was in the process of arranging Betsy's wake and funeral services.

To his right sat his sister Bernice, ever mindful of her younger brother, as though he was incapable of caring for himself. She had cooked dinner and he was grateful for her help. To his left was Mrs. Churchill, more of a nuisance, who he wish would return to her house rather than interfere in a situation he felt was really none of her business. On the sofa in front of him sat three people he would have also wished were not present: Mrs. Eleanor Whitney, and two police detectives from the Albany City police, Inspector Harris and Lieutenant Taylor.

It was still cold and cloudy, the snow had tapered, but the wind continued unabated. Carl glanced at the living room windows, hearing the harsh winds rattle the windowpanes, wishing he were alone. He did not invite Mrs. Churchill nor Mrs. Whitney and other than their general inquisitiveness, he could not fathom why they were in his house. Certainly, he did not turn them away when they came about an hour ago. He looked at the two detectives, who were putting him through another endless round of questions. He had spoken with them over the weekend and yesterday but now, Tuesday, he wanted nothing more than to be alone with his grief, his mourning for his daughter, who despite her faults, he still loved and cared for. He looked up as he realized the inspector was speaking to him.

"Mr. Donovan, your daughter may not have been the victim of an accident. That's why my partner and I are here again to speak to you." Inspector Harris cleared his throat and had been scribbling in a small notebook. "Mr. Donovan, where were you when your daughter climbed to the top of the staircase at the Hall?"

Carl sipped his tea, more to camouflage his expression. Why did this turn into a police investigation? He took his time in answering. "I was in the atrium. I was dancing for a while, but when my daughter climbed to the top of the staircase, I urged her to come down. Betsy had a mind of her own and did pretty much whatever she wanted."

"Do you think it wasn't an accident, Inspector?" Mrs. Churchill asked.

Inspector Harris looked her way. He was a tall, rather handsome middle-aged man, with a head of thick wavy brown hair and deep brown eyes. His rank as an investigating officer gave him the opportunity to handle a multitude of cases, including murder, arson and theft. His partner, Lieutenant Taylor, sat next to him on the sofa. He too was of roughly the same age, tall and broad-shouldered, with thinning brown hair speckled with gray and blue eyes. Their demeanor was professional and perseverant as though they had seen the worst that

Albany could offer and were accustomed to it.

Lieutenant Taylor answered Mrs. Churchill's question. "We can't say at this point. We were assigned this case after hearing what Mr. Alan Cartwright told the police yesterday."

An uncertain quiet fell over the room until the inspector broke it by mentioning how Alan found the fire escape on the fifth floor ajar, the footprints on the landing and the snowy footprints leading to the staircase. No one saw the relevance of this information, until Mrs. Whitney asked if it pertained to Betsy's fall. The inspector turned in her direction.

"That's what we're attempting to learn, Mrs. Whitney. I'd like each of you to tell us your relationship with the deceased and where you were the evening of Friday, the twenty-ninth."

Bernice cleared her throat. She commented that she had been dancing in the atrium, enjoying the wonderful music. She had no idea that the fire escape had been opened on the fifth floor, to which Carl, Mrs. Churchill and Mrs. Whitney all reiterated. No one as far as they knew, had gone up to the fifth floor.

"Your son showed visitors around the building," Inspector Harris said to Bernice. "That's when he noticed the fire escape door slightly ajar."

"I still don't see what that has to do with Miss Donovan's death," Mrs. Churchill said, slightly annoyed. "You make it seem like this is a murder investigation, Inspector."

"My brother is still in mourning for his daughter," Bernice said, clearly alarmed at Mrs. Churchill's insinuation. "I ask that you respect us in our time of grief."

Inspector Harris nodded. "Of course, Mrs. Cartwright, but we are undertaking an investigation to learn what happened to your niece. It may have been simply an accident."

"I cannot imagine it being anything else, Inspector," Mrs. Churchill remarked dryly.

"My son did not mention a fire escape door being ajar," Bernice commented. "If it was relevant, he would have told me. He didn't mention it that evening or over the weekend."

"This is the first I'm hearing about it," Carl said. "I don't see the relevance, Inspector. Maybe a maintenance man forgot to close it all the way."

Inspector Harris had been scribbling in his notebook. He asked Mrs. Whitney for her relationship with the deceased. Eleanor commented that she hardly knew Miss Donovan and that she was dancing in the atrium, like Mrs. Cartwright, when she heard the commotion of Miss Donovan on the top of the staircase, about to slide down the railing.

Carl grimaced. "My daughter was the quintessential flapper. She liked to enjoy herself and frolicked around, showing off."

"Mrs. Churchill, were you present at the time of the accident?" Lieutenant Taylor asked.

Mrs. Churchill set her lips firmly. "I was appalled at first at the dancing there, as we did not plan to have dancing in the atrium at the same time as the marathon was occurring in the ballroom. But people were enjoying themselves and it was rather harmless, so Mr. Ferguson decided to let them continue. I was watching the attendees dance when I heard Miss Donovan on top of the staircase, about to slide down the banister." She paused. "I will admit, Inspector, I was not fond of either Miss Donovan or that hideous Miss Barker. Please excuse me for saying that, Mr. Donovan. I found your daughter's manners extremely uncouth and impolite."

Carl smiled wanly at Mrs. Churchill. "I understand, Mrs. Churchill. My daughter had a way of getting under people's skin."

"Does anyone have information that can help us with the investigation into the murder of Miss Barker?" Inspector Harris asked. "We are still investigating her death and appreciate anything you could tell us."

Carl, Bernice and Eleanor looked at each other, surprised and speechless. Finally, Carl mentioned that they did not know what happened to Miss Barker and frankly, he did not see a connection between her death and the death of his daughter.

"Had any of you been to the fifth-floor landing earlier in the evening?" the Inspector asked.

Carl looked at the women sitting around him. None of them registered the least acknowledgement that they had been anywhere in the Hall except the ballroom and the atrium, where all the activity was occurring.

The inspector asked for their addresses, noting that they lived close by. Mrs. Cartwright and her son Alan were two doors away and Mrs. Churchill was three doors away. Mrs. Whitney and her daughter Evangeline lived on Columbia Street, just around the corner. He finished writing in his notebook and closed it with a snap. "Please accept our condolences on the loss of your daughter, Mr. Donovan. I understand this is a difficult time for you and your sister. Thank you for speaking with us this evening. We will most likely need to speak with you again in the near future."

The police officers rose to leave, thanking them again for their time. Bernice showed them to the door and then returned to the living room, where Mrs. Whitney and Mrs. Churchill also announced they needed to leave. Carl did not encourage them to stay. Bernice saw them to the door, then standing in the living room entranceway, told her brother she would clean up in the kitchen. She turned the radio to WGY, and the sounds of Bessie Smith and Helen Kane filled the room pleasingly. She soon departed, leaving Carl alone, deep in distorted thoughts.

Could someone really have been responsible for Betsy's fall? Then her death would be a homicide, not an accident. Carl shuddered inwardly and sipped his lukewarm tea.

Evangeline closed the ledger book in which she had been entering figures. To her right was a large pile of receipts and bills, which she had finished and to her left another pile which she had yet to begin. Glancing at the wall clock in her office, she noticed it was after six o'clock.

Evangeline decided she had spent long enough at Whitney's. She wanted to contact either Alan, Ed, or John. She sat back and thought of the eligible young men with whom she would like to spend time, especially now that Betsy and Penelope Barker were out of the picture. Of course, Norma was still around, but for some reason she did not find her a threat or vindictive as the other two. Her thoughts turned to Lester Cavanaugh, someone she admired for quite a while. Lester was so charming, cunning, handsome and such a neat dresser but he was too much a ladies man, openly brash, arrogant and even dangerous. Evangeline admitted she rather found his dangerous side appealing. Ed was more settled and even homespun, certainly articulate and good-hearted, although she knew he drank, but so did Lester and John. Alan was tall, handsome and intelligent, like the others, and there certainly were qualities about him she admired. Perhaps his intelligence and good looks, which he did not flaunt, unlike Lester. On the other hand, John also caught her eye, and it was convenient that he was only just down the block at the Strand Theater.

She turned the banker's lamp off on her desk and put on her fur coat and cloche hat. She climbed the stairs to the main floor, waving good night to several employees and was soon on the sidewalk. North Pearl Street was busy even for a Tuesday evening. She was about to cross at the light to catch an uptown trolley, when impulsively she turned toward the Strand Theater.

She pushed open the door of the luxurious theater and entering the lobby, asked the young man at the ticket window for John Whitmore. Fortunately, he had not left for the day. She was told his office was on the third floor; Evangeline did not realize the theater had a third floor. When asked if she had an appointment, Evangeline told him she did not, but said she was a friend. The young man phoned John to let him know she would be seeing him.

A screening of the Charlie Chaplin film *The Gold Rush*, still popular from last year, drew quite a crowd, as evidenced by the nearly sold-out theater. As she climbed the stairs to the third floor, Evangeline noticed framed autographed pictures of Ethel Barrymore, Mary Pickford, Douglas Fairbanks and Charles Farrell impressively lining the wall.

Arriving at his office, Evangeline saw his door open. John looked up and putting aside some papers, rose and greeted Evangeline pleasantly, welcoming her into his office.

"I worked late this evening and I wanted to stop by to see you," she explained as she sat in the chair in front of his desk. "Mother's helping Mrs. Cartwright and Mrs. Churchill prepare dinner for Mr. Donovan, so I didn't want to go home to an empty house."

John lit a cigarette, offered one to Evangeline, who graciously accepted it. He leaned over his desk, lighting it with his gold lighter and then settled back on his chair and looked at the pretty girl in front of him. Evangeline equally looked back at the handsome young man behind the desk.

"John, I'm concerned about what happened to Betsy. How could she just loose her grip and fall? She was an expert at riding down banisters, she had done it pretty of times before!"

John knocked ash from his cigarette into an ashtray on his desk. "I don't really know what to think," he said slowly. "I'm still confused by what happened."

Evangeline puffed on her cigarette, rather impatiently. "The newspapers said there'll be a police investigation. I heard that on the radio, too."

He puffed thoughtfully, looking at Evangeline, wondering if she was easily swayed as Betsy and Penelope. He had dated her a few times, but nothing much came of it. Of course, she lived with her mother, but Betsy lived with her father and that never stopped her. Personally, he found Mr. Donovan a self-centered, money-hungry executive who cared only for himself.

While he considered himself a ladies man, John did not quite put himself in the same category as Lester, who he knew had charmed and conquered most of the eligible and even ineligible women in downtown Albany. What a lounge lizard, he thought. Where did he hear that spoken before to describe Lester? From Betsy, of course, that night at the speakeasy, when she threw her drink in Norma's face and all hell broke loose. He came out of his reverie to hear Evangeline still talking about Betsy's accident.

"If there is a police investigation, we need to be careful. Especially Norma, who fought her at the speakeasy that night. Of course, we've all had issues with Betsy and with Penelope."

John finished his cigarette and in an attempt to change the subject, mentioned he was about to leave for the day. It was getting late, and he wanted to return to his apartment. Personally, he did not feel like discussing Betsy Donovan or Penelope Barker at the end of his workday.

Outside on North Pearl Street, it was still blustery and cold. John and Evangeline crossed at the light to catch a north bound trolley, which approached within minutes and to their relief was not too crowded.

"Poor Mr. Donovan," Evangeline commented. "I do feel bad for him at the loss of his daughter, regardless of Betsy's character. Must be devastating for him."

John glanced at her, his cap low, looking what Evangeline thought rather mysterious, almost as though he had something to hide. "I wouldn't worry about Mr. Donovan," he said curtly. "He knows how to play his cards straight. He isn't the kind, gentle man you may think he is."

Before she could answer, the trolley stopped at State Street. Evangeline got up, wished John good night, and then hastily walked to the front of the trolley. She stood on the sidewalk watching as it disappeared up Washington Avenue, past the capitol.

Crossing in front of city hall, the Court of Appeals and the Albany County Courthouse on her way to Columbia Street, Evangeline thought about John's apparent harshness toward Mr. Donovan. She wondered if there was something he was too unwilling to mention.

Alan spent a restless evening at home. His mother left a message on the kitchen table, that she was at her brother's, making dinner. She had prepared baked pork chops and a salad, which she left in the icebox. Having finished eating and still feeling rather agitated, with Betsy's death weighing heavily on his mind, he decided to call Ed, Lester, John and Norma.

He spent a few minutes in the hallway, trying to reach his friends. The operator tried John's apartment but there was no answer. When the operator put through the call to Norma's rooming house, Alan spoke to the proprietress, who mentioned Miss Smith was not home and that she would take a message. Finally, the operator called Ed and then Lester. Successful in reaching them, he invited them to visit. As Alan expected, Lester suggested a speakeasy, but he told him he was not up to par tonight, and he preferred to stay in. Within the half hour, Alan, Ed and Lester was seated at the kitchen table, smoking, talking, and drinking coffee, fortified by Lester's flask. They were immersed in a poker game, as Lester was quite an expert card player. As he won hand after hand, Alan wondered if there was anything he was not an expert at. Certainly, seducing women was one of his specialties. He changed his thoughts quickly as he heard the front door open.

It was his mother arriving home from his uncle's house. Glancing at the wall clock, Alan noticed it was seven fifteen. He did not think she would be back so early. As he heard her footsteps in the hallway, almost to the kitchen, he braced himself for whatever comments she would make upon seeing Ed and Lester. He did not have time to warn Lester to hide the flask, and sure enough, his mother noticed it first thing upon entering.

"Well, is this a party, Alan," she demanded, rather hotly. She noticed the coffee cups and the flask in front of Lester, a hint that there was something stronger than just coffee in the cups. A strange silence followed until Lester, rather jovially, broke it by greeting Bernice.

"Hello, Mrs. Cartwright, nice to see you again. Ed and I came here to play poker with Alan and shoot the breeze." He slurred his words and Bernice could tell he was slightly drunk, much to her chagrin. She turned her eyes to her son, who extinguished his cigarette and explained he had called Ed and Lester and invited them over.

She looked at the young men at the table and then smiled in spite of herself. "Of course, dear," Bernice relented, knowing the stress of Betsy's death had affected him. These were her son's friends and there was nothing wrong with an innocent card game, although she did not approve of the flask at Lester's side.

"Mother, the police spoke to us again today," Alan told her. "They think Betsy's fall may not have been an accident."

Bernice was about to leave when she turned from the doorway and looked at her son. Lester and Ed also looked at Alan, as though they had not quite heard what he said. Bernice set her mouth firmly and asked her son what he told them.

"We were all questioned by the police," Alan explained, finding relief in his cigarette. "I don't know what more they'll accomplish, but there are detectives assigned to investigate."

"What's there to investigate?" Ed questioned. He looked forlorn and perplexed, his usual upbeat expression rather sad, despite the liquor and the card game. He took another swallow of his coffee; feeling rejuvenated, which Bernice was sure, was tainted with whiskey.

Lester agreed. "I think they're wasting their time," he said, a cigarette between his lips. He had loosened his tie, as though the card game made him sweat. His blondish hair fell over his forehead, rather disheveled but on Lester, it did not matter much, as he exhibited a powerful appearance.

Bernice stood still in the doorway. "Yes, I know about it, Alan, I just came from your uncle's house and the police were there, speaking to us. It just so happened that Mrs. Churchill and Mrs. Whitney were there, too."

"Mrs. Whitney and Mrs. Churchill?" Lester said, surprised. "Why would the police want to speak to them? I wouldn't consider them good witnesses. Mrs. Churchill's blind as a bat."

"Because they saw Betsy fall," Bernice said, rather firmly. "Did you tell Lester and Ed about the fire escape door left ajar, Alan?"

Alan wished she had not mentioned the fire escape door. He wondered if she said it on purpose, to involve Lester and Ed, perhaps she thought them responsible for Betsy's fall. Now that it was out in the open, he explained about discovering it ajar, and the snowy footprints leading to the staircase. Lester did not see the connection. Ed asked him what he meant.

Alan hesitated before replying. "The police think someone may have put snow or ice on the banister, causing it to be slippery. It would've made Betsy loose her grip and fall."

"Of all the cockamamie things," Lester slurred, puffing away at his cigarette and swallowing coffee with great relish. "I don't believe that for a minute!"

Ed agreed. "It does sound pretty far-fetched, Alan."

Bernice remained planted in the doorway, looking at her son as he socialized with the young men at the kitchen table. She mentioned she would be in the living room, leaving them to play their poker game.

The game continued for a good hour longer, until they finally decided to break it up. Lester, as usual, won the most and Alan and Ed admitted he was quite a poker player. Joining them in the hallway as they put on their jackets and caps, he bid them good night, watching them walk onto Elk Street, and then closing the front door firmly, the lock in place.

He joined his mother in the living room, where she was reading *The Albany Evening Journal* and listening to the radio. He sat in an armchair across from her and waited to hear what she would say about Lester and Ed, playing poker and drinking out of a flask. To his surprise, she said next to nothing.

"I'm glad you have Lester and Ed to spend time with, dear," Bernice told him, looking over the top of the newspaper. "Although I do not approve of Lester and his drinking habits, at this difficult time, we need company."

Alan felt a great relief, as though a burden was lifted off him. "They mean no harm and I trust them." He hesitated. "Suppose someone did cause Betsy to fall? Then it would be murder."

Bernice continued reading the paper, not looking up at her son. "Indeed, dear, it would be murder. Honestly, like Lester and Ed, I find it hard to believe but given the nature of your cousin and her vindictiveness, I wouldn't be surprised if that was just the case."

"You're saying you agree that someone put snow on the banister to make it slippery?"

"I'm not saying anything of the sort, dear," Bernice said, folding the paper and putting it on the coffee table. Wishing to change the subject, she turned toward the radio. "Would you find the station that has Sister Aimee? I think her sermon would do me good at this time."

Alan got up and turned the dial until he found the station broadcasting the sermon of Sister Aimee McPherson, one of his mother's favorites. Settling back in his armchair with the paper and another cigarette, Alan decided after a half hour he would go to bed, saying good night to his mother and climbing the stairs rather eagerly.

He turned on the radio in his room, finding a station playing great jazz. He knew having two radios in the house was a luxury, but since he and his mother did not enjoy the same programs, he found it a convenience to buy one for himself. Alan loved Duke Ellington and the music filled him with anticipation, making him shortly forget about the recent turmoil. He stretched out on his bed and was enjoying the music so much that he didn't realize the time.

He glanced at the alarm clock and saw it was one o'clock. He got up and padded over to the window to see if it was still snowing. Lifting a slat of the blind, he was reminded when he thought he saw Betsy. Expecting to see no one, he was quickly surprised.

Practically across from his window, on the other side of Elk Street, he saw Lester, talking to a woman. Her back was to Alan, so he could not see who it was, but he definitely saw Lester. He seemed to act more drunkenly than ever, but who was the woman with him?

He observed him speaking quite heatedly with the woman, who-ever she was, and attempting to get away from her. Alan wished she would turn his way, as he could not see her from his angle. He saw Lester trudge off in the direction of Washington Avenue, the woman trailing after him, like a lost dog seeking its master. Alan continued watching until he could no longer see them as they passed in back of the Boys Academy.

Most likely a girl he met somewhere. Having more than enough of Lester's shenanigans, he crawled back to bed. He had a full day of work tomorrow, and sleep was imperative.

Drowsiness finally overcame him. His last conscious thought was of Betsy falling hideously to her death on the atrium floor.

CHAPTER TWELVE

I t was a week later, Tuesday, the ninth of February and still no breaks in the case of the murder of Penelope Barker. It had been two months since her death and Albany City Police were at a loss for new information. Police detectives conducted countless interviews; everyone assembled in the cast including the manager of the Ivory Theater, who had worked with Miss Barker. No one could shed light on the circumstances surrounding her death. Most commented that Miss Barker kept to herself and did not socialize with the cast outside the theater. Her neighbors reiterated this information. She was described as secretive and manipulative and was avoided at all costs. When asked if she had a steady beau, the only name mentioned was Mr. Lester Cavanaugh, whose name was also associated with Miss Betsy Donovan.

At police headquarters on Central Avenue in Albany, Inspector Harris patiently read a police report on the murder of Penelope Barker over and over, hoping to find something that could lead to a breakthrough. It was unlike the inspector to let a crime go unsolved this long and he was desirous to find the culprit. He then picked up another report, this on the death of Miss Betsy Donovan. He had noted his interviews with the deceased's father, aunt, cousin, Mrs. Jeanne Churchill and Mrs. Eleanor Whitney. The initial reports by officers on the scene that night stated that Miss Donovan may have simply fallen, but Mr. Alan Cartwright shed light on a surprising revelation; that of the fire escape door ajar on the fifth floor, the same floor where Miss Donovan attempted to display her agility in sliding down a banister.

Ridiculous, the inspector thought wryly, if he had a daughter, he would never allow her to act in such an insolent manner. Of course, the flappers were above the law, or so they thought, and their parents usually had little if any control over them.

Having met Mr. Carl Donovan, he assumed that was just the case with him. While he understood his state of mourning, he was able to deduce that Mr. Donovan could not control his daughter and rather than trying to tame a savage beast, immersed himself at his accounting practice. There was no talk of a mother, so he assumed he and his wife were divorced and apparently estranged. Such a waste, if only her father had better authority, perhaps it would not have happened.

The issue of Miss Barker's murder was paramount and of the utmost importance to the inspector and his colleague. They had been assigned the case by their superior and since Miss Donovan's death, had been assigned to her calamity, too. But was her death premeditated? Was it actually a murder investigation?

At that moment, the door opened and his partner, Lieutenant Taylor walked in. He had a cigarette in one hand and a file in the other, which he placed on the inspector's desk. He sat in a chair in front of his desk and was apparently eager to tell him of his recent findings.

"I've spoken to more people who work at Harmanus Bleecker Hall," he said. "No one knew Miss Donovan, but most knew of Miss

Barker. A few commented that she had visited the Hall a few times and was very flamboyant, to the point of rudeness."

Inspector Harris sighed. "We have a murder that is two months old with no leads. And a possible homicide, with an atrium full of people who witnessed it, but no one can tell us anything."

"Except Mr. Cartwright," Lieutenant Taylor put in.

Inspector Harris nodded. "Mr. Cartwright discovered the fire escape ajar on the fifth floor and the snowy footprints leading to the top of the staircase. Does it mean someone rubbed snow on the banister to make it slippery so that when Miss Donovan decided to show off her skill she would lose her grip and fall to her death?"

Lieutenant Taylor puffed at his cigarette, knocking ash into an ashtray on the desk. "That could just be the case. We've spoken to the father, the aunt and the two older ladies. They couldn't tell us much. The older woman refused to believe it was not an accident. Usually people like that have something to hide."

The inspector agreed and then glanced down at the reports again. "There's a name that keeps popping up. It's Mr. Lester Cavanaugh."

The lieutenant nodded. "People at the Hall mentioned he's on the board of directors and that he dated Miss Barker and Miss Donovan. I looked in our files and noticed he's on probation for bootlegging. I'm sure he hasn't stopped his illegal business."

"And they have him as a board member? What's he do for a living?"

"He works at the public library on Dove Street. Can't imagine someone like him working in such a sedate environment. I spoke with his probation officer yesterday. He's been clean for a while and is trying to go straight."

"Anything else of interest?"

Lieutenant Taylor extinguished his cigarette and leaned back in the chair. "I spoke to associates who worked with Miss Donovan at

Albany Savings Bank. They told me she was quite a flirt and enjoyed the company of men around town."

"Goes to show her father could not control her," the inspector remarked dryly.

The lieutenant nodded. "A few commented they heard Miss Donovan caused a scene in a few public places, like Whitney's and at a speakeasy on Howard Street. She was involved in a catfight with a girl named Miss Norma Smith at the speakeasy, who works at Harmanus Bleecker Hall and is also on the board there. Apparently, Miss Donovan and Miss Smith did not get along. Seems Miss Donovan and Miss Barker did not have good reputations in this city."

"And their names are linked to several people who were present at the dance marathon that night. I'd like to speak to Mr. Cavanaugh and Miss Smith. We don't know yet if these deaths are related or if Miss Donovan's death was just an accident." He paused thoughtfully and then continued as though talking to himself. "Could be Miss Donovan knew something and was silenced." He blinked and realized the lieutenant was waiting for him to say more. "I'll call Mr. Ferguson and set up a meeting so we can make headway on this case."

Lieutenant Taylor mentioned he had files to work on and left the office. Inspector Harris lifted the handset on the candlestick phone but hesitated before giving the number to the operator.

The vicious murder of Miss Barker, Miss Donovan's sudden death…He tried to convince himself he would soon learn the truth in both cases. But as he spoke to the operator and waited for the call to go through, his apprehension would not dissipate.

Alan sipped his coffee and looked at his uncle as he finished the last of his mother's pot roast. He certainly had quite an appetite, he thought, watching as Carl helped himself to second portions. But then given the tumultuous days of Betsy's death and the recent wake and funeral services, Alan was concerned his uncle would take longer to recuperate. He was glad he and his mother were close by to provide much needed support.

It was just after seven o'clock and Alan and Bernice joined Carl at his home, where Bernice cooked a pot roast and all the trimmings, including roasted potatoes and hot garlic bread. It was quite a meal and was complimented by Bernice's chocolate cake and coffee.

Conversation ensued about the cold snap that did not seem to break, more snow predicted, work related issues and of course the family and friends who attended Betsy's wake and funeral. Bernice had helped her brother with the arrangements and the services. Carl had sent a telegram to his ex-wife that went unanswered, as far as he knew, she most likely did not receive it and if she did, did not reply to it.

Alan lit a cigarette and enjoyed the chocolate cake and coffee, glad to spend time with his uncle and his mother, who he found rather sullen and more demur.

"Best meal I've had in weeks," Carl said, wiping his mouth on a napkin. "You're just the best cook a brother could ask for, Bernice."

Bernice smiled. "Thanks, Carl. We've been concerned about you. I'm glad you're feeling better and returned to work, too."

Carl nodded. "It's made this horrendous ordeal more tolerable. Fortunately, I have a great staff that took care of business while I was out."

Alan offered him a cigarette and Bernice refilled his coffee cup. He asked Alan about events at the Hall to which Alan had little to tell him.

"Mr. Ferguson is reluctant to book any new talent," he said. "With the negative publicity we've had the last two weeks, he wants to wait for everything to settle down."

"Didn't you mention the Marx Brothers would return?" Carl asked him.

Alan nodded. "Hopefully in the near future. Right now, we're showing a double feature all week; *A Slave of Fashion* with Norma Shearer and *Cheaper to Marry* with Conrad Nagel. So far, ticket sales have surpassed what Mr. Ferguson and I had hoped. We wondered if Betsy's death would keep people away."

Carl puffed at his cigarette, looking at his nephew and sister. "Those films wouldn't keep anyone away. Norma Shearer and Conrad Nagel are top stars."

"Women adore Conrad Nagel," Bernice added, rather dreamily. "There are always articles about him in *Photoplay* and even *The Saturday Evening Post.*"

"Perhaps Mr. Ferguson will reschedule the dance marathon," Carl said. "It was quite a disappointment when he canceled the remainder of it."

"The refunds have been time-consuming to say the least," Alan commented. "When people started to realize what had happened, especially after the police and the ambulance arrived that night, it pretty much meant the end of the marathon."

Bernice nodded. "I think he did the right thing by canceling it."

"Do you think it's worth it to hire a private investigator, Uncle Carl? It'll clear up any remaining questions; especially if it's determined that it was just an accident."

"A private investigator?" Bernice spoke before her brother had the chance. "Why in the world would we want to do such a thing? It was an accident. It's not like it was murder."

Carl was silent for some time. Sipping his coffee, he looked at his nephew and his answer was grave yet assuring, taking Alan and his mother by surprise.

"I think it's a good idea, Alan. I had not thought of hiring a private investigator. We don't know the circumstances leading up to Betsy's death. The police move so slow in this city, it could take weeks or months if they find anything out, if there is anything to find out. The footprints on the top of those stairs could mean someone put snow on the banister."

"The police insinuated just that," Alan reminded him.

Carl nodded. "God knows my daughter had plenty of enemies. And wasn't it ironic that her enemies were all there that night? Anyone could've rubbed snow on that banister, you know."

"We would have seen someone at the top of the stirs," Bernice insisted.

"Not necessarily," Alan said, causing Bernice to look at her son almost angrily. "The atrium and the ballroom were crowded that night. If someone went up to the top of the right staircase, I doubt if anyone would have paid the slightest attention."

"It would be a considerable expense, Alan," his mother mentioned, determined to make a point. "Have you considered the cost of hiring a private investigator?"

"Not to worry about the expense, Bernice," Carl told his sister. "If a private investigator can clear up the circumstances surrounding my daughter's death, then I agree to it."

Bernice offered more coffee and Carl suggested they relax in the living room. Bernice started to clean the kitchen, while Alan and Carl entered the spacious living room. Alan turned the radio dial until he found *The Atwater Kent Hour*, Carl's favorite program.

"A private investigator," Carl mused, sipping his coffee, lighting a cigarette. He sat in his armchair near the fireplace, listening to the radio, glad for the company of his sister and nephew.

"I think it's foolish," Bernice said, entering the living room and sitting opposite her brother on the sofa. She let her son know of her disapproval.

Alan was immersed in the evening paper, while enjoying the sounds of *The Atwater Kent Hour*. Carl mentioned how grateful he was for their company and that a private investigator may be just what was needed to clear his mind about his daughter's death. Carl and Bernice listened to the soothing symphonic music, chatting amongst themselves. The uncertainty of Betsy's untimely death remained foremost in their minds, an inexorable and troublesome burden.

In the boarding house where she resided, Norma Smith paused by the window in her room overlooking State Street. She looked out and noticed it was busy as usual, full of traffic and pedestrians. Hastily she grabbed her fur coat and cloche hat from her closet, and then satisfied with her evening plans; she abruptly descended the staircase to the second floor. She wanted to avoid old Mrs. Webster, the proprietress, as she was extremely nosy and meddlesome. Undoubtedly, she would ask her where she was going on such a cold evening and Norma would be hard pressed not to tell her to mind her own business.

Furtively, she cast a quick glance at herself in the large antique hallway mirror. She had applied fresh lipstick and rouge and was rather pleased with her appearance. She straightened her pretty cloche hat on her delicate head and silently opened the door to be welcomed by gusty winds and intermittent snow showers.

Descending the snowy steps, she looked back at the handsome old brownstone she called home. It was indeed a beautiful building and so well kept by Mr. and Mrs. Webster, but the less she saw of them the better. She paid her rent on time and preferred not to socialize with them. The location was ideal to Harmanus Bleecker Hall and downtown Albany was within walking distance.

This evening Norma's plans took her to Lark Street, a neighborhood with a rather unconventional atmosphere. Walking briskly up State Street, reaching the corner with Lark, she turned left. She frequented a coffee shop, where government officials often met. Norma considered it an excellent place to meet eligible men.

She was about to cross at the corner of Lark and Hudson when Evangeline and her mother were coming toward her in the opposite direction. She smiled in recognition although she would have preferred not to see them or anyone else she knew.

"Norma, nice to see you," Evangeline said. She was carrying a bag full of groceries, and she was practically shivering in the cold.

Norma smiled at Evangeline and commented that it certainly was cold. While speaking she was aware of Mrs. Whitney sizing her up. Another one she wanted to tell to mind her own business.

"How are you, Mrs. Whitney?" Norma forced herself to say pleasantly.

"I'm just fine, Miss Smith," Eleanor said warmly, looking every bit the matron, yet pleasing in her winter coat and cloche hat, ever protective of her daughter. "You look very pretty, Miss Smith. You must be meeting someone. We don't want to keep you, dear."

"I'm going to the hat shop further down Lark," she lied. "They're cleaning one of my most prized hats, and they called to let me know it was ready."

"They're open so late?" Mrs. Whitney asked, looking around.

Norma nodded. "Evening hours on Tuesdays," she said which she knew was the truth.

"So terrible about poor Betsy, isn't it, Norma?" Evangeline said, as though she felt any sympathy. Even her mother looked at her oddly.

Norma nodded. "We'll get on with business at the Hall."

"A shame the dance marathon was canceled," Evangeline lamented. "It was rather fun that night until Betsy fell, shocking everyone."

"We must support Mr. Donovan during this difficult time," Mrs. Whitney said.

"And how upsetting about Miss Barker, too," Evangeline continued. "Right around the corner from here on Lancaster Street."

Mrs. Whitney shook her head. "The city just is not safe anymore. We must be careful." She paused. "Would you like to join us for coffee, Miss Smith?"

"Oh, thank you, Mrs. Whitney, that's very kind of you, but I must be off," Norma said, smiling. "So good to see both of you. We must get together soon, Evangeline."

Evangeline returned the smile, saying she looked forward to seeing her again. Mother and daughter continued on Lark Street toward State Street while Norma walked toward Madison Avenue. She bundled her scarf and fur coat around her to keep warm, feeling rather irritable at seeing the Whitneys, but her thoughts kept her from feeling the cold.

Foolish of Evangeline to mention Betsy and Miss Barker, as though she sympathized over their deaths. Norma knew Evangeline had issues with Betsy and Miss Barker, so why mention them and pretend that she cared? Just idle small talk, she thought miserably. She put the Whitneys out of her mind as she reached her destination.

The coffee shop, while respectable from the outside, catered to an avant guard clientele, bringing out the bohemian side of the neighborhood. Dance bands flourished and music helped to keep patrons happy, although it was well-known that liquor could be purchased clandestinely. Prohibition be dammed, Norma thought descending the stairs and entering the busy coffee shop. She greeted a few regulars and then spotted the man she was looking for.

"Hello, dear," she said sweetly coming up to the handsome man at a corner table.

"Hello, Norma," Lester said, smiling, looking at her provocatively.

She did not need to know the purpose of their meeting. Like Betsy and Penelope Barker, Norma knew she was one of Lester's many conquests, but she was attracted to him, finding him handsome and dangerous, qualities that appealed to her. She knew Evangeline was attracted to him as well, but then what woman wasn't? While Lester was in his mid-thirties, past his formidable twenties, he still gave a stunning appearance, and he knew it. His suit was immaculate and his rugged good looks captivated women who turned his way.

They ordered coffee and Lester slipped the waiter a twenty-dollar bill for something a little stronger added to their beverages. They continued conversing, smoking, laughing and drinking the whiskey-laced coffee. Lester spotted a few friends and he and Norma were soon conversing with them, discussing work and picnics this summer in Washington Park.

Finishing his coffee, Lester turned to Norma and suggested they go to his place before it got too late. They walked out onto Lark Street during a snow shower. A trolley arrived and during the ride downtown, Norma linked her hand through his arm affectionately. She was reminded how much she liked Lester, but then she liked Alan, John and Ed, too. Such decisions, but not tonight.

Alighting from the trolley, they walked south on Broadway, reaching Lester's brownstone. Norma felt a little tipsy and almost slipped climbing the snowy steps, laughing lightly as Lester helped her. He unlocked the front door, and they disappeared inside.

They did not know they had been watched. Down the street, an obscure figure moved silently away.

CHAPTER THIRTEEN

Downtown Albany was a scene of chaotic activity during the morning rush hour and a heavy snowfall only contributed to the frenzy. Looking down State Street hill from the capitol, the snow fell steadily, creating almost a picture-perfect tranquility of whiteness. But at the corners of South Pearl Street and Broadway, there was the inevitable sounds of city life, mingled with the harshness of winter maneuvering. Horns blared; executives rushed to arrive at their offices, trollies clambered for space, filling up quickly to accommodate pedestrians.

None of this city racket intruded into the office of Sloane Sheppard. Carefully tucked away in a corner on the fifth floor of the Albany City Savings Bank building, directly in the middle of downtown at 100 State Street, in a rather small and nondescript room, Sloane blocked all outside interference from allowing him to concentrate fully on his work.

Finishing with a recent divorce case, Sloane put a folder aside and glanced toward the windows overlooking State Street. Another cold, blustery, snowy day, typical for February. He leaned back in his swivel desk chair and lit a cigarette, glad to take a few moments of respite. He ran his own business and although tempted at times to hire a secretary, to relieve him of mounting paperwork, Sloane preferred to accomplish it all himself.

An Albany native, Sloane lived in an apartment on upper Madison Avenue, across from Washington Park and while still in the city proper, it was away from the downtown core. Though a sought-after bachelor, at thirty-six, and despite the invitations that were showered on him, he spent many evenings quietly working at home on research projects. He completed a master's degree in library science from the State Teachers College and his skills in research aided him in his investigations. He embarked on a career in private investigations and after completing courses from a local trade school, he obtained a license as a private investigator with the State of New York, which he proudly framed and hung on a wall in his office.

Sloane was a well-known member of the downtown Albany business community. In a city riddled with crime and violence, especially since the Great War and the advent of prohibition, he had gotten to know the underworld of Albany like few others. Politicians, government scandals, gangsters, prostitutes, bootleggers, child kidnappings, speakeasies, murderers, show girls and con artists—he had observed them all in the capital city.

A powerful figure, both physically and professionally, Sloane stood at six feet two inches tall, and his strong physique aided him in his crusade in apprehending criminals. He worked often with the Albany City Police, having insight into different areas that as a private investigator were more easily accessible than to a police officer in uniform. His professional strength was his ability to resolve cases, achieving resolution for his clients. His business prospered and Sloane had few free days to himself.

Dressed impeccably in a solid white shirt, tie and vest, his wavy black hair, rugged, chiseled face and brown eyes exhibited a formidable presence. Never undaunted, he knew a few people in the Albany community considered him too young in his profession, but Sloane let his track record of success speak for itself.

He glanced at the calendar on his desk. Today was Wednesday, February 10, 1926, and he had an afternoon full of appointments. As it was too cold to go out and not to waste time, he decided to send out for lunch. He extinguished his cigarette and was about to call in an order to the deli on South Pearl Street when someone knocked on his office door.

"Good morning, Mr. Williams," Sloane said, smiling at his dependable mailman.

Mr. Williams, the mailman, relatively new to this route, although a postal employee for over twenty years, smiled in return. "Here you go, Mr. Sheppard. Nasty day today, too much wind and snow. I hear there's more coming, too!"

"It's only February, Mr. Williams," Sloane joked. "We've got more winter on the way."

Getting up from around his desk, Sloane took the letters he held out to him and wished him a good day. Once settled behind his desk, he thumbed through the envelopes until he came to one from the Albany City Police. Realizing it came from Inspector Harris, he ripped it open without using his letter opener and carefully read the contents.

So the police are asking for my help in the murder investigation of Miss Penelope Barker, he thought. He had read about her death in the paper last December and already had spoken to Inspector Harris and Lieutenant Taylor a few times by telephone. They were requesting his assistance again as they had so far uncovered no new leads and to quote the inspector "the investigation had stalled."

The police were also seeking his assistance in determining the cause of death of Miss Betsy Donovan. Sloane pondered where he had heard that name mentioned, and then remembered reading in the newspapers about her premature death during the dance marathon at Harmanus Bleecker Hall last month. He sat for several minutes, looking at the snow falling outside his window. He reached for his pack of Lucky Strikes and lit one, drawing in the smoke to his lungs and exhaling with great trepidation.

In cases of unnatural death, including accidents, he knew the police were always involved. He remembered the newspapers stated it was an accident, as Miss Donovan had fallen to her death, while attempting to slide down a banister. Certainly foolish on her part, he thought. She must have lost her grip, causing her to fall. He was surprised something of that nature would occur at Harmanus Bleecker Hall. Looking at the letter again, he owed Inspector Harris a response. He had already spoken to him about the first death but knew nothing about the second. He was not sure if he wanted to get involved, as he had several cases to attend, and his agenda for the next several weeks was quite full.

Donovan, Donovan, he turned the name over and over and then remembered Mr. Carl Donovan, a prominent accountant here in downtown Albany. He may have met him once before but could not place him. Certainly, a prosperous man, so his daughter must have been secure financially. If he remembered correctly, they lived downtown too, on prestigious Elk Street.

Most likely a flapper acting irresponsible, Sloane thought. He assumed Mr. Donovan's daughter frequented speakeasies. The speakeasy scene in the city had become notorious; he saw more trouble emanating from those establishments than good.

He would gladly assist his contacts at the Albany City Police, as they had obliged him numerous times in the past. Rather than writing to the inspector, Sloane decided a telephone call was better. He picked up the handset on the candlestick phone and asked the operator to connect him with the police headquarters on Central Avenue. In a relatively short time, he was connected to Inspector Harris's office, but both the inspector and Lieutenant Taylor were out on an assignment. A police officer asked if he could take a message.

Sloane identified himself, keeping his cigarette between his lips and between puffs told him that he was available to assist with the murder investigation of Miss Penelope Barker and the death of Miss Betsy Donovan, as Inspector Harris requested. The officer recognized his name immediately and thanked him for his call and his offer to help. He would relay the message to Inspector Harris as soon as he arrived back to headquarters.

Sloane replaced the handset, placing the candlestick phone on the corner of his desk, puffing thoughtfully at his cigarette. It could be a long investigation since no new leads had surfaced on Miss Barker's murder. And the death of Miss Donovan. Was it even worth his time? Unless there was much more to it, that perhaps even the police had yet to discover.

Sloane sighed, irresolute, finishing his cigarette. His concern turned to files and reports on his desk awaiting his attention.

That afternoon, just before five o'clock, Mr. Ferguson called an unscheduled meeting. Mrs. Russell told Alan he was summoned to the conference room. Alan had been looking through the city directory for private investigators. With a sigh, he closed the directory and thanked Mrs. Russell.

Entering the hallway and approaching the conference room cautiously, he looked at the assembled people around the long table. He sat down and greeted everyone but felt a strong undercurrent, and then noticed the police officers he spoke with previously, seated next to Mr. Ferguson. Their presence created a rather uncomfortable atmosphere.

Alan looked at Lester, Ed and John and thought there was just about any place in the world they would rather be than sitting with officials from the Albany City Police. He wondered if Lester felt especially uncomfortable, given his previous brushes with the law and his current probation status. He was surprised they took time off from their jobs. Perhaps Mr. Ferguson insisted they attend. Judging from the expressions of Norma and Mrs. Churchill, they also did not appreciate this unanticipated meeting. Certainly, Mrs. Churchill was firm and resolute, appearing more matronly and Alan thought she looked older. Perhaps the ordeal with Betsy aged her but then he did not think it would affect her that badly. Lester, Ed and John looked mellow, as though Betsy's calamity had sapped them of their inner reserve and left them unsettled. Only Norma appeared nonchalant, a cigarette in her hand. She *should* care, given her relationship with Betsy and the fight they had at the speakeasy, with plenty of witnesses. But then why should that even matter, it certainly was not a murder investigation. But was that why the police came here today? Suddenly, Alan felt chilled, and he knew it was not from the bitter winds outside. He turned his attention to Mr. Ferguson who began to speak, holding everyone transfixed.

"I called this board meeting today at the request of Inspector Harris and Lieutenant Taylor of the Albany Police. They'd like to ask everyone about the evening Miss Donovan died."

Inspector Harris cleared his throat, introduced himself and his colleague. He requested their full cooperation while they attempted to learn the truth. He turned his attention first to Lester.

"Mr. Cavanaugh, were you acquainted with Miss Donovan?" he asked Lester.

Lester lit a cigarette and had it between his lips. "Yes, of course, Inspector. Betsy and I went out quite frequently."

"I understand she said, 'Lester you're mine' that evening, as she was attempting to slide down the banister."

Lester smirked, depositing ash in an ashtray. "That's just Betsy talking. She was rather silly at times. I don't know what she meant by that remark."

"You're on probation, Mr. Cavanaugh?"

Alan thought that if Lester could kill someone it would be at that exact moment. From his expression alone, he could tell Lester did not like that personal part of his life mentioned in front of everyone. Even Alan thought it could have been done privately, without an audience. But Lester, ever the sly fox, played his cards right as always and answered the inspector coolly.

"Yes, that's correct; Inspector, but I don't see what that has to do with the death of Miss Donovan. If you wish to pursue that further with me, I'd prefer to discuss it in private."

Inspector Harris nodded. "You also were intimate with Miss Barker, I understand."

"Intimate? Well, Inspector, Miss Barker and I had a relationship, but it has nothing to do with Miss Donovan," Lester said quite firmly. "Honestly, my personal life is not the issue here."

"Perhaps it is, Mr. Cavanaugh. You were involved with both women, who met premature deaths. You are on probation and have a criminal record with the Albany City Police." He paused. "You must be familiar with the streets of this city. You are also a board member so you must know the layout of this building quite well."

Alan could tell Lester was losing his patience. To his surprise, he said nothing and continued smoking, locking eyes with the inspector, a sneering look on his face.

Lieutenant Taylor mentioned what Alan had told them when they first interviewed him; the fire escape door left ajar, with footprints on the landing that led to the top of the right staircase, where Miss Donovan was to slide down the railing.

"We've spoken to Miss Donovan's father, Mrs. Whitney and Mrs. Cartwright," the lieutenant said. "They could not remember seeing anyone at the top of the stairs, except, of course, Miss Donovan."

"We tried to convince her not to attempt it," Ed said. "But she was adamant."

Norma agreed. "Betsy liked to put-on, especially when there were a lot of men around. She liked to trap men in her lair and use them, then move on to someone else."

"But she mentioned that Mr. Cavanaugh belonged to her," Inspector Harris persisted.

Norma almost laughed. "As Lester said, that was just Betsy rattling on. It didn't mean anything. I don't think she would've been happy with just one man."

Inspector Harris asked if anyone had noticed the fire escape door ajar that evening or if they had the opportunity to go to the fifth floor. Blank faces all around; no one had seen anyone on the fifth floor landing, or noticed the fire escape door ajar, except Alan when he showed guests around the building.

"Mr. Whitmore, I understand you knew Miss Barker," the inspector continued. "Were you also intimate with her as well as Miss Donovan?"

"Inspector, to save you time," John said, keeping his patience. "Lester, Ed, and I dated Miss Donovan and Miss Barker on several occasions. Alan also dated Miss Barker. I can't speak for anyone else, but I was intimate with both." He hesitated, his mind reeling. "Miss

Barker caused problems for nearly everyone, spreading malicious gossip and Miss Donovan did the same. They seemed to enjoy wreaking havoc for others."

"Where are you employed, Mr. Whitmore?"

"I'm an assistant manager at the Strand Theater. Miss Barker played at our venue a few times and she was always difficult. She created scenes when something didn't go her way."

"What sort of gossip did they spread, Mr. Whitmore?"

John sighed. "Miss Barker said I was fired from my previous position, which was not true. She used that as blackmail against me, as long as I gave into her demands. She expected me to give her star billing at the theater. She talked about me to others in the theater community that I was incompetent and should be fired from the Strand. The same for Miss Donovan. She wanted me to help her make bathtub gin at her house. She told people I did help her, but it wasn't the truth. Betsy also was a liar."

Lieutenant Taylor was scribbling in a notebook. "Miss Smith, did you get along with Miss Donovan? Did you know Miss Barker?"

Norma squirmed somewhat in her seat, finishing her cigarette. "No, I did not get along with either one. Before you hear it from another party, you may be interested to know that Betsy and I had an altercation at a speakeasy recently. She threw gin in my face and she and I went at it. She accused me of stealing Lester from her, all the while thinking he belonged to her."

"She must have had deep feelings for you, Mr. Cavanaugh," Inspector Harris said.

Lester shrugged it off. "Betsy used people to get what she wanted. She didn't care about anyone except herself."

"Mr. Flynn, what was your relationship with Miss Donovan? Did you know Miss Barker?"

Ed was caught off guard. Rather meekly, he said that he did know Miss Donovan and Miss Barker and that he also had dated them. He mentioned he was employed at city hall and had little contact with either Miss Donovan or Miss Barker.

"I know Betsy talked about me to different people," Ed said, thinking back to Betsy's conniving ways. "She spread a rumor that I was involved with Mrs. Whitney, while I was dating her daughter, Evangeline." He paused, as he realized everyone was looking at him. "She broke Evangeline and I up and enjoyed doing so. Evangeline heard about it and was really hurt. I told her there was no truth to it, but our relationship was over."

"Mr. Cartwright, you mentioned you found the fifth floor fire escape door ajar that evening and snowy footprints leading to the top of the staircase. Why did you not report this to Mr. Ferguson when you discovered it?"

All eyes turned to Alan. He could feel Mr. Ferguson's wrath even in the silence that followed. He took his time in replying.

"I was showing Senator Miles and his wife around the Hall when I discovered it. I thought nothing of it at first. I figured the maintenance crew hadn't secured the door."

"The fact that the snowy footprints led to the staircase suggest that someone was on the fire escape and walked to the head of the right set of stairs," the inspector continued. "Perhaps that person rubbed snow on the banister, causing Miss Donovan to fall."

"But nobody knew ahead of time that Betsy would demonstrate her sliding down a banister, Inspector," Ed said, to which they all agreed.

"There were no footprints on the fire escape steps, just on the landing outside the door," Alan told the policemen. "Honestly, I thought nothing of it."

The lieutenant asked for their addresses and reluctantly they supplied the information. Inspector Harris noted that Ed lived close to the Donovans on Elk Street as did Alan Cartwright, and his mother and Mrs. Churchill. He noted that John lived in an apartment on State Street and Norma also lived on the same street, in a well-respected boarding house. Lester, he noticed, lived the furthest on Broadway. He then turned his attention to Mrs. Churchill.

"We've spoken already, Mrs. Churchill, but I would like to know if you have anything else to add that could shed light on these investigations?"

Mrs. Churchill set her mouth firmly and spoke, quite intuitively. "As I told you, Inspector, I had no regard for either Miss Barker or Miss Donovan. Miss Barker was extremely rude to me on several occasions. Miss Donovan spread rumors that I was a senile old woman that should be locked up in a state mental hospital." Her face twisted harshly. "Hardly a motive for murder, Inspector, although I will say I was quite disturbed over her comments."

Norma spoke in her defense. "Not to worry, Mrs. Churchill. Betsy spread rumors about everyone, like John said. She told people that I bribed Mr. Ferguson into hiring me at the Hall."

"With such a bad reputation, she managed to perform well at the Albany Savings Bank where she was employed," Lieutenant Taylor commented. "From people we spoke to who worked with her, she was quite efficient in her daily activities there and was well liked by customers."

"That's because they didn't know her," Norma put in.

Inspector Harris cast a quick glance at Mr. Ferguson, who he realized was embarrassed and losing his patience. He concluded by reiterating that they will most likely speak with them again and he thanked them for their time and attention this afternoon.

The meeting broke up; chairs were scraped back as everyone stood to leave. Alan proceeded to his office for his coat and cap, noting Mrs. Russell had already left for the day. Ed, John and Lester met him in the hallway and together with Norma, they descended the stairs to the first floor and the main entrance. Mrs. Churchill trailed behind them but did not join them.

Outside, they were greeted with intermittent snow showers and bone chilling cold. They chatted amongst themselves and soon dispersed in different directions. Within a short time, Alan arrived home and realized Ed and Mrs. Churchill had not followed him. Strange, since they also lived on Elk Street. Once inside, he greeted his mother, basking in the wonderful aroma emanating from the kitchen. He removed his jacket, cap and shoes and joined her for dinner.

It was about an hour later, while Alan and his mother were in the living room with coffee and the evening newspaper, that John called, clearly alarmed. He told Alan that Norma had been injured in a horrific accident on State Street. She was taken by ambulance to Albany City Hospital, where her condition was listed as serious. He added that doctors were uncertain if she would survive the night.

CHAPTER FOURTEEN

The emergency room at Albany City Hospital was rather quiet that Wednesday evening. Few major calamities were present until the arrival by ambulance of a young woman, suffering a bad concussion. Immediately a nurse and the attending doctor examined her and make a preliminary prognosis. After more than a half hour, a nurse entered the hallway, looking around for next of kin. She saw a middle-aged woman, pacing back and forth, obviously perplexed and overcome, grief lining her face.

"Oh, nurse, will she be all right?" Mrs. Whitney asked her worriedly.

"Are you related to the victim?" the young nurse asked.

Eleanor shook her head. "No, but I know Miss Smith and came upon the accident."

At that moment, Alan and John walked hurriedly down the hall, stopping as soon as they saw Eleanor and the nurse. Alan explained they were friends of Miss Smith. The nurse told them the doctor would be with them shortly. Alan looked at Eleanor, confused, asking her to explain what she knew.

"I was at the library and when I left I heard a great commotion," she explained. "There was a crowd gathered and when I looked closer, I recognized Miss Smith lying on the ground. Someone called an ambulance and I decided to take the trolley here to inquire about her." She paused. "I called Mr. Whitmore to let him know Miss Smith had met with an accident."

John smiled and thanked her. "That's good of you, Mrs. Whitney."

The emergency room doctor, an older man who looked as though he had treated every ailment known to humanity, looked at them solemnly. He introduced himself as Dr. Osborne. He told them Miss Smith's vital signs and prognosis had improved. She suffered a concussion and needed to remain in the hospital for observation, at least for a few days. Other than that, she was quite fortunate. No broken bones, no fractures. He asked if anyone saw what happened. Eleanor explained what she told Alan and John, to which the doctor merely nodded and then disappeared behind the swinging doors of the emergency room.

"I called Evangeline earlier to tell her what happened," Eleanor explained, almost tearfully. "She also was terribly upset. Oh, it was just terrible!"

Alan tried to console her. "Why don't you sit down over here, Mrs. Whitney?"

They sat in chairs lined against the wall before the emergency room doors. No one spoke until John unleashed a torrent of vituperation seemingly aimed at nobody in particular.

"First, Miss Barker was murdered, and they still haven't found the killer yet and then Betsy falls from the railing. And now Norma falls on State Street and is lucky to be alive!"

Alan agreed. "But Norma's accident has nothing to do with Penelope or Betsy. You make it seem like it's somehow related."

"I heard someone say she slipped on the ice," Eleanor said wearily. "A woman in the crowd said she just missed being struck by a car. She could've been killed!"

With an increasing sense of urgency, John spoke again. "Something's going on around us, Alan. I want to know exactly what it is."

"Yes, I'd like to know, too," a female voice spoke.

They looked up to see Evangeline in front of them. Alan thought she looked pretty and feminine in her fur coat and cloche hat, her brown hair escaping on the side, but very daintily. He also noticed her worried expression, dark eyes and solemn face. She looked at them sitting together and asked again, what exactly happened.

Eleanor looked up at her daughter as though just realizing she was there. She explained to her what she already told the nurse, the doctor, Alan, and John. Evangeline mentioned she came to take her mother home. Eleanor gathered her purse and stood.

Alan assured her he would call them if Norma's condition changed for the worse. He watched as mother and daughter walked down the hallway toward the exit, and then noticed the doctor appearing again to speak to them.

"Miss Smith's prognosis has improved," he explained again. "Initially, my colleague and I were uncertain of her condition, as it appeared a serious concussion. But her youth and vitality have contributed to her improvement. As I mentioned earlier, I'd like to keep her here for observation for a few days."

Alan expressed his gratitude. John explained that Norma had no immediate family and that they were her close friends. The doctor asked them to complete the required paperwork.

While they approached the nurses' station and Alan began to write contact information for himself and John, he wondered again where Ed and Mrs. Churchill had gone after the meeting. He assumed Ed would catch up with him, or at least he and Mrs. Churchill would not be far behind since they also lived on Elk Street, unless they went somewhere else. Glancing at John, wouldn't he have seen or heard an accident as he and Norma lived on State Street, just a few houses away? Unless John also had other plans, most likely a speakeasy or a house party after the meeting this afternoon. Sometimes he thought John inconsiderate and untrustworthy, especially after touching liquor, although at the moment he did not think he was intoxicated.

He completed the forms and returned them to the nurse. John suggested they remain at the hospital in case Norma needed them, but the nurse informed them she was sleeping. She assured them they would be contacted at once if any adverse changes occurred.

Reluctantly, they decided to leave. Once outside, braving the snow and frigid air while waiting for the trolley, Alan could not help but think again that something, somewhere was terribly wrong with this whole picture—and that it was right in front of him—but at the moment, he could not determine precisely what it was.

On Thursday morning, the day dawned cold, but the sun peaked through the clouds, offering some hope of a clear day. In an effort to assist residents, city snowplows were enforced and scraping of shovels on sidewalks and streets was virtually everywhere this morning in downtown Albany.

Alan stretched lazily in bed, yawned, not quite awake. He was up before his alarm went off and slipping into his slippers and robe, he went downstairs to the kitchen. He found his mother already up and his uncle sipping coffee and reading the morning newspaper. Bernice turned to greet her son.

"I made oatmeal for us, Alan," she said, depositing a piping hot bowl on the table, along with a cup of coffee. The newspaper was scattered around the table.

Alan sat down across from his uncle, greeted him sleepily. Carl nodded, lifting his eyes from the paper quickly and then putting them back down again. He had no sooner sipped the coffee and taken his pack of cigarettes out of his robe pocket when his mother addressed him, rather seriously, as she sat down at the table.

"I already called the hospital to inquire about Miss Smith," she told him.

"What did they say?" Carl asked, putting the paper aside.

Bernice swallowed some coffee. "She is awake and asked for breakfast, which is a good sign. Her vital signs have improved, and she may be released this weekend." She paused. "Poor dear, I don't really know her, of course, but what could have happened to her?"

Alan tried to take it all in, still not quite awake. He then remembered what happened to Norma; how John called him last night and how he met him at the hospital. He lit a cigarette, sipped coffee and asked his mother what more the hospital told her.

Bernice shook her head. "Nothing else, except that Miss Smith was fortunate that she didn't have a more serious concussion. Ed called and told me he contacted Mr. Ferguson to tell him of Miss Smith's accident. He also was extremely upset."

"The streets are too snowy and icy," Carl said with strong disapproval. "It's no wonder more people don't slip and hit their heads."

"I also called Mrs. Whitney to see how she was coping," Bernice said. "She was still quite upset over the ordeal, understandably."

"Kind of her to go to the hospital to check on Miss Smith," Carl observed.

Bernice agreed. "You would have done the same, Carl, if you were there. I would have too and my son, also." She smiled at Alan.

"We are caring people, like Mrs. Whitney." She paused. I'm so glad we live near each other, Carl. You can always come here whenever you want."

Carl smiled, thanking his sister. "The best sister and nephew a man could ask for."

"I also called Mrs. Churchill, but there was no answer," Bernice said. "I don't know where she would be so early in the morning. Does she go to the Hall every day, Alan?"

"No, she's only part-time," he told her. "She usually starts after nine o'clock."

"Perhaps she had errands to run," Carl suggested.

"This early on such a cold morning?" Bernice said. "That's unlike her."

Alan and Carl wondered about Mrs. Churchill and oddly, the conversation ended, and an awkward silence followed. Alan broke it by exhaling a large cloud of smoke and announcing what he had reminded them of recently.

"I'd like a private investigator to look into Betsy's death. Granted, Betsy and I weren't especially close, but I do think there's more to it, honestly."

Carl nodded. "You have my consent, Alan and don't worry about the expense."

Bernice was obstinate. "I made my feelings clear on that. I don't feel it's necessary. Isn't that what the police are for? And do you really believe Betsy's death was not an accident?"

Alan yawned, still quite sleepy, his hair disheveled. He took time in replying. "I don't know, Mother. That's why a private investigator will clear it all up."

Carl agreed. "My daughter deserved better than what happened to her. If someone is responsible for her fall, I want that person held accountable." His tone verged on anger and Alan looked at his uncle sympathetically.

"Before Mr. Ferguson called a meeting yesterday, I looked in the city directory and found Mr. Sloane Sheppard. He works on State Street, so his office is convenient. I'd like to explain to him our concerns."

Carl thought for a moment. "Mr. Sheppard? I believe I know him. From what I hear about him, he is quite the best around."

Alan nodded, extinguishing his cigarette. "When I called Lester and Ed last night after I got back from the hospital, they even thought it was a good idea. Let's face it, the police in this city have let crimes go unsolved for months, even years. Look at the Penelope Barker murder case. They still haven't found who killed her and it's been since December."

"Must you mention that woman in my house, Alan?" Bernice said. "You know I never cared for her, that she was nothing but trouble. She spread gossip about me, trying to ruin my reputation at the capitol."

Carl told them how Penelope Barker wanted him to cut excuses on her taxes, but he would not have it. "She didn't play fair, even with the IRS. She'd cheat any chance she got." He sipped his coffee. "Contact this Mr. Sheppard, Alan. It'll be the best thing."

Alan nodded and then announced he needed to prepare for the day. He retreated upstairs and after shaving and showering, dressed in his usual business suit. Upon descending the stairs, he arrived at the kitchen and noticed his mother and uncle were still at the table, drinking coffee and conversing. Bernice finished her coffee and mentioned she too needed to dress for work. As Alan was about to leave, she reminded him to be careful, that there was a murderer loose in this city. Carl reiterated the need for extra vigilance, mentioning the rise in city crime.

But Alan, turning toward the front door rather indifferently, had already become immersed in his own disturbing thoughts.

Upon arrival, Alan greeted Mrs. Russell as he entered the outer office and then proceeded to his desk. He was surprised that within ten minutes to see Mrs. Churchill in the doorway, obviously perturbed and wishing to speak to him. He wondered what she had on her mind.

"Hello, Mrs. Churchill," he said cordially, ready for just about anything.

Mrs. Churchill sat in the chair in front of his desk. "I heard about the accident that befell Miss Smith last night," she said. "Mr. Ferguson told me about it. Most unfortunate. Kind of Mrs. Whitney to go to the hospital to check on her."

Alan sat at his desk, moved the telephone and fiddled with a few papers to stall for time. He was not sure what she wanted him to say, except that he also found it most unfortunate. He waited for her to arrive at her point if she was indeed making one.

"I do not understand why so much misfortune occurs to today's youth," she expostulated. "First, Miss Barker and then Miss Donovan and now Miss Smith suffered a horrendous accident. Terrible publicity for the Hall, too."

Alan was in shock. "It has nothing to do with our work here."

"The papers could tie it in with the accident of Miss Donovan," she answered grimly. "I know how they operate. They seek sensationalized stories to sell papers."

Alan saw her point. Calamities happened to two people related to Harmanus Bleecker Hall: one a guest and the other an employee. He then noticed Mr. Ferguson in the doorway. From his expression, he could tell he was disturbed over the recent events.

"Alan, I am genuinely concerned about Miss Smith. I also called the hospital and was relieved that her condition has improved, and she should be released soon. However, her work needs to be completed. I would appreciate if you would undertake a few of her assignments."

"Of course, Mr. Ferguson," Alan said.

"And I also would be happy to oblige," Mrs. Churchill added.

Mr. Ferguson nodded. "There is another matter of concern. One of our kitchen workers claims she knows something about the accident involving Miss Donovan." He hesitated. "She would not tell me anything, so I am inclined to brush it off as nonsense. You may know her. Her name is Miss Sarah Evans, a rather high-strung girl, a good cook, but overzealous." He cleared his throat. "Already rumors are starting. People are talking and Miss Evans is just one of many. When I went to my bank yesterday, I heard people gossiping about Miss Donovan and Miss Barker. Then on the way home last night on the trolley, I heard more people talking. A woman said that she thinks someone at the Hall is responsible for both deaths." He sighed in frustration, as though he was at wit's end. "I don't know what else to do to clamor this gossip."

"There is nothing we can do, Mr. Ferguson," Mrs. Churchill spoke sensibly. "People will talk, and the evil tongue has no remorse. But we know the truth and that should sustain us."

"Mrs. Churchill introduced me to Miss Evans that night," Alan said. "I've seen her around the building. Maybe I'll speak to her and see if she really does know something."

"Do you intend to visit Miss Smith later today, Alan?" Mrs. Churchill asked him.

"I plan to call the hospital to see if she will be released soon," Alan told her. "Although I don't know if I will go there today." He paused, and then regretted what he was about to say. "I want to contact a private investigator to look into Betsy's death."

Both Mrs. Churchill and Mr. Ferguson looked at him oddly. From their expressions alone, he could tell they did not approve of his endeavor but then he did not need their approval. He told him just that as soon as they both objected, as politely as possible.

"What you do on your time and with your money is your business, Alan," Mr. Ferguson told him rather sternly. "But I believe the police are handling this, so I do not understand why you wish to include another party to investigate, if there is anything to investigate."

"My uncle thinks it's a good idea," Alan added which silenced them both. "Betsy was his daughter, after all and he deserves closure and peace of mind."

With that, they could not argue, and Mrs. Churchill rose from the chair and proceeded to her office down the hall. Mr. Ferguson told Alan he would comply with a private investigator as needed, but reiterated he did not wish to have the Hall sensationalized in any way. Alan assured him that a private investigator would not leak anything to the press, to which the older man was doubtful, but he acquiesced, nonetheless. He left Alan, chatting briefly with Mrs. Russell in the outer office before returning to his own office on the fifth floor.

Alan lit a cigarette, drew smoke into his lungs and exhaled with great frustration. He wondered about Penelope Barker and his cousin Betsy. Was the same person who killed Miss Barker also responsible for Betsy's accident and Norma's incident, too? He wondered if anything more would happen and to whom. It was an unsettling feeling.

That evening, after dinner, Alan met Lester, John and Ed at the speakeasy on Howard Street. He told his mother he planned to meet John at his apartment on State Street. He was in no mood to hear her lecture about the dangers of speakeasies. He hated lying to her, but he was at the stage where he did not feel he needed to explain everything he did to his mother.

Sitting on the trolley, heading down State Street, Alan's thoughts were confused and chaotic and he wanted nothing more than a stiff drink to settle his nerves. He realized he was craving liquor much more frequently but then given the recent tumultuous events, he was not surprised. He did not let his mother know that, however.

Exiting at the corner of South Pearl Street, he saw Ed and John in the distance. At the same time, he noticed Lester coming up from lower State Street. They greeted each other and made their way to the speakeasy, and upon descending the stairs, Lester, ever the lead man, knocked on the door, gave the password and soon they were inside.

Through a haze of cigarette smoke, Alan looked around and was surprised it was not too busy for a Thursday night. It was dark as usual, there was no band tonight, but still there was a small crowd, enjoying the liquor and the atmosphere.

They found a corner table and ordered drinks. Lester felt in his pockets for cigarettes and realized he had finished his last pack. Ed brought his and offered them around the table. They chit chatted about work, enticing girls, Duke Ellington's hit songs, the latest movies, Lillian Gish and Mary Pickford, their home life and social life, until the inevitable topic of Norma's accident. Ed exclaimed how fortunate she was not to have been injured seriously.

"I'm glad Mrs. Whitney was there to see her at the hospital," John said.

"I'm surprised she'd go to the hospital," Lester said, almost gulping down a beer and soon getting the waiter's attention to order another. "Evangeline demands so much from her."

"Where were you when the accident happened, John?" Alan asked him, sipping his whiskey and puffing at his cigarette. He was feeling better as the liquor sustained him.

"After the meeting, I crossed Washington Avenue and headed down Lark Street to State. I don't know where Norma went, I assumed she was somewhere in the area."

"I went to a corner store to buy cigarettes," Ed said. "I didn't see her leave."

"I got on the first trolley when I left the Hall and headed for home," Lester said. "I didn't see her either, so I have no idea what happened to her."

"Nobody seems to know what happened," Alan said, causing a rather uneasy silence between them. "It had to be just an accident. She slipped on the ice."

He noticed several women at the bar, turned in their direction, looking at the handsome young men at the corner table. Sure enough, Alan knew Lester would smile and encourage them, apparently, he knew a few of them, but oddly, he did not go over to them and instead remained planted at their table, deep in thought.

They sat brooding, each concerned about the recent events, wondering what else could happen to cause such havoc. Ed asked Alan if he still planned to hire a private investigator.

He nodded. "I haven't had the chance to call yet. I looked in the city directory and found one I'm interested in. His name is Mr. Sheppard."

Lester mentioned he had heard of him, but neither John nor Ed were familiar with him. Ed asked them what they remembered about the night of the dance marathon. Alan spoke first.

"You mean Betsy's accident? I don't remember much of anything. It happened so fast."

"Your mother mentioned you found the fire escape door ajar on the firth floor," Lester said, finishing another glass of beer. "The police mentioned it, too. Do you think it means anything?"

Alan shrugged. "The police who questioned us may think it does. The maintenance crew shovels the fire escape but when I looked, I didn't see that it was shoveled, only footprints on the landing, leading to the top of the staircase."

"Which means someone could have rubbed snow on the banister, causing Betsy to lose her grip and fall," John remarked.

"You really think that?" Ed said, horrified. "We didn't know she'd demonstrate her sliding down a banister to the whole atrium!"

John took a gulp of whiskey. He puffed at his cigarette, before answering Ed.

"I don't know what to think, Ed. Norma's accident, Betsy's death, Penelope's murder in less than three months. I don't know what the hell is going on around here."

"I have to be careful," Lester said. "I'm still on probation, so I can't take any chances."

"Who are you seeing now, Lester?" Ed asked him.

Lester smiled, coyly, already asking the waiter for another. "No one in particular. You know me, Ed. I keep my eyes open. I play the field."

They laughed and ordered another round and Alan felt rather light-headed from another whiskey. He found his tongue even looser, and he wanted more than anything to tell Lester he had seen him chatting with Betsy early one morning from his bedroom window as well as with another woman, too. But he knew if he did, Lester would not tell the truth and would even turn on him, and although he considered him a friend, he did not trust Lester and wondered what he was up to, if cornered for any reason. He knew better than to back Lester Cavanaugh into a corner.

They continued chatting, drinking and smoking, but Alan felt an unmistakable danger somewhere near, almost poised and waiting. It was not Ed, John or Lester, but then Lester must know things he was not telling. Too many bizarre happenings and no resolution in sight.

John announced he was ready to call it a night and Lester agreed it was time to get home. After all, tomorrow was another workday. Once outside on the street, it had finally stopped snowing, but the wind had increased, creating an almost subzero wind chill. Lester trudged off in the direction of Broadway, mentioning he would call them tomorrow.

Alan followed John and Ed along South Pearl Street, and crossed to State, where they waited for a north bound trolley. The icy wind brushed Alan's hair across his forehead, and he pushed it back, under his cap and shrugged deeper into his coat to stay warm. After what seemed an eternity, they boarded and found seats in the back. As Alan settled in for the short ride up State Street, he looked at the semidarkness of downtown Albany, few pedestrians about. Crime had plagued our city, he thought grimly. A murderer was loose somewhere, perhaps even nearby.

Ed mentioned he planned to visit Norma in the hospital tomorrow after work and Alan told him he would meet him there as he wished to see her, too. Upon reaching Academy Park, Alan and Ed got up and said goodbye to John, before making their way to the front of the trolley and getting off. While cutting though the park, Alan listened while Ed was talking, but something immediate clawed at his mind. Ed hurried ahead of him, saying he would talk to him tomorrow; he wanted to get out of the cold and eagerly entered his apartment house on the corner of Elk Street. Alan looked back at the capitol, ablaze in floodlights, illuminated brilliantly. He thought about Lester, his liaisons with so many women, including Penelope, Betsy, Norma and Evangeline. John was a ladies man, too, but Alan did not think he was up to Lester's level. But they must know more than they told. They were too unscrupulous to take at face value.

Upon reaching home, Alan wondered what secrets Lester and John kept hidden and why.

CHAPTER FIFTEEN

I t was on Saturday, the thirteenth, that Norma was released from the hospital.

John received a call from the head nurse, informing him that Miss Smith was being discharged. He then called Alan and together they hopped on a trolley, bound for Madison Avenue. Getting off at the corner of Madison and New Scotland Avenue, they walked the short distance to Albany City Hospital. Upon entering the lobby and giving the nurses at the reception their names, they were directed to the set of elevators. They told the elevator attendant to bring them to the third floor, and soon enough, they were in Norma's room, where she was dressed and ready to leave.

"I am so glad to see both of you!" she exclaimed. Color had returned to her face, and she appeared her old self, even jubilant. "I can't wait to catch up on everything!"

The doctor entered at that moment and was pleased with the progress Norma had made. He cautioned her about not overdoing any work and to take things easily, at least for a few days. A nurse entered with a wheelchair and although Norma insisted she did not need it, they mentioned it was standard hospital procedure. Reluctantly, she sat in the wheelchair with Alan and John beside her. They rode down the elevator and finally reached the lobby. The elevator attendant opened the gates, and the nurse wheeled Norma through to the main doors. She thanked the nurse and then walked with Alan and John outside.

John suggested a taxi to which Norma started to protest, but Alan concurred and approached a cab as it was waiting in front of the hospital. Once settled, they chatted briefly, although Norma was still rather overcome and was not too talkative. The cab pulled up in front of the brownstone on State Street, Alan paid the fare and then he and John helped Norma up the stairs and inside. Climbing the stairs to the second floor, Norma fumbled with her purse, finding the key and upon opening the door, felt an overwhelming gladness to be at her home, or at least the place she called home. John helped her to an armchair overlooking State Street. Alan asked if he could get her anything, but Norma just shook her head, glad to be home.

Alan sat on the sofa and John lit cigarettes for them, walking around the small yet adequately furnished room. He turned and asked her to explain to them what happened the other night. Norma nodded, exhaling a cloud of smoke.

"I don't really know what happened. I was about to cross at the corner of State and Dove, where a perfume store had a sale of my favorite cologne. I wanted to get there before it closed."

"So you went there after Mr. Ferguson's meeting on Wednesday?" Alan asked her.

Norma nodded. "As I was about to cross State, I slipped or thought I slipped and next thing, I was on the ground and I don't remember anything else, except waking up in the hospital."

"What do you mean you *think* you slipped?" John asked, turning to look at her.

"There was a lot of snow and ice on the pavement, but I thought I felt something press against me. Of course, there were others waiting to cross too, so it probably was just someone else, who accidentally bumped into me. Goodness knows I've had that happen plenty of times while waiting to cross streets in this city."

An uncomfortable silence ensued until someone abruptly knocked on the door. As though puzzled who it could be, and Norma hoped it was not Mrs. Webster, John went to the door and opened it. Before him stood Mrs. Whitney, carrying a large pot and Evangeline holding a dish covered with aluminum foil. John moved aside allowing them to enter.

"Hello, Miss Smith," Mrs. Whitney said, smiling and depositing the pot on the kitchen table. "I made beef stew, as I knew you were just home from the hospital. Evangeline made corn bread, too."

"That's very kind of you, Mrs. Whitney," Norma said gratefully. "And thank you also, Evangeline for coming here today."

"I called the hospital to inquire about you," Eleanor said, taking off her fur coat. "They told me you were being released so I thought you'd need some nourishment."

Looking around at the small room, the kitchen was adequate, but Alan reminded himself it was just a boarding house, with more kitchen privileges downstairs. He moved aside on the sofa allowing Eleanor and Evangeline to sit next to him.

"I hope you like corn bread, Norma," Evangeline said rather awkwardly.

Norma smiled. "Thanks, Evangeline, I do like it. And I'm sure your mother's beef stew is the bees' knees for sure!"

Eleanor smiled. "Are you feeling better, dear?"

Norma extinguished her cigarette and shook her head. "I just need to rest for a while. I wish I could remember what happened, but I don't remember anything, really."

"It's best not to get worked up," Alan said. "It'll come back to you eventually."

"I remember standing at the corner and falling, hitting my head and then I woke up in the hospital." She paused. "What do you remember, Mrs. Whitney?"

"I came out of the library and saw a crowd. I asked someone what happened, and they mentioned a girl fell and hit her head. I recognized you and went back into the library and asked them to call an ambulance."

"When do you plan to return to work, Norma?" Evangeline asked her.

Norma shrugged. "Maybe Monday, but I'm not sure. I want to rest today and tomorrow, and I'll see how I am Monday morning. I'll call Mr. Ferguson and let him know how I feel."

Eleanor mentioned she and Evangeline needed to leave, as they planned to shop on Lark Street. They wished Norma well and were out the door, down the stairs and out on the sidewalk. Alan and John remained with Norma for about an hour more, making sure she was settled and secure, then John mentioned he needed to leave.

Alan put on his jacket and cap firmly on his head and looked worriedly at Norma. "Are you sure you'll be all right? You have my number in case you need me."

Norma assured them she was fine. She had plenty of food, the radio, her cigarettes and magazines, so she planned to rest for the remainder of the day. She promised she would call him if something came up. As John opened the door, Mrs. Webster stood at the entrance.

"I heard you were back, Miss Smith," she said heartily. She also carried a plate, containing homemade bread and cookies.

Norma thanked Mrs. Webster and then introduced Alan and John to her proprietress. Mrs. Webster left the plate on top of the kitchen table. She insisted that if she needed anything to come downstairs at once.

Alan winked at Norma as they left, joining Mrs. Webster down the stairs and to the entrance. John asked her to call him in case Norma needed them, writing his number on a tablet she handed him. He mentioned his apartment was only a block north on State Street. They bid her goodbye and stepped out onto State Street.

It was a busy Saturday and looking to his right, Alan saw crowds forming on Lark Street. He noticed John had walked to the corner of State and Dove and he joined him there.

"Strange, isn't it?" John said, looking down at the pavement. They moved aside allowing pedestrians to pass. "You're in a crowd, you get pushed and no one would notice a thing!"

Fumbling in his pocket for his cigarettes, Alan hastily lit one and shuddered.

Later that afternoon, Alan called Lester, who invited him over for a drink. He felt extremely restless, with too much on his mind. He needed to get out, at least for a while, to clear his mind.

After hanging up the phone, he told his mother he would be going to see Lester, but naturally omitted the drinking part. It was close to seven o'clock and he and his mother had already finished eating. Carl had called and mentioned he would stop over later this evening. Bernice asked her son if he planned to go out with Mr. Cavanaugh, but Alan, observing his mother relaxing in the living room with coffee and the evening paper, told her he was not sure of his plans yet. He did know that he was not in the mood for a sedate evening at home, at least not tonight.

He donned his jacket and cap and once outside walked through Academy Park, crossed Washington Avenue and waited in front of the capitol for a southbound trolley. Finally, one arrived and for a Saturday, he was surprised it was not too crowded. It arrived at the corner of State Street and Broadway, and he disembarked.

It was still bitterly cold, and Alan lowered his cap and bundled his jacket in an attempt to stay warm. Walking past the opulent Delaware and Hudson Railroad Building, he came upon a row of fashionable brownstones, wondering how Lester could manage to live there. Certainly, only people with good incomes could afford the rents and the magnificent views of the Hudson River. He didn't think the money he earned at the library justified living in such splendor. Then he remembered Lester's bootlegging activities earned him quite a penny. He wondered if his probation officer was aware that he still dabbled in that undertaking.

Pressing the buzzer, the downstairs door opened, and Alan entered, climbing the two flights to Lester's apartment. He knocked and the door was open by Lester, who already looked glassy-eyed, clearly at the brink of intoxication. He seemed glad to see Alan and beckoned him inside.

Alan removed his jacket and cap, leaving them on a chair and then followed Lester into the well-furnished living room. The radio console was on, tuned to a station playing great jazz, and the sounds of Duke Ellington, Louie Armstrong and Ruth Etting filled the room.

Lester disappeared into the kitchen, returning with a glass of whiskey and cigarettes. He handed the glass to Alan and lit a cigarette for him. He sat on the sofa while Alan sat in a comfortable armchair. Alan noticed he looked pristine as usual; a white dress shirt highlighted his muscled arms, along with pleated dress slacks, he looked dapper, straight out of a fashion magazine. His blondish hair fell over his forehead, rather disheveled but on Lester it didn't matter.

A pleasant apartment, Alan thought glancing around, wondering how many women Lester brought here in the past. He also wondered why Lester never pursued a female to marry. He was certainly handsome enough and could have had any woman he wanted, but he was a lounge lizard, in his own words. Penelope, Betsy, Norma and Evangeline were a few of his many conquests. Of course, Alan had dated Penelope, Norma and Evangeline as well, but they and many other females were seemingly attracted to Lester and his unscrupulous, dangerous attributes. Observing him, smoking nonchalantly, as though he had not a care in the world, Alan wondered why he associated with him. He knew Lester enjoyed his company. Even though he considered Lester a friend, he knew he harbored secrets, his criminal past was abhorrent to him. They were quiet for a few moments before Lester spoke, puffing at his cigarette and sipping his whiskey.

"How's Norma? You called me earlier to let me know she's home now."

Alan drank more of the whiskey. "She's a lot better. She just needs to rest." He paused. "Lester, what do you remember about the night Betsy died?"

Lester grimaced, obviously in no mood to discuss one of his many girlfriends. "I didn't see anything different, as I told the police. Like everyone else, I saw her on top of the fifth floor, about to slide down the banister when she lost her grip and crashed to the floor."

Alan winced as he said crashed. "I found the fire escape door ajar with footprints leading from it to the top of the stairs. Of course, that doesn't really mean anything."

"Like the police told us, maybe someone did something to cause her to fall," Lester said, finishing his cigarette. He gulped down what was left in his glass. "Didn't they suggest someone could've rubbed snow on the banister causing her to lose her grip?"

Alan nodded. "There has been too much going on since December. First, Penelope is murdered, then Betsy dies and now Norma has an accident."

"You think they're related? That's absurd, Alan."

Lester got up and grabbed the whiskey bottle from the kitchen table, refilled his glass and went over to Alan and poured more into his glass. Alan thought of asking him whom he met early in the morning in Academy Park when he saw him from his bedroom window. He admitted he did not feel comfortable in asking such personal questions. He knew Lester was always up to something, and he would undoubtedly tell him it was none of his business.

"The police haven't caught who's responsible for Penelope's murder," Alan said. "Now, they may think something's up with Betsy's death." He paused. "I don't think they are looking into Norma's accident, but John mentioned earlier that anyone could bump into someone, and nobody would notice!"

"That's John's opinion," Lester said bitterly. He had his cigarette between his lips. "Sometimes I wonder about John. He had gripes against Betsy and Penelope. I've seen him angry at times, too. I don't really trust him."

"We've all had gripes with Betsy and Penelope," Alan said, extinguishing his cigarette in an ashtray by his side. "So have Evangeline and Norma. I don't think Mrs. Churchill liked them any more than we did."

"I know Mr. Donovan didn't like Betsy dating me," Lester said. "I don't think anyone would've been good enough for daddy's little girl. He was very protective of her."

"I think my uncle turned a blind eye when it came to Betsy," Alan said regretfully. "I don't think he ever spoke up to put her in her place."

"Well, too late for that now, isn't it?" Lester said almost mockingly. "Maybe Norma or Evangeline had more than enough of Penelope and Betsy."

"You really think that?" Alan was stunned.

"Or maybe that old battleax Mrs. Churchill did Penelope in," Lester said jeeringly and blew a large cloud of smoke. He hesitated, feeling a need for more liquor. "Why don't we go to the speakeasy, Alan? You know, make some new female friends."

Obviously, he was ready to start his usual Romeo tirade with willing females. Alan finished his cigarette and told Lester that he would go for an hour. Lester grabbed his shoes and socks, put them on and asked Alan to help straighten up the kitchen.

Lester washed a few glasses while Alan threw away an empty cigarette pack lying on the counter. Lester went to the hallway for his jacket and cap and called to Alan to join him. Alan told him he would be there in a minute. As he threw the empty cigarette pack in the garbage, his eyes fixed on several pieces of paper, crumpled up but still readable, lying in the trash can. Picking them up, he realized they were letters written to Lester, from an apparently anguished female. He scanned them quickly and then, hearing Lester approach, stuffed them in his shirt pocket.

"All set to go, buddy?" Lester asked, handing Alan his jacket and cap.

Alan joined him to the door and after locking it they made their way downstairs and outside, across Broadway to the speakeasy on Howard Street. He was unaware of the significance of the discovery he just made, which he shoved in his shirt pocket.

The next day, Sunday, the fourteenth, in the afternoon, Alan decided to visit Norma, as it was Valentine's Day. He did not think she had plans, as she was still recuperating from her concussion. He glanced at his watch as he got off the trolley, heading for State Street. It was going on four o'clock, so he was sure Norma would be resting. He did not think she would be gallivanting around the city. His mother made cookies, which Alan carried with him. Norma was happy to see him.

"Nice of you to visit me two days in a row, Alan," she said, smiling. "I called Mr. Ferguson, and he told me to take a few days' rest." She welcomed Alan in her room and motioned him to sit on the sofa.

"Happy Valentine's Day, Norma," he said and smiled. "I think it's a good idea for you to rest. You have plenty of magazines and the radio."

Norma smiled. "I read *True Story* and *Vanity Fair* faithfully." She was quiet for a few moments. "Alan, what do you think is going on? I mean, first Penelope and then Betsy. Do you really think there's more to Betsy's death than we first thought?"

Alan lit a cigarette for himself and one for Norma. "I really don't know. I plan to hire a private investigator, with my uncle's consent, to look into things. Betsy had enough enemies, where someone who had something against her could've hastened her fall."

"In what way?" she asked him.

Alan knocked ash into an ashtray. "I found those snowy footprints leading from the fire escape to the top of the stairs. The police suggested someone could've rubbed snow on the railing, causing Betsy to lose her grip and fall."

Norma shook her head. "We discussed that at the meeting with Mr. Ferguson and the police last Wednesday. We didn't know ahead of time that she would be doing that ridiculous banister slide. She didn't mention it while I was in the atrium."

Alan was perplexed. "There's something going on, Norma and I don't know what it's all about. Somebody is hiding something. That's why I am hiring a private investigator, There may be nothing and Betsy did indeed fall. On the other hand, he may find something we weren't aware of." He hesitated. "The police may want to question you again. Since you and Betsy had that fight at the speakeasy, you may be a suspect if they determine her fall wasn't accidental."

Norma shrugged. "Will this private investigator look into Penelope's murder, too?"

"I plan to mention it, but I don't know if her death and Betsy's are related. I'm sure he's aware of Penelope's murder as it's been in the local headlines."

They sat quietly for a while, not knowing what to say, a thousand thoughts passing through their minds. Norma asked him if there was anything coming up at the Hall that she should know about. Alan mentioned they were still showing movies and the returns had been quite profitable. He told her Mr. Ferguson did not intend to reschedule the dance marathon, as he felt the negative publicity from Betsy's death would hurt the Hall's reputation. Norma nodded skeptically, not agreeing with him and yet seeing his point. She knew it had been a long road to host the marathon and an even more difficult course to cancel it and refund money to the participants.

Alan extinguished his cigarette and after another hour of discussing the Hall, his mother, current movies, Mary Pickford and Rudolph Valentino, he decided he would leave. He stood and hugged Norma, wishing her a speedy recovery.

"I'll be fine, Alan," she assured him. "I've got your number and Mrs. Webster has been terrific. Please thank your mother for the sweets." She hugged him and wished him well.

Down the stairs and outside on the sidewalk, State Street was quiet for Sunday, late in the afternoon. He decided to walk to Elk Street, despite the bone chilling cold. As he increased his stride heading south on State, he found the fresh air invigorating.

Poor Norma, he thought compassionately. He was surprised John, Ed and Lester had not paid her a visit today. She would have mentioned if they had stopped by. On Valentine's Day, he figured Lester would give her a dozen roses. Even John and Ed would bring her a gift. Of course, it was only late in the afternoon, so maybe they would visit her before evening. Certainly, kind of Mrs. Whitney and Evangeline to bring her food, too.

He stopped at the corner of State and Dove Street to light a cigarette, cupping his hands while holding the match. He realized that was the spot where Norma fell and hit her head. It was quiet there now, as the library was closed. He continued south on State, when suddenly he heard a young, high-pitched female voice call his name. Turning, he recognized Sarah Evans coming up behind him.

"Hey, Mr. Cartwright!" she said, rather breathlessly. "Or I should say Alan. Say, you really are a handsome guy! You must be at least six feet tall! I like your jacket and cap. Really dapper!"

Alan stood still, puffing at his cigarette. He did not know Sarah Evans well except for her work at the Hall. She was twenty at a guess. Her short, bobbed hair was unbecoming, no makeup, she appeared rather excitable and most likely not very dependable, although she was productive the night of the dance marathon. She was still talking to him, rattling on and on about something.

"…heard lots going on that night. You'd be surprised. But then I decided not to say anything. I'm pretty clever, you know. Anyway, when I saw what happened, I realized afterwards what I heard." She smiled modestly. "Certainly pays to be at the right place at the right time!" She continued looking up at Alan, smiling. "Funny, how things turn out, ain't it? Well, it's been great chatting with you, Alan. I'll see you at the Hall sometime. Ta ta for now, handsome!"

Alan drew on his cigarette, seeing his breath in the cold air. He had no idea what she was getting at. He watched as she casually skipped toward Dove Street. Shaking his head and puffing away at his cigarette, he reached South Swan Street, crossed to Washington Avenue, and continued past the State Education Building to Academy Park.

Certainly a flapper, he thought. He paid her no more attention until Monday evening.

CHAPTER SIXTEEN

Alan picked up the telephone on his desk and was about to speak to the operator but hesitated.

It was late Monday morning, cold and blustery, with snow predicted for later in the day. He arrived at Harmanus Bleecker Hall to begin his workday as usual. He told his mother that he planned to contact Mr. Sloane Sheppard to make an appointment. His uncle, having breakfast with them again, highly encouraged it, reminding Alan not to worry about the expense.

It was quiet for a Monday and Alan's workload was not too heavy. He and Mrs. Russell divided their tasks along with Norma's amongst themselves, pleasing Mr. Ferguson enormously. He had called Norma earlier in the morning and she mentioned she planned to return to work on Wednesday, which also pleased Mr. Ferguson.

Alan had been in contact with the agents of Ruth Etting and Marion Harris, hoping to book them for appearances. Mr. Ferguson stressed the importance of continued business at the Hall, attempting to dispel any negative publicity from the recent death of his cousin Betsy. The *Albany Evening Journal* ran another article about her fall, claiming negligence on the part of the Hall staff, further irritating Mr. Ferguson.

Alan had looked again in the Albany city directory for the listing of Mr. Sloane Sheppard, private investigator. He also looked at other agents, but Mr. Sheppard's office was right on State Street, a convenient location. He took a deep breath and gave the number of Mr. Sloane Sheppard to the operator. To his surprise, the call was answered on the second ring. He swallowed hard and with much courage, began to speak.

"Is this Mr. Sloane Sheppard? My name is Alan Cartwright and I'd like to speak to you about something of importance to me."

In his office on State Street, Sloane put aside a few papers and listened to the young voice on the other end of the line. In his routine as a private investigator, Sloane Sheppard was used to people from all walks of life. From this voice, he deduced it was that of a young man, rather cultured, refined, but a little anxious, certainly apprehensive. He could dismiss the call after hearing what he had to tell him or inquire further.

While listening to the young man speak, Sloane looked at the pile of folders on the edge of his desk. Besides two appointments this morning, the afternoon was free for him to be caught up on his paperwork. He glanced at the filing cabinet against the wall, which he knew needed his attention. He realized the young man was still speaking.

"…so I don't know what to think, Mr. Sheppard. It happened so fast. My cousin Betsy fell from the fifth floor at Harmanus Bleecker Hall, where we had a dance marathon. She was just showing off, like she usually liked to do."

Alan waited anxiously for Sloane to speak. He had never contacted a private investigator and did not know what to expect. The smooth voice on the other end of the line assured him he made the right choice.

"I've been in touch with the Albany police, Mr. Cartwright," Sloane told him. "They've asked for my assistance with the murder of Miss Penelope Barker. They also mentioned the death of your cousin,

Miss Donovan. They don't know if there is foul play involved, but as usual in cases of accidental deaths, they make an inquiry."

"So you know about it already?" Alan asked, rather surprised.

Sloane lit a cigarette, depositing the match in an ashtray already overflowing with butts. "Yes, but I will be glad to meet with you to discuss this further." He glanced at his calendar and mentioned that he was free for most of the afternoon. He explained about his fees and how he expected payment. Alan listened and told Sloane he could see him this afternoon, about four o'clock. He told Sloane he worked at Harmanus Bleecker Hall so he could be at his office in no time. After a few additional remarks, the conversation ended. Alan replaced the handset on the candlestick phone and sat back in his swivel chair, with much to think about before his appointment with Sloane.

The afternoon wore on and as the four o'clock hour approached, Alan felt a certain tension. He told Mr. Ferguson and Mrs. Russell of his appointment and left Harmanus Bleecker Hall just as the afternoon rush was about to start. Hopping on a trolley, he arrived at the corner of State and South Pearl, and then walked until he reached the Albany City Savings Bank Building at 100 State Street. He looked at the wall directory and spotting the listing for Sloane Sheppard on the fifth floor, he entered an elevator, telling the attendant the floor he wanted. He watched as the gates closed, and the lift slowly creaked upwards. Upon opening the gates, the attendant closed them again on its way down. Alan looked around at the various doors along a rather dimly lit hallway. Finally, he found the door marked SLOANE SHEPPARD INVESTIGATIONS. He knocked and within a few moments, Sloane opened the door.

At first glance, he was favorably impressed with Mr. Sheppard. Certainly, a formidable presence, tall, clean-shaven, professionally and impeccably dressed and even imposing, rugged looking, but attentive. He shook hands with Sloane and the detective invited him into his office. He sat in the chair in front of his desk, while Sloane went back around to sit in his chair. Alan removed his jacket and cap, still nervously, feeling rather overwhelmed.

"What can I do for you, Mr. Cartwright?" Sloane leaned back in his swivel chair and regarded the young man opposite him.

Alan sighed, and with great fortitude, explained what he knew to have happened to Betsy, her sliding down the railing and losing her grip, causing her to fall to her death on the atrium floor. He told Sloane about his position as the assistant manager at Harmanus Bleecker Hall, the arrangements for the dance marathon and how Mr. Ferguson decided to cancel it, after his cousin's death. He mentioned the fire escape door ajar and the snowy footprints leading to the top of the stairs. He mentioned Norma's fall and suffering a concussion last Wednesday on State Street, although he did not think it related to Betsy's accident. But he remarked he thought something strange was going on, but he didn't know what. He mentioned Penelope Barker's murder, although he did not think it was related to his cousin death. Upon finishing, he felt relieved, twisting his cap in his lap, while waiting for Sloane to speak.

"I plan to assist Inspector Harris with the murder of Miss Penelope Barker," Sloane told him. "Although I don't see how that ties in with your cousin's death." He paused. "I will help you if I can, Mr. Cartwright. But from what you have told me, there would be little I can do." Sloane then speculated on the snowy footprints on top of the staircase.

It was exactly what Alan feared. This rugged-looking man, with his courteous manner and penetrating, brown eyes, would not be satisfied until the whole story was laid bare, every nook opened with a knife. But then that was the hallmark of a dedicated investigator.

"Do the snowy footprints really matter, Mr. Sheppard?" Alan asked, confusedly. He explained again the circumstance under which he discovered them, and the fire escape left ajar.

"In cases of suspicious death, everything matters," Sloane said grimly.

On Monday evening, the low clouds that had moved in late in the afternoon finally broke and unleashed a torrent of snow, blanketing the city. A maze of whiteness swallowed up downtown Albany, the pedestrians, the street lamps, the traffic and trollies, so that figures no more than a few feet away were merely dark shapes lost in a winter oasis. Pedestrians jostled along North Pearl Street, wondering when winter would end its merciless stranglehold on the city.

Arriving home from work before the storm hit, Alan joined his mother, his uncle, Ed Flynn and Mrs. Churchill in the kitchen for a sumptuous dinner of lamb, sweet potatoes and his mother's fabulous chocolate cake. Mrs. Churchill commented how Bernice found the time to cook so much while working at the capitol library. Bernice smiled and told her she had it all prepared the night before; she simply popped it all into the oven to cook. Ed told Bernice her cooking was the best and accepted a second helping of the rich cake.

Alan told them about his visit with Mr. Sheppard earlier in the day, which met with approval from his uncle and Ed, but skepticism from his mother and Mrs. Churchill. He mentioned Mr. Sheppard would want to speak to everyone who knew Betsy, to attempt to determine what caused her manner of death.

"We already know what happened to her, Alan," Mrs. Churchill said, sipping coffee. "I admire your tenacity to this endeavor, but I feel it is a waste of your time."

"I don't know what I could tell him," Bernice said. "She just fell from the railing, and it was quite horrible. I don't even like to think about it."

"Maybe he'll learn things we don't know about," Ed said, adding sugar to his coffee.

"Like what?" Mrs. Churchill addressed him, rather appalled.

Carl extinguished his cigarette and picked up his coffee cup. "I appreciate all that you're doing, Alan, you are to be commended. But it may be that Mr. Sheppard has nothing to learn."

"You believe your daughter's death was something other an accident?" Mrs. Churchill asked him incredulously.

Carl shrugged. "My daughter had enemies. Certainly, Miss Smith was not her friend. I do not trust her. And you, Mrs. Churchill, were not fond of my daughter, either."

Mrs. Churchill simply pursed her lips, rather curt, but said nothing in reply. There was a certain tension in the room and Alan felt stifled and wanted to get away from it. It had been over an hour that Mrs. Churchill and Ed were at the house. He listened to their conversation, making comments as appropriate. Truthfully, he did not feel like listening to his mother, his uncle and Mrs. Churchill. Although he considered Ed a friend, he was not in the mood to listen to his comments.

About a half hour later, Mrs. Churchill glanced toward the kitchen windows and noticed the snow coming down steadily. Bernice had yet to draw the curtains and as Alan got up to look out the windows, it was a picture-postcard scene, enveloping Academy Park in white, with few pedestrians about.

Mrs. Churchill announced she would leave and entered the hallway for her coat. Ed also told them he needed to leave, finishing his second helping of the chocolate cake and slurping the rest of his coffee. Bernice and Alan joined them, wishing them good night as Mrs. Churchill and Ed walked outside and down Elk Street. Carl told them he would stay another night in the spare room on the third floor. Alan grabbed the *Albany Evening Journal* from the hallway table, announcing he was going to his room. He made the excuse he wanted to read before going to bed. He wearily climbed the stairs to the second floor, finding sanctuary in his bedroom.

Closing the door, he wanted nothing more than to block everything from his mind, too much had been happening and he felt overwhelmed. He threw the newspaper on his bed, removed his shoes and socks and took off his pants, shirt, tie and vest. He fluffed his pillows and turned his radio to his favorite station playing jazz. Lighting a cigarette, he stretched out on his bed in his shorts and tee shirt, his mind replaying his conversation with Mr. Sheppard.

Was it worth his time and money or just a waste as his mother and Mrs. Churchill believed? He was not fond of Betsy, but her death was hideous, and he still had nightmares over it. Her fall, the terrible scream and her broken body lying crumpled on the atrium floor kept repeating in his mind. So perhaps Mr. Sheppard would find out what happened if there was indeed anything more to find out.

He got up, left his cigarette in the ashtray on the nightstand and realizing he was cold in just his underclothes, went for his pajamas in his wardrobe. While buttoning his pajamas, he noticed the shirt he wore when he went to Lester's on Friday night. It was on a hanger and the letters he stuffed in the front pocket were still there. He had forgotten about the letters. Curiously, he took them out and noticed there were three letters. He settled on his bed, stretching comfortably. He reached for his cigarette, unfolded the letters and began to read. It took a few moments for the shock to hit him. Someone enamored with Lester. The contents and tone repulsed Alan.

My darling Lester

I long to be with you again, dear, to be in your arms and to hold you
as before. You mean so much to me and I wish to see you, soon.

He noticed it was dated in December, before Christmas. He put
this letter aside and looked at the second. This was much more explicit,
containing references he found embarrassing.

Lester,

This charade must stop. I want you as I have wanted no other
man. You mean so much to me and I am deeply in love with you. I
implore you to stop your foolishness with Miss Donovan and devote
your time and attention to me, as I long for you, my darling, I long
for your embrace and to feel you in my arms as before. I am madly
in love with you, Lester, and desire you. I will wait for you but
not for long, as I will take action to make sure you are mine. You
belong to me dear and I to you.

Alan saw that this letter was dated January 22. A third letter, brief
like the first, conveyed the same tone and was dated February 8, just
last Monday.

Lester, my darling

It will not be long until we are together. I know the perfect life
that will be for us, someday soon. We will love each other like never
before, for we belong together, a match made in heaven.

Thumbing through them again, Alan noticed none were signed.
Certainly, the handwriting was feminine and very stylish, on good
stationary, too. Who would write such graphic letters to nefarious

216

Lester, the proud seducer, who enjoyed his dominations and thought only of himself. Most likely, he ignored them, even laughed at them. Obviously, the letters meant nothing to him, as he had thrown them in the trash. However, after reading them again, Alan thought they meant something. He did not know what to do with them, but he realized they were important, but just how important he was not yet sure. He decided to put them in the drawer of his nightstand and forget about them, at least for now.

With his cigarette between his lips that helped to dispel his nerves, he picked up the *Albany Evening Journal*. Political news, President Coolidge in the White House, continued prosperity in the stock market and upon turning the pages, he noticed advertisements for the new *Model T Ford, Listerine, Wonder Bread, Hershey Chocolate* and *LifeSavers*. Looking at local stories, he read about Mayor Hackett's visit to Cuba, the Albany YMCA and various church functions. He then noticed a small paragraph in the police section.

It was reported that apparently a young woman fainted while waiting for the trolley on Lark Street during the morning rush. A local businessman summoned an ambulance and while examining her at Albany City Hospital, a knife wound was discovered on her abdomen. She remained unconscious and died in the emergency room. The woman was identified as an employee of Harmanus Bleecker Hall, Miss Sarah Evans of Albany.

CHAPTER SEVENTEEN

Sloane Sheppard arrived at Albany City Police headquarters the next morning. He had called Inspector Harris from his apartment, to tell him he planned to see him regarding the murder of Miss Penelope Barker. Looking at his calendar, he moved appointments to give him ample time to work on this case and to inquiry into the death of Miss Betsy Donovan.

He did not own a car, finding it more of a nuisance, especially in winter with the difficulty of maneuvering on snowy streets. Instead, he relied on Albany's efficient trolley service. Hopping on a northbound trolley on Madison Avenue across from his apartment building, he soon arrived at the corner of South Allen and got off, walking a few blocks to the corner of Central Avenue, where he hopped on another southbound until he arrived at the intersection with Quail Street.

Upon entering and speaking with the young officer at the front desk, he was directed to an office in the back. Anticipating his arrival, Inspector Harris came out and shook hands with Sloane and then welcomed him into a rather small and cramped but efficient looking office.

"Good to see you again, Mr. Sheppard," the inspector said. "We appreciate your assistance with the Penelope Barker case. We also have questions about the recent death of Miss Betsy Donovan during the dance marathon at Harmanus Bleecker Hall. Could be just an accident, but in such cases, as you know, the police are initially involved."

Sloane asked the inspector for the details on the murder of Miss Barker. He was told she returned from the Ivory Theater after a performance in early December to her apartment on Lancaster Street and was stabbed multiple times on the steps leading up to the front door. A couple found her around two in the morning. She was dead at the scene. As far as Miss Donovan was concerned, she slipped and fell to her death at Harmanus Bleecker Hall during the dance marathon last month. She demonstrated how to slide down a banister and apparently lost her grip and landed on the atrium floor, quite a steep fall. While there appeared no foul play, Mr. Alan Cartwright had observed the fire escape door open adjacent to the stairs on that floor and snowy footprints leading to the top of the stairs. The inspector concluded that there existed a possibility of snow or ice on the railing causing Miss Donovan to lose her grip, causing her fall.

"Is there a possibility that Miss Donovan was intoxicated, which might have caused her to lose her balance on the railing and fall?" Sloane asked.

Inspector Harris nodded. "There is that possibility. But we've been told Miss Donovan was quite an expert on sliding down a railing, so even if she were inebriated, I don't know if it would have affected her so called performance." He paused. "We received word that a Miss Sarah Evans, an employee at Harmanus Bleecker Hall, was stabbed early yesterday morning during rush hour on the corner of Lark Street and Madison Avenue while waiting for the trolley. Police at the scene questioned several people who were there, and nobody saw anything, which is usually the case in situations like this."

"You think that is related somehow to the other deaths?" Sloane asked him.

Inspector Harris was stolid, impassive. "We don't know yet. I wonder if there is a pattern somewhere, but what it is, isn't clear to us. That's why we asked for your assistance."

Sloane nodded. "Mr. Cartwright came to see me yesterday and explained about the death of his cousin, Miss Donovan. He wants me to look into it, with his uncle's blessing. Apparently, he may think there is more to it than meets the eye."

"We don't know if the murder of Miss Barker and this accident of Miss Donovan, if it was an accident, are related. There were no witnesses to the murder of Miss Barker and as for Miss Donovan, there were a phalanx of witnesses to her fall, but no one saw anything unusual."

"And no witnesses to the murder of Miss Evans, either," Sloane added.

The inspector nodded. "During the morning rush, it'd be relatively easy to push or stab someone in a crowd. Although with so many people, you'd think someone would have noticed."

"Mr. Cartwright mentioned Miss Norma Smith, also a Hall employee, fell and suffered a concussion last Wednesday," Sloane said. "He didn't think there was anything suspicious but remarked he thought something strange was going on, to use his exact words."

The inspector nodded again. "So do I, Mr. Sheppard. Something strange indeed is going on and I don't know what the hell it is."

Sloane cleared his throat. "I'll start by determining if there is a connection between Miss Barker and Miss Donovan. I need to inquire who their friends were. From what I've been told Miss Donovan made quite a few enemies."

"Ditto for Miss Barker," the inspector informed Sloane. "From interviews we conducted with her fellow actors and employees of various theaters around Albany, she was not one to reckon with. She was involved with Mr. Lester Cavanaugh, who is on probation for bootlegging here in the city. He also was involved with Miss Donovan, and many other women in the area."

"I'd like to speak to Mr. Cavanaugh," Sloane said. "First, I'll speak to the manager of Harmanus Bleecker Hall, who I understand is Mr. Ferguson. The snowy footprints at the top of the stairs are important. It may mean nothing, but it could be a significant clue."

"So you believe someone rubbed snow or ice on the railing?"

"That's exactly what I plan to find out," Sloane said, heading for the exit.

He left the inspector's office, a firm and resolute look on his face.

As the day wore on and word got around about the murder of Miss Sarah Evans, nearly everyone at Harmanus Bleecker Hall was in an uproar. To calm nerves of his immediate staff, Mr. Ferguson called an important meeting later that afternoon, summoning Alan, Mrs. Churchill, Harvey the maintenance man and several employees of the kitchen to tell them what happened to Sarah Evans.

"What more can happen?" Mrs. Churchill lamented, clearly upset. "This does not look good for the Hall, Mr. Ferguson. Almost as though a dark cloud is over us!"

"I saw Miss Evans Sunday afternoon on State Street," Alan told them. "I was leaving Norma's and she called out to me."

"What did she say, Alan?" Mr. Ferguson asked.

Alan tried to remember. "Something about being in the right place at the right time, or something like that. I don't really remember. She was pretty strange, actually."

Mr. Ferguson mentioned the negative publicity for Harmanus Bleecker Hall and implored everyone not to spread rumors regarding the two recent deaths. After a few more words, the meeting adjourned, with everyone silently leaving the conference room.

Mrs. Churchill drew Alan aside in the hallway. "Do you think Miss Evans knew something, Alan, which can help the police with their investigation?"

Alan shook his head. "I don't know, Mrs. Churchill. She didn't allude to anything, really."

"Did you contact that private investigator you mentioned?"

They walked to the top of the stairs and upon looking down toward the main entrance, Alan at that moment saw Sloane enter the building and pass into the atrium. He saw him stop a secretary and ask for the office of Mr. Ferguson. He looked up and noticed Alan and Mrs. Churchill.

"Mr. Sheppard," Alan said, catching his breath, surprised at seeing Sloane.

"Hello, Mr. Cartwright," Sloane said, climbing the stairs to the second floor. He shook hands with Alan upon seeing him. He nodded hello to Mrs. Churchill.

"Mr. Sheppard, this is Mrs. Jeanne Churchill," he introduced Sloane to her. "She works here at the Hall as an executive."

"I'm retired, Mr. Sheppard," Mrs. Churchill said rather firmly. "I spent over thirty years here. It dismays me that so much negative publicity has been attributed to this fine establishment, a pillar of success in our community."

Sloane looked at Mrs. Churchill. He knew her type well; an Albany native, of prime stock, firm and resolute in her opinion and intolerant of those who disagreed with her, most likely old money, well-off, and a widow.

"Why don't you come to my office, Mr. Sheppard?" Alan said. "And please call me Alan."

Sloane followed him down the hall to his office, where he met Mrs. Russell. He then followed Alan into his office and to Alan's surprise, Mrs. Churchill joined them. She seemed intent on making a point with Sloane as she sat in the chair in front of Alan's desk. Alan went to the sidewall and brought another chair for Sloane to sit in, then sat at the swivel chair at his desk. He looked at Sloane with a mixture of trepidation and fear.

"Thank you, Alan," Sloane said. "First, let me reiterate that I will do what I can to look into the details of your cousin's death. There is nothing to indicate it was anything but an accident. Perhaps she was intoxicated which contributed to her losing her balance."

"Of course it was an accident," Mrs. Churchill said firmly.

Alan looked up at Mr. Ferguson as he stood in the doorway. He could not read the expression on his face, although he could tell it was not a happy one. He introduced him to Sloane who stood and shook hands with him.

"Alan tells me you are investigating the death of Miss Donovan," he said rather acidly. "I do not see that the Hall should be involved in any way, Mr. Sheppard. As I told Alan, what he does outside of this establishment, is his business."

"Perhaps not, Mr. Ferguson," Sloane said equally acidly. "Since Miss Donovan's death occurred here at the Hall, it is imperative I speak to as many people as possible who were here that night." He paused. "First, I'd like to see the spot where Miss Donovan was positioned and fell."

Alan came from around his desk and asked Sloane to follow him.

To his surprise, Mr. Ferguson and Mrs. Churchill also joined them. Climbing the three flights to the fifth floor, Alan showed Sloane the fire escape, how the door was ajar and the snowy footprints that led to the top of the staircase. He showed him the railing where Betsy positioned herself and looking down; they saw the spot where she fell to her death. Mrs. Churchill stood back, as she suffered from vertigo and did not want to stare down at the lower floor. Mr. Ferguson was extremely perturbed over the whole ordeal and wanted nothing more for Mr. Sheppard to finish his inquiry and leave the premises. He tolerated his presence but intended to tell Alan that he would prefer him not to take up their time during business hours.

Sloane meanwhile was examining the railing, quite steep as he looked down toward the atrium, He then looked back at the fire escape, which he could easily see how someone could put snow or ice on the railing, making it slippery enough for Miss Donovan to fall. However, the questions remained; how did someone know that she would be demonstrating her sliding down the rail? Was she encouraged to do it at a certain time? He asked these questions to Alan, Mr. Ferguson and Mrs. Churchill and received blank stares in return,

"Betsy was dancing and showing off as usual," Alan told him. "I don't remember when she decided to slide down the banister. She got everyone's attention and the next thing we knew; she fell down to the atrium."

Sloane nodded. "She must have let someone know of her intent. If snow was put on the railing, it would melt eventually and dry up after a while."

"Mr. Sheppard, please," Mr. Ferguson said impatiently.

"That would mean someone must have asked her to demonstrate it," Alan suggested. "That would give him enough time to put the snow on the railing."

"Ridiculous," Mrs. Churchill said with tight lips. "I've never heard anything so preposterous. Really, Alan, and you are a graduate of the college here in Albany. I would think you would know better than to draw such forgone conclusions!"

"He may be right, Mrs. Churchill," Sloane said. "This banister does not seem to me that it would be slippery, unless something was applied to it to make it so. Someone must have suggested to her to demonstrate it. Since the atrium was crowded, wouldn't someone have seen something up here that night?"

"Not necessarily," Alan told him. "It was a busy evening, and everyone was dancing, enjoying the music. The marathon was in the ballroom and people were in the atrium dancing, too, although not part of the competition."

"If people saw someone near the railing, I doubt if they would have paid any attention," Sloane said, seeing the picture clearer, still looking at the railing and the sheer drop below. "If it was as crowded and busy as you say, they would have been focused on the dancing and the merriment, not on the upper floors."

He asked Alan, Mr. Ferguson and Mrs. Churchill about Miss Sarah Evans and her role at the Hall. Alan explained she was a cook, employed in the kitchen and that they had little to do with her. He explained that he saw her on Sunday afternoon after visiting Norma at her boarding house and that Miss Evans seemed aloof, secretive.

"She told me she didn't realize until later what she heard. I don't know what she meant."

"Possibly she witnessed something that led to Miss Donovan's death," Sloane concluded.

"Miss Evans was highly unreliable, Mr. Sheppard," Mrs. Churchill offered. "She was foolish in her work, and I suggested she be terminated."

Alan mentioned speaking to the other kitchen workers. He led

Sloane down the stairs, Mr. Ferguson and Mrs. Churchill joining them. Sloane looked at the railing again, and the steep drop to the atrium below, envisioning the horrendous sight when Miss Donovan plunged to her death that night.

After thanking Mr. Ferguson and Mrs. Churchill for the information they imparted, Sloane followed Alan to the basement, where the kitchen was located. Mr. Ferguson returned to his fifth floor office while Mrs. Churchill scurried off to her own on the second floor.

Few kitchen workers could add anything to the persona of Miss Sarah Evans. Most commented they knew little about her, except she was dependable to an extent and got her work completed. Another young woman acknowledged and practically repeated everything that had already been said about Miss Evans.

"What more can be done, Mr. Sheppard?" Alan asked as they climbed the stairs to the atrium. It was rather quiet now at Harmanus Bleecker Hall. Many employees left for the day and Mr. Ferguson and Mrs. Churchill managed to calm the nerves of those still in the building.

"I'd like to speak to your uncle," Sloane told him. "I'll call him when I return to my office. I have a client to see first." He paused. "You will let me know if you remember anything else from that evening. Please mention to your mother that I will need to speak with her, too."

A certain hardness pulled at Alan's mouth and his eyes were astute. "Of course, Mr. Sheppard. I'll tell my mother you wish to speak to her." Alan watched as Sloane left the building. He then returned to his office, dismayed, apprehensive and confused.

Sloane sensed the anxiety inherent in Alan, but felt it was too early in the investigation to reassure him of any outcome. He could not say that his cousin's death was just a terrible accident or murder. Her death was quite possibly the result of someone's involvement, and he intended to stick to the facts to arrive at a conclusion. He could not avoid the murders of Miss Barker and that of Miss Evans, which could be intertwined with the death of Miss Donovan.

Hopping on the first southbound trolley, Sloane arrived on State Street and eagerly entered the opulent office building, seeking shelter from the cold in the warm lobby. The elevator attendant brought him to the fifth floor, and he found more solace in his office. He took off his jacket and hat, leaving them on a corner chair. He partially unbuttoned his vest, loosened his tie and undid the top button of his shirt. Feeling oddly claustrophobic, he opened the window an inch, letting in the chilly air. He looked down on State Street, noting the heavy traffic, the crowds on the sidewalk.

His next appointment, a middle-aged woman seeking custody of her young son from her husband in a divorce proceeding, appeared in the doorway and the next half hour Sloane was consumed with the facts of this rather arduous case. As the particulars were complete, Sloane assured her he would be in touch, accompanied her to the door, and wished her well. He returned to his desk and picked up the candlestick phone, asked the operator to call the Donovan Accounting Agency on Broadway. Glancing at the wall clock, it was quite late, and he did not think anyone would answer. To his surprise, Mr. Donovan answered himself. When he identified himself, Carl was hesitate at first, and then welcomed him to his office at a time convenient to him. Sloane mentioned he was free now and Carl told him he would be expecting him.

Locking his office door, and taking the elevator down to the lobby, the attendant lifted the gates and Sloane eagerly made his way through the lobby and outside onto State Street. The sidewalks were full, and he had to jostle through the crowds.

He cut across Lodge Street to Pine Street, turning left onto North Pearl until he came to Columbia Street. Arriving at the corner with Broadway, he found the Peter Schuyler Building, with its wrought-iron gates imposed over the windows, across from Union Station, where commuters hurried to catch evening trains home.

Never having reason to enter the Peter Schuyler Building, he realized the entire building was the Donovan Accounting Agency. As it was late in the afternoon, only a few people remained. A pleasant young woman looked up from her desk and asked Sloane if she could help him. He mentioned the agency would soon be closing.

"My name is Mr. Sheppard. I called Mr. Donovan, and he is expecting me."

The young woman nodded and disappeared down a short hall, returning within moments, telling Sloane he could see Mr. Donovan. Sloane walked down the hallway and turned into a small but elaborately furnished office, with a commanding view of Broadway and Union Station. The man seated at the desk rose, shook hands with Sloane, and beckoned him to sit in the chair in front of him. He looked inquiringly at Sloane.

"Thank you, Mr. Donovan, for seeing me today," Sloane began. "Please accept my condolences on the loss of your daughter under tragic circumstances. Your nephew came to see me. I've spoken to the police and plan to assist to the best of my ability."

Sloane looked carefully at the man behind the desk. Certainly, professional, his suit and the gold watch on his vest spoke of good quality. Rather a fatherly figure, maybe about fifty or so, but Sloane could tell a life of unspeakable burdens had caused premature agedness, his brown hair speckled with gray, shadows under his blue eyes created an older appearance, and Sloane thought he could pass for sixty or older. His attitude was of some indifference, although acknowledging Sloane's inquiries, he preferred to be left alone.

"I appreciate your assistance, Mr. Sheppard," Carl said. "I believe I met you years ago, when you were just starting your practice, but I'm not sure the details."

Sloane mentioned he also remembered meeting him but did not recall the event. He was a member of the Albany Business Council, to which Carl also mentioned his affiliation. He concluded it was there they had previous met, but he put that aside and brought up the matter of his daughter's premature death.

Carl extinguished his cigarette and sighed rather deeply. He told Sloane everything he knew about the evening in question; Betsy's fall from the banister, her relations with several young men including Mr. Lester Cavanaugh, Mr. Edward Flynn and Mr. John Whitmore. He told Sloane his daughter was a notorious flapper and enjoyed such a lifestyle; drinking, smoking, going to parties, speakeasies, jazz clubs and petting parties. He told him she was employed at the Albany Savings Bank and seemed to enjoy her work. She appeared to get along with her colleagues and never said anything untoward about them to him.

Sloane asked about her mother. Carl grimaced and mentioned he and his wife were divorced years ago and in fact were estranged. She had no contact with her daughter and preferred it that way, as she lived in the western part of the state.

"My daughter had enemies, Mr. Sheppard," Carl continued. "I won't beat around the bush with that. She seemed to enjoy wreaking havoc for others. She was jealous of other women who paid attention to men she dated, especially Mr. Cavanaugh. She considered him her beau, although I hardly believed he felt the same toward her."

"Was sliding down a banister something she did often?"

Again, Carl grimaced. "Yes, that was one of my daughter's infuriating habits. True flapper, as she called it. She considered it all in jest, of course, although personally I could not tolerate it."

"Do you think something may have contributed to her fall? Perhaps she was intoxicated?"

Carl shrugged. "My nephew told us he noticed the fire escape on the fifth floor of the Hall ajar and snowy footprints leading to the top of the stairs. That doesn't mean anything, of course." He paused. "I wasn't under the impression my daughter had been drinking that evening. I've seen Betsy inebriated. I can truthfully say she was not under the influence of alcohol at that time." He paused again, rather anxiously. "What do you think, Mr. Sheppard?"

Sloane had lit a cigarette and drew smoke, releasing it thoughtfully. "I'm not sure at this point, Mr. Donovan. It seems far-fetched that someone would rub snow or ice on the railing before your daughter decided to slide down it."

"Someone would have had to know she was going to do it," Carl suggested. "I read in the morning paper about the murder of a Hall employee, a Miss Evans."

"I've spoken with Mr. Ferguson and Mrs. Churchill," Sloane told him. "And of course, with Alan. They did not know Miss Evans well, and neither did anyone else employed there."

"Do you think there is a connection with her murder, the murder of Miss Barker and the death of my daughter, Mr. Sheppard?"

"Again, I am not sure. I am investigating the death of your daughter, to determine if foul play was involved."

An uncertain tension hung in the air and Carl shifted in his swivel chair uneasily. He commented on the rise in crime and violence in downtown Albany and that the streets seemed no longer safe for anyone, even during daylight hours. He commented he did not know Miss Barker but admitted his daughter and Miss Barker had a falling out, over Mr. Cavanaugh. They were both enamored of him and Betsy believed he belonged to her. She was very possessive of anything she felt belonged to her, including men.

From his tone, Sloane wondered if he knew more than he was willing to admit, that perhaps there were things so painful that he preferred not to mention them. Certainly, his divorce seemed to embitter him. His daughter unquestioningly initiated enough problems with so many people that he wondered if there was more he was not mentioning.

"My daughter also had a falling out with Miss Norma Smith at a speakeasy not long ago," Carl told him. "I believe it was over Mr. Cavanaugh again, too. They fought, according to my nephew. A regular catfight, right in the speakeasy. Betsy threw liquor in Miss Smith's face, and they went at it. Disgraceful, to say the least."

"Was Miss Smith injured?" Sloane asked him.

Carl shook his head. "No, just her pride, I'm sure. She suffered a concussion recently when she was crossing State Street. She fell and hit her head and was taken to the hospital. I understand she is doing much better now."

"Alan told me about Miss Smith," Sloane said. "The pattern so far seems that these women have been involved with the same man, Mr. Lester Cavanaugh."

Carl agreed. "I warned my daughter to stay away from him, that he was nothing but trouble. The gangster quality in him seemed attractive to her, rather foolishly. And I'm sure that is the same for other women he manipulates."

Sloane asked him about his home on Elk Street. Carl told him his house was an exquisite brownstone of three floors which he and his daughter kept sparkling, certainly a source of pride and one to cherish. He maintained good relations with his neighbors, including Mrs. Jeanne Churchill also of Elk Street and his sister, Mrs. Bernice Cartwright his nephew Alan, who lived just three doors down also on Elk Street. He was acquainted with Mr. Edward Flynn, who lived in an apartment on Elk Street, although he did not know him well. His daughter had dated Mr. Flynn quite steadily but as was usually the case, it ended rather abruptly, although he could not say why. He knew Mr. Flynn worked at city hall, so his apartment on Elk Street was conveniently located to his work, just a five-minute walk away.

"Who else was your daughter involved with?" Sloane asked.

Carl thought. "Betsy had many boyfriends over the last several years, but she was infatuated with Mr. Cavanaugh, who as I mentioned she believed was her beau. She also dated Mr. Edward Flynn and Mr. John Whitmore. Mr. Whitmore is a manager at the Strand Theater." He paused. "Personally, I found Mr. Cavanaugh unscrupulous, untrustworthy and not the right kind of young man for my daughter. Mr. Flynn was probably the best of the three. Mr. Cavanagh has a criminal record. I believe he is on probation for bootlegging, but I hardly think that has stopped his criminal activities. Mr. Whitmore also appears to have a deceitful nature." He paused, as though about to add more but decided against it. He looked down at the papers on his desk, as though to take his mind off his troublesome daughter.

Sloane had taken a small notebook from his jacket pocket and scribbled down the names of the people Carl mentioned. He asked him if there was anything else he could tell him about his daughter that could be helpful. Sloane thought he was worn out, as though his daughter's death and the circumstances involved had rid him of any vitality he may have had left. He gave Sloane his address and home telephone number and mentioned he could contact him again if necessary.

He shook hands with Sloane, saw him to the front door and thanked him again for stopping by.

Outside, in the frigid air, the street lamps illuminated the snowy sidewalk brilliantly and the rush hour was in full swing. Sloane briskly walked up Broadway past Union Station to catch a northbound trolley, his mind full of contradictory thoughts.

The murders of Miss Barker and Miss Evans weighed heavily on Sloane's mind, but he did not see a connection with the death of Miss Donovan. Or the accident to Miss Smith. Nevertheless, Alan mentioned if they were somehow related. His wondered if Mr. Donovan was reluctant to mention something concerning his daughter.

At that moment, a trolley pulled up. Eager to escape the cold, Sloane quickly boarded and settled into a seat for the ride home.

CHAPTER EIGHTEEN

On Wednesday, Sloane continued his investigation by stopping at city hall. He was well acquainted with the staff and the building itself, having utilized its resources on numerous occasions. City records were stored there so he had many reasons to frequent the place. Finishing up with a client by ten o'clock, he walked over to city hall with the intention of speaking to Mr. Edward Flynn.

He learned that Mr. Flynn worked in the Office of Licensing and Permits, so with the excuse that he needed to check on his investigator license, he climbed the stairs to the second floor. He was pleased the Office of Licensing and Permits was not terribly busy. A young man came forward and asked how he could help. Sloane asked if he could check on his investigator license, having given him his name and date of filing. The young man disappeared behind a large wooden card catalog and within a few minutes returned, stating that Sloane Sheppard, private investigator was on file as licensed by the State of New York, dated June 15, 1917, just nine years ago. The young man explained there was nothing more he needed to keep his license, which Sloane already knew, as it was valid for life unless invalided for cause. He was about to return to the card catalog when Sloane asked if he were Mr. Flynn. Rather startled, Ed told him he was Mr. Flynn. Sloane asked if he could speak with him about the death of Betsy Donovan. Ed looked around, hoping none of his associates had overheard. He went to the office of his supervisor and announced he would be on a short break, then returned to where Sloane stood in front of the counter.

"There's an empty office down the hall," Ed told him. "We can talk there."

Sloane followed him until they came to a small room furnished with a desk, a few chairs and a file cabinet. The windows overlooked Academy Park. Ed sat behind the desk while Sloane sat in the chair in front of him.

Looking at the young man, Sloane could tell he was obviously nervous, most likely not used to an interrogation of any sort. Sloane was rather reminded of Alan; he guessed Edward Flynn around thirty. He was dressed in a shirt, tie and vest, and clean-shaven, his brown hair center parted and slicked back, his green eyes alert. He exuded an overall air of vitality and intelligence.

"Her death was an accident," he said before Sloane had the chance to speak. "She just fell from the railing. Do you think otherwise, Mr. Sheppard?"

Sloane cleared his throat. "Alan Cartwright has hired me to look into his cousin's death. I am also assisting the police with it, as well as the murders of Miss Barker and Miss Evans."

Ed frowned. "Who is Miss Evans?"

Sloane told him she was an employee of Harmanus Bleecker Hall, who was stabbed early Monday morning during rush hour on the corner of Madison Avenue and Lark Street. Ed looked puzzled and told Sloane he did not know her, and that this was the first he heard of it.

"What was your relationship with Miss Donovan, Mr. Flynn?"

Ed took out a cigarette from the pack in his pocket, lit it and blew smoke nervously. He did not offer one to Sloane but sat thinking what to tell him. He appeared disturbed and chose his words carefully.

"Betsy and I dated for a while. She broke it off after she found someone new. She was interested in John Whitmore and Lester Cavanaugh. Their backgrounds were more appealing."

He continued puffing at his cigarette, knocking ash into an ashtray. He remained tight-lipped and Sloane could tell it would be a difficult interview. From experience, people like Mr. Flynn usually had something to hide, something they were unwilling to reveal. He decided to wait to see what more he would tell him,

"Did she tell you the reasons for breaking up with you?"

Ed shook his head. "No, she never did. Betsy was like that. She used people to get what she wanted. If she wasn't satisfied with something, she'd move on to something else. She worked at the Albany Savings Bank. I'm surprised she was able to hold her job."

"Why do you say that, Mr. Flynn?"

"Because Betsy was difficult to deal with. As long as things went her way, then all was fine. That included her relations with men. She bullied nearly everyone, even her own father."

Sloane figured as such. Obviously, Miss Donovan had the upper hand when it came to her father, who he surmised was more tolerant than most men would be in his position.

"What did you see the night of the marathon when Miss Donovan fell to her death?"

"I was in the atrium. I was dancing with a few ladies and then Betsy called down for everyone to watch her. She wanted to demonstrate her ridiculous sliding down a railing. She called out to Lester that he belonged to her or something like that and the next thing, she lost her hold and fell onto the floor. It was a really hard fall. There was no way she could have survived." He shuddered slightly. "It was really horrible, Mr. Sheppard."

Sloane nodded. "How long have you worked at city hall, Mr. Flynn?"

Ed explained he had worked at city hall since graduating from the State Teacher College in 1917. He lived in an apartment on Elk Street, which was extremely convenient to his place of work. His parents were deceased, and he had no brothers or sisters, few relatives were scattered about, but he did not maintain contact with them. He was good friends with Alan Cartwright and John Whitmore. He also was on friendly terms with Lester Cavanaugh, Norma Smith and Evangeline Whitney. He mentioned how Betsy had had issues with each of them; how she had thrown her drink in Norma's face at the speakeasy on Howard Street, causing a catfight.

"Because of Lester," Ed mentioned sourly. "Lester has caused a lot of problems in this city. He's on probation and personally, I don't trust him. I associate with him, but I don't consider him a good friend."

"Apparently Miss Donovan considered him more than just a friend," Sloane commented.

Ed nodded. "Maybe she wanted to marry him, although I don't consider Lester the type to settle down. Betsy was jealous of Norma and Evangeline. She spread rumors about them as she did about John and me, causing friction amongst us. She enjoyed causing trouble for others."

"Why do you think she would do that, Mr. Flynn?"

Ed shrugged and extinguished his cigarette. "I couldn't say, Mr. Sheppard. She made enemies and her father would be the first tell you that. I don't know her reasoning, except that she was self-centered, an egomaniac. She wanted Lester and was determined to have him, too."

"Miss Whitney was not on good terms with Miss Donovan?"

"That's an understatement," Ed almost laughed. "Neither was

Evangeline's mother. Her name is Mrs. Eleanor Whitney. She works here in city hall, at the Department of Public Works. Why don't you ask her yourself?"

Sloane detected a touch of sarcasm in his voice. He realized he had learned all he could from this rather impertinent young man. He handed him his business card and asked if he remembered anything further to contact him. He stood and thanked him for his time.

Ed seemed relieved upon opening the office door. "I'll be glad to show you where the Department of Public Works is located," he told Sloane as they entered the hallway.

Sloane mentioned he knew where it was and thanked him for his help. He watched as Ed returned to his front office rather quickly, leaving Sloane in the middle of the hallway, pondering his next move. He walked down the stairs into the busy lobby, where people were going back and forth to different departments. The Office of Public Works was located on the first floor, which Sloane knew well, having used its services extensively over the years. At that moment, he could not place Mrs. Whitney. Approaching the office, he entered a busy area, a long counter with several people behind it, assisting clients with varied requests. A young man approached Sloane and asked how he could assist him. Sloane asked for Mrs. Eleanor Whitney. He nodded to a middle-aged woman at the end of the counter, assisting a man with something that seemed quite urgent. Sloane approached just as she was finishing with the customer. She then turned her attention to him and asked what she would do for him. Sloane introduced himself and expressed that he wished to speak to her as he was investigating the death of Miss Betsy Donovan.

Eleanor nodded and told Sloane to follow her to another office, which she used when processing paperwork. They passed a few rooms until arriving at a small office at the end of the hallway, which was labeled ARCHIVES. Eleanor opened the door and Sloane followed, sitting across from her at a small table.

He could tell it was not used often, there was a damp feel to the room and it contained only a file cabinet and the table at which he sat. He looked at the middle-aged woman at the other side of the table. Pleasing and attentive, although certainly matronly, he did not know if she was a widow or a divorcee, she had a daughter, so he waited to hear what she would tell him.

"I'm afraid I cannot tell you anything much, Mr. Sheppard," Eleanor said. "It's commendable that Alan is having Betsy's death investigated, but I feel it is a waste of his time."

No beating about the bush with her, Sloane thought wryly. He wondered if her attitude toward law enforcement extended to the local police as well.

"What makes you say that, Mrs. Whitney?"

Eleanor pursed her lips. "Miss Donovan was an extremely difficult young woman. She had few friends, although she enjoyed the company of several men here in the city. She was rude to my daughter, Evangeline, and to me several times. My daughter works at Whitney's and once Miss Donovan created a scene about something, I don't remember the details. She was a most difficult young woman."

Sloane thought that sounded like a repeated phonograph record. He expected to hear the same from everyone he interviewed. He asked her what she remembered from the night she died.

"Miss Donovan climbed to the top of the stairs and wanted to show off her skill in sliding down the rail," Eleanor said. "Personally, I found it ridiculous. She called down to everyone to watch her. Next thing, she slipped and fell, a terrible scream, crashing to the atrium floor below."

"Where were you when this occurred?"

"In the atrium, looking up at Miss Donovan, like everyone else."

"Was anyone else on the top flight of stairs when she was sliding down the railing?"

Eleanor shook her head. "Not that I could see." She paused. "Is Alan paying you for investigating his cousin's death?"

Sloane kept his composure. "Of course, Mrs. Whitney. I am also assisting the police with the murders of Miss Barker and Miss Evans."

"Yes, I read about that poor girl in the paper," Eleanor said. "I didn't know Miss Evans but it's so sad, so young, too."

"Were you acquainted with Miss Barker?"

"I knew of her, from her local theater productions. I did not know her personally. She also was difficult, according to various people around town. She and Miss Donovan did not get along. I believe they had a row in public, too."

"Like Miss Donovan and Miss Smith recently," Sloane commented, waiting for her reaction. He was not disappointed.

"Miss Smith has tolerated a lot from Miss Donovan," Eleanor said in Norma's defense. "I'm not close to Miss Smith, but she is more down to earth than Miss Donovan or Miss Barker ever were. She and Alan are rather close, and I believe they dated on and off for a while.' She hesitated as though reluctant to impart more information.

"Miss Smith suffered an accident recently," Sloane prompted her to continue.

Eleanor nodded. "I happened to be coming out of the library and saw a crowd. I went to the hospital to inquire about her injuries. I brought her some food, too when she arrived home."

Sloane changed course and asked her about herself, how long she had worked at city hall and where she was from originally. Eleanor mentioned she was an Albany native and had worked at city hall for close to thirty years, she was divorced and her daughter Evangeline, lived with her. She had prospered in her position in the bookkeeping department at Whitneys. And her mother was incredibly pleased with her accomplishments.

"I'm sorry I cannot help you further," Eleanor said, wishing to conclude the discussion. "I only saw Miss Donovan fall from the railing." Her tone implied she wished not to be contacted again, but Sloane was not to be put off. He handed her his business card, which she reluctantly put in her pocket.

"If you remember anything more, Mrs. Whitney, please contact me. I'm assisting the police as well as investigating on behalf of Mr. Alan Cartwright."

"I've already spoken to the police," Eleanor told him firmly.

"You may be contacted by them again," he told her equally firmly.

Eleanor got up to leave. "I must return to work now, Mr. Sheppard. I cannot be away from the desk for too long. We are quite busy at the moment."

Sloane opened the door, and they walked down the hallway. Upon entering the outer office, she was summoned almost immediately for assistance with numerous requests. She was quickly consumed by various duties, forgetting that Sloane had even been behind her as they entered.

Sloane made his way to the outer hallway and down the stairs to the lobby, thinking about the interviews he just conducted with Mr. Flynn and Mrs. Whitney, certainly more odd and ambiguous people in the ongoing investigation into the sudden death of Miss Betsy Donovan.

Next, Sloane headed straight over to the Strand Theater on North Pearl Street to see John Whitmore. As it was only three o'clock, Sloane did not expect the theater to be busy. Upon entering, he was favorably impressed with the grandiose lobby, with its plush carpeting and crystal chandelier. He approached a young man behind a ticket booth.

"I'd like to see Mr. John Whitmore. My name is Mr. Sloane Sheppard, and I am a private investigator. I was told he is employed here."

The young man looked twice at Sloane, his tall, commanding presence rather intimidating. He merely nodded and picked up the handset on the candlestick phone, calling Mr. Whitmore, letting him know a Mr. Sheppard was in the lobby and wished to see him. When the young man inquired, per Mr. Whitmore, what it was regarding, Sloane told him it concerned the recent deaths of Miss Donovan, Miss Barker and Miss Evans. Almost frighteningly, the young man imparted this information into the handset, looking up at Sloane after receiving approval from Mr. Whitmore. He explained to Sloane how to get to his office.

Entering the stairway and climbing to the second floor, Sloane walked along a short passage, arriving at the office of John Whitmore. He introduced himself and John welcomed him to a chair, offering him coffee, which he refused.

"Thank you, Mr. Whitmore, for seeing me on short notice. I was hired by Alan Cartwright to look into the recent death of his cousin, Miss Betsy Donovan. I am also assisting the police with the homicides of Miss Penelope Barker and Miss Sarah Evans."

John had lit a cigarette and blew a fine cloud of smoke toward the ceiling. "I read about Miss Evans in the morning paper. Another scandal for the Hall."

"Why do you say that, Mr. Whitmore?"

John continued smoking, a satirical look to his face. "Mr. Ferguson had good intentions with the dance marathon, and it was going smoothly, until Betsy fell to her death and ruined it." His tone was firm, almost defiant as though Betsy's fall was the death knell for the event.

Sloane tried to read the young man seated behind the desk. Another handsome guy, he realized, like Alan Cartwright, Lester Cavanaugh and Ed Flynn, certainly appealing to women of any age. His height, fine physique, professional dress and chiseled facial features would entice any female. Sloane detected confidence, diligence and a touch of arrogance. He waited for him to add more and when he did not, Sloane decided on his usual course of action, asking him about himself, his background and his role at the theater.

John explained he was originally from Schenectady and had lived in Albany after graduating from the State Teachers College. He was employed as a teacher but then turned his attention to the theater, which he always enjoyed, landing a managerial position at the Strand. He liked his position, meeting actors, and often collaborating with Alan Cartwright at Harmanus Bleecker Hall for upcoming talent to appear in Albany. He had known Alan for several years and considered him a good friend. He lived in an apartment on State Street, not far from Norma Smith.

"What do you remember about the night Miss Donovan died?" Sloane asked him.

John explained that he had been working at the dance marathon, per Mr. Ferguson's instructions and was in the atrium, dancing with a few girls. He then heard Betsy call down to everyone to watch her as she slid down the banister. She lost her grip and crashed down on the floor, horribly. He knew she was dead, she did not move a muscle.

"Did you see anyone else with her at the top of the stairs?"

John continued smoking. "No, she was alone, although it was kind of dark at the top of the stairs. I suppose someone else could've been there, but I didn't see anyone."

"Alan mentioned he noticed the fire escape ajar and snowy footprints leading to the top of the stairs. Did you have occasion to go to the upper floors that night?"

John shook his head "I don't work at the Hall, Mr. Sheppard. I have no reason to go to the upper floors. If that fire escape was ajar, that's their concern. They should've been more mindful of the building before and during the event."

"Did you know Miss Barker and Miss Evans? Do you know Miss Whitney?"

"I dated Penelope a few times, as well as Evangeline Whitney. Mrs. Whitney is rather domineering of her daughter, which turned me off on seeing her anymore. I don't think she was particularly fond of me. Betsy was jealous of Evangeline and spread rumors about us to anyone who would listen. I didn't know Miss Evans. Norma Smith and I also dated for several months, but Betsy interfered in our relationship, too, causing a lot of strife for Norma. I dated Betsy rather steadily, but as she did with Ed Flynn, she dropped me like a hot potato as soon as she found someone new. Betsy used people and didn't care who she hurt in the process."

"Would you say she was infatuated with Mr. Cavanaugh?"

John knocked ash into an ashtray. "Most likely. She shouted down to us that night that they belonged together, or some such nonsense. Personally, I don't know what she ever saw in him, as she knew he had a criminal record. Apparently, it didn't bother her; although I'm sure it bothered her father."

"Do you know Mr. Donovan?"

John crushed his cigarette and sighed. "Yes, I know him. He is not what he is cracked up to be. He gives the impression of a hard-working businessman, but underneath he's conniving and ruthless. He is quite wealthy, and his business is prospering. He couldn't control his daughter and he told me to my face straight out that he didn't think I was good enough for her. That contributed to Betsy and I breaking up."

Sloane detected some bitterness in his tone. He could picture Carl Donovan protective of his daughter, but would he insult a suitor to the point of rudeness? As though reading his mind, John continued.

"He didn't want his daughter to associate with theater people, which I found ridiculous. It was just an excuse for Betsy not to bother with me anymore. I don't think Mr. Donovan approved of any man his daughter associated with."

"Including Mr. Cavanaugh? From what I've been told, they were always together."

John looked at him carefully. "Lester managed to seduce a lot of women, but he was never serious about them. But she took it the wrong way."

"I understand Miss Smith had an accident recently," Sloane commented.

John explained to him the circumstances of Norma's accident and that her condition had improved dramatically. He believed she planned to return to work on Wednesday. He saw her often, as her boarding house was just a block from his apartment on State Street.

Sloane had made a few notes in his small notebook and then closed it with a snap. He realized he could not get more from John Whitmore, and he may not have anything else to add. He gave the impression of being an innocent bystander, which Sloane thought, he probably was. He had suffered Miss Donovan's wrath and even that of her father, and he detected some scorn toward Mrs. Whitney, too. He handed John his business card, asking him to contact him if he remembered anything else helpful to the investigation. He then rose and shook hands with him, thanking him for his time.

"Evangeline could tell you more about Betsy," John offered, seeing

Sloane to the door and to the hallway. "She works at Whitney's as a bookkeeper, although she may have left by now." He glanced at his watch, noticing it was past four o'clock.

Sloane mentioned since Whitney's was nearby he would stop to see Miss Whitney. He entered the stairway and upon reaching the lobby, headed for the entrance. Walking less than a block, he entered the imposing department store, finding it full of shoppers and browsers, which he expected, as Sloane occasionally shopped in the men's department. He inquired for Miss Evangeline Whitney and was directed to the lower floor, where the business offices were located. He found the accounting offices and knocked on a door bearing her name. Evangeline looked up and smiled.

Sloane introduced himself and stated the reason for his visit. Evangeline set aside a few papers and motioned for him to sit at the chair in front of her desk. He looked at her carefully; certainly, a pretty picture, a well-dressed businesswoman, just enough makeup, her bobbed hair arranged tastefully, and a pleasing scent of Chanel No. 5. He imagined many young men would find her attractive. He wondered why she was not married or at least engaged.

"It was really terrible," Evangeline said. "Betsy fell to her death, and I saw it all! It was just horrible, like a nightmare."

"You were in the atrium when she fell?"

Evangeline nodded. "I was dancing and enjoying himself." She did not add anything more and remained strangely tight-lipped, as though afraid to continue. She asked Sloane about himself and his work, which he knew from long habit, was a cover-up for a reluctance to provide more information.

Sloane told her he was looking into the death of Miss Donovan as Alan Cartwright initiated his inquiries; he was also assisting the police. In cases of accidental deaths, the police are involved until there was no question of foul play. He also mentioned he was investigating with the police the murders of Miss Barker and Miss Evans. Evangeline shuddered slightly.

"I read about Miss Evans in the paper," she told Sloane. "I didn't know her."

"You knew Miss Barker?"

"I wouldn't say I knew her. I saw her several times when I was out for the evening. She was quite a drinker and had a mean temper, too."

"Did you see any altercations with Miss Barker or Miss Donovan?"

"I heard that Betsy and Penelope had a row once, but I never saw it. Betsy and Norma had a fight at the speakeasy on Howard Street recently. She was jealous of Lester paying attention to Norma and threw her drink in her face."

Sloane nodded. "I spoke with your mother earlier at city hall. She mentioned she made a scene here at Whitney's."

"Yes, she accused me of stealing John and Lester from her, both of whom I dated. She was difficult with the salesgirls, too."

Sloane tried to get the picture right. "You, Miss Smith and Miss Donovan dated at one time Mr. Flynn, Mr. Whitmore and Mr. Cavanaugh, is that correct?"

Evangeline nodded, reluctantly. "Yes, I was quite serious with John for a while, but now we're just friends. Betsy interfered with our relationship. She also interfered when I dated Ed and Lester. Apparently, she thought Lester belonged to her. She was extremely jealous of other girls, including Norma." She hesitated as though wanting to add more but changed her mind.

"What is your relationship with Alan Cartwright?"

"Alan and I also dated. We still go out on occasion. Betsy seemed to enjoy wreaking havoc, causing friction by talking about us to others, as she did when I dated John, Ed and Lester. She and Alan were complete opposites in personality and demeanor."

"Do you know Alan's mother? Do you see her often?'

"Yes, I know her," she answered simply.

"I spoke to your mother at city hall. She seems quite proud of you."

Evangeline nodded, adding nothing more. He did not press her for more information. He detected a slight resistance. He asked if she enjoyed working at Whitney's and the convenience of living so close to work. Evangeline told Sloane she liked her bookkeeping position and appreciated the brownstone on Columbia Street, where she lived with her mother, which was within walking distance of North Pearl Street.

Sloane reached in his pocket for his business card, handing it to Evangeline across the desk. He asked her to contact him if she remembered anything about Miss Donovan. Evangeline smiled prettily, seeing him to the door and the stairs to the main floor. He reached the main entrance just as the store was announcing it would soon close.

Outside, it was dark; the evening rush hour was in progress with snow falling intermittently. Pedestrians huddled in coats, a throng of traffic and trollies clogged the streets, and windows poured light boldly onto the sidewalks. A chilly wind off the Hudson River blew patches of snowy fog about.

Sloane walked up North Pearl Street, crossing at the light to State, arriving at the Albany City Savings Bank Building. Once in his office, he settled at his desk and looked at reports needing his attention. Lighting a cigarette, deep in thought, his mind drifted to Mr. Donovan, Mr. Flynn, Mrs. Whitney, Mr. Whitmore and Miss Whitney.

Certainly an odd bunch, he thought wryly. Miss Whitney seemed hesitant to speak about her mother and Mrs. Cartwright. He wondered if there was something she was reluctant to mention that warranted further inquiry.

CHAPTER NINETEEN

Inspector Harris looked at the report he received from the Albany County Morgue. It contained the results of the autopsy on Miss Betsy Donovan. He had spoken with Lieutenant Taylor and then called Mr. Donovan earlier, as he wanted to discuss the results with him. Instead of cooperation, the inspector heard a torrent of vituperation, demanding to know why the police were privy to his daughter's autopsy, as it was a family issue. The inspector reiterated that in cases of accidental death, the police have access to pertinent records to determine cause of death. If an accident were indeed the cause, then the investigation would be concluded. He reminded Mr. Donovan he expected his full cooperation during the investigation.

It was Thursday, the eighteenth and another cold, blustery day, although a weak sun tried to break through the clouds. It was mid-morning and Inspector Harris was at his desk with Lieutenant Taylor seated in front of him at Albany City Police headquarters, sorting through the various notes they wrote on the Donovan case as well as the homicides of Miss Barker and Miss Evans. So far, they were unable to reach a satisfactory conclusion.

"We need to determine if these deaths are related," Lieutenant

Taylor said. His tone hinged on frustration, as though all of his resources were used up.

The inspector agreed. "Quite possibly, the common link is Mr. Lester Cavanaugh. I didn't particularly like him when we were at Harmanus Bleecker Hall. He seemed evasive and indifferent, almost as though it was all a joke to him."

"Perhaps he knows more about what happened to Miss Donovan than he lets on."

"He's on probation for bootlegging; his criminal record in Albany is extensive."

The inspector nodded. "I spoke with Mr. Ferguson earlier. Miss Smith has returned to work. We need to ask her a few questions, too."

"As for Miss Donovan's death, someone could have put something on the banister, causing her to lose her grip and fall. I realize that's a long shot."

"The snowy footprints leading from the fire escape to the top of the stairs certainly point in that direction," the inspector said logically. "Perhaps someone encouraged Miss Donovan. No one claims to have seen anyone else on the fifth floor at the time."

"When we spoke to the kitchen staff, nobody could offer anything of importance," the lieutenant said. "I remember Miss Evans distinctly. She was rather aloof, and I thought she seemed to be hiding something. I should've pressed her for more information."

Inspector Harris shook his head. "Most likely she was right there when it happened."

"And most likely saw or heard something and decided to blackmail the murderer."

"Who must've been there and witnessed the entire thing, too."

"Nobody saw anything when Miss Barker was killed. It was during the overnight hours and the streets were quiet, but someone came up behind her and stabbed her multiple times."

"Somehow, there is link between these three women. The only problem is that all of the people involved knew Miss Barker and Miss Donovan. Therefore, it would be difficult to pin the blame on one person. We need more facts."

"I'll contact the Harmanus Bleecker Library where Mr. Cavanaugh works," the lieutenant suggested, standing.

Inspector Harris cleared his throat.. "In the meantime, I'll call Mr. Sheppard. He's interviewed several people already. He should know about the autopsy report, too."

Lieutenant Taylor left the office, leaving Inspector Harris alone at this desk. He sat brooding for several moments, and then turned his attention again to the notes. He reached over to the candlestick phone on the corner of his desk and picking up the handset, asked the operator to dial Mr. Sloane Sheppard at the Albany City Savings Bank Building. In no time, the phone rang and was answered promptly by Sloane.

"Mr. Sheppard, this is Inspector Harris of the Albany City Police. I'm calling in reference to the recent murders and the death of Miss Donovan."

In his office on State Street, Sloane listened carefully, anticipating news that would change the course of this investigation and would lead it in the right direction. He put down a cigarette and loosened his tie; he knew it would be a long day. With his normal caseload, including working for Alan Cartwright, and the assistance he was giving the city police, he had little free time and expected to work late into the evening.

"We believe the death of Miss Evans is somehow related to the other two," Inspector Harris told him. "Perhaps she saw something and decided to blackmail the murderer."

Sloane took a sip of his coffee, only lukewarm, and then related to the inspector the interviews he had with Mr. Flynn, Mrs. Whitney, Miss Whitney, Mr. Whitmore and Mr. Donovan. He had yet to speak with Mrs. Cartwright or Mr. Cavanaugh. He planned to contact Mr. Cavanaugh and Alan Cartwright, to see when his mother would be available.

Inspector Harris expressed his gratitude to Sloane for his invaluable assistance. He then told him about Betsy's autopsy report, which he recently received from the Albany County Morgue. He called Mr. Donovan to discuss it, but unfortunately, he was clearly adamant that his daughter's autopsy was personal. The inspector explained that Mr. Donovan had received it before they did which, Sloane assumed, would explain his indifference on Tuesday when he spoke with him. Inspector Harris mentioned the cause of death as severe head injuries, hip fractures, numerous broken bones and a broken neck. He then caught his breath and spoke hoarsely.

"There is something else you should know, Mr. Sheppard."

"What is that, Inspector?"

"At the time of her death, Miss Donovan was with child."

Alan carried a tray containing coffee, cups, a sugar bowl and cream into the living room, where his mother, uncle, Norma and Lester were sitting, after enjoying a delicious dinner prepared by Bernice. It was early evening on Thursday. Bernice had called her brother to invite him for dinner as well as Norma Smith. Norma asked if she could bring Lester. At first, Bernice hesitated, and then relinquished and told Norma that was fine. She would look forward to their arrival.

Settled in the spacious living room, on the comfortable sofa and the deep armchairs with the chintz coverings, the radio console was tuned to WGY, which played wonderful jazz tunes. The atmosphere was relaxing and inviting. No one spoke of Betsy, Penelope Barker or Sarah Evans, as though they welcomed a much needed respite from the turmoil of the last several weeks.

Bernice added sugar to her coffee cup after accepting it from her son. "I admit I didn't bake the pie, Carl. I bought it at the market on Lark Street."

"It was the bees knees, for sure, Mrs. Cartwright," Norma exclaimed, grateful to have dinner at their house. She was seated on the sofa and looked around the living room contentedly.

Lester lit a cigarette, after depositing the match in an ashtray, sipped his coffee, and addressed Bernice. "Thank you, Mrs. Cartwright, for having me for dinner, along with Norma. I can't say too many people have cooked dinner for me recently."

Bernice smiled, ever the perfect hostess. "You're welcome, Mr. Cavanaugh."

"You have a lovely home, Mrs. Cartwright," Lester said, looking around the well-furnished living room. "And it's convenient for your work and Alan's, too."

Bernice commented how she and Alan enjoyed living on prosperous Elk Street, one of the finest addresses in Albany. Her brownstone was furnished comfortably and its convenience to the capitol and Harmanus Bleecker Hall was advantageous for them.

Carl remarked on the growth in downtown Albany, that Union Station was increasing its train schedule to accommodate passengers from all parts of the state and the Hampton Hotel was almost sold out every night.

It was at that moment the doorbell rang. Bernice glanced at her son, who almost dropped his coffee cup. He had forgotten to mention that Sloane Sheppard would be stopping by this evening. He put his cup on the coffee table, almost spilling it onto the floor.

"I forgot that Mr. Sheppard is stopping by this evening," he explained, feeling rather foolish. If he could have dug a hole to hide himself, he would have at that moment. "I spoke with him earlier today and he wanted to meet you, Mother."

Bernice put her cup on the coffee table. Rather than exuding anger, especially not in front of guests, she merely told her son to answer the door and not keep Mr. Sheppard waiting outside in the cold. As he entered the hallway, Alan could hear his uncle scowling over the intrusion of Mr. Sheppard and Norma and Lester asking who he was and what he wanted from them.

"Convenient for Mr. Sheppard that you and Lester are here," Carl remarked to Norma.

Upon opening the front door, Alan stood aside to let Sloane enter, taking his coat and hat and welcoming him into their home. He led him down the hallway to the living room, where everyone looked at him as he stood in the entranceway. Alan introduced Sloane to his mother and Norma and to Lester, who stood and shook hands with him. Alan also introduced Sloane to Carl, who did not stand, but simply mentioned he had spoken with Mr. Sheppard on Tuesday.

Making room for him on the plush sofa, Sloane sat next to Norma and Lester, while Alan sat in an armchair near the fireplace, next to his mother and uncle. Sloane thanked them for having him this evening and before he could speak, Bernice offered him coffee and pie, which he declined. A strange silence ensued until Bernice asked him what they could do for him. She was unused to any law enforcement present in her pristine house. Although she would tolerate Sloane's presence this evening, Alan could tell his mother was not thrilled.

"We've had a relaxing evening, Mr. Sheppard," Carl said, puffing rather anxiously on a cigarette. "I'm sure you mean no intrusion, but we really do need a break from any discussion of my daughter's unfortunate demise."

"It is not my intention to intrude, Mr. Donovan," Sloane said. "I am investigating the death of your daughter, as well as the murders of Miss Barker and Miss Evans. I had yet to meet Mrs. Cartwright." He paused. "And I appreciate the chance to meet Miss Smith."

Alan looked at Sloane carefully. He wondered what information he had to impart. First, he asked them what they remembered about the night in question.

Bernice commented she had been in the atrium, enjoying the festivities when she heard Betsy call down from the top floor to watch her slide down the railing. That was all she remembered, until she crashed down onto the atrium floor. Norma and Lester also reiterated what Bernice said, not knowing she planned to do that ahead of time. Bernice also mentioned she had no idea what Betsy planned to do that evening, adding that perhaps she was slightly drunk and just acting rather recklessly. To Sloane's surprise, her brother shared her opinion.

"My daughter may have been drinking that night," Carl said reluctantly. "Although I spoke with her just before it happened, and I didn't have the impression she was intoxicated."

"She called out that you belonged to her, Mr. Cavanaugh," Sloane commented.

Lester puffed on a cigarette. "As I told the police, Mr. Sheppard, that was just Betsy talking. She thought she could control me and plenty of other men, too."

"What happened to Miss Evans, Mr. Sheppard?" Norma asked.

Sloane explained that Miss Sarah Evans was found stabbed on the corner of Madison and Lark while waiting for the trolley to go to work. At first, it seemed she simply collapsed but while in the emergency room, it was discovered she had been stabbed.

"I spoke with her Sunday afternoon, after I left you, Norma," Alan said. "I saw her on State Street. She told me she had seen or heard something before Betsy fell, but she didn't go into detail."

"Foolish girl," Carl said, rather impatiently. "If she had information that could've helped, she should have said something."

"More than likely she was blackmailing someone, Mr. Donovan," Sloane said gently. He had lit a cigarette, exhaling a great cloud of smoke. "The police believe her murder ties in with the murder of Miss Barker. But so far we have yet to discover if these homicides are related to the death of your daughter."

"Nonsense," Bernice spoke up. "How could Betsy's fall down the railing have anything to do with the other two?"

"You had an accident recently, Miss Smith?" Sloane said, ignoring Bernice's comment.

Norma nodded. "Mrs. Whitney and her daughter Evangeline have been most kind." She explained how Eleanor and Evangeline prepared food upon her return from the hospital and of Eleanor's concern for her welfare. "She came to the hospital to check on me, too."

"Do you remember what happened?" Sloane asked her.

"No, not really," Norma told him. "I fell on State Street and the next thing I remember was waking up in the hospital. Mrs. Whitney said I slipped and fell on the icy street."

"We're glad you're much better now," Carl added and smiled.

"Where do you work, Mrs. Cartwright?" Sloane asked her.

Bernice spoke about her work at the capitol library, how she researched bills and articles for the legislators. Norma mentioned her secretarial duties at Harmanus Bleecker Hall. She enjoyed her work, meeting different actors who graced its stage. She lived in a boarding house on State Street, within walking distance.

While she spoke, Sloane had the opportunity to take a better look at Norma Smith and Lester Cavanaugh. He was surprised Alan and his mother would have them or at least Mr. Cavanaugh in their home together, as they must know the unscrupulous background of Lester Cavanaugh. And even Norma Smith, who fought with Miss Donovan at the speakeasy. Certainly proved she had a temper, although now she seemed composed and even subdued. Perhaps her recent accident changed her. Of course, Alan considered them his friends. Apparently Miss Smith and Mr. Cavanaugh seemed comfortable together, so he assumed they were an item, at least for the time being. He could understand the insecurity of Miss Donovan, who must have resented Norma Smith's interest in Lester Cavanaugh

He then listened as Lester talked about his work at the Harmanus Bleecker Library. He saw for himself that Lester Cavanaugh was quite a handsome young man. His muscular physique and wavy blonde hair would attract any female. Sloane figured he was about his own age, mid-thirties and clever. And a criminal, with a shady past. On the other hand, didn't Miss Smith know of his background? Obviously, it did not bother her if she was aware of it.

"You will excuse me, Mr. Donovan, but I feel I must share information which the police told me earlier. It is vital to the investigation." He paused, looking at Carl. "According to the autopsy report, Miss Donovan was expecting a child at the time of her death."

It was a bombshell totally unexpected. A stunned silence pervaded the room. Alan was rendered speechless, Bernice sat with her mouth open, and Norma and Lester were quiet, but not surprised. Lester continued smoking as though nothing could phase him. His wry expression told Sloane he merely found it amusing. Only Carl was rather indignant. He made it clear to Sloane not to mention such unpleasantness to just anyone, as it was a personal matter.

"Betsy never mentioned she was expecting a child," Alan said, still in shock.

"She wasn't even married," Bernice said. "A child born out of wedlock is disgraceful."

"Were you aware of this, Mr. Donovan?" Norma asked him.

Carl shook his head. "I wonder if Betsy even knew. She would've told me."

A stunned silence ensued as though they were absorbing the news Sloane just shared. Bernice asked him politely if there was anything further. Her tone implied she would prefer he leave, as though she had heard enough shocking news for one night. Sloane thanked them for their time, stating that he would contact them again in the near future.

Norma also mentioned she would like to leave, as it was getting late. Bernice went to the hallway for their coats while Alan saw Sloane to the front door. Sloane shook hands with Carl and reiterated he would follow up with him soon. He put on his coat and fixed his hat squarely on his head. He thanked Alan for having him visit this evening.

Glancing at Bernice, Carl, Norma and Lester in the hallway, Sloane wondered what information they withheld and what more he had to learn before this investigation was over.

Mrs. Eleanor Whitney finished looking at the *Albany Evening Journal*, finding extraordinarily little of interest. Political and economic news always bored her, and she did not feel like reading the latest on President Coolidge or the projected financial upswing for 1926. She skimmed the entertainment news; Greta Garbo was making her American debut in *Torrent*, opening this month. She was proclaimed the new Hollywood starlet, even surpassing Clara Bow. Charlie Chaplin's hit film *The Gold Rush* was still on demand at Harmanus Bleecker Hall. Eleanor decided she would eventually see it.

She and her daughter had eaten dinner and were now spending the evening hours in the living room, drinking after dinner coffee, reading and listening to the radio. The fireplace was lit, creating a warm atmosphere. She was ensconced in her favorite armchair, while her daughter sat opposite her on the comfortable sofa, reading as usual her favorite magazine *True Story*, while sipping coffee and listening to the latest hit songs on WGY radio.

Sensing her mother's eyes on her, Evangeline looked up. "Is there something wrong, Mother? Are you not feeling well?" Her tone was a mixture of annoyance and concern.

Eleanor smiled weakly. "I am worried about the recent violence in our city, dear."

Evangeline shrugged. "You mean that Evans girl or whatever her name was? I didn't know her. Could've just been a robbery or something."

"Perhaps," Eleanor said, sipping her coffee. "Are you seeing Lester again, dear?"

Evangeline did not take her eyes off *True Story*. "I don't know, Mother. Now he's smitten with Norma, which is fine by me. Norma had a bad accident and if she wants to spend time with Lester, then so be it."

Eleanor was surprised by the finality in her voice. "I do believe Alan Cartwright would be the special man you're seeking. He is intelligent and so handsome, too."

"When I find the man I want to settle with, I'll let you know," Evangeline said, rather irritability and to the point. "In the meantime, I am not in any rush." She hesitated, as she realized her mother was rebuffed by her words. "You are available to date local men, Mother. Certainly, Mr. Donovan is someone you should consider."

Eleanor felt hostility inside boiling to the brim, but she controlled it by clearing her throat. "I believe I had already mentioned, I am not interested in Mr. Donovan. Please do not mention him to me again."

"Now that Betsy is out of the way, I thought you would consider him," Evangeline said simply. "Unless there is someone else on your mind. What about that Mr. Peters who works at city hall? He's a widower and extremely attractive, Mother."

"Yes, I know, dear," Eleanor said patiently. "But Mr. Peters and I have different interests. I wouldn't worry about finding me another man. When the time comes, I'll let you know." She paid her daughter back in the same coin, further infuriating her.

Evangeline sighed, closed the cover of *True Story* and announced she was going to bed. Eleanor got up and hugged her daughter and told her she too planned to retire for the evening soon. Evangeline wished her mother good night, making her way out of the living room, up the stairs to the second floor and her lovely bedroom, overlooking Columbia Street.

Once in her room, she kicked off her shoes and lit a cigarette from a pack in her nightstand, sitting on the edge of her bed. Her mother could infuriate her, but there was something else hammering away at her mind. Something that had been at the forefront of her mind for weeks since the dance marathon before Betsy climbed those stairs.

Of course, there were so many people in the atrium and the ball-room, too. The music blaring, people dancing, talking, such merriment before Betsy crashed to the atrium floor, a broken body laying practically at their feet. Alan might know. Yes, dear Alan, that handsome man just around the corner. She should grab him while she had the chance. She finished her cigarette and went to bed, hopelessly holding on to that thought.

It was after eleven o'clock and Alan could not sleep. After Norma, Lester and Uncle Carl left for the night, his mother had gone to bed already and he stayed up listening to the radio and finishing the evening newspaper. He knew she was not particularly pleased that Mr. Sheppard had paid them a visit, but he could tell she was too tired to start a discussion. Alan went to bed less than an hour after his mother, but now, after tossing and turning restlessly, he got up and began pacing the floor.

He never imagined a crime of murder so close to home. It disturbed him and he found his everyday activities were in a turmoil; his concentration at work was even impacted. He lit a cigarette and looked out the window, again feeling the icy draft on his bare feet, expecting to see Lester chatting with someone. Even a cold night would not stop Lester from gallivanting around the city. But he did not see him or anyone else when he looked out.

He glanced at the nightstand and realized the letters he found in Lester's garbage were still there. Keeping his cigarette between his lips, he reached over to the drawer and took them out. He looked at them again, reading them repeatedly, practically to the point of memorization. He shivered slightly, realizing the significance of what he held in his hands.

He had forgotten the letters. Perhaps he ought to show them to Mr. Sheppard. Lester had so many different admirers he would lose track of them. The lounge lizard, as Betsy called him that evening at the speakeasy. His criminal history could make him a prime candidate as a murderer. Alan knew he was involved with local gangsters, who were notorious for using unscrupulous means to achieve their goals. Was Betsy a threat to him somehow? Did she know something about Lester that he did not want revealed?

Alan blew smoke, knocked ash into the ashtray on his nightstand and felt a sudden uneasiness run up his spine. The letters were so chilling to him that he hesitated to handle them again. Something told him that the writer of these repulsive letters was also the same person who had brutally killed two people, caused the death of his cousin Betsy and was even responsible for Norma's accident. And quite possibly, whoever wrote these letters would not hesitate to kill again, if threatened in any way.

He extinguished his cigarette, and unable to keep his eyes open any further, felt sleep and mental fatigue overwhelm him. He returned the letters to the drawer, turned off his bedside lamp, crawled into bed and within a few seconds, drifted into a deep but troubled sleep.

CHAPTER TWENTY

On Friday morning, Sloane was at his desk early, as he anticipated the arrival of a new client regarding a child custody suit. A man was seeking parental care of his young son from his wife, who had abandoned them for another suitor. It was the initial consultation and Sloane was unsure if he would take the case. He lit a cigarette and sipped his coffee while reviewing the case notes.

It was a cold day in downtown Albany, but the sun was breaking through, a sign that spring would arrive within a few weeks, although residents were used to prolonged winters, that dragged into April. It had finally stopped snowing, and Sloane contemplated eating lunch at the diner on South Pearl Street.

Preparing his notes and contracts for the new client, he was nonplused when the candlestick phone on his desk rang, rather shrilly, as though whoever was calling make it known it was important. Picking up the handset, he heard the rather excitable voice of Alan on the other end.

"Mr. Sheppard, I'm glad you're in your office. This is Alan Cartwright. I have to speak to you about certain things that have come up, that may pertain to my cousin's death."

"Of course, Alan," Sloane told him. He put aside his notes and the contract for his appointment and asked Alan what he could do for him.

Alan took a deep breath and told Sloane about the love letters he found in Lester's trashcan. He discovered them last Saturday and had forgotten about them until last night. He did not know if they were significant. There was no signature on them, so he did not know who wrote them. He had them with him and wanted his opinion.

Sloane paused before speaking. If there was no signature, what value were these letters to the investigation? He heard Alan almost pleading with him to come to the Hall today, if possible, to look at them. He told him he was unable to come to his office until after work, but Sloane, glancing at his calendar, told Alan he would stop by today after lunch.

When that time came, Sloane arrived at Harmanus Bleecker Hall after one o'clock and proceeded to Alan's office, where he told Mrs. Russell he was expecting him. He entered his office, shook hands with Alan and sat in the chair before his desk.

"Thank you, Mr. Sheppard for coming here today," Alan said rather gravely. Without hesitation, he took the letters from his drawer and handed them across his desk to Sloane. Sloane took them and read them carefully, then looked up into Alan's expectant face.

"Whoever wrote these is definitely infatuated with Mr. Cavanaugh," Sloane remarked. "We don't know who wrote them as there is no signature." He paused. "How do you see these as significant, Alan?"

Alan puffed at a cigarette. "I think Betsy wrote them to Lester and he just threw them out."

Sloane looked at the letters again. "The first was written in December and the second on January twenty-second. The third is dated February eighth. Miss Donovan could not have written the third because she was already dead. The handwriting appears the same on all three. Therefore, she could not have written them."

Alan sighed, continued smoking, feeling extremely agitated. "I thought there was a possibility. Who else could write such sordid letters to Lester? She called down to us in the atrium that Lester belonged to her, although I do not believe he felt that way toward her."

"There is the possibility that Mr. Cavanaugh was the father of her child."

"I'm sure Lester isn't the only man who could fit that bill," Alan said dryly. "Betsy didn't hesitate in flirting with men. She knew how to lure a man and she was often successful, too."

"Have you told your uncle about these letters?"

Alan shook his head. "I didn't want to burden him with anything else. The funeral was too much for him and he's just getting back on his feet."

Sloane nodded, looking at the letters again. He asked Alan about Mr. Cavanaugh and if he knew whom he was involved with now.

"Norma is involved with Lester, but for some reason, I can't see her writing the letters. Besides, they're together all the time and they seem to care for each other. Evangeline could have written them, but that isn't really her style."

Sloane studied the letters again. "I'd like to keep these letters and show them to Inspector Harris." He folded them and placed them in his coat pocket.

Alan looked up at that moment to see Mr. Ferguson in the doorway, along with Mrs. Churchill. They greeted Sloane cordially. Mr. Ferguson cleared his throat and addressed Sloane.

"Alan informed me earlier that you would be stopping here this afternoon, Mr. Sheppard. I have something to relate to you concerning Miss Donovan's behavior the night of the dance marathon. Something that you may want to investigate further." He glanced at Mrs. Churchill who picked up where he left off.

"We spoke with Mrs. Truman, a cook in the kitchen here," she told Sloane, her tone serious. "She and her daughter were present the night of the dance marathon. Her daughter was a friend of Miss Sarah Evans,"

Sloane did not see what this information had to do with the death of Miss Donovan, but he waited for her to continue.

"Mrs. Truman told us her daughter and Miss Evans may have overheard something pertinent that night, although she would not specify what. She may not know herself."

And look what happened to Miss Evans, Sloane thought. He waited for Mrs. Churchill to continue. Instead, she handed Sloane a piece of paper with the address of Mrs. Gerard Truman, on Jay Street, not far from Harmanus Bleecker Hall. She commented that Mrs. Truman had left early to care for her daughter, who was at home and not feeling well. Apparently, she was still upset over Miss Donovan's fall, having witnessed it and not realizing what she had heard previously.

"Mrs. Truman told us that if you wish to speak to them, they will see you," Mrs. Churchill said. "We do not know what her daughter saw or heard, but at this point, it may be of some help."

"How old is Mrs. Truman's daughter?" Alan inquired.

"Around eighteen or nineteen. She attends the State Teachers College but has been so distraught over Miss Donovan's fall that she has hardly left their apartment."

"Mrs. Truman is a valued employee here," Mr. Ferguson commented. "If she said her daughter overheard something, I believe her. She didn't say anything earlier because she didn't know what her daughter saw. Her daughter isn't comfortable in speaking to the police."

"Alan informed us that Miss Donovan was expecting a child at the time of her death," Mrs. Churchill commented. "It is most unfortunate that her death occurred here at Harmanus Bleecker Hall. I am afraid this fine institution's reputation will forever be tarnished over this calamity."

"Most likely Betsy didn't know either," Alan said. "Her father wasn't aware of it. We don't know who the father was. With Betsy, it could've been several men."

"Perhaps anyone who is capable of passion is indiscreet," Mrs. Churchill remarked stiffly. "As Alan said, I am sure Miss Donovan had many suitors, so the possibilities would be endless."

Sloane looked at the address on the piece of paper Mrs. Churchill handed him. He was familiar with Jay Street, just off Lark Street. He would stop first to see Mr. Cavanaugh and then proceed to Jay Street to speak to Mrs. Truman and her daughter. At this point in the investigation, he needed to unearth as much information as possible and with the letters Alan discovered in Lester's trash, he saw a pattern, but the link needed to discover the culprit was still missing.

Sloane stood and thanked Mr. Ferguson and Mrs. Churchill for the information. He thanked Alan for his time and promised he would be in touch soon. Leaving three rather startled faces looking after him, Sloane left the office, nearly bounded down the marble stairs on his way to the exit, determined to find the answers to what really happened the night Miss Donovan died.

Ed paused in his work at city hall and glanced out the window overlooking Lodge Street and Washington Avenue. His office had a spectacular view of Academy Park, a mass of snowy whiteness, covering park benches and the magnificent fountain.

Soon the Boys Academy would dismiss for the day. Ed marveled at the students who erupted from the building like a locust. He saw his apartment building at the very end of Elk Street, convenient to his work. And convenient for other encounters, too, he smirked.

Putting his feet up on his desk, during a momentary lull, Ed relaxed with a cigarette, exhaling a fine trail of smoke. He had established contact with a local bootlegger who supplied him with liquor as needed. The illegal liquor trade was rampant in Albany and the bootleggers worked together, including Lester, who was locally one of the most prolific. His mind then drifted to Mr. Sheppard, who came here to speak to him. Of all the nerve, coming to his place of work to interview him about Betsy, Penelope and that Miss Evans, whoever she was. Maybe he'll call Alan later, to get his opinion on Mr. Sheppard. After all, he hired him to investigate this sordid business.

He felt no sympathy for Betsy or Penelope; two troublemakers who got what was coming to them. Both had spread malicious gossip about him needlessly and Betsy and Penelope used him as they used so many men. He continued smoking meditatively when suddenly Evangeline and her mother walked into his office. Taken aback, he took his feet off the desk and expressed surprise at seeing them. He asked what he could do for them.

"I came by to see mother," Evangeline said simply. "We decided to stop by to see you."

Ed looked carefully at Evangeline and noted her pretty features, so impeccably dressed, wearing a fine string of pearls and lovely earrings, rather alluring in her simplicity. Mrs. Whitney was tall and matronly, rather overbearing but pleasant, wearing a simple black dress and rather heavy lipstick. Her face was creased as though the recent burdens had taken a toll.

"It's great to see you both," Ed said uneasily, not sure where this was headed. He was not used to many visitors in his office, certainly not the Whitneys.

"We should invite Ed to dinner, Mother," Evangeline told her.

Ed smiled, extinguishing his cigarette. "Thanks, Evangeline, I'd like that. Do you have plans for tomorrow? Maybe we can see a movie at the Strand or have dinner at Keeler's."

Evangeline told Ed she did not have plans for tomorrow and would love to see a film and have dinner with him. She told him to call her this evening and they would make plans for tomorrow. He was surprised since he thought she had her eyes set on Alan. He could not read Mrs. Whitney, standing protectively next to her daughter, a prominent frown to her face. Of course, he was sure Mrs. Whitney knew he drank and frequented speakeasies, but didn't everyone nowadays?

"The League of Women Voters is meeting Saturday evening," Eleanor said, ever the community activist. "I plan to attend, and Mrs. Churchill may, too. Women have the right to vote now, and it's important our voices be heard."

Ed was surprised to hear her staunchness pertaining to women's rights. He never imagined Mrs. Whitney or Mrs. Churchill involved in women's rights. He paid little attention to women getting the vote. Besides, in 1920, he was in college, so the last thing he thought about was women's voting rights.

Evangeline said she needed to return to the department store and Eleanor to her office. Saying goodbye, they turned to leave. Ed mentioned he would call her tonight and then got back to work. Soon he was consumed with reports, memos and telephone calls. Before long, the workday was over, and it was time to leave.

While he put on his jacket and cap, he overheard a woman in the outer department say the League of Women Voters was meeting Sunday evening at the State Education Building. Ed thought Mrs. Whitney mentioned tomorrow evening. He wondered if she had mistaken the day or perhaps had other plans, like looking to see what her daughter was up to.

Sloane entered the Harmanus Bleecker Library on Dove Street. He knew the library well and had spent much time researching and using the archives. He approached the circulation desk and asked for Mr. Lester Cavanaugh. The clerk recognized Sloane, greeted him warmly, and told him Mr. Cavanaugh was in the back room, sorting newspapers. Sloane thanked her and made his way to the newspaper area, where several patrons were at tables reading the local and out-of-town papers. He spotted Lester near a cart with a plethora of newspapers. He approached him and mentioned he wanted to speak to him.

Lester looked at Sloane and had to bite his tongue to tell him to leave him the hell alone. He had spoken to him that night at the Cartwrights, so what more did he want from him? Of course, he did not say that, but merely pushed the cart against the far wall and told Sloane to follow him to a small office down the hall where they could talk in private.

Settling himself in a chair across from Sloane, Lester lit a cigarette and asked him what he could do for him. His tone hinged on annoyance, which was not lost on Sloane. He cleared his throat and came directly to the point.

"I want to speak to you about your relationships with Miss Barker and Miss Donovan."

Lester shrugged, drawing on his cigarette. "Nothing to tell."

"I believe there is," Sloane said father firmly. "You were involved with both women, who must have mistaken your interest in them for infatuation. Perhaps that has been the case with other women as well."

"What are you getting at?" Lester said perturbed.

Sloane took the letters from his coat pocket and handed them to Lester. He asked him to explain them and from the look on his face, Sloane could tell he was surprised and deeply disturbed, as though a long held secret had become known. Sloane waited for an answer.

"Betsy wrote these, Mr. Sheppard. She thought I would promise to marry her. Maybe she did know she was going to have a child. And maybe the child was mine. That's why she felt I belonged to her." He looked at the letters as though he had never seen them before. "Where did you find these? They belong to me and are personal."

Sloane explained how Alan showed them to him after finding them in his trash can. Since he threw them out, they could not have meant anything to him, Sloane pointed out. This knowledge infuriated Lester even more and remarked that his personal business belonged to him, no one else. Sloane reminded him this was a murder investigation and that he intended to retain the letters. He planned to turn them over to the police shortly. He also mentioned that Betsy could not have written the letters, since the third, dated just last Monday, was written after her death.

"And you think I killed Penelope and caused Betsy to fall?" Lester said with a slight smirk, blowing smoke toward the ceiling.

"Where were you the night of the dance marathon?" Sloane sked him.

"I believe I supplied this information already. I was in the ballroom and then went to the atrium to see what was going on. I joined in on the dancing with a few ladies and then I heard Betsy call down that she was going to demonstrate sliding down a banister. She shouted that I belonged to her or some such nonsense before she lost her grip and fell to the atrium floor."

"Is that all you saw?"

Lester nodded. "It was pretty horrible. I really prefer not to discuss it."

Sloane nodded. "If you have information, you must share it with me or the police."

When Lester still did not speak, Sloane continued. "A Hall employee, Miss Sarah Evans was stabbed while waiting for the trolley on the corner of Madison and Lark. She told Alan she heard something that night while in the atrium. Most likely she saw the person responsible for causing Miss Donovan's fall." He paused, seeing the startled expression on Lester's face. "After I leave here, I am going to see a Mrs. Truman and her daughter, who work in the kitchen at the Hall. According to Mr. Ferguson, Mrs. Truman's daughter heard something that could implicate someone and bring this case to an end."

"There were a lot of people in the atrium and it was really noisy," Lester told him. "I really don't remember seeing anything incriminating."

"Alan found the fire escape on the fifth floor ajar and snowy footprints leading to the top of the stairs," Sloane reminded him. "That may mean someone put something on the banister, making it slippery for Miss Donovan to lose her grip and fall to her death."

"You mean snow or ice on the railing?" Lester said incredulously. "But wouldn't it melt? It wouldn't remain slippery all night."

Sloane agreed. "Unless someone encouraged Miss Donovan to slide down the banister immediately after the snow was applied to it."

Sloane asked him again whom he thought wrote the letters, but Lester shook his head. He told Sloane he had received numerous letters from women over the years and he did not remember who wrote them all. He mentioned he had been involved with several women in Albany but did not recognize the handwriting, which is why he threw them away.

"Were they mailed to you?" Sloane asked.

Lester shook his head. "No, if I remember correctly, they were stuffed under my apartment door when I got home from work."

"So whoever wrote them came to your apartment three times; once in December, the second in January when the second was written and just last week, when the third was written. And you didn't see who could've come to your apartment?"

Again, Lester shook his head. "No, I go to the YMCA to lift weights after work and when I'm not there, I usually go to a speakeasy with friends. Or I have a date with Norma, sometimes Evangeline or someone else." He made it sound as though his social life was so active that he could have no idea who was responsible for the letters, which, Sloane thought, was most likely the case. A man who used women and reaped the benefits. So carefree and worldly, a man who would never settle down, who infatuated women left and right but left them hurt and dejected, often rebellious and even lonesome.

Sloane put the letters back in his coat pocket, thanked Lester for his time and stood to leave. He walked to the front lobby of the library, leaving Lester in the hallway to stare after him.

Outside on Dove Street, Sloane walked until he came to Jay Street. He looked for the house number and found it easily enough; a pleasant brownstone with three apartments on each of its three floors. He pressed the buzzer, and the downstairs door opened. Finding the right apartment on the second floor, he knocked and waited.

The middle-aged woman who answered was not pretty in a common sense. She exuded a motherly persona, certainly protective of her daughter. Her voice was gentle and inviting.

"Are you Mr. Sheppard? I am Mrs. Truman. I spoke with Mr. Ferguson. He mentioned you would stop by. Please come in." She moved aside, allowing Sloane to enter the apartment. She led him down a short hallway to the living room, where a young woman sat anxiously, looking apprehensive, listening to the radio and looking at a magazine. Realizing she was the daughter, Sloane smiled, hoping to put her at ease.

"Winnie, this is Mr. Sheppard. He's come here to see you."

Sloane looked around and admired the comfortable furnishings, the radio console in the far corner, overlooking the street. Off to the right was a bedroom and to the left was the kitchen. Mrs. Truman welcomed Sloane to sit on the sofa, next to her daughter, while she sat in an armchair opposite. She did not offer him coffee but merely looked at him inquiringly, wondering what he would say to them.

"Thank you for letting me come here today, Mrs. Truman." He turned to the young woman next to him on the sofa. "May I call you Winnie? My name is Sloane Sheppard, and I am a private investigator. You can call me Sloane if you wish. I am looking into the deaths of Miss Penelope Barker and Miss Betsy Donovan."

Winnie Truman remained quiet. Sloane thought she was about eighteen or nineteen, rather pretty, but withdrawn and serious. Her brown hair, worn in the bob style, was fixed neatly but the worry on her face was overpowering.

In his work as a private investigator, Sloane had the ability to set people at ease, to help them open up and confide in him, despite the fear and apprehension. His commanding presence assured the young woman she was dealing with someone trustworthy.

Mrs. Truman mentioned her daughter was a student at the nearby State Teachers College and was preparing for a career as an English teacher. Sloane commended Winnie on such a rewarding career choice. He then mentioned that Mr. Ferguson told him she might have information important to tell him, but that she had been unable to attend classes due to her anxiety. Sloane encouraged her to confide in him, to tell him to the best of her ability what she remembered from that night.

"You were present at the dance marathon, Winnie?" he asked gently.

Winnie nodded. "Sarah and I were there to help with the food. My mother spent most of her time in the kitchen, while Sarah and I helped in the ballroom." She paused. "Afterwards, Sarah and I went to the atrium to see what was going on. Lots of people were dancing and it was a lot of fun." She stopped, as though afraid to continue.

"What else do you remember?" Sloane asked her.

"Well, Sarah and I were near the stairs, just watching the dancing. We thought of dancing too but remembered we were working and didn't think Mr. Ferguson would like that. But then that girl climbed to the top of the stairs and shouted down to everyone and then she just fell horribly to the floor!" She shuddered, as though reliving the moment in her mind.

Sloane nodded, feeling compassion for this young woman, who witnessed more than just the fall. He prodded her kindly for more information. "What more can you tell me, Winnie?"

She frowned, deep in thought. "Sarah and I heard someone tell that girl to slide down the railing! Just like that! We didn't realize until afterwards what we heard."

Sloane looked at her carefully. "You must tell me more, Winnie."

"Mr. Sheppard, this is really too much for my daughter," Mrs. Truman interrupted.

Winnie intervened. "No, I'm all right, Mother." She turned to Sloane, with newfound strength. "I was too frightened to speak to the police." She shuddered slightly. "Sarah was foolish and was killed." She hesitated, and then nodded. "But if I can avenge Sarah's killer, I'll tell you what you need to know, Sloane."

Sloane nodded, grateful he had earned her trust.

It was after seven o'clock, another cold and wintery evening. Alan and his mother were busy in the kitchen, cleaning up after dinner. Carl was in the living room, relaxing with the evening paper and coffee. Bernice suggested to her son that he join his uncle as she could finish the rest herself.

Alan entered the living room to see Carl on the sofa, listening to *The Atwater Kent Hour*, while thumbing through the *Albany Evening Journal*.

"You gave Mr. Sheppard the letters you told your mother and I about," Carl commented.

Just then, Bernice entered, overhearing what her brother asked.

"Why didn't you tell us earlier about the letters, Alan?" she asked him.

Alan thought his mother had a way to lay terrible guilt on him. He was used to it, but this time felt indignant. He did not feel he needed to explain his decision to remain silent.

"Honestly, I forgot about them," he explained. "Until last night. So I showed them to Mr. Sheppard today when he came to the Hall."

"And what does he plan to do with them?" Carl asked.

Alan shrugged. "Talk to Lester, I guess. I really don't know."

"Since they were addressed to Mr. Cavanaugh, I imagine that is exactly what he will do," Bernice said firmly. She paused, and then changed the subject. "Tomorrow is Saturday and I'm having Mrs. Churchill and Mrs. Whitney for lunch and to play cards. Sunday evening there is a meeting at the State Education Building of the League of Women Voters, but I don't think I'll attend. Mrs. Whitney and Mrs. Whitney may go. Beforehand, I'd like to have Miss Smith over again. She seemed so forlorn and lonesome the last time. She doesn't have family so perhaps a nice home cooked meal will help her since her recent stay in the hospital."

Alan and Carl agreed that was a good idea. Bernice explained Sunday afternoon would be best, when she could get everyone together and she would make the arrangements. Alan extinguished his cigarette and announced he planned to visit John at his apartment on State Street and would stop to see Norma and extend the invitation for Sunday afternoon. He went for his jacket and cap, returning to the living room.

"I won't be long, Mother," he announced, buttoning his jacket, his cap firmly on his head.

He turned toward the front door, making his way through the snow in Academy Park and Washington Avenue. Crossing at the light at Dove Street, he turned right onto State and reached John's apartment building. He pressed the doorbell and the front door buzzed, allowing him to enter. Climbing the stairs to the second floor, he realized he had

---

only been to John's place once before, so he did not quite remember it. When John answered, he was nonplussed to see Lester, Norma and Ed in the living room, talking, smoking, laughing and sharing bottles of whiskey, which were almost depleted. John took his jacket and cap, welcomed him to an armchair and soon put a glass of whiskey in his hand. Alan sipped it and found it soothed his shattered nerves. He continued drinking until Lester addressed him, rather forcibly, causing Norma, Ed and John to look his way, rather surprised at the tone of voice he would use in speaking to Alan.

"Alan, why the hell did you give that Sheppard fellow letters I threw out? You had no business going through my trash!"

Alan took a large gulp of whiskey and lit a cigarette. "I didn't go through your trash, Lester. I threw out an empty cigarette pack and noticed the letters on top, so I thought I'd look at them."

"How convenient," Lester remarked dryly.

"Maybe I wrote them," Norma said, sitting next to Lester, her hand on his knee. "I do love you so, Lester dear. I have written you letters before, but I don't know if those are mine."

"Maybe Betsy wrote them," Ed suggested.

"Or Penelope," John added.

"Or one of my many admirers," Lester laughed drunkenly.

"Then I wrote them," Norma said, "but I didn't think you'd throw them out, Lester dear!"

Her jovial tone helped to alleviate the tension in the room. Lester held her hand rather tight, while sipping the whiskey and puffing at his cigarette.

"Maybe they don't mean anything at all," John said. "Lots of women write love letters, you know. I've had my share of them. I end up throwing them away, too."

"Well, I didn't kill Penelope," Norma said, rather defensively.

"Although I would have liked to. She was nothing but an interfering bitch."

"She tried to break us up a few years ago, remember?" Lester said to Norma.

She nodded. "Yes, I remember quite well. Betsy did the same thing."

"Likewise with Evangeline and me," John added.

"Sounds like Betsy, too," Ed put in.

"I have no sympathy for them," Norma said coldly, finishing the whiskey in her glass. "They caused so much havoc in our lives. Too bad what happened didn't occur sooner."

"Can't we talk about something more cheerful?" Ed said firmly, rather exasperated. "I find discussing murders and deaths rather dark topics."

"Darker than the night, buddy," Lester mumbled, taking a big gulp of his whiskey.

There was an awkward silence for a few moments until Norma mentioned Betsy's unborn child. Her tone was defiant and even mocking.

"Maybe that's why she felt you belonged to her, Lester. One way to hold onto you."

Lester shook his head. "It could've been others, Norma. I wasn't the only one."

"What do you think, Alan?" Ed asked him, refilling his glass. "You got this Sheppard guy involved. And you're paying him to check things out."

Alan felt inquisitive eyes on him. He noticed Lester drinking heavily. From long experience, he knew Lester could be devious when intoxicated, even dangerous, and given his apparent anger toward him at the moment, he did not feel comfortable in his presence.

"I don't really know what to think," Alan answered truthfully. He tried changing the subject. "Mother wants to invite you for lunch on Sunday, Norma. Are you available?"

Norma crushed her cigarette and smiled. "Another of your mother's great meals? Of course, I'd like that. Please tell your mother I'd be delighted to come. She is the best cook ever!"

"We'll all stop by," Lester slurred his words, putting his arm around Norma, rather drunkenly. "As long as Mrs. Cartwright doesn't mind. Your mother is the best cook ever, Alan. John and Ed, you guys, too."

Before Alan could say anything, John turned on his phonograph player and put on the new 78 record of Duke Ellington. Before long, Norma and Lester were in the middle of the floor, dancing. Ed poured more whiskey and Alan lit another cigarette. John asked Alan about work at the Hall and if he planned to see Evangeline soon. Alan wondered if he wanted to see her himself.

"I'm going out with Evangeline tomorrow night," Ed told them, finishing the whiskey in his glass and reaching for the nearly empty bottle. "We're going to Keeler's and to the Strand to see Greta Garbo's new film."

John told him it was quite a sellout. "Greta Garbo is the bees' knees. We're showing Colleen Moore's latest film, too. Tickets are selling like hot cakes."

Norma and Lester finished dancing, or what Alan thought was mere transpiring the floor, as Lester was clearly inebriated, and Norma was practically holding him up. They plopped down on the sofa, holding on to each other, laughing and finishing the liquor in their glasses.

Alan extinguished his cigarette, finished his whiskey and announced he had to leave. Ed offered to walk with him, but Alan could tell he wanted to drink more. John told him to stay, but Alan was adamant on leaving. He told them he would call tomorrow with the details for the meal on Sunday. Oddly, he felt as though he could not wait to leave these people he considered friends.

John saw him to the door, handed him his jacket and cap and stood with him in the hallway. Alan told him he would call him tomorrow and then rather eagerly headed for the stairs. Once outside, he lit a fresh cigarette, breathing in the smoke and refreshing cold, seeing his breath in the frosty night air. Something was bothering him, and he felt extremely irritable.

He made his way down a rather dark and nearly deserted State Street toward the capitol. Lester was infuriated with him for showing the letters to Mr. Sheppard. Norma claimed she wrote those letters. But wouldn't she have signed them? A sudden horrid thought came to Alan. Was Norma responsible for the recent deaths? She could have caused Betsy's death. Lancaster Street, where Penelope was murdered, was just around the corner. Would she kill for Lester's affection?

Reaching the State Education Building, he continued on Washington Avenue and walked through Academy Park to Elk Street. He was so deep in thought that he did not notice someone in front of the capitol, across the street, carefully watching his every move.

CHAPTER TWENTY ONE

On Saturday, Bernice was busy in her kitchen, preparing lunch for Mrs. Churchill, Mrs. Whitney and her brother Carl. She had contacted them last evening and insisted her brother attend as well, although he was reluctant at first. She assured him lunch and a game of bridge made for a wonderful and relaxing afternoon on a cold winter day, after which Carl accepted her invitation.

It was late morning when Alan entered the kitchen, after cleaning his bedroom, vacuuming the rugs, taking out the garbage and shoveling the front steps. He told his mother that Norma accepted her invitation for a meal on Sunday. He then asked if the others could attend. Bernice looked up from the counter and asked him exactly who were the others.

"Lester, John and Ed," Alan told her, pouring a cup of coffee and sitting at the kitchen table. "They were at John's apartment last night."

"Did you invite them, Alan?" Bernice said a trace of annoyance in her voice.

Alan shook his head. "No, Lester sort of suggested it."

"Well, I don't plan to make anything special," Bernice admitted. "Beef stew and potatoes, something easy to prepare. I'm sure Miss

Smith will be glad to have a home cooked meal after her terrible ordeal."

"I'll tell them to stop over for coffee and dessert," Alan suggested.

Bernice smiled. "That would be better, dear. I'll do likewise with Mrs. Churchill, Mrs. Whitney and Evangeline."

"It was great that Mrs. Whitney and Evangeline have been helpful," Alan remarked.

Bernice nodded. "Perhaps you should get together with Evangeline, now that…" She broke off and did not finish speaking.

"You mean now that Betsy and Penelope are out of the way," Alan finished for her.

"They interfered in nearly everyone's relationship," Bernice said, anger seething below the surface. "Betsy may have been my niece, but that was as far as it went."

"What did you have against her, Mother?" Alan asked, sipping coffee.

Bernice joined him at the table. "Your cousin had a nasty habit of spreading malicious gossip. Even while I was married to your father. I told my brother I didn't trust her and that his divorce left her a bitter, disrespectful, spiteful girl." She paused. "I believe she caused problems for her father while in high school."

Alan listened to the harsh words as he sipped his coffee. From his own experience, he knew what his cousin was like, but he never realized the anger she stirred in his mother. He thought of asking her to elaborate but he could tell the subject was too painful, so he decided not to say anything. How did his uncle withstand such behavior from his daughter? Most likely, there were stories neither he nor his mother knew pertaining to Betsy and her father. He wondered how often she infuriated him and what recourses he took to amend it.

The candlestick telephone in the hallway rang shrilly. Alan got up to answer it and was surprised to hear the voice of Sloane Sheppard on the other end. He greeted Sloane pleasantly and waited to hear what he had to tell him.

"Alan, I believe I know what happened to Miss Donovan the night of the marathon," Sloane told him. "And I have a good idea who was responsible for the murders of Miss Barker and Miss Evans. I plan to speak to Inspector Harris of the Albany City Police later today."

"Mr. Sheppard, that's great news," Alan said, feeling a burden lifted off him. "Can you tell me what you know and how you put it all together?"

"Not at the moment," Sloane cautioned him. "I spoke with a Hall employee who was a witness to Miss Donovan's fall. Tomorrow afternoon I'd like to stop by to speak to you and your mother. I'll wait until I speak to Inspector Harris. I want to know what he advises is the best course of action. Most likely he and Lieutenant Taylor will make an arrest relatively soon."

"But we all witnessed Betsy's fall. What did the kitchen worker see that we didn't?"

"She overheard something that helped in the investigation."

"Do you still have the letters I showed you about Lester?"

"Yes, I intend to give them to the police as evidence. They helped pinpoint the culprit."

"Then you do know who is responsible?" Alan asked, his voice rising with excitement.

"Why don't I stop by in the afternoon tomorrow," Sloane told him, not wishing to divulge information over the telephone. "I'll speak to you and your mother then."

Alan mentioned his mother planned a meal for Norma tomorrow, if he did not mind seeing her as well. The others might stop by for dessert in the later afternoon.

Sloane rang off, telling Alan he would stop by around four

tomorrow afternoon. He hung up the handset, replaced the telephone on the hallway table and returned to the kitchen to find his mother at the table reading the morning paper.

"That was Mr. Sheppard," Alan explained. "I invited him here tomorrow afternoon. He's figured out what's been going on and wants to tell us about it."

Bernice looked up from the newspaper. "That certainly is news."

At that moment, the doorbell rang, and Alan went to the hallway to answer it. He returned shortly with his Uncle Carl, Mrs. Churchill and Mrs. Whitney. Bernice smiled upon seeing her guests and welcomed them, as they sat around the kitchen table.

"Thank you for having us for lunch, Bernice," Mrs. Churchill said, her cheeks rather flushed from the cold.

"The coffee smells wonderful, Bernice," Mrs. Whitney said pleasantly, settling at the table.

Bernice served turkey sandwiches and salad, followed by coffee and cake. Alan enjoyed a sandwich and mentioned they were having Norma over tomorrow for a meal. Bernice extended the invitation to include them for coffee and dessert in the afternoon.

"You are the perfect hostess," Mrs. Whitney smiled, sipping coffee. "I think I can make it, although I may attend the meeting of the League of Women Voters. Or is that tonight?"

Mrs. Churchill corrected her. "It's tomorrow night. But if the meal is for Miss Smith, I certainly don't want to intrude."

After much persuading, it was agreed that Carl, Mrs. Churchill and Mrs. Whitney and Evangeline would stop by for coffee and dessert tomorrow afternoon. Alan also mentioned Lester, Ed and John might stop over as well.

"You'll have a full house, Bernice," Carl remarked and smiled.

Bernice shrugged. "I'll do it for Norma Smith, poor dear. I always

say a good meal is the best
way to stay warm during the winter months."

Alan got the deck of cards from a cupboard and asked if he could join the bridge game. Bernice welcomed her son, and the game soon began. While shuffling the deck, he mentioned Mr. Sheppard contacted him, having reached a conclusion regarding Betsy as well as Miss Barker and Miss Evans. He planned to stop by tomorrow afternoon, after first speaking with the police, to relay his findings.

"So you may be here when he arrives," Alan said. "I'm sure you'll want to hear about it."

"Indeed we will," Mrs. Churchill said, looking at her cards.

"Did he say how he reached his conclusion?" Carl asked his nephew.

"It was the letters written to Lester," Alan said. "And he mentioned he spoke to someone who works in the kitchen at the Hall. She saw or heard something, which I guess clinched it."

"What letters, Alan?" Mrs. Whitney asked.

"Letters a woman wrote him," Alan told them. He realized they were looking at him rather intently, making him feel uncomfortable. "They weren't signed, but someone sent one in December, one in January and another this month. I found them in his trash and retrieved them. I gave them to Mr. Sheppard. I don't think Lester was happy with me for doing that."

Bernice got up from the table to retrieve the coffee pot to refill everyone's cup and offer more dessert. Alan thought there was a certain tension at the table, as though they were repulsed and disturbed by Lester's letters and the news that Mr. Sheppard had reached a conclusion. He would have thought they would be just the opposite; at least a resolution was forthcoming.

They continued playing bridge in relative silence, an unspoken anxiety among them.

Evangeline fastened a string of pearls around her neck and smoothed down her dress. She combed her brown hair and looking at herself in her vanity mirror, was pleased at her appearance. She applied Chanel No. 5 and just enough lipstick.

She looked out her bedroom window overlooking Columbia Street. It was busy as most Saturday evenings were in downtown Albany. Crowds flocked to restaurants, theaters, department stores, boutiques and of course the well-hidden but inevitable speakeasy.

She felt exhilarated that she was spending the evening with Ed Flynn. She had always liked him and now that Betsy and Penelope were no longer around, she had fair play with Ed. They had dated a few times in the past and she looked forward to getting to know him better.

Brushing her hair as she looked in the mirror, her mind returned to the night of the dance marathon. She tried hard to forget it, but it was still fresh in her mind. Foolish Betsy, demonstrating her sliding down the railing, as though anyone cared. What made her decide to do that in the first place? Of course, she was such a showoff. She wanted to impress Lester and Evangeline did not think he even noticed until she called down to him.

But then she lost her grip and came hurtling down to the atrium floor, practically at their feet. It was just terrible, the way she fell, screaming horribly. Evangeline thought of the people around her, looking up at Betsy at the same time. Then her thoughts turned to that Miss Evans or whatever her name was and another young girl, who were at the foot of the right staircase. She remembered her eyes drifting to that area and seeing someone else there but could not recall whom. She remembered her mother nearby, and Alan, John and Ed somewhere in the vicinity but could not find where Mrs. Cartwright or Mr. Donovan had gone. She remembered Lester shouting up at Betsy not to slide down. Her father might have done the same; it was all too frightening to think about. She thought Norma was there too, but she was not sure. Poor Norma, such a freak accident, if it was an accident. She wondered if she really did slip on the ice or if she was pushed. But who would do such a thing and why?

Suddenly, she sat upright in the chair. She realized someone was in the distance, whose back was toward them, talking to Betsy *before* she ran up the stairs and those girls saw it, too. But the girls not only saw but they must have *heard* what was said to Betsy. In fact, no one paid much attention to Betsy at all, although she was rather flamboyant dancing, until she shouted from the top of the stairs and was about to slide down the railing. Did someone edge her on? Is that what the conversation at the foot of the stairs was about? If snow were applied to the railing, and Alan saw snowy footprints from the fire escape leading to the top of the stairs, of course she would lose her grip and fall!

She shuddered, reliving the scene in her mind. That Miss Evans and the other girl were standing at the foot of the stairs, just before Betsy ran up them. Someone else was standing there, too, but it was dim, and she couldn't see precisely who it was. Evangeline got up fitfully, looking out the windows. With the loud music, the tenebrous lighting, the dancing and the crowds in the atrium, she didn't notice anything unusual.

Soon Ed would be here, and she would enjoy the evening with him. Mother was at Mrs. Cartwright's house, although she imagined she would be home soon. Unless she took an evening walk, one of her favorite pastimes. She knew Mrs. Churchill, Mr. Donovan and Mrs. Cartwright enjoyed walking, too. Mrs. Churchill was rather matronly, but pleasant enough. Mr. Donovan had had his hands full with Betsy and was always preoccupied. Betsy was out of the way now so maybe he would change. Mrs. Cartwright was such a nice lady and lucky to have Alan with her. She smiled thinking of dear Alan, so handsome and intelligent. She understood what he meant to her, but she was enamored with Ed and John, too. Unless one of them killed Penelope, Miss Evans, and caused not only Norma's accident but Betsy to fall, too.

From the second floor, Evangeline heard the front door open. Her mother called up to her. She felt better hearing her familiar voice, and hurriedly left her bedroom, on the way down the stairs to greet her.

CHAPTER TWENTY TWO

An unexpected warmth slowly replaced the frigid air on Sunday. Temperatures were expected to climb into the forties, with plentiful sunshine, causing the mounds of snow to finally begin to melt, creating muddy streets, footpaths and sidewalks.

In his apartment on Madison Avenue, Sloane rather sleepily opened the blinds in his bedroom and living room, squinting from the bright sunshine. It was just nine o'clock and he had gotten up less than an hour ago. Sloane admitted Sunday mornings were his tranquil time. No rushing to catch the trolley, no reports to consider, no appointments to keep. He could relax on his sofa, drink plentiful cups of coffee, listen to the radio and smoke innumerable cigarettes while reading the Sunday edition of the *Times Union*.

Sloane came out of his bathroom, feeling replenished after a hot shower and dried himself vigorously. His jet-black hair was tousled and still wet. He knotted the towel around his waist and then stepped over to the bureau in his bedroom, where clean clothes awaited him. He had no sooner put on underclothes than the telephone rang from in the living room.

Rather surprised, as he was unused to calls on Sunday mornings, he approached the instrument with some trepidation. Although clients could search for his number in the Albany City Directory, he knew most did not reach him at his apartment. He had contacted Inspector Harris at Albany City Police headquarters yesterday; he assumed it was he returning his call. Upon grabbing the candlestick phone and sitting on his sofa, he was proven correct when he unhooked the handset and heard a familiar voice on the other end.

"Mr. Sheppard, this is Inspector Harris. I was not on duty Saturday. I got your message and am returning your call first thing. You mention you have information pertaining to Miss Donovan and the murders of Miss Barker and Miss Evans?"

Sloane put his feet up on the coffee table and reached for his pack of cigarettes. "Yes, Inspector, I believe I have resolved this issue for Alan Cartwright pertaining to his cousin's death."

"And the murders of Miss Barker and Miss Evans, too?"

Sloane lit a cigarette with one hand while holding onto the handset with the other. He flicked his lighter and exhaled a trail of smoke. "Yes, including Miss Smith's accident, which I don't believe was an accident at all. I believe the same person was responsible."

"Lieutenant Taylor and I visited Harmanus Bleecker Hall again yesterday and did not learn anything new," Inspector Harris informed Sloane. "Mr. Ferguson mentioned a kitchen employee who might have seen something, but she was afraid to speak to us. He told us he recommended she speak with you. I've had other officers speak extensively with Mr. Cavanaugh, but he is a dead fish out of water. If he knew anything, he won't admit to it."

Sloane puffed at his cigarette. "I did speak with the kitchen employees Mr. Ferguson mentioned who were at the dance marathon, a Mrs. Truman and her daughter." He explained the revelations Winnie Truman made to him. He explained about the love letters written to

Mr. Cavanaugh that Alan discovered in the trash bin in Lester's apartment and how either Miss Barker or Miss Donovan could not have written them.

"The handwriting is the same," Sloane explained. "Unfortunately, there is no signature. When I questioned Mr. Cavanaugh, he was very noncommittal. He wasn't sure who had sent them. He found them at separate times slipped underneath his apartment door. He claims he was never home when they were delivered. Usually he goes to the YMCA after work."

"He didn't know who wrote the letters? Surely, he must have some idea."

"He told me it could have been several women," Sloane said.

Inspector Harris whistled. "Quite the ladies' man, isn't he? He's a tough character and we can bring him in on bootlegging alone. He is still on probation."

Sloane negated that idea. "I plan to visit the Cartwrights later today at their house on Elk Street. Can you and Lieutenant Taylor be there this afternoon, say around four?"

"What do you have planned, Mr. Sheppard? From what you have told me, we are ready to make an arrest. Before that, I'd like to see the letters to Mr. Cavanaugh as evidence."

Sloane knocked ash into an ashtray. "I'll bring them with me. I want to present to Alan and his mother what I have shared with you. Afterwards, we'll see the person and make the arrest."

Inspector Harris told Sloane that he and Lieutenant Taylor would be at the Cartwright's house this afternoon about four o'clock. Sloane extinguished his cigarette, replaced the handset and put the candlestick phone on the coffee table. He then went into the bedroom, put on his robe, and entered the kitchen to fix coffee. While waiting for it to boil, he returned to the living room and stretched comfortably on the sofa.

He picked up the newspaper and scanned the headlines. A feeling of fulfillment came over him. Another case resolved.

Norma looked in awe at the delicious meal Bernice had prepared. A magnificent beef stew, with rich brown gravy, potatoes and carrots, followed by rice pilaf, salad, and Bernice's wonderful chocolate cake for dessert.

"Mrs. Cartwright, this is really too much," she exclaimed happily.

Alan, his mother, Carl, Norma and Lester were heartily enjoying the meal. They were seated at the dining room table and Bernice was pleased her efforts were a success. She commented she wanted to wait to serve her chocolate cake as Alan mentioned the others would arrive later in the day. It was a most relaxing atmosphere and Alan noted everyone was enjoying the meal. His mother laid out her best table-cloth and the dining room was exquisite. He asked Norma how she was feeling after her terrible ordeal.

"Alan, you see me every day at work," she said, smiling, sitting next to Lester. "But thank you for your concern. I am much better and feeling like myself again. The hospital staff was the best. And taking a few days of rest helped me get back on my feet."

"The city should maintain the streets better," Carl said rather harshly. He finished his salad and sipped a glass of ginger ale. "You could've been struck by a car."

Norma agreed. "It happened so fast, I only remember waking up in the hospital. Mrs. Whitney and Evangeline were so helpful. Are they closer to finding out what happened to Betsy?"

Alan paused, uncertainly. "Mr. Sheppard called yesterday and told me he knows what happened. He plans to come here later today to tell us what he uncovered."

Carl nodded in approval. "That's great news. I want the circumstances of my daughter's death to be cleared up. If someone is responsible, I want that person brought to justice."

"Did Mr. Sheppard tell you anything more, Alan?" Norma asked.

Alan shook his head. "No, he didn't want to divulge information over the telephone. So he wants to meet with us today. I told him to stop by later in the afternoon."

Lester cringed slightly. "The police have spoken with me numerous times about Betsy, Penelope and that Evans girl, who I didn't even know. They seem to think I was involved."

"In some respects, you *are* involved," Carl said, rather forcibly. "My daughter may have been carrying your child. Those letters to you may have been written by the person responsible for these deaths." He paused, rather vehemently. "I am not saying you are responsible, of course."

Lester continued eating the rice pilaf and the beef stew on his plate without lifting his head, saying nothing. An uncomfortable silence ensued. At that moment, Alan felt incredibly sorry for Lester Cavanaugh. As he had done with Norma, he suddenly realized a different side to Lester. Perhaps he was lonesome, without family, using women to fill a void, a desperate need for companionship. Maybe he wanted attention, and deep down was insecure. His only diversions were seducing women and getting drunk. Perhaps that is why he got involved with bootleggers. He continued eating, feeling differently toward Lester on the other side of the table, seeing a different side to him.

Bernice mentioned if anyone wanted more of the stew and the rice pilaf. Carl asked for seconds, as did Lester and Alan. Bernice went to the sideboard where she had placed the pot containing the beef stew, and dishes with the rice pilaf and the salad. She filled their plates, and then refilled their glasses with more ginger ale.

"I'm surprised you didn't invite Mrs. Churchill, Mother," Alan said, watching as she spooned more rice pilaf onto his plate. "Was she not available today?"

"Mrs. Churchill is busy at the church," Bernice told them, returning the food to the sideboard. She sat back down and sipped her ginger ale. "She promised to stop by for coffee and dessert this afternoon."

Lester asked Alan about performances at Harmanus Bleecker Hall. Alan commented that attendance had dropped after Mr. Ferguson's decision to cancel the dance marathon, especially with the negative publicity in the newspapers and on the radio but was slowly picking up again. They were concentrating on showing first rate films like *Ben Hur*, *The Big Parade* and *The Phantom of the Opera*, which were drawing in good ticket sales. He hoped to book the Marx Brothers, Fanny Brice and Paul Whiteman and his orchestra for performances in the near future.

"I talked to Mr. Ferguson about rescheduling the dance marathon," Norma said, spearing a tomato with her knife. "I don't think he was interested."

"There was too much negative publicity after my daughter's death," Carl said. "The newspapers and the radio picked up on it. I can see Mr. Ferguson's point in canceling it."

"It didn't help that Barbara La Mar died at the same time," Norma added. "One of the best actresses around. People flocked to see her in *Thy Name is Woman* two years ago."

Bernice agreed. "Such a gifted actress and so young, only twenty-nine. Someday they'll treat tuberculosis, although I don't know if I'll be around to see it."

"Mother, you'll be around for a long time," Alan said good-naturedly.

"Do you enjoy your work at the library, Lester?" Carl asked him.

Lester wiped his mouth on a napkin and took his time in replying. "It's challenging, especially when I am asked to retrieve archives. Albany is rich in history, and I am impressed with the documents on file there."

Bernice offered more stew and rice pilaf, but everyone had had plenty. She announced she would serve dessert and make fresh coffee. Alan noticed his uncle, Lester and Norma chatting amicably. He lit a cigarette and sighed in contentment. Within a few hours, he would remember the luncheon as the only placid part of the day.

The sun was still shining brightly as the afternoon progressed. Ed and John arrived at almost the same time as Mrs. Whitney and Evangeline. Alan greeted them at the front door, took their coats, and welcomed them into the kitchen. Bernice turned from the counter and smiled.

"Please come in and enjoy my chocolate cake. The coffee will be ready soon."

"You really are the best cook ever, Bernice," Mrs. Whitney told her admirably.

"Thank you, Eleanor," she said gratefully. "You're looking lovely today. Likewise, Evangeline, you are such a pretty girl. Alan, would you turn the radio on in the living room and we'll have our coffee and cake there."

Alan ushered their guests into the living room, where he turned on the radio console and soon the wonderful hit songs of Duke

Ellington and Ruth Etting enchanted them. Eleanor and Evangeline sat on the sofa while Norma and Lester sat in the armchairs near the fireplace. Ed, John and Carl sat in extra chairs Alan brought in from the kitchen.

Bernice entered with a tray containing plates of chocolate cake. She asked for Alan's assistance in retrieving the coffee and he scurried off to the kitchen, returning with a tray, containing a coffee pot, cups, a sugar bowl and a jug of cream. Bernice served plates with the cake while Alan poured coffee. Eleanor accepted a cup and sipped the coffee, commenting how delicious it tasted while Evangeline marveled at the moistness of the chocolate cake.

Carl explained his sister inherited their mother's culinary expertise. Ed, John, Norma and Lester also enjoyed the rich dessert and soon asked for refills on the coffee.

"Where's Mrs. Churchill?" Ed asked, sipping coffee.

Bernice smiled. "She was busy at the church earlier. She's involved with community projects and the women's movement in Albany. Her volunteer work means a great deal to her."

Eleanor agreed. "The League of Women Voters meets tonight. I may attend, as it certainly is important now that we have the vote."

"Mother, I didn't realize you were part of the women's movement," Evangeline said, wiping her mouth on a napkin. "Are women's rights important to you?"

Eleanor looked at her daughter. "Of course, dear. We have the right to vote and that is only the beginning. It is time for a woman's voice to be heard."

"I hear it is quite an event," John said, finishing his cake. "I read in the paper that Carrie Chapman Catt will be delivering a speech later today in front of the capitol."

"She's here in Albany?" Ed asked, rather astonished. He sipped coffee and nibbled at the cake. "What better place to make a speech than in front of the capitol building."

Evangeline agreed. "I didn't think women would ever get the vote! I voted for President Coolidge in 1924 and I was glad he won. Mr. Harding died so unexpectedly."

"President Harding was a good man," Carl mentioned. "Unfortunate he died in office."

"A sad loss to the country," John added. "Let's see who'll run in '28."

"I plan to vote again in the next election," Norma said, smiling up at Lester. "Maybe by 1928 I'll be Mrs. Cavanaugh. Lester and I are talking about getting married."

Alan almost dropped his plate with the chocolate cake and looking around the room noticed the others were also in shock. Norma and Lester getting married? This was news to him. Of course, Lester would never open up to him, but he always thought they had a certain comradery. He was surprised he never mentioned it. He listened as Lester addressed them.

"Well, Norma is talking about a wedding, but I haven't decided on marriage quite yet," he said, a mixture of annoyance and shyness in his tone. He threw Norma a look that Alan could only describe as resentful as though he preferred her to remain quiet. "For now, Norma and I are a couple." His eyes went to Evangeline, her mother and to Bernice.

Alan detected shock, incredulity and even annoyance from them. Of course, he was rather taken aback by Norma's announcement too, but why would it apparently bother the others, including his own mother? He glanced at his uncle, who looked with extreme distaste at Lester, obviously still concluding he was somehow responsible for Betsy's premature death. Mrs. Whitney was aghast, and Evangeline seemed repulsed. Even Ed and John were surprised. John registered what Alan thought was anger, as he knew he liked Norma and having dated her, most likely would have wanted to continue doing so. Ed kept his cup to his lips, as though to hide his expression.

"Did you have a nice time last night, dear?" Eleanor asked her daughter, trying to change the subject. "Where did you and Ed go?"

"We went to Keeler's and then the Strand," Evangeline said with a trace of annoyance, "I believe I mentioned that this morning at breakfast."

"Of course, dear," Eleanor said, feeling foolish. "I had forgotten."

"The Strand's a great theater," Ed said rather awkwardly.

"We work hard to keep it pristine," John said with pride.

Alan thought the pleasant atmosphere of a little while ago had evaporated, replaced by uneasiness. Norma's announcement had a distant impact, and it was evident amongst the people assembled. Glancing at his mother, he noticed she had stopped eating the chocolate cake and only sipped her coffee.

"Do the police have any idea what happened to Penelope, Alan?" John asked him.

Alan explained briefly what Sloane had shared with him yesterday. He mentioned Mr. Sheppard would be here later in the day. Judging by the expressions on everyone assembled, Alan could tell this announcement also had a pronounced effect. He did not offer anything more until Norma mentioned the love letters.

"I wrote dear Lester love letters," she said, rather foolishly. "I gave them to him, professing my love. So I don't know why the police are making a song and dance about them."

"I wouldn't worry about love letters, Norma," John said. "Nothing sinister about them."

"You threw them away, Lester dear," Norma said coyly. "But Alan retrieved them and gave them to Mr. Sheppard. Soon the police and the whole city will know, too!"

Changing the subject quickly, Lester asked, "Who's the girl from the Hall that claims she saw something?"

Alan explained about Mrs. Truman's daughter, who might have seen or heard something that night. He tried to read the people in front of him but was not successful.

Eleanor sipped her coffee thoughtfully. "Albany has certainly changed over the years. Sometimes I don't like to take my evening and early morning strolls. Too much crime and violence. It's just awful nowadays." Her glance went to Norma and to Lester, lingering a bit longer on Lester.

Alan began to see a different picture but could not clarify his thoughts. He wondered if someone present knew or suspected something, but who was it and what did he or she know? He glanced at Evangeline as she sat on the sofa next to her mother. She looked sullen, as if the recent murders, Betsy's death and Norma's supposed wedding announcement were too much for her.

The ringing of the doorbell interrupted the clinking of forks on plates and brief small talk. From in the hallway the grandfathers' clock struck four.

Bernice went to the hallway to answer the front door. From in the living room, a mumbling of female voices could be heard along with footsteps approaching the living room. Soon Bernice returned with Mrs. Churchill by her side. She greeted everyone pleasantly.

"I was busy at the church just now," she exclaimed, catching her breath and sitting in the armchair that Lester vacated for her. "Thank you, Mr. Cavanaugh." She paused, wondering if she had interrupted something. Her cheeks were flushed as she looked at everyone assembled. She could tell there was a certain tension in the room.

"Would you like a piece of chocolate cake and coffee, Mrs. Churchill?" Alan asked her.

Mrs. Churchill took off her gloves and left them on her lap. The soft voice of Bessie Smith emanating from the radio console was a pleasing sound in the background. "No, dear, I don't have much time. You'll excuse me, Bernice, for arriving late. I want to go to the capitol to hear Carrie Chapman Catt deliver a speech." She glanced at her watch. "It should be starting soon. There is already quite a crowd gathered."

"She's really here in Albany?" Norma asked.

Mrs. Churchill nodded. "Yes, the League of Women Voters is meeting later today, and Mrs. Catt is giving a speech in front of the state capitol. So I can only stay a few minutes before I head over to hear her speak." She paused. "Afterwards, I'll come back for a piece of your delicious chocolate cake." She smiled at Bernice.

"It's a perfect day for it," Evangeline said, looking toward the windows, as the sun warmed the room comfortably.

"WGY plans to broadcast her speech but since we live across the street, I'd rather see her in person," Mrs. Churchill said.

"I'd like to go, too," Bernice said. "Anyone else care to join us?"

To Alan's surprise, Lester, Norma, John, Ed, Eleanor and Evangeline mentioned they would go to hear Carrie Chapman Catt speak in front of the capitol. Feeling outnumbered, Carl reluctantly told them he would go, too.

"I've never attended a function of the League of Women Voters," Carl mentioned as they went for their coats in the hallway. "Should be interesting to hear her speech."

Mrs. Churchill agreed. "Carrie Chapman Catt is quite a brilliant woman. She founded the League of Women Voters just six years ago. She speaks for all people, and it will benefit the city and the state."

"I should clean up in the kitchen first," Bernice said, excusing herself. She turned off the radio console and was prepared to go to the kitchen when Alan stopped her.

"I'll take care of that, Mother," he told her. "You go ahead first and then I'll join you."

"I'll be glad to help you, Alan," Eleanor said pleasantly. "I'll join everyone at the capitol afterwards. May I use the bathroom upstairs, Bernice?"

"Of course, Eleanor," Bernice said and smiled. "Please, help yourself."

"How exciting," Evangeline said breathlessly, putting on her fur coat and cloche hat in the hallway. "I've never attended a rally, especially one for women's rights!"

"I'm eager to hear her speech," Norma said, shrugging into her coat.

"Certainly good for Albany," Lester said.

"It should draw a good crowd," Bernice commented, wrapping a scarf around her neck.

Ed and John had put on their jackets and caps and were walking out the front door, followed by Norma, Lester, Evangeline and Carl. Bernice told Alan she would see him in front of the capitol and then with Mrs. Churchill headed across Academy Park and the majestic capitol building.

Alan joined them at the front door and in the distance past Academy Park he saw quite a crowd gathered in front of the capitol steps. He closed the door, shutting out the still chilly air and returned to the kitchen to clean up. At the sink, he washed the dessert plates and coffee cups, followed by the utensils. He heard Mrs. Whitney come down the stairs and enter the kitchen from the dining room, carrying the pot of beef stew, placing it on the counter. She then returned to the dining room to collect the plate containing the rice pilaf. She placed that also on the counter and Alan thanked her for her help. He heard her scrap the dish containing the rest of the rice pilaf.

Dear Mrs. Whitney, a good soul, he thought as he dried the dishes and cups, a caring mother to Evangeline, too. Certainly, kind of her and Evangeline to help Norma when she returned home from the hospital. He felt her presence near him, as she opened one of the kitchen drawers. Then he realized she was much nearer than he thought. He turned and saw her standing before him, holding a large carving knife in the air. At first, he did not quite take in the scene before him but then in a fraction of a second he knew. He knew what was about to happen, what had already happened and who was responsible—and he was alone without anyone else in the house.

"Where are the letters, Alan?" Eleanor said menacingly, intense anger on her face.

Alan fumbled for words. "I don't have them. Mr. Sheppard gave them to the police."

"I don't believe you," Eleanor hissed. "You think you know everything, you're always so self-righteous. I want the letters now! Go get them!"

"I don't have them, Mrs. Whitney," Alan repeated.

"Lester belonged to me, not to your trampy cousin or bitchy Penelope. I got rid of them for good. Those letters could ruin my reputation in this city. I'd be a laughingstock at city hall. People could figure out I wrote them! You had no business showing them to that damn investigator!"

Alan again told her he did not have them, but he realized he could not reason with the enraged woman standing before him. He eyed the carving knife as she held it high in the air, aimed at him, and he knew she would not hesitate to use it.

"I'll say a burglar broke in and killed you," she threatened him. "I was upstairs freshening up and didn't hear a thing. Your mother knows I went upstairs, so my alibi is secure. When I came downstairs, I found you dead in the kitchen. They would believe me. So give me the letters, now!"

Alan was too shocked to speak. Sensing his silence as unwillingness to cooperate, Eleanor flung herself upon him, pinning him against the sink with her free hand. Alan fought her off, grabbing hold of the knife, desperately trying to wrench it out of her grip. They struggled for the deadly weapon and still Eleanor hung onto the knife, and Alan resisted, fighting her off.

Just then, Alan heard the front door open and footsteps rapidly approaching from the hallway. Sloane Sheppard burst in, followed by Inspector Harris, Lieutenant Taylor and two officers of the Albany City Police. Sloane quickly aided Alan and with their combined effort, they easily mastered Eleanor, and while she struggled viciously, she was soon overtaken. Sloane wrestled the carving knife from her, while at the same time the police officers swiftly restrained her in handcuffs.

By this time, Bernice, Mrs. Churchill and the others had returned, seeing the police car parked on Elk Street and realizing they had entered the house. Confused as to what was happening, they stood in the kitchen doorway as Inspector Harris spoke gravely.

"Mrs. Eleanor Whitney, I arrest you the murders of Miss Penelope Barker, Miss Sarah Evans, for causing the death of Miss Betsy Donovan, and the assaults on Miss Norma Smith and Mr. Alan Cartwright."

Alan put his hand over his eyes, stunned and out of breath. He couldn't see Mrs. Whitney, but he could hear her agonizing voice. The sound of her wailing and proclamation of innocence faded as they escorted her from the house and outside to the police car.

Alan leaned against the sink as his mother approached him. At the same time, Evangeline slumped forward in a dead faint.

CHAPTER TWENTY THREE

I t was an hour later, and the darker stage of twilight settled over the city. Sloane sat in the living room, along with Alan, Lester, Norma, and Ed. Carl and John had built up the fire and it warmed the room comfortably. Bernice made a fresh pot of coffee and Mrs. Churchill assisted bringing the trays to the living room.

Inspector Harris, Lieutenant Taylor and the police officers left, with Eleanor in custody. While escorted to the police car, she broke down, sobbing heavily, and admitted her responsibility in the murders of Miss Penelope Barker and Miss Sarah Evans. She admitted threatening Miss Barker and putting snow on the railing causing Betsy's fall. She confessed to pushing Norma on the icy pavement and her intention to kill Alan, unless he gave her the letters she believed he kept.

After fainting from learning the truth about her mother, Evangeline was carried to the living room by John and settled on the sofa, where Bernice fetched her smelling salts. Ed produced a flask containing whiskey he kept in his jacket pocket and together with the smelling salts Evangeline was brought back to consciousness. Carl insisted on calling his personal physician, but Evangeline assured him she was much better. She sat up, sipped more of the whiskey from Ed's flask, and drank the coffee Bernice handed her. Alan went over to the windows and drew the curtains and upon turning to join them listened as Sloane began to speak.

"I apologize for the shock, Miss Whitney. I understand this has been a terrible ordeal for you. I can only offer my explanation of what motivated your mother to commit murder."

Sloane looked at the faces assembled around him, sensing their uneasiness and yet their anticipation of finally learning the truth. He lit a cigarette, accepted a cup of coffee from Mrs. Churchill and continued speaking.

"Apparently Mrs. Whitney believed you belonged to her, Mr. Cavanaugh." He turned his attention to Lester. "She knew you had been involved with Miss Barker and Miss Donovan. With them eliminated, she believed she had a better chance to cement a relationship with you."

"Is it true you and mother had an affair?" Evangeline asked him weakly from the sofa.

Lester lit a cigarette and blew smoke frustratingly. "Yes, but for a very brief time. I told her I was not interested in a relationship, but she mistook my attention. I realized she was extremely lonely and vulnerable and wanted my affection on a permanent basis." He paused. "I never encouraged her. I feel responsible for what happened."

"It isn't your fault," Carl said, standing near the fireplace. They looked at him in surprise. "Mrs. Whitney was obviously unbalanced to do what she did!" He hesitated, realizing the force of his words. "She tried to kill my nephew. Alan, are you feeling better now?"

Alan was seated in one of the extra chairs he brought in from the kitchen, next to Sloane, Ed, and John. He was still in shock, although too shaken for anger. He was safe, and that was what mattered. But there were still many things he did not understand.

"I'm fine, Uncle Carl," he said and forced a smile. He had also lit a cigarette and drank some coffee, finding the caffeine helped to restore some vitality in him.

Sloane continued speaking. "She killed Miss Barker in December, when she arrived at her apartment after performing at the Ivory Theater. She wanted to eliminate her as she knew Miss Barker was involved with Mr. Cavanaugh. But then she realized Miss Donovan was also involved with Mr. Cavanaugh. This proved a bit more difficult. She figured it would be risky to attack her on Elk Street as the Cartwrights lived here as well Mr. Flynn, Mrs. Churchill and of course, Mr. Donovan. The Whitneys lived on Columbia Street, just around the corner. She might have felt it was too convenient. The night of the dance marathon gave Mrs. Whitney an idea on how to eliminate Miss Donovan. Unfortunately, for her, two witnesses overheard Mrs. Whitney encourage Miss Donovan to demonstrate her sliding down a railing. The fire escape door ajar and the snowy footprints that Alan discovered were caused by Mrs. Whitney, who had rubbed snow and ice on the railing, making it slippery enough for Miss Donovan to lose her grip and fall to the bottom of the atrium."

"Wouldn't we have seen her on the top of the fifth floor?" Ed asked.

Sloane shook his head. "It was dim on the upper floor. With the music, the dancing and everyone in the atrium and the ballroom having a good time, I don't think anyone would have even noticed her ascending the stairs. Even if someone noticed her rubbing the snow and ice on the railing, I doubt if it would have caused the least bit of attention. The focus that evening was the dancing in the ballroom and the atrium and Mrs. Whitney used it to her advantage to kill Miss Donovan.

"She had to make Miss Donovan perform her sliding down the railing before the snow melted. It worked well for her, as Miss Donovan eagerly climbed the top of the stairs and got everyone's attention before she lost her grip and fell down to the atrium floor."

"So why was Miss Evans killed?" John asked.

"Miss Evans and Miss Truman overheard Mrs. Whitney encourage Miss Donovan to slide down the railing. As employees of Harmanus Bleecker Hall, they discovered the snowy footprints at the top of the stairs, but thought nothing of it, until Miss Donovan fell to the floor below. Miss Truman was too shocked to say anything but Miss Evans, realizing what she overheard and the significance of the snowy foot-prints, decided to approach Mrs. Whitney. Most likely, she demanded hush money. Mrs. Whitney would not allow a kitchen helper to stand in her way, so she stabbed her one morning, while she waited for the trolley at the corner of Madison and Lark Street. It was risky, but she felt her love for Mr. Cavanaugh was worth the risk."

Sloane turned to Norma. "Miss Smith, she also perceived you as a threat. She was responsible for your fall on State Street. She hoped by eliminating you, as she had done with Miss Barker and Miss Donovan, she was one step closer to the man she loved."

"You mean she *thought* she loved," Lester added irritably. "I don't believe Eleanor Whitney loved me or anyone else for that matter, except herself. I found her a selfish, self-centered woman and I repeat-edly told her I did not want to continue seeing her, but she refused to listen to me. The age difference between us did not matter to her. She was obsessed in continuing to see me, even while I dated Evangeline. I didn't recognize the handwriting on those letters, so I decided just to throw them out. If I had known they were from her, I would have told her to stop."

Sloane nodded. "She became extremely paranoid about the letters. She realized they would incriminate her and wanted them back. She believed you still had them, Alan, which is why she attacked you in the kitchen."

"I told her I gave them to you," Alan said. "She didn't believe me and was consumed with rage. She admitted she had killed Penelope and Betsy." He paused, then turned to Lester. "I saw you talking to someone early in the morning from my bedroom window. I couldn't see who it was, but it was a woman."

Lester looked at Alan with a hard, set expression. "I talked to Betsy in Academy Park, late at night, after we had been out. She made demands on me, and I told her I was not seeking a permanent relationship. The other time was with Eleanor. She wanted to marry me and start a home life, but I told her I was not interested in seeing her anymore. She was too possessive."

An uneasy silence settled over the people in the living room until Norma spoke, seated next to Lester. Her tone was carefree and the fact that a murderer was uncovered in her presence did not diminish her mood. "Lester and I are serious about each other," she told them. "Penelope and Betsy did their best to end our relationship, but Mrs. Whitney would have killed me to break us up. Nevertheless, that is behind us now."

"That's why she wanted to help Alan clean the kitchen," Mrs. Churchill said, seeing the picture accurately. "With us out of the house, she could have killed him."

Alan nodded. "She told me she would tell everyone she found me dead in the kitchen, that a burglar had come in while she was upstairs."

"Such a stupid plan, and it could've worked," Lester said rather disgustedly. "Especially with most of the neighborhood at the capitol to hear Carrie Chapman Catt's speech."

Sloane commented that the trouble with her diabolical scheme was that she had gone to extremes. She felt safe with Miss Barker and Miss Donovan out of the way, but she did not reckon on Miss Smith causing a threat. With two murders already behind her, she would not have stopped at eliminating Norma Smith.

"She followed you, Miss Smith," Sloane told her. "At the corner of State and Dove, she pushed you in a crowd. Most likely she lied about being in the library. She went to the hospital to see if she succeeded in killing you. She gave the impression she cared, even visiting you when you returned home. She hoped you were killed, as she perceived you as a threat to her relationship with Mr. Cavanaugh."

"What will happen to Mother, Mr. Sheppard?" Evangeline asked concern in her voice.

"She will be charged with murder but most likely given the circumstances, she may be incompetent to stand trial and declared insane. Such cases may include a mental institution."

Evangeline fought back tears. "Mother wanted another man in her life, but I had no idea she was fixated on Lester. At the dance marathon, I saw someone talking to Betsy *before* she ran up the stairs. Her back was to us and in the distance, with the dim lighting, I couldn't see who it was. I understand how she could've killed Miss Barker and Miss Evans. She'd take early morning and evening walks." She sobbed softly. "She must have really loved you, Lester."

Lester had gotten up and walked over to the windows overlooking Elk Street, obviously disturbed. He remained in front of the window, his back to them, saying nothing. He then turned and approached Carl. His expression was solemn. "Mr. Donovan, I had no idea Eleanor was so taken with me. I owe you an apology."

Carl shook hands with him. "I am glad Miss Smith's life was spared as well as my nephew."

"Thank you, Mr. Sheppard," Alan said, shaking Sloane's hand. "You saved my life."

"You're a tough guy, Alan," Sloane told him. "I'm glad I was able to resolve this case. I hope you have closure now that the truth is known."

Carl also thanked Sloane for his assistance, shaking his hand warmly. Bernice mentioned Mr. Sheppard was welcome to stay and enjoy the luncheon. Alan led Sloane and the others to the dining room, the horrendous incident he went through momentarily forgotten.

On Tuesday morning, the local newspapers carried the headlines of Mrs. Eleanor Whitney, implicated in the murders of Miss Penelope Barker, Miss Sarah Evans and also Miss Betsy Donovan, which was now classified as murder.

Alan was at the breakfast table with his mother, dressed for work, reading the morning paper. Life went on as usual, but he was still in some shock from his ordeal Sunday afternoon and the revelations Sloane presented to them. He put down his cigarette, folded the newspaper, put it aside, and accepted a plate of scrambled eggs and home fried potatoes from his mother. She refilled his coffee cup and handed him the jug of cream. He asked her why she was making such a large breakfast on a weekday. Bernice smiled at her son.

"No trouble, dear. I'm going in later this morning, so I have time. The assembly isn't in session, so it's been rather slow." She paused. "Have you seen Evangeline?"

Alan sipped coffee, tightened his tie, buttoned his vest and shirt cuffs. "No, not since Sunday, when Mr. Sheppard was here."

"I called her earlier, before you got up," Bernice told him. "I don't like her in that big house by herself. She should be here soon."

"You invited Evangeline here?" Alan said, rather surprised.

The doorbell rang at that moment. "That might be her," Bernice said.

Alan put down his coffee cup and pushed back the chair. Early morning company was not quite to his liking. Walking to the front door, he hoped it was not Mrs. Churchill. It could be Uncle Carl stopping by before work or indeed Evangeline.

He opened the front door to brilliant sunshine and a chilly breeze blew in. Evangeline stood before him, daintily and pretty in her fur coat and cloche hat, rather downtrodden but hopeful, smiling bravely, the recent ordeal still fresh in her mind. She shivered slightly. Alan did not feel the cold. He smiled at her and drew her to his arms, where she belonged.

THE END

ACKNOWLEDGMENTS

Historical fiction requires research to accurately portray the period. Tony Opalka, historian for the City of Albany, answered my questions pertaining to Albany in the 1920s. I appreciate his explanation of the Albany trolley system at that time. The reference librarians at the New York State Library and the Albany Public Library were helpful in providing information and locating sources. Albany city directories from the 1920s were particularly helpful. My presentation on *Albany in the 1920s* at the Albany Public Library was well-received. I am grateful to the librarians for giving me the opportunity to present my research. I would also like to thank my mother who worked at Whitney's Department Store as a bookkeeper (not in 1926!) She provided valuable information on Whitney's and North Pearl Street.

The 1920s Mystery Series by Michael Sinclair

An Unfortunate Coincidence
The Consequences of Murder
Murder in Cucumber Alley
Darker than the Night

Available on book websites, in department stores
and through bookstores worldwide.

Printed in the USA
CPSIA information can be obtained
at www.ICGtesting.com
JSHW012031101023
49711JS00008B/79